Reed reached across the table and caressed her hand with his thumb.

As shivers shot through Kristen's body, she looked into Reed's deep, smoky eyes.

"How do we do this long distance?"

His voice dropped to a husky timbre.

Well, okay, who needed oxygen anyway? "I-I don't know." She searched his face. "I guess the bigger question is do we want to do this, given the long distance?"

A charged silence filled the air and time seemed to stop as her question hung in the space between them.

Finally, Reed squeezed her hand. "The distance complicates things, but I'm not ready to let you go."

The look in his eyes nearly scorched her skin, and his words held her in awe as they pounded in her head.

"You don't realize how addictive you are, do you?"

Praise for Darlene Deluca

"Kristen Hanover is a winsome heroine and *THE STORY BETWEEN US* is a satisfying romance that will warm your heart and renew your belief in the hope of happy endings."

~Marie Bostwick,
NYT and USAToday bestselling author

~*~

"An utterly charming tale of life, loss, and finding love in unexpected places. A heartwarming and delightful read from start to finish!"

~InD'tale Magazine

~*~

"I couldn't put this sweet story down. The characters are so lifelike. I found myself pulling for this couple to make it. Darlene's stories never disappoint!"

~Toni A.

~*~

"*THE STORY BETWEEN US* is a sweet poignant story about loss, love, and finding sparks that last. I recommend this 5-Sparkler book to anyone looking for a romance that tugs at the heartstrings in all the right ways."

~Sparkling Book Reviews

The Story Between Us

by

Darlene Deluca

The Story Between Us

Cover Art by *The Wild Rose Press, Inc.*

The Wild Rose Press, Inc.
PO Box 708
Adams Basin, NY 14410-0708
Visit us at www.thewildrosepress.com

Publishing History
First Sweetheart Rose Edition, 2020
Trade Paperback ISBN 978-1-5092-3257-4
Digital ISBN 978-1-5092-3258-1

Published in the United States of America

Chapter One

They were waiting.

A line of people stretched almost to the front door from the children's area of the bookstore—people waiting for *her*.

"Your adoring fans," Valerie whispered.

With flutters in her stomach, Kristen Hanover grinned at her literary agent as the two peeked into the popular Dallas store from a backroom doorway. Kristen loved this shop. The children's area featured cute reading nooks depicting scenes from well-loved children's classics. The whole place beckoned children inside and invited them to discover stories and let their imaginations take them to exciting new places. Magic happened here.

She stole another quick glance at the line. *Adoring fans*. Kristen still could hardly believe all those people wanted to speak to her. While her previous releases garnered lukewarm response in sales and attention, her newest children's book launched four months ago to rave reviews. She intended to enjoy the surprise wave of success and make contact with as many fans as possible.

Stepping forward, she took her place behind the table and pulled from her purse the bright-orange marker she used for signing books.

The store manager faced the crowd. "Welcome,

everyone. We're so excited to present our guest this evening. From Shiloh, Oklahoma, Ms. Hanover is the author of four delightful children's books. She has degrees in creative writing and sociology from the University of Tulsa. Ms. Hanover enjoys horseback riding and making up stories. Please welcome Kristen Hanover."

The sound of clapping filled the room. The manager beamed at Kristen then unhooked the small velvet rope, signaling the event was under way.

For more than an hour, Kristen hardly put down the marker or drank any of the water the store provided. No awkward gaps appeared in the line. While she visited with the customer in front of her, movement in her periphery vision caught Kristen's attention.

A young boy bounced in line waiting for his turn.

Kristen smiled but kept focused on the customer at the table.

"Christmas gifts." The woman presented three copies of the new book.

Kristen mentally pinched herself. Three copies to a single customer had to be a first. "Thank you so much. I sure hope they enjoy the books." Turning back toward the line, Kristen was surprised to find the fidgeting boy already standing at the table.

With both hands, he placed a copy of *What Will You Be?* on the table and shoved it forward with a lopsided grin, his bright blue eyes shining.

"Hello there," Kristen said. "What's your name, my friend?"

He put his chin in a hand and leaned in close.

The bill of his Rangers baseball cap pushed into Kristen's personal space.

"Dylan."

"Pleased to meet you, Dylan." She flicked her glance to the man standing beside the boy, who she assumed was Dylan's dad. *Wow.* No wonder the kid was such a cutie. With a tall, solid build and unruly curls, the man looked as if he'd come straight off a professional soccer field—except for the suit and marigold-yellow tie that dangled around his neck. At seven forty-five. Had he just come from work?

Beneath raised brows, his slate-blue eyes stared.

Oops. She might have lingered a bit too long with her assessment.

"Dylan wanted to get his book signed."

His deep voice reminded Kristen why she was there, and heat rushed to her face. She grabbed for the orange pen. "Yes, of course."

"You're coming to my class tomorrow." Dylan said.

"Oh, my gosh! Well, I sure am looking forward to being there." Her schedule included an appearance in the classroom of her longtime friend Jana Baxter the following afternoon. School visits were always a fun time. While Kristen appreciated parents bringing kids to the bookstore—and buying her books—she preferred the low-key time with the kids in a classroom setting. "Mrs. Baxter is your teacher?"

Dylan bobbed his head vigorously.

Kristen glanced at the boy's dad, surprised to see a hint of impatience in his otherwise gorgeous eyes. Apparently, he wasn't excited about being dragged out tonight. From the looks of things, he'd only gone home long enough to pick up Dylan. Maybe he hadn't eaten dinner and felt a little grumpy.

Turning to the inside title page of the book, she wrote, *"For Dylan, a very special book buddy."* She signed her name then stood and extended a hand. "I'm Kristen. You must be Dylan's father. Thanks so much for coming this evening."

With a slight nod, he grasped her hand. "Good to meet you, Kristen. I'm Reed Armstrong, Dylan's uncle."

Ah. He must've promised the kid some kind of outing, thinking it'd be baseball or ice cream, not a trip to the bookstore. Kristen stifled a laugh, not sure whether to feel sorry for him or annoyed he didn't seem to appreciate time spent in a bookstore. Pulling away her gaze, Kristen turned back to her young fan. She lifted the book and held it toward Dylan. "Have fun reading that with your mom and dad or your uncle," she told him.

Dylan's smile disappeared, and he looked down. "Thank you," he mumbled.

His uncle leaned forward, clearing his throat. "I'm Dylan's guardian."

Kristen's mouth dropped open. She registered his low, tired tone but had trouble processing that bit of information. Why would an uncle be—*Oh, no way.* Her heart stuttered. Had this kid seriously lost his parents? "I…But—?"

The man glanced around, tapping a fist against the table. "Dylan's parents and little sister were killed in a car wreck."

He spoke the shocking words quietly so that only Kristen could hear.

Then he patted Dylan's shoulder. "We'll read it tonight. How 'bout that?"

Dylan looked up at Reed, and his smile returned. "Okay."

Kristen glanced behind Reed Armstrong, and the woman next in line shifted, her folded arms saying time to move on. A good dozen people still waited. Kristen drew a deep breath, feeling as if a tornado suddenly descended and sucked up all the air—or at least all the fun. She needed to let Dylan go. With sadness and about a million questions weighing on her mind, she touched his arm. "I'll see you tomorrow, okay?"

Again the boy nodded, his shy smile lighting his face.

His uncle nudged him along.

"Bye," Kristen said softly, noting the slight hiccough in Dylan's gait as the pair retreated. Frowning, she took a long drink from her water bottle—and a moment to mentally regroup. She forced a smile and hoped the next person in line couldn't tell the difference. But she lost her focus, thinking ahead to the classroom visit tomorrow—would Dylan's presence change the dynamics?

****

In the car, Dylan chattered about the book that obviously captured his imagination. Maybe he was loosening up a little—maybe indulging this book obsession would help Reed connect with his nephew. He needed to make some progress. Reed glanced in the rearview mirror with a smile as he started the ignition. Nice to see the kid excited about something. He'd been quiet and withdrawn since the accident that took his parents and younger sister two months ago. No surprise there. The horrific accident also left Dylan with multiple injuries, including a huge gash to his head and a few pins in one leg—not to mention confused and distressed.

Ditto that. Reed was still in shock. Still couldn't believe his sister, brother-in-law, and little niece were gone, and he was legal guardian of his six-year-old nephew. Suddenly, Reed became the person responsible for Dylan's upbringing and well-being. Sometimes, the thought practically strangled him. Truth was, taking Dylan scared the hell out of him. He knew nothing about raising kids and didn't know his nephew that well. The six-hour distance between Dallas and Amarillo where his sister and her family had lived made for infrequent visits. Holidays and long weekends at the ranch were about the only times they'd seen each other in recent years.

When Dylan was born, and Amy asked, Reed told her without hesitation he'd be honored to be listed as the boy's potential guardian. He never imagined it would happen. Of course, he wanted to do what was best for the kid, but he wasn't even sure what that looked like.

"She's really nice," Dylan said.

"What?" Reed asked, his train of thought broken. "Who's nice?"

"Miss Hanover."

Reed couldn't place the name. Who was—

"The book lady."

"Oh. Yes, she was." He nodded then signaled to switch lanes.

"Pretty, too. Isn't she pretty?"

Reed visualized the woman behind the table at the bookstore. He remembered her friendly smile—remembered the concern in her *pretty* green eyes when he explained their situation. Those two apparently made a quick connection. But then he'd seen how people reacted to Dylan. A person would have to have a black heart and no soul not to feel bad for the kid. Except for Jessica, Reed's now *ex*-girlfriend. Sure, she felt badly for Dylan but not badly enough to stick around and be inconvenienced by a child. At the time of the accident, they'd only been dating a few months, but her quick departure had been a surprise.

For Reed, ducking out wasn't an option. With no warning and no experience with kids, Reed had to find a way to incorporate a child into his life. "Yep, she is," he answered. He wondered if Dylan had a crush on the children's author. Was he headed for his first heartbreak at age six? Reed glanced in the mirror again. He had enough on his plate already. Maybe the infatuation would run its course quickly. "Hey, buddy, you ready to drive to the ranch tomorrow and see Grandpa?"

The kid didn't answer.

Reed was sidetracked by his cell buzzing in his pocket again. He resisted looking at it. Ever since the accident, he'd vowed never to text while driving and to limit talking, which could be a distraction even with hands-free capability.

"I just want to stay here," Dylan said.

Reed pulled the car into the driveway of his small but high-end condominium, keeping his sigh inside. Adding Dylan cramped the space, but Reed had no time to explore other options. They were fortunate the complex sat between an upscale residential area and the expressway. The location meant a good school for Dylan and easy access to work for Reed. For now, the condo would have to do.

Inside, he switched on lights as he moved from the kitchen to the living room. He turned his attention to his phone while he pulled his laptop from its case, then he glanced at the kitchen clock. "Hey, Dylan, we're running kind of late. Do you want anything else to eat before bed?" He recalled the half-eaten burger left on Dylan's plate earlier.

"Like what?"

Reed shrugged. "I don't know. What sounds good?" He wasn't sure about the choices. He'd have to make time for another trip to the grocery store. "What about peanut butter and jelly?"

"No. I'm not hungry."

"Go ahead and brush your teeth then put on your pajamas." Reed plugged in the computer and scrolled through emails.

But Dylan didn't move.

Reed searched his face. "What's the matter?"

"You said tonight was bath night."

Reed heaved a sigh. So he had. But was a bath really necessary? Or was the bath a bedtime stall tactic? The book signing took up their evening, and Reed still had work to do. He raked a hand through his hair. He needed Dylan settled so he could switch gears and concentrate. And damn, he could use a cold beer. Facing Dylan, he offered a conspiratorial smile. "How dirty are you? Did you wrestle alligators in the swamp today?"

The boy giggled. "Nope."

"Did you go to the beach and squish sand between your toes?"

"No." He backed away and fell into a cushioned

armchair.

"Any dirt on your clothes?" He reached out and tugged on Dylan's shirt. "What about in your nose?"

Laughing, Dylan shook his head. "No, Uncle Reed. You're goofy."

"So you must be the cleanest kid in Texas. Let's call it a night." He scooped his nephew into his arms, careful not to jostle his legs too much, and hauled him to the small bedroom that used to be an office. "Okay, chop-chop." He supervised the teeth brushing, then scooted Dylan toward the bed. "In you go." He pulled back the light blanket.

Dylan climbed in but remained upright. "What about the book?"

"What about it?"

"You said we could read my book tonight."

Reed blew out his breath. He had to learn to keep his mouth shut. Or at least trade words like 'yes' and 'sure' for 'maybe' and 'we'll see.' This kid remembered everything. He glanced around. "Where is it?"

"In the living room."

Mustering his self-control, Reed managed not to groan as he retrieved the book then perched on the side of the bed and turned to the first page.

Dylan reached for the book. "I want to read some."

Reed envisioned ten minutes turning into thirty. "Nah. I'll do it." *Wait.* Did kindergartners read now? Did the kid even know his ABCs? "You know how to read?"

"I can read this."

Reed stared hard at Dylan. "How'd you learn to read already?"

The no-duh look Dylan shot Reed included an eye-roll. "Pre-school. Me and Mom read every night."

Good news, since Reed planned to buy Dylan a bare-bones cell phone to contact him if necessary. Maybe he could send and read simple text messages. Resigned to his fate, Reed handed over the book and reminded himself that Dylan enjoyed reading, and reading together could be a bonding activity. But his mind wandered while he half-listened to Dylan read.

"Look!"

Dylan's shout interrupted Reed's thoughts.

"That's her."

Reed looked across the page to where Dylan pointed to a glossy color photo of the author at the back of the book. The photographer did a nice job. Cinnamon-colored hair framed her face, and her wide, cheery smile lit the page. On closer inspection, he noticed the smattering of light freckles across her cheeks. He skimmed the bio underneath. Huh. A farm girl. She now lived in Denver but grew up not far away in Oklahoma. Made sense. She had that Sundance nature-girl look. Though he'd vowed to put thoughts of women and relationships on the back burner, Reed noted no mention of a husband or children in her bio.

Eyes sparkling, Dylan looked up at Reed. "When she comes back, can we go see her again?"

Reed smiled. By the time she came around again, Dylan would probably be way beyond the picture book stage and embarrassed by his little crush. "Sure." He caught himself. "We'll try." He pulled up the blanket and put a hand on Dylan's shoulder. "Listen, buddy. We're going to the ranch after school tomorrow. Grandpa's expecting us. But you don't have to ride the horses, okay?"

"Promise?" Dylan mumbled. He clenched the blanket in one fist and raised his other hand to his mouth.

Reed wasn't sure whether the kid sucked his fingers or chewed his nails, but he saw the gesture whenever Dylan got tired or anxious. "I promise."

Switching off the light, Reed blew out his breath and left the room. Because Dylan shut down every time Reed mentioned the ranch, he'd been stalling on heading out there. But he couldn't put the trip off any longer. He'd promised to help his dad with projects around the property. Normally, they'd ride horses. But with Dylan in tow, that plan wouldn't work. He was scared of the horses—a fact that annoyed his grandfather. Reed knew from personal experience "sissies" were not welcome or tolerated on the ranch. His father could be harsh and stern. No coddling was how a boy grew up to be a man.

Reed's stomach tightened. Now that he thought about his dad's attitude, he wondered if Dylan was afraid of more than the horses.

****

Thirty minutes after the store manager declared the book signing officially over, Kristen pulled her cornflower blue hatchback into a parking spot at the hotel, still riding the high of the well-attended book event.

"Time for a celebratory nightcap," Valerie said.

"Absolutely." Kristen climbed out of the car and fell into step with Valerie. A good night's sleep was high on Kristen's agenda, but she was too keyed-up to fall asleep right away. Besides, despite a couple of awkward moments and the sad encounter with the little boy Dylan, this book signing was worth celebrating.

Inside the plush hotel lobby, Kristen spied an available table in the bar. "Will this high-top work?" Kristen's agent carried herself with fierce confidence but stood only about five-foot-four in heels. Tall tables weren't ideal.

"It's fine." Valerie tucked a strand of long, dark hair behind her ear then reached for the wine list. "That crowd tonight was amazing. Sounds like we got some good press and distribution around here."

"Because they consider me a "local" author even though I grew up across the state line." Kristen let out a long breath. A good crowd was gratifying and nice for the ego, but these events took both physical and mental energy and left the well nearly dry.

"Sorry I can't be there tomorrow," Valerie said. "But I know you've got this routine down."

"No worries." Kristen waved a hand. "Jana is always so organized. I knew way back in high school she'd be the perfect teacher."

Valerie handed her the wine list. "Well, have a drink. You deserve it."

"Thanks." Kristen ordered a glass of her favorite New Zealand chardonnay.

Moments later, the drinks arrived, and Valerie lifted hers toward Kristen with a flourish. "Here's to a successful tour. You hit a homerun with this book for sure."

"I'll drink to that." Kristen grinned and sipped her fruity wine as a little thrill of excitement rushed through her. "The numbers are still looking good?" Could she possibly revisit the financials? Reconsider the sale of the farm?

Her brother repeatedly crunched the numbers and said he saw no cost-effective way for her to buy the farm—that she'd be throwing away her money and jeopardizing her future. He and his wife weren't the least bit interested in hanging onto the farm.

The sale would help her financially, too, of course. She could finally get a place of her own without roommates. But...the farm was special. She could almost smell her mother's pot roast cooking in the oven and the sweet scent of freshly cut hay. Those acres of pecan trees and farmland and the quaint two-story clapboard house with its wrap-around front porch were home.

"Absolutely." Grinning, Valerie set down her drink and put up a hand. "The numbers are holding steady, and I'm betting they'll keep rising." She leaned closer, patting Kristen's arm. "Ride this wave, my friend. Enjoy tonight then get back to work."

Valerie's encouraging good news made Kristen determined to remain optimistic but proceed with caution. The lukewarm response to her earlier books left her skittish about the viability of being a full-time author.

"By the way, you looked really nice tonight." Valerie flicked a hand toward Kristen. "Love that outfit."

"Thanks. It's one of my faves." She'd splurged on new clothes for the tour. Tonight, she wore an orange pantsuit with a hand-dyed scarf in shades of pink, yellow, and orange. Kristen loved bright colors and chose orange as her signature hue. For the classroom gig tomorrow, she'd trade the more professional look for comfy leggings and a tunic. A school visit always included playtime—and probably crawling around on the floor. Free play was the fun part, and Kristen— *Oh, wait*. She groaned inside. She always worked to block out the parents and focus on the kids, to be in the moment, and not worry about whether she looked foolish to the adult members of the audience. But tomorrow…

Her thoughts drifted back to the book signing. What if Dylan's hunk of an uncle showed up?

Chapter Two

Without looking toward the back of the room, Kristen took her place at the front of Jana's classroom. She settled into the hard molded-plastic chair and felt every hour of the book tour in her muscles.

While Kristen listened to Jana give an introduction, she also waved to the group of children sitting cross-legged on the floor, assembled to hear her story. Just looking at them gave Kristen a buzz. Forget the sore muscles. Today was the last classroom visit of the tour. These kids wanted to have some fun—and so did she.

Kristen searched the group, looking for a familiar face. She did a double-take, and the pang to her chest hit hard. Among the gathering of mop-headed kindergartners a student with a shaved head caught her attention. *Oh, no.* Even from several feet away, Kristen saw a fresh, jagged scar running from the top of his hairline to the left ear. Alarm bells clanged in her mind at the memory of the Rangers hat covering Dylan's head at the bookstore last night.

The car accident. The accident that took Dylan's parents and sister must have also injured him. Her chest clenched. What did that poor kid see? Did he even remember? So much trauma—something a person that age shouldn't have to experience. She glanced toward the back of the room, scanning the row of parents. Reed Armstrong was absent. Swallowing hard, Kristen forced her gaze to move on, surveying the crowd before resting once again near the center of the room. She smiled when she made eye contact with Dylan, and her heart lifted at the shy smile and wave she received in return. *What an adorable kid.*

The sound of clapping startled her. She'd missed her cue. Turning toward Jana, Kristen gave a little laugh. "Thank you so much, Mrs. Baxter." She faced her expectant audience. "Good afternoon, you guys." She leaned forward, grinning. "Are you ready for a lesson?"

A few kids nodded, but many blank faces stared back.

They were never quite sure whether she was kidding or serious. "Hmm." Kristen sat back in her chair and pretended to think. Leaning toward the group again, she put her hands on her hips. "Are you ready for some fun?"

Shouts and smiles erupted.

Okay. They were in. Now she had to deliver. She pulled a book out of her neon green tote bag and read the title in a clear voice, loud enough to be heard but still pleasant. "*What Will You Be?*"

Like all of her books, the story line centered on pretending and creativity using ordinary objects and settings kids could find in their backyards to make up fun stories of their own. The books encouraged unplugging and getting outside, looking at their world in new ways—and always with the emphasis on having fun.

As she read the words, Kristen held the book high for the students to see. With larger groups, she often set up a slide show to give the kids a better view. But with a smaller group, she drew them closer for a more intimate experience.

Every few pages she stopped, and the students joined her in a chant-and-clap routine. *One. Two. Three. Now what can I be?* Each time the story restarted, the characters morphed into a new scene.

Reading the story took only about twenty minutes. When Kristen finished, she put the book in her lap. With a clap of her hands, she grinned at the kids. "The end."

Jana stood and began the applause. "All right, everyone, let's put our hands together and give Miss Hanover a big thank you."

Kristen stood, too. "Thanks for being such a great audience. Now, what questions do you have for me?" Things could get weird here. Rarely did the questions have anything to do with her books or writing.

According to their usual routine, Kristen took over the Q-and-A session.

Hands shot into the air.

Kristen pointed to a girl in the back row.

"What's your favorite kind of cookie?" the girl asked.

"Oh, that's an easy one," Kristen said. "Chocolate chip with nuts. Like my mom used to make." She immediately regretted her words—and where they took her. Those cookies would always remind Kristen of her mother. Almost a year ago, her mother succumbed to her illness after a courageous two-year battle. So many reminders still hit Kristen unexpectedly. She drew in a deep breath and forced her attention back to the kids.

The questions went from cookies to pizza to breakfast cereal and other foods until Dylan raised a hand.

"Hey, Dylan, hit me with a question."

"Do you have a dog?"

Kristen thought of the farm again. Her family always had dogs and cats running around, but Kristen's favorite "pet" was Star, a gentle mare temporarily pastured at a neighboring farm with three more remaining horses. Once the book tour ended and the farmhouse was emptied, she had to find them permanent owners. The lease arrangement on the farm was about to expire, and the sale of the property loomed ahead. "I don't," she said. "Not anymore. But I like dogs. Do you?"

The boy nodded.

Several other children jumped in, naming their favorite animal or shouting out their dog's name.

"Boys and girls, I think that's enough about me," Kristen told them after a few more minutes. "We want to have plenty of playtime, right? Let's get those wheels in motion and turn our imaginations loose." She grabbed her bag and dumped the contents onto the floor, then whirled. "One. Two. Three," she chanted. "What will *you* be?"

The chant was their cue and had the effect of spontaneous combustion. The kids jumped up and reached for objects.

A tall girl with long pigtails waved a pencil. "I'm the drummer in a band."

Within seconds, several other students pretended to play violins, trumpets, and air guitars.

A moment later, Dylan grabbed Jana's white sweater from the back of her desk chair and pulled it over his head then lunged toward Kristen. "Grrrr," he shouted.

The awkward movement made her wonder if the boy couldn't put weight on his knees. Did he have lingering impairments from the accident? Kristen crouched and put a hand to her chest. "Oh, my goodness! You must be a polar bear." She rocked back on her heels. "Where do you live, Mr. Polar Bear?"

"The North Pole."

"Of course! And what do you eat, Mr. Polar Bear?"

"I eat fish!"

"Yum, yum." Kristen rubbed her stomach. "And what else? What is your most tasty meal?"

The kid stared, eyes wide.

He was apparently stumped, so Kristen put a hand to her mouth as if to tell a secret. "Why, seals are the most scrumptious, extra-delicious."

Dylan's face fell. "I like seals." He threw down the sweater. "I don't want to be a polar bear."

Uh-oh. Kristen snatched the sweater and twirled, keeping the sweater above them. "Now, sir, you are an Eskimo in your igloo." She was rewarded with a wide grin. *Whew*.

"That's right," Dylan said. "My house is made out of ice."

"Ooooh," Kristen said. "Ice is nice."

Another student pulled the sweater from Kristen's hands and wrapped it around Dylan's shoulders. "Look! Now he's a snowman."

Kristen didn't know where his idea was going but figured she should take charge. Dylan might not want the other kids using him as a prop. She grabbed the sweater again and tossed it on a desk. Then she put her open book on top of her head and straddled a backward chair in one of her popular go-to moves. "Hey, I have a hat," she told the group. "I'm a cowboy. I'm on my horse at the rodeo."

"Giddyup," another boy shouted, moving behind her. "Giddyup."

The free play continued for another twenty minutes.

Then Jana rang a bell. "Boys and girls, I'm afraid we're out of time with Miss Hanover. Please move back to the center circle. Let's give another round of applause and show our appreciation for her visit today."

With a sigh of relief, Kristen thanked her audience. She'd never been so glad to end a session. The concern over Dylan created an element of stress to what should've been nothing but fun and games. Thankfully, she only had one classroom visit today. Sometimes the agency scheduled a morning and an afternoon presentation to squeeze as much as possible into a day—which explained the sore butt cheeks.

Moving toward the back of the room, Kristen wiped clammy hands on her pants. She always found socializing with parents more difficult. On one hand, she imagined herself as their peer, but sometimes a nagging voice inside her head told her she was a fraud. What did she know about kids, really? Still, she forced a smile and went down the line, shaking hands with the adults while the children prepared to end the day.

Once the school bell rang, Jana waved the kids toward the door. "Thanks so much, Kristen. What a fun way to end the day. I'm really sorry about cancelling for happy hour, but I've got to rush to this meeting. Call me before you leave town, okay?"

"It's not a problem, Jana." But Kristen would

definitely call later. Probably didn't matter at this point, but she'd like to know more about Dylan. Kristen walked to the front of the room to gather her bag of objects. When a tug on her arm interrupted her, she spun a hundred and eighty degrees and looked into Dylan's big, blue eyes. "Hey, Dylan. Isn't it time to go?"

"That was fun," he said.

As a lump formed in her throat, Kristen squeezed his hand. Moments like this with the kids made her job the best. "Good. I'm glad you enjoyed it."

"Me and my mom read all your books. And we pretended a concert on the deck, just like in *Stay and Play*."

Wow. Talk about a tug on the heartstrings. "Oh, Dylan, I'm so happy you enjoyed the books with your mom." Kristen swallowed hard. "You keep using that fun imagination of yours, and I'll see you next time, okay?"

With another step forward, he threw his arms around her neck.

Whoa. She didn't see that coming. Kristen tossed one arm around the kid and put the other against a chair to keep her balance.

In the next instant, he turned and ran from the room.

Well, his run was more like an awkward gallop. Shaking her head, Kristen chuckled. *What a sweetheart.* A sense of melancholy stole over her, and all of a sudden, she didn't want to stay at the hotel another night. The farm beckoned her. She couldn't ditch Valerie before dinner, but she could decline drinks and then hit the road. The drive from Dallas to the farm in

Oklahoma would only take a couple of hours.

As much as she dreaded the tasks awaiting her, she needed the weekend at the farm.

****

By the time Reed finally tossed their bags into the back of his SUV, his watch read almost six o'clock. "Dylan, let's go," he hollered. If this trip was going to be a hassle, he might as well get it over with as soon as possible. At the same time, if the trip could provide a chance to unwind, he was more than ready to bring that on.

Dylan appeared in the garage carrying his school backpack.

"Why the backpack?"

"My stuff." Dylan held up the bright blue pack.

Reed frowned. "I thought your stuff was in the suitcase."

"My other stuff." He gave a quick shrug then climbed into the car without further explanation.

Reed shook his head. *Whatever.* He couldn't imagine needing to take toys and "stuff" to the ranch. But then he'd never had all the cool new electronics growing up. The ranch had its own forms of entertainment. For a kid, the place should be exploration heaven.

"You know, we'll probably be outside most of the time." Reed backed the car onto the street. "You can find a lot to do at the farm." Late September and temps still hovered in the mid-eighties. He could play outside until dusk. "Hey, you brought a hat, didn't you?" Reed hit the brakes. He'd forgotten to double-check that detail, and doctors' orders were to protect Dylan's head from sunburn.

"Two," Dylan said.

Good. Reed could hardly keep up with all the dos and don'ts on top of juggling a schedule that now included pediatric appointments, physical therapy, school pick-up, papers, and projects.

Dylan lasted only about thirty minutes into the drive. As soon as the car hit open road, his head bobbed and he went silent.

Reed appreciated the solitude and opportunity to think. If he didn't get a couple of situations in the office settled, he might be facing some field visits. As director of research operations for Viking Oil, he already was overdue for one in Houston but putting it off as long as possible. Travel presented a quandary. He'd already taken off way too much time. He needed to find some kind of nanny or babysitter for Dylan who didn't shut down at six o'clock or for random "service" days. Finding someone meant identifying potential candidates and interviewing—all of which took time. First thing Monday, he'd have his administrative assistant start looking. *Other duties as assigned.*

An hour and a half later, Reed pulled off the county road onto the long gravel drive that led to the main house.

Dylan woke immediately.

"Hey, buddy. We're here. It'll be bumpy for a minute."

Instead of sitting up and looking out the windows, Dylan shrank into his seat.

Not for the first time, Reed wished he'd talked to his sister more, kept in touch regularly, and knew Dylan and the family dynamics better.

Dylan hovered beside Reed as he lifted their

suitcases from the car then headed up the walkway.

Without knocking, Reed set down one case and opened the heavy front door of the sprawling ranch house, ushering Dylan inside the grand entryway. The vaulted ceiling featured windows high above the door, which flooded the room with natural light. On the facing wall, a large, vibrant landscape in bold acrylics welcomed visitors.

Nora, a longtime family friend and housekeeper, jogged around the corner. "There you are!" Making a beeline for Dylan, she knelt and wrapped him in her arms. "Hello, sweet thing."

Dylan let go of Reed and turned his face into Nora's shoulder.

"Hey, Nora," Reed greeted her. "Wasn't expecting to see you tonight."

She stood and patted his arm. "Oh, I told your father I'd come by for a couple of hours and at least make sure y'all got fed. Besides, I didn't want to miss you two." Wiping a hand on her apron, she kept the other on Dylan but leaned toward Reed. "How's he doing?" she whispered.

Her unexpected presence and question caught Reed off guard, and a sense of gratitude rushed through him. He could use an ally in the concern and care for his nephew. He was tempted to beg Nora to stay the whole weekend. "Doing all right, I think," he said under his breath. *As good as could be expected under the circumstances.*

"Sounds like our guests have arrived," a raspy voice boomed from the hallway.

"Dinner is just about ready." Nora winked at Dylan before turning toward the kitchen. "I've got cookies and ice cream, too."

"Hey, Dad." Reed grasped his dad's firm hand.

"Son."

They always greeted each other by shaking hands. But Reed frowned when his father also held out his hand to his grandson, dwarfing Dylan's when the boy slowly raised his. A man's handshake for a little boy. Something about the exchange didn't seem right.

"Well, get your bags and stay awhile."

"Yeah. Let me run these upstairs."

"I'll be on the porch."

Upstairs, Reed set his own bag in his old room while Dylan made a pit stop.

"Hey, Dylan," Reed called. "Which room did you sleep in when you came here with your mom and dad?"

Dylan appeared in the doorway. He glanced around then shrugged. "Can I sleep in here?"

No, absolutely not, was Reed's immediate reaction. He really did not want to share a bed with a squirming six-year-old. "The house has lots of bedrooms, buddy. Why don't we go pick out one?" He scooted Dylan back into the hallway. Right next door should be fine. Reed peeked inside. The décor was on the feminine side, but—

"Hey, Uncle Reed!"

Reed turned to find Dylan in the doorway across the hall.

"Look. Two beds."

Reed crossed over. Yeah—two twin size beds. Folding his arms, he was about to mention the fact, but Dylan's wide eyes stopped him. Instead, Reed sat on the edge of the closest bed and faced his nephew at eye level. "You don't want to stay in a room by yourself?"

Dylan shook his head, and his lower lip jutted forward.

The expression hinted at a potential meltdown and sealed the deal. Reed put a hand on Dylan's shoulder. "No problem. We'll sleep here tonight."

The smile returned to Dylan's face. "Okay."

Reed couldn't help wondering if he was being a pushover as his father's favorite saying came to mind. *Toughen up, Buttercup.* But he couldn't use that on Dylan—at least not yet. As much as sleeping in a twin bed sounded like a kind of hell on earth, he listened to his gut tell him it was the right thing to do.

Two hours later, fed and ready for sleep—or at least a little solitude—Reed sank onto the bed, wincing as his feet hit the wooden footboard. Keeping the expletive inside, he rolled over and closed his eyes, willing sleep to take him soon.

Reed awoke the next morning to find Dylan peering at him, only inches from his face, as if he could telepathically wake him. Funny, but a little creepy at the same time. He turned to look at the bedside clock but knew it didn't matter. Sunlight streamed into the room from the edges of the curtains. He'd never get back to sleep, anyway. "Morning, Dylan." He swung his cramped legs to the edge of the bed. "You hungry?"

Dylan nodded.

Reed wondered how long he'd been waiting and whether the kid was afraid to go downstairs alone. "You don't have to wait for me, you know." When Dylan didn't respond, Reed let it go. "Let's get dressed and see what Grandpa's doing."

Downstairs, Reed's dad sat at the table along with a plate full of muffins and rolls. Two of the dogs got up and sniffed around, but a quick word from Reed stilled them—except for the thumping of the tails. "You can pet them." Reed handed Dylan a glass of orange juice.

Dylan perched on a chair.

"Have a bite to eat then come over and help get the horses ready," Dad said.

In a sideways glance, Reed saw Dylan's head whip around. "Sure," Reed said. "Dylan can ride with me, or we can follow you in one of the jeeps." He hoped his words sounded matter of fact, as if that plan was expected.

His father's brows pulled together, but he said nothing. The door closed behind him.

Thirty minutes later, Reed drained his glass and walked with Dylan to the barn. The smell of fresh hay—as familiar to Reed as the back of his hand—permeated the air around them, and a horse whinnied from farther inside.

"Come here, Dylan." His grandpa issued the order inside the barn.

Dylan turned wide eyes to Reed.

He saw the fear radiating from his nephew's eyes and stepped toward him. Ignoring his dad, Reed lifted Dylan so he could pet the horse's head. "Come say hello, big guy." Maybe his nephew just needed to spend a little more time in the barn getting used to the horses. Amy had been horse-crazy as a girl, but Dylan apparently didn't get those genes. Reed knew his sister's family hadn't visited the ranch often in the last few years. He remembered Amy saying traveling was too difficult with the baby, and the four-and-a-half-hour drive from Amarillo took too much time for an ordinary weekend.

Dylan slowly reached out a hand but pulled back when the horse nudged forward.

"These horses won't hurt you, boy," Grandpa said. "This here's Penny. She's small and knows exactly what to do. You won't have any trouble with her. Why, your mom used to ride her—"

"Dad, I told him he didn't have to ride a horse. Let's leave it at that." Reed sensed pressure would make it worse—as would shaming him. His dad's ice-blue eyes and weathered scowl bore into Reed.

"Why'd you tell him that? He's old enough to learn. No grandson of mine is—"

Reed held up a hand to cut him off. He didn't often argue with his dad, but he wasn't breaking his promise to Dylan. "Come on. Think about everything the kid's been through and what he's dealing with. Can't we cut him a little slack?"

"Slack?" Dad spat the word. "No room on a ranch for slack. You know that. He won't get anywhere in this world being soft. A man's—"

"I get it." Reed set Dylan on the ground slightly behind him. "But he doesn't need to be a man when he's six years old."

His dad turned the scowl on Dylan. "And take off that silly ball cap. You need a cowboy hat to—"

"Dad, come on." Reed's temper rose. "Even if he did ride, he'd need a helmet. You know he had a concussion, and the doctors—"

"The doctors want to cover their butts," his dad muttered. "Won't get a damned thing done."

Reed's hopes of having his own fast, exhilarating ride across the grasslands evaporated on the breeze like his father's words. No way could he leave Dylan alone

28

with him. "We'll do what we can." Annoyance crept into Reed's tone. "And we can get online and start looking for the horses you mentioned." He turned to Dylan. "Is your backpack in the jeep?" Reed's new plan was to keep Dylan engaged in activities out of the way.

As soon as his dad finished saddling the horse, Reed and Dylan followed in the open-air jeep. Reed could almost taste the haze of dust churned up by the wheels.

An uncomfortable veil of tension hung in the air when Reed stopped and met his father at the north gate and pulled supplies from the vehicle. Finally, Reed cleared his throat. "So you lost Cheyenne, but why do you want three new horses?" The old paint lived on the ranch as long as Reed could remember. The horse's heart gave out shortly after the car accident, but amid the family's tragedy, the animal's death was barely acknowledged.

"Some fool notion of Roger's. Wants to rent out the cabins and let people ride while they're here."

Nearly choking, Reed reached into the cooler for a bottle of water and took a long drink. He stared at his father. "You're kidding me."

His father returned a scorching look. "I'm not. Says he can make a lot of money. I told him they better stay off the south slope and away from the cattle. I'm not having a bunch of greenhorns out here to play cowboy."

If his father said he was selling out for a luxury resort, Reed could not have been more surprised.

"He and Nora got those cabins fixed up real nice now. Might as well make some money off 'em."

"Sure," Reed croaked. He hid his smile and

wondered how in the hell his father's friend and most trusted ranch hand ever slipped that one past. Maybe he and Dylan could go check out the cabins this evening. The small homes used to house married help, but over time and with changes in the business, they fell empty.

"You know as much about horses as Roger, so you can take care of that part. Get us some that are trained and anybody can ride."

"I'll see what I can do." As if he had time to deal with ranch business. He didn't, but maybe he could find a horse that Dylan would like.

Once the work began, Reed sensed his dad relaxing as he went through the familiar motions. Even Dylan seemed to have a good time, handing the men tools and watching them. He also spent plenty of time picking up rocks and hanging out in the jeep. That he could entertain himself and stay out of the way cheered Reed immensely. Next time, maybe he could bring Dylan just for fun, when his father didn't have a list of chores. Reed hammered a nail into place then stood back, looking around. The grassland extended as far as he could see. Unfortunately, work never ended on the ranch.

At lunchtime, Reed stretched out under the shade of a huge oak tree, enjoying the brief reprieve from the sun on his skin.

His dad and Dylan ate their cold turkey sandwiches with little conversation.

Later, when long shadows spread across the land, Dylan approached Reed and his dad with fresh bottles of cold water.

Reed took the water, wiping sweat from his brow. "Thanks, buddy."

"Are you done now?" Dylan asked.

Reed didn't miss the hopefulness in his voice or his eyes. He tugged on Dylan's hat. "Almost. You hungry again?"

"Yeah. Let's go back to the house."

"All right. Just a few more minutes."

Once the tools were loaded, Reed started the jeep. Just shy of the house, he noticed an unfamiliar car in the driveway. Looked like they had unexpected company. At least his dad hadn't mentioned expecting anyone else for dinner. He turned the jeep toward the shed and saw someone sitting on the porch. Squinting, he tried to make out the figure. Didn't look like Nora. Reed let Dylan help put away the tools while his dad cared for the horse. Then he took Dylan's hand and walked to the back of the house.

A woman in tight jeans and a floral top waved from the patio.

"Who's that?" Dylan asked.

"No idea." They were almost at the steps when Reed recognized Dylan's Aunt Celia, Amy's sister-in-law. Reed met her a few times over the years and most recently saw her at the funeral.

"Hi, y'all!" She held out her arms. "Hey, Dylan, give your auntie a hug. How are you, Bumblebee?"

Reed winced at the high sing-song voice and couldn't help noticing that Dylan's greeting was less enthusiastic than his aunt's, though he did accept the hug.

"Hi, Aunt Celia."

Reed extended a hand. "Hello, Celia. What brings you out here today?" He nearly recoiled when she ran her thumb across his. *Was that intentional?* He couldn't be sure, and the moment passed.

She flicked her hair off her shoulder and offered a smile. "Well, a little birdie told me you two would be here," she gushed. "So I thought I'd drop by for a visit. I've been wanting to check on this precious boy." She squeezed Dylan to her side.

Reed didn't know a lot about Celia, but he knew his sister didn't trust her, that she'd had some reliability issues, and that she had to be pushing forty but acted as if she were still in her twenties. Single, no kids, and kind of a rolling stone. He didn't know if she worked or how she made a living, but he did know she'd been upset when she discovered Reed was named guardian of Dylan and executor of her brother's estate, of which Dylan was the sole heir. And no one "dropped by" the ranch. In the middle of nowhere, the place was a destination.

"When nobody answered the door, I called Nora, and she told me to come on in," Celia said. "I hope that's okay."

"What have we got here?"

Reed turned when his father joined them.

Celia perked up. "Hello, Jack."

His dad nodded. "Celia."

"I hope you don't mind me crashing your little party."

"Not much of a party," Jack told her. "We best get cleaned up. Help yourself to a drink."

Reed could tell by the tightness of his dad's voice he wasn't thrilled with Celia's drop-by. Her voice and tendency toward baby-talk probably sent him up the wall. He elbowed Dylan. "Let's get upstairs, buddy."

"Oh, I can help Dylan if you want." Celia stretched

an arm toward Dylan.

"Nah. We got this. You have a seat and relax."

Upstairs, he pointed Dylan toward the hallway bath. "Wash your hands and put on some clean clothes, okay?"

Fifteen minutes later, with Dylan tagging behind, Reed joined his dad and Celia on the wide back porch that offered a spectacular view of the ranch. Celia held a glass of wine, and his dad already had a bourbon. Reed backtracked to the kitchen and pulled out a beer and a soda. He popped the tab and handed the soft drink to Dylan.

"Are y'all ready to eat?" Celia asked. "I've got Nora's instructions, and the lasagna is in the oven."

So Celia was joining them for dinner. Did that mean she'd spend the night, as well? Reed forced a smile. "Sounds good. Thanks."

"Dylan, Sweet Pea, how's your leg?"

Dylan shrugged.

"Doing better," Reed said. "Still no running, though."

"When will they let those darling curls grow back?"

Reed practically squirmed on Dylan's behalf. She acted as if the kid was a toddler. "Hopefully after our check-up on Monday."

"Oh, good. Poor thing. How's school? Do you like your teacher?"

Dylan nodded, then his face brightened. "And guess what? We had an author come to our class. We got to meet her, and she signed my book. She's really nice."

Oh, yeah. Reed almost chuckled. If Celia wanted in

on this deal, she could listen to Dylan go on and on about the children's author, and she could read the book with him tonight. "Hey, Dylan, why don't you get your book? I bet Aunt Celia would like to see it."

He scrambled off his chair.

"No running," Reed said.

The book kept Celia and Dylan occupied for several minutes.

But Reed could tell Celia was getting bored when her glances toward the men became more frequent.

Finally, she smiled at Dylan. "You are reading so well, Bumblebee. I'm proud of you. Now why don't you come inside and help me get ready for dinner?" She turned toward Reed and his dad. "Would y'all excuse us, gentlemen?"

The sugary smile made Reed cringe. As soon as they were out of hearing range, Reed tipped his head toward the door. "What's up with that?"

Dad shrugged and took a long drink from his glass. "No idea. She's called a couple of times to check on the boy."

"Huh. I never got the feeling she was close to Amy and Brian."

"Son, I don't have the first damned clue. You got a problem with her?"

Reed hesitated. "I really don't know. Guess it's fine for now."

"She can watch Dylan tomorrow while we ride out west. We got a couple dozen new calves. Thought he might like to see those, but if he won't get his butt up on a horse, guess he'll miss out."

Reed wasn't sure what would be worse—leaving Dylan with Celia or forcing him on a horse. Neither option sounded good. At this rate, the kid would never want to come back to the ranch.

Dinner was nothing short of exhausting. Celia's voice grated on Reed's nerves, and with every passing minute, the weekend was less and less relaxing. He had half a mind to load up Dylan and head back to Dallas. At least his place would be quiet, and he wouldn't be sleeping in a toddler-sized bed.

As Celia served dessert of cherry ice cream and sugar cookies, she smiled at Reed. "So, how are you handling the doctor's appointments and everything, Reed?"

Was that a leading question or just polite conversation? He didn't mean to push her away, exactly, but the last thing he needed was interference. Celia's presence didn't give him good vibes. "Doing fine. So far, no problems." The doctor's appointments had finally scaled back, and since school started, the two worked out a basic routine. But he had to admit, the crazy schedule felt a lot like treading water.

"That's great. But you know, I'm in Dallas too, and I'd be happy to help. I could run errands or pick up after school. That sort of thing." She reached across the table and squeezed Dylan's hand. "I sure don't want to lose you guys. I mean, we're still family, right?"

Reed sucked in his breath. He'd never considered her part of his family, but he supposed she was part of Dylan's. Since the accident, their family had dwindled significantly. But at the moment, the family they had felt like too much. Celia and his dad were each overbearing in their own way. Did Dylan need more people in his life, or was it in his best interest to restrict exposure to these two?

Chapter Three

Mug of tea in hand, Kristen wandered outside into the soft morning light and perched on the top step of the wooden porch that ran across the front of the farmhouse. The rocking chairs that sat on the porch for years were taken inside after her mother's death. Kristen considered dragging one out, but for now, the step was fine. It'd always been one of her favorite places to hang out.

From this spot, she could see the main road and neighboring fields. Most of the Hanover land sat behind and to the east of the house. Her mother always loved that the house faced south, exposing the front to as much sunlight as possible. Even in winter, she kept the door open, allowing light and heat to stream in through the outer glass door.

Smiling at the memory, Kristen stretched her legs down the steps. She expected the weekend to be full of memories, and she wanted to enjoy them. Later in the day, she had to face tasks and the business at hand. Staying in the moment, she closed her eyes, wanting to feel her mother's presence.

When a rumbling truck interrupted the quiet a few minutes later, Kristen moved down the steps and into the yard. The dry grass crunched beneath her feet. Even though the estate still paid for basic maintenance like mowing, the place looked deserted and empty.

Amazing how quickly the change happened. She turned and viewed the house with a critical eye.

The house was missing her mother—and her mother's creative and caring touch. Normally, colorful mums lined the steps this time of year. At least the roses that made a hedge in front of the porch were still in bloom. She inhaled their sweet scent then glanced toward the house. If she could find scissors and a vase, maybe she'd cut some and take them inside to enjoy their fragrance.

Wait. For that matter, why couldn't she take a whole plant? Her mother's beds were profuse with flowers from early spring until winter. Fall was a good time for transplanting. She could dig up a few of the flowers and take them on her last day here. When she finally got a place of her own, she could move them again and always have her mother's flowers with her.

The shed was probably full of old pots and containers, but Kristen wasn't crazy about exploring in there. As she grimaced toward the old structure, something scurried past. And just like that, the idea for a new book sprouted in her head. A simple trigger was the way ideas formed. Out of thin air, a seed took root. She mulled over the idea. The farm could be the backdrop for her next book. Instead of focusing on pretend play, the story could be about looking at something and really seeing what's there. Instead of *What Will You Be?,* she could make the title *What Can You See?*

Thoughts tumbled in. Don't just see a tree—see the leaves and branches, a perching bird, or perhaps a nest. She could present kids with the challenge to look at a house. Would they see just see a house, or flowers and windows? Curtains in the windows? Colored trim? Would they notice details such as shutters? A porch? Flower pots? A chimney?

Grinning, she hurried up the steps and into the house to find a notepad. Re-energized, Kristen refilled her cup, cranked up some tunes, and turned her attention to the appointments of the day. Sam Crenshaw, local farrier and horse trainer, would meet her at the Andersons' place to look at the horses. She needed his expertise on what to say about each one in an ad and how to price them. Later this afternoon, the people from the auction house would arrive to look over the contents of the house.

As she closed her calendar, she remembered the call she promised Jana—and another idea surfaced. Perhaps the new book could feature a special needs child, like someone on crutches or in a wheelchair. Her thoughts turned to the little boy Dylan, and Kristen grabbed her cell phone. Resuming her perch on the steps, she punched in Jana's number.

"Hey, Kristen. How are things at the farm?"

"I'm having a nice, slow morning just lounging around. Without the city noise, I can hear all the farm sounds. A hummingbird flew by so close I heard its wings move."

"Sounds wonderful."

"I even thought of an idea for a new book."

"That's exciting. You'll have to keep me posted so I can get it for my kids when it comes out."

Kristen laughed. "You know I will. But remember, from idea to bookstore is a long road."

"A new project to work on is fun, anyway."

"For sure. Hey, speaking of your kids, that little

boy in your class, Dylan, came to my book signing."

"Did he really? That's great. With his uncle?"

"Yeah." Regret washed over her, and she rested her head against the porch railing. "I feel so sad about his parents."

"They told you?"

Kristen let out a groan. "Well, I opened my big mouth and told Dylan to have fun reading the book with his parents."

"Oh. Don't feel bad. You couldn't have known. His situation is unusual, and having him in class is a challenge. He has to wear a hat and a leg brace at recess. No running, which is hard for a boy, and I have to be on guard constantly for any signs of bullying or anyone making fun of him or saying something that might upset him. But he's a sweet kid, and I think having him in class will be good for all the students in the long run."

A loud truck loaded with hay bales rumbled by, and Kristen put a finger to her ear. "Do you know what happened?"

Jana let out a deep sigh. "Pretty sad stuff. He was hurt, and his parents and little sister were killed in a car accident. I guess he doesn't have much family. The only people listed as relatives in the file I got, besides the uncle, were a grandfather and an aunt. And neither is cleared for release."

"What's that mean?"

"They can't pick Dylan up from school."

"So the good-looking uncle's not married?" Hard to believe he was unattached—but interesting.

"I don't think so. A wife isn't named on the pick-up list. I think he's a little shell-shocked. I'll know more next month when we have parent-teacher conferences."

"Right. I'm sure parenthood is a huge adjustment. It's too bad. I can't imagine losing both parents at that age." Her throat tightened. "I'm having a hard enough time dealing with the loss now."

"I'm sure it's difficult getting the farm ready to sell."

"Yes, but kind of therapeutic, too. I'm getting there."

"I can't even picture the house without your mom."

"I know. Hey, I'll be in Fort Worth next week if you want to meet up. Maybe Friday night? I have my final signing Saturday morning before I head back here."

"I'd love to. I'm so sorry yesterday didn't work out. Let me check with Adam, and I'll get back to you. Maybe we could do something late after Kayla goes to bed."

"Sounds good. I know leaving her is hard when you've been working all week." A full-time job and an eighteen-month-old daughter kept Jana in a perpetual busy zone. Kristen ended the call, but her thoughts were still on the boy. How would a child that age even begin to process the accident and loss? How alone in the world Dylan must feel. And how would that manifest itself? Anger? Fear? Sudden tears stung her eyes. Would he even remember his parents? The tears came hard, and Kristen dashed into the house for tissues. No one remembers much before kindergarten. He'd be left with vague memories and faded photos. She hoped he had lots and lots of pictures.

Dabbing at her eyes, Kristen sniffled. Valerie

warned her early on about getting emotionally attached to fans. She wasn't attached, but she did care. In the bathroom, she splashed cool water on her face. How could caring about a kid ever be wrong?

****

When Kristen arrived at the Anderson barn, she saw Sam had a notebook in hand. Looked as if the assessment was under way. The heels of her cowboy boots crunched against the loose gravel driveway as she approached.

Nate Anderson, her family's long-time neighbor, turned her direction.

"Here she is." The lanky man with a friendly face met her in a few quick strides and wrapped her in a hug. "Hey, Kristen. Good to see you."

"You, too, Nate." She pulled back and gestured toward the weathered barn. "How's the hooved Hanover gang doing?"

"I think they're checking out just fine."

"Good news. You've been so great to keep them." The estate paid boarding costs, of course, but moving the horses a mile down the road and not worrying about them was a huge relief. She took a few steps forward to greet the farrier, a silver haired gentleman who always reminded Kristen of a character from an old western movie.

Sam smiled and extended a hand.

"Thanks for meeting me on a Saturday, Sam."

"My pleasure. I don't think you'll have any problem selling these. The old mare, maybe. She might not take to traveling much. We'll have to see what comes along."

"Right." Kristen pressed together her lips. *Okay.*

This conversation stung already. The "old mare" was Rosie, the horse Kristen's mother rode almost daily until she became sick.

Nate rested a hand on Kristen's shoulder. "Maybe we can work something out, Kristen. We might be able to keep Rosie."

"Really?" Hope blossomed in Kristen's heart. "Has anyone been riding her?"

Nate blew out his breath. "Well, not as much as I'd hoped, but Laurie's taken a liking to her."

"Oh, that's wonderful." Having Laurie, Nate's high-school-aged daughter, show Rosie some love and take care of her, would be the perfect scenario. "I'd love to keep her here if you think it would work out."

"You two can make that decision." Sam handed Kristen a sheet of paper. "These are the places we like to post ads," he said. "The horses look good. I just need to get them out and see how they handle."

"Of course." She gave the notes a brief glance then watched Sam lead the horses from their stalls.

Without comment, he saddled them and put them through their paces.

"Bentley acts like he wants to take off," she told Nate in a loud whisper.

"They might be a little jittery. I'm sorry I couldn't get them out and exercise them more."

"Nate, don't apologize. You've done us such a favor."

When Sam dismounted the last horse, he pulled a pad of paper from his pocket.

"I'll take Cinnamon on back to her stall." Nate reached for the reins.

Arms crossed, Kristen dug the toe of her boot into

the dirt and fidgeted while she waited for Sam's assessment. She and her brother, John, didn't need a lot of money for the horses, but Kristen wanted them to go to good places. They needed to be gentle, responsive to commands, and in good health for that to happen.

From the corner of her eye, Kristen watched Sam.

After a few more minutes, he tore off a couple of papers and headed toward her.

She held her breath.

"These are nice horses," he said. "They're in good shape and handle real well. Should attract some buyers."

Relief flooded through Kristen. "Oh, Sam. That's great news."

He handed her his notes. "Here's what I'd say about 'em and the prices I'd start with."

Nodding, Kristen skimmed the paper. The numbers looked reasonable. "Excellent. Thanks so much, Sam. You're still good with handling the posts and calls?"

"Not a problem. I'll get on the advertising and be in touch if I get any nibbles."

Kristen spent the next hour talking to the horses while she petted, fed them, and added fresh straw to their stalls. She lingered with Star, letting the mare nuzzle against her neck and hair. "We'll go for a ride, girl, I promise. If I don't get back today, I'll be here in the morning." She returned to the house only twenty minutes before the people from the auction company were due to arrive. When the doorbell rang, she drew in a gulp of air and pasted on a smile. Kristen invited them in and after introductions were made, she left them to the task.

After her mother's death, Kristen and her brother

took most of what they wanted—and items that might tempt a thief—from the house. Everything else was simply covered with sheets. With restless energy, Kristen picked up her story notes from earlier and went outside. The jingle of her phone broke the silence thirty minutes later. Kristen checked the caller ID then answered the call. "Hey, John."

"Hi. Just checking in. How'd everything go?"

"The appraisers are here." Kristen kept her voice low.

"Oh. I thought the assessment would be over by now."

Kristen rolled her eyes. Nothing subtle about that comment. "I told you I'd call. They're still in the house, John. They also need to look at the stuff in the barn when they're done here."

"What about the horses?"

"They're fine."

"Kristen, you know what I mean. What did Crenshaw say?"

She counted to ten and studied a billowing cloud that looked like a giant piece of popcorn building to the south. "So, you don't want to know how the horses are doing, just how much they're worth?"

"That's right."

Kristen heard the hard edge in John's voice and bit back a retort.

"I'm not emotional over every little thing like you are," he said. "We just need to settle the estate. Does he think he can sell the horses?"

"Of course. But he won't know how much until he places the ads and gets some responses. The process might take a few days." She couldn't help the annoyance in her voice.

"Look, Kristen, if you can't handle this, I'll make arrangements to get down there."

Kristen bristled and marched into the house for a cold drink. "I didn't say I couldn't handle it, but I am saying you can lighten up. I'd like the sale handled with some grace and tact, the way Mom would want."

"Fine. Call me when you know something solid."

The line went dead, and Kristen swore under her breath. She didn't want to fight with him again, but she didn't like being pushed and pressured. Didn't he have a shred of sentimental feeling for any of their past?

Leaning against the counter, she rubbed her temples. The items in the house weren't just stuff—they represented history. These things were pieces of their lives. Kristen was acutely aware they would all be gone soon—and her brother and his family were all the family she had left. On that sad note, she opened a bottle of peach-flavored sparkling water and stepped back outside to shake off the foul mood.

Much later, when the people were gone and Kristen was alone with her thoughts and space, she finally relaxed. She sat on the porch and watched dusk turn to darkness. Gazing up at the stars in the clear night sky, she let her mind wander to her young readers and her quest to connect with them. The possibilities poured in. A story about starry nights? About listening?

Was the farm the energizing force that got her creative juices flowing? Or did she owe the surge to the quiet solitude of being in nature? She used to think she'd have the farm forever—imagined writing retreats in the country and having a little getaway now and then where she could unplug and refresh. Drawing up her knees, she locked her arms around them and breathed in the crisp air. Maybe she could find a quiet getaway in other places, as well. Occasionally renting a cabin in the woods or on a secluded shoreline would be far cheaper than keeping and caring for this old house and farm. Would new environments spawn new ideas and adventures?

Did the house deserve more than someone lost in its memories? Perhaps a new family, new life, new possibilities? Kristen released a heavy sigh. Maybe her brother was right—time to cut the emotional attachment. She wished she knew whether cutting the strings meant gaining a new perspective—or losing a chunk of herself.

Chapter Four

Kristen met Jana at a small bar that had a quaint, local feel and sat about halfway between Jana's school and Fort Worth. A noisy Friday happy hour was in full swing, but she caught sight of an empty bar table and beckoned Jana to follow. For Kristen, catching up with her friend was an added bonus to finishing the book tour. "This is perfect." She hitched onto the chair. "Cute place."

Jana took a sunny yellow envelope from her purse and waved it at Kristen. "Here. I have to give you this before I forget."

Reaching for the envelope, Kristen frowned. "What is it?"

"A note from Dylan, the little boy in my class."

"Oh, that's sweet."

"Wait. Maybe I should get a picture of you opening it so I can prove I delivered it. I'm sure he'll want a report."

Kristen laughed. "What are you talking about?"

Jana held up her phone camera. "Okay, open the envelope."

Kristen slit the back tab and unfolded the paper inside.

Jana snapped several photos. "That is one fierce fan you've got there. He almost had a meltdown at school the other day because he missed signing the card the kids made for you. He had a doctor's appointment on Monday so he missed a few hours of class. By the time he found out, I'd already mailed the card."

Kristen ordered a lemon drop martini then turned her attention to the paper. The drawing of a seal and stick-figure child was rudimentary, but the writing was legible. "He writes well for his age." She re-read Dylan's words.

Dear Miss Hanover, Thanks for coming to my class. Your books are very good, and I like to read them. Your friend, Dylan

"Aw, he's so adorable." Kristen held up the paper. "Can you do video on your phone?" She glanced behind her. "Just keep the camera tight on me so we don't have bottles showing in the background. Probably not good for my image."

"Good thinking."

With Jana's phone pointed at her again, Kristen held up the paper and waved. She leaned in close to record her voice over the crowd noise and music. "Hello, Dylan! Thank you for your nice note. I hope to see you again some time. Keep up the reading."

"Whew." Jana tucked away the phone. "Hopefully that will take care of the problem."

"Sorry he made a fuss," Kristen said. "He's such a cute kid."

"No worries. I think he's fine now. I just didn't expect it to be a big deal, you know? I assured him the card was from the whole class, but I guess he was still upset at home that night, and I got an email from his uncle."

"Oh, Jana. I'm really sorry." Kristen wasn't surprised that Dylan was super-sensitive right now. Her concern over the boy and his uncle came rushing back.

The waitress delivered their drinks.

Jana lifted hers toward Kristen with a grin. "To problems with easy fixes."

"Hear, hear," Kristen sipped the tart drink then squeezed in a little more lemon. "Was the uncle cool about it?" She had a feeling the handsome and self-assured Reed Armstrong could come off as brusque or curt, even if he didn't intend to. At least he was standing up and advocating for his nephew. Standing up and advocating were positive. Maybe the two would bond and be okay. Though their situation might be none of her business, Kristen couldn't stop worrying about Dylan—or his uncle, for that matter.

"Yes. He was very polite. Actually, I'm glad he let me know because I hate for things like that to fester. I'm already on pins and needles with Dylan."

"I'm sure you're doing fine. You'll probably end up being really important to him—kind of like a mother figure. He'll always remember the special lady who was his kindergarten teacher and helped him through a rough time."

"Same with you," Jana said. "Think of all the kids who'll hold onto your books so they can read them to their kids someday. It's pretty cool."

"I hope so." Of course Kristen knew books were boxed and forgotten in dusty attics, too. But if she could claim she'd influenced even a single kid and set him or her on a course of reading and creativity, then she'd feel she'd made a difference in the world.

"So, back to the farm tomorrow?" Jana asked.

"Yep. After the last book signing. Some people are coming to look at the horses we're selling."

"Ouch. I know that's hard. You sure about selling all of them? No way to take Star to Denver?"

Kristen still agonized over those questions. Letting the horses go was hard, but she wanted to do what was best for them, even if the best hurt her heart. "I've thought about keeping her, but I don't think it'd be right. She's old for traveling and starting over. Taking her away from the others seems cruel. Believe it or not, horses make friends. These guys are buddies. Also, boarding is expensive, and I live in the city. Driving to a barn would probably take an hour, and I couldn't give her the attention she deserves."

She considered moving to a rural area, but she'd committed to teaching a writing class at the local community college next semester, and a long commute didn't appeal. Though they called second semester "spring" semester, spring accounted for only about a month if Denver weather was true to form. The teaching gig came up before her latest book hit the market with surprising success.

And the success was not guaranteed. A silver lining to the sale of the farm was the financial cushion it would provide. That cushion could mean the difference between a flexible, creative lifestyle and an eight-to-five office job. She didn't ever want to go back there. Ready or not, tomorrow she'd turn the final page of the book tour and begin the last chapter of *Life on the Farm*. Could she close the book for good?

****

Reed opened the door to the bookstore and looked around, hoping the line wasn't as long as the last one. He and Dylan had a busy day ahead and the detour to Fort Worth put him in a time crunch. He heard the soft lilt of laughter as soon as he and Dylan stepped into line. Though he couldn't see her yet, he heard the genuine smile in her pleasant voice—a sharp contrast to the shrill, high pitch of Celia's voice, which curled his toes last weekend. The lovely Miss Hanover's voice had a warmth that was easy to listen to. So far, he approved of Dylan's taste in women.

Reed belatedly wondered about book signing protocol. Since Dylan already owned all of Kristen Hanover's books, he brought one from home to be signed. Hopefully that wouldn't be a problem. Reed's personal library consisted mainly of business-related and non-fiction books, though he did read an occasional thriller or historical novel. He'd never attended another author's book signing.

When the people in front of Reed moved toward the author table, Miss Hanover looked their direction.

The smile faltered as her eyes widened.

Only a second passed before the surprise of recognition turned into a puzzled expression that wrinkled her brow. She probably wondered if she should call security. At this point, he and Dylan might seem like stalkers. Truth be told, that's what Reed felt like. He gave a slight nod and hitched a hand in his pocket. He put his other hand on his nephew's shoulder to restrain him from rushing the table.

But as soon as the mother and daughter moved on, Dylan broke free.

Though Dylan's gait wasn't smooth, Reed found keeping the kid from running almost impossible.

"Miss Hanover, it's me again."

The woman grinned and reached out to Dylan.

Reed couldn't help noticing her painted nails were

a perfect match to the pink polka dot scarf around her neck. Combined with the pink and orange blouse she wore, she looked like an artist—fun and creative.

"Well, it sure is. I'm so glad to see you again, Dylan. How are you?"

Dylan's head bobbed. "I brought another book."

"Excellent." Her gaze flickered up to Reed.

He caught the appreciation in her clear green eyes—the acknowledgment that he was making the effort to indulge Dylan's interests. A ridiculous sense of accomplishment rushed through Reed. Did Miss Hanover not think he was on the verge of ruining his nephew's life? Nearly every woman he'd met since becoming Dylan's guardian had some kind of condescending advice or look of doubt. And they all conveyed the same poor-baby message. Not that he particularly cared what strangers thought. No, he wasn't a parenting expert, but the automatic assumption that as a man he couldn't raise his nephew rankled.

She took the book from Dylan, then she stood and held a hand toward Reed. "Nice to see you again. I hope getting here wasn't too much trouble."

"Not at all," he lied, thinking of the road trip ahead of them. "You've got a big fan here, Miss—"

"Kristen, please. And it's Reed, right?"

That she remembered his name gave him pause. He rather liked the sound of it coming from her lips in that soft, cheerful voice. Of course, she was a writer, trained to be observant and remember details. She probably remembered everything. "Right." Leaning against the table, Reed went into bystander mode, watching the interaction between Kristen and his nephew. The kid lit up around her, that's for sure.

"Hey, Dylan, I love the picture and note you made for me. Thank you."

Reed's glance snapped to Kristen. "You already got it?"

Kristen reached for, but missed, the orange pen rolling away. "Yes. Jana—er, Mrs. Baxter is a friend of mine. We met last night, and she gave me the note."

The pen dropped to the floor, and Dylan dove under the table. "I'll get it."

"You're a friend of Dylan's teacher?" Groaning inside, Reed leaned closer while Dylan was distracted. He lowered his voice. "Listen, can we keep that fact between the two of us? Dylan has this infatuation thing going, and it could become a nuisance."

Kristen pressed together her lips for a moment before speaking. "I-I'm sorry. I was just— He's a sweet kid, and I don't want to hurt his feelings."

Her eyes clouded, but Reed needed to make her understand. "You live in Denver, right?" When her cheeks colored, Reed blew out his breath. "Don't worry, we're not stalking you. Saw the information on your book jacket. Look, the crush isn't your fault. I brought him today because I don't want to hurt his feelings, either. But by next week, he'll hopefully be on to something else. No offense."

"None taken," she said softly.

Dylan bounced up with the pen in hand.

Kristen turned back to him and clapped her hands. "So, Dylan, tell me, which book is your favorite?"

"I like this one," he said. "But I like the new one best." He put his hands on top of his hat and screwed up his face. Then he shook his head. "I like them all."

Laughing, Kristen walked around the table. Then

she crouched to his level and pulled him into a quick hug. With a tug on the bill of his cap, she looked into his eyes. "Dylan, you made my day. Now I better get back to work and sign some more books. You take care, all right?" She held her hand out to Reed again.

He squeezed it gently—her soft touch sending a surprise humming through his veins. "Thank you." He lingered just a beat before moving on. Outside, he helped Dylan climb into the car while agreeing for the umpteenth time Miss Hanover was pretty, and Miss Hanover was really nice. He was tempted to give Dylan a geography lesson and point out the distance between Denver, Colorado, and Dallas, Texas, but he refrained.

Next up, a couple of errands and then lunch. Then they'd head north. He planned to get everything out of the way today. He had a hot date with his couch, a couple of cold beers, and the Dallas Cowboys on Sunday. Reed was about to swing into the car when his phone buzzed. "Reed here." He picked up though he didn't recognize the number.

"Mr. Armstrong? This is Sylvia McGill from *The Clarion*."

"Excuse me? The what?"

"*The Clarion*. We're a community magazine in Amarillo."

Reed rolled his eyes. Why did he answer this call? "What can I do for you, Sylvia?" He figured he already knew the answer.

"We'd like to schedule an interview with you about the accident that took your sister's family."

"Sorry, Sylvia. There's nothing more to tell."

"Well, we do feature articles. We were thinking of a follow up. You know, now that a few months have passed. An update on how your nephew is doing. People were so concerned about him."

Reed's jaw clenched. When would these people let the story go? Leave them alone? "I'll have to decline, Sylvia. Not interested. You have a good day." Rude or not, he ended the call before the woman could respond. He was so done with the media. If an ambulance chaser wasn't after them, a reporter wanted a profile piece or a human-interest angle. He blocked future calls from the number and started the car.

Following the directions of his GPS, Reed pulled the SUV onto a rutted gravel road about ten minutes after his three-thirty appointment. Spotting the barn in the distance, he drove past the house, a trail of dust billowing behind them.

Seeing a man step from the barn, Reed rolled down the windows and shut off the engine. He swiveled to face Dylan. "Why don't you stay in the car for now while I go look at the horses? I'll just be right out here."

Dylan nodded. "Okay, Uncle Reed."

Yeah, he didn't figure he'd get any pushback. He hoped the horses were gentle enough that Dylan might get more comfortable around them one of these days. Maybe he'd have better luck with horses that weren't already associated with the ranch and Grandpa.

Reed went around the car and greeted the older man with a weathered face that told of years on a farm in the elements. His lean form and worn hat reminded Reed of his dad. He extended his hand and received a firm shake in return.

"Good to meet you Reed," Sam Crenshaw said.

"Hope we haven't kept you waiting."

According to his website bio, Sam was an award-winning farrier and horseman. On the phone, he'd sounded competent and knowledgeable. Reed was about to see whether his assessment was correct or the three-hour trip had been a waste of time. Starting from Fort Worth added an hour to the drive.

"Come on in, and we'll introduce you to the horses."

Reed stepped forward, but movement from inside the barn caught his attention.

A woman led a horse through the open doorway and into the sunlight.

Reed stopped in his tracks. *What the hell?* His heart skipped a beat, and he blinked, taking in the petite form in denim jeans and cowboy boots. Red highlights shone in her hair as the sun hit it, and she could easily have passed for a college girl.

She adjusted the horse's halter and gave the animal a little pat before starting Reed's direction. Her eyes widened, and she also stopped short.

Stunned, Reed stared until the slamming of the car door broke the déjà vu moment.

"Miss Hanover!" Dylan shouted.

Chapter Five

Thoughts tumbled through Kristen's head, but none of them made any sense. What in the world were Dylan and his uncle doing at the farm? She could believe they were, in fact, stalking her, except for the look on Reed's face. He seemed just as surprised as she was. She held out a hand to a grinning Dylan. "Okay, I give up. What brings you guys out here?"

Sam poked his head around Cinnamon, his brows pulled together. "Y'all know each other?"

Kristen glanced from Sam back to Reed. "Are you here to look at my horses?"

Turning toward Sam, Reed spread his hands in the air. "Is that right?"

"Mr. Armstrong, this is Kristen Hanover, owner of the horses we've discussed." Sam gestured toward Kristen. "I've been handling details of the sale for her. This here's Cinnamon, a mighty fine horse. She's strong but gentle. And follows directions. Perfect for trail rides."

"Trail rides? That's what you want the horses for?"

Reed nodded. "On my dad's ranch. They wouldn't be doing ranch work. Well, maybe some light work riding fences or something. But mostly, they'll be for guests who want a pleasure ride."

"I see. People with no riding experience?"

Reed hitched his shoulders. "I expect a little bit of

everything."

"These are your horses?" Wrinkling his nose, Dylan stared at Kristen,

Kristen had to laugh. The kid must be totally confused. "Yes, buddy, they sure are. But I can't keep them anymore, so I'm looking for a good home for them."

With wide eyes, Dylan swung toward Reed. "Grandpa's ranch!"

"That's what we're talking about."

"Dylan." Kristen bent to his eye level. "Do you like horses?"

He cast his eyes downward and kicked at the dirt.

Uh-oh. He didn't look like a fan. Kristen shot a glance at Reed, who silently shook his head.

"I guess so," Dylan mumbled.

"Yeah? Me, too." Maybe she could offer some encouragement. It'd be a shame for the kid to grow up going to his grandpa's ranch and not like horses. "Want to meet my horse?" When he looked up, his eyes were filled with doubt—maybe fear.

Sam held out some papers toward Reed. "Here's the background on her. Gives you the last assessment from the vet, too."

Kristen flashed a smile at Dylan. "Why don't we go see my horse while these guys talk? She's really friendly. I promise." She wanted to meet the prospective owners. She wasn't handing over the horses to just anyone. Though she wouldn't mind seeing what kind of horseman Reed Armstrong was, maybe she shouldn't witness the critical scrutiny that would take place. "Would that be all right?" Kristen addressed Reed.

"Sure."

Dylan took her hand.

He seemed reluctant, but Kristen was happy to have something else to do. She steered him into the barn and down to the fourth stall where Star stood peeking over the railing. Dylan tightened his hold on her hand as they got close.

Stopping, Kristen bent her knees again. "Dylan, this horse won't hurt you. I would never let that happen," she said gently. "But if you're scared, we can go back." When he remained silent, she tried again. "It's okay to be scared, sweetie. Horses are big, powerful animals."

Nodding, he put a fist to his mouth. "They're really big."

So the size of the animal was the problem. Kristen glanced toward the open doors, wondering about Dylan's experience with horses. She figured he'd had a scare. Probably at his grandpa's ranch. "The thing is, you have to learn the rules, just like when you're starting in school or learning to drive a car," Kristen said. "You have to learn what to do. When you started school, were you a little bit nervous because you didn't know Mrs. Baxter or where your classroom was? You didn't know the other kids?"

His head bobbed again.

"Well, being around horses is kind of the same. You have to learn how to be safe around them. I bet if you wanted, your uncle would get you some lessons." She lifted Dylan and let out an exaggerated groan. "Oh, man. Talk about big. You weigh a ton." She held Dylan on her hip, turned slightly away from the stall, as she ran a hand over the white patch on Star's forehead.

59

"This is Star. I've been riding and taking care of her since I was thirteen years old, but since I don't live here anymore, she needs a new home."

"How come?"

"Because my mother died, and—" *Oh, damn*. She clamped a hand over her mouth, kicking herself inside.

Dylan's face fell, and his lower lip trembled. "My mom died, too."

Tears burned Kristen's eyes, and she pulled him close. "Oh, sweetie. I know. I'm so sorry." She leaned against the door of the stall and took a minute to regroup. Star nuzzled her hair, and Kristen shifted Dylan to the other hip. "Look, she's tickling me."

"She's tickling?"

"Yeah. That's how they play. I think she wants me to pet her again." She stroked the horse while Dylan watched. "Would you like to touch her?"

"Okay," Dylan whispered.

"Put your hand right beside mine." Kristen held her breath and took a step closer to Star.

Dylan placed his hand against Star's coat and patted a couple of times. But as soon as the horse raised her head, Dylan's hand shot back, and he burrowed into Kristen.

"Don't worry," Kristen said. "She's letting you know she likes when you pet her. See? If she didn't like you to touch her, she'd back up or turn away." She gently turned him so she could see his face. "Isn't that what you would do?"

Activity at the entrance drew Kristen's attention.

The men led Cinnamon back inside the barn then guided out Bentley.

Reed paused when he caught sight of them.

"Uncle Reed, come see Star."

He smiled and waved. "Hold on. I'll be there in a couple of minutes."

While they waited, Kristen grabbed a stalk of hay for Star to munch on. Dylan was reluctant at first, but she enticed him to also take a stalk. "You don't have to get close. Just hold it up, and she'll take it."

When Star began chewing at the piece Dylan held, he swiveled, a grin spreading across his face.

"See there?" With a little laugh, she squeezed him closer. "You're doing great."

A few minutes later, Reed joined them.

Kristen gratefully transferred Dylan into his arms. She shook her arm to get the blood flowing again. Dylan's weight had become a strain, but she'd wanted him to feel secure.

"This is Star," Dylan told Reed.

"I know. She looks like a nice horse."

"She is. She's the one Miss Hanover likes to ride."

Kristen sensed Reed's gaze, but she didn't look up. If the conversation turned personal, chances were, she'd get emotional. "Do you want me to bring her out?"

"I don't think we need to," Reed said.

She counted to ten to steady herself then glanced up.

Reed cocked his head toward the exit. "You want to talk business for a minute?"

"Sure." Kristen dusted her hands on her jeans then stepped in front of Reed. She raised her brows at Sam.

He gave a slight nod in return.

"I'd like to take them all," Reed said. "If that's good with you. Sam mentioned you'd like to keep them together."

Kristen put a hand to her chest. "I'd love to keep them together. Can—" She moistened her lips, thinking what to say without sounding like a control freak. "Can you tell me a little more about the ranch?"

"Uncle Reed, I'm thirsty." Dylan tugged on Reed's arm. "I need to use the bathroom."

"Oh, um…" Kristen looked toward her neighbor's house but didn't see anyone outside. "Listen, why don't we run over to my place? It's just a mile up the road. We can get this guy taken care of, and you can take a look and see if you want any of the tack as well."

Reed turned to Sam. "We all set here? I can have the horses picked up next weekend. Maybe sooner."

She waited while the men shook hands, then Kristen headed for her car. "Follow me." Moments later, she unlocked the back door to the farmhouse and ushered her guests inside. "Here we go." She dumped her purse on the counter then motioned Dylan down the hallway. "This way, big guy." She flipped on the light then closed the door behind her. "Time for cold water all around," she told Reed back in the kitchen.

"I wouldn't turn it down," he said with a wry smile.

She opened the fridge and grabbed three bottles then handed one to Reed.

"Thanks."

Leaning against the counter, she pushed back the hair that escaped her French braid and took a long drink. "Sure doesn't feel like fall yet, does it?" Kind of a lame conversation starter, but she was still getting her head around the fact that these two were actually at the farm and in her house—and that Reed wanted to buy all her horses. This morning, he was ready to be done with her. Now, they'd have a permanent connection. Sort of. She glanced over to find his gaze fixed on her.

"Pretty warm," he agreed.

She flushed under his scrutiny. And getting warmer...

When the bathroom door squeaked open, Kristen pushed off from the counter. "Hey, sweetie. Here's some cold water." She twisted off the cap and handed Dylan the bottle.

"Thank you."

"Let's head to the barn, and you guys can tell me about your ranch." She motioned toward the back door, but just before they got there, Dylan stopped.

Turning, he looked at Kristen with wide eyes and pointed. "Miss Hanover, somebody colored on the wall."

Kristen swallowed past the sudden lump in her throat. She'd been walking by that wall for years and didn't take much notice anymore. She'd have to remember to snap a picture before she left. New owners would paint over the image in a heartbeat.

With a soft smile for Dylan, she reached out and ran a hand over the amateurish painting of a dog and flowers around a tree. "We sure did. My mother let me and my brother do that a long time ago. See these marks and dates on the tree trunk? That's how she kept track of how tall we were each year. It's called a growth chart."

"That's awesome."

"How old are you?"

"Six."

She heard the pride in his voice. "Stand here and let's see how tall you are." Against the wall, she put her hand above Dylan's head. "Okay, step out. Look at that, you're a couple of inches taller than I was at six."

His smile widened. "I'm going to be tall like my dad."

Oh, man. Kristen choked up every time the kid mentioned his parents. Taking a deep breath, she tugged on the bill of the cap again. "I bet you are."

"Come on, sport," Reed said. "We still have a couple of things to do."

Outside, Kristen unfastened the padlock on the barn doors.

Reed stepped in to slide the door.

"Thanks." Though vacant for several months, the barn still smelled of hay, leather, and horses. For Kristen, those scents would always conjure memories of the farm. Inside, she squinted until her eyes adjusted to the dim light. "Tack is to the left." She pointed toward the open door opposite the stalls. "Several saddles and blankets. How many horses do you already have at the ranch?"

"We lost one recently so I think there are three."

"Hey, Miss Hanover."

Kristen turned to see Dylan holding up a rusty metal watering can.

"What's this?" he asked.

"Just an old water—" She saw the mischievous light spark in his eyes. *Well, duh.* Grinning, she took the can. "This, sir, is a frosting foozle, and I am a baker. I use this to pour ooey gooey frosting onto cakes and donuts."

Dylan grabbed it back, puffing out his chest. "But see, I am a big, big giant, and this salt shaker is the right size for me."

Laughing, Kristen clapped her hands. "That's very good, Mr. Giant. And you rhymed, too."

Reed poked his head out of the tack room. "All of the saddles go?"

So much for playing around. Kristen hesitated a moment, torn between entertaining Dylan and settling the business at hand. She joined Reed in the small room, surveying the shelves lined with dusty gear. She focused on one saddle in particular—the one she'd used for years, bought with her own savings in high school, and formed to her figure.

Reed reached for a blanket. "These are in good shape. I think we can take all of these off your hands."

His words rung in Kristen's ears with finality, and she hesitated again. Taking them all?

His brows arched.

In that instant, she decided once and for all, she would keep her saddle. "I think everything in here can go except the dark caramel saddle here." So what if she was being sentimental? So what if she didn't have a horse? Maybe one day she would again.

Kristen hovered while Reed spent about fifteen minutes looking at the tack—about fifteen minutes too many for Dylan.

"Are you guys done?"

Dylan collapsed against the wall as if his spine suddenly failed.

"Uncle Reed, I'm hungry."

His voice took on a slight whiney tone, and Kristen sympathized. Standing around waiting on grown-ups was no fun. She wished she had some kid-friendly snacks to offer, but her cupboards were bare.

"Yep. Almost done." Reed turned back to Kristen.

"Go ahead and have Sam add all of these to the bill of sale."

"Sounds good. I'm sorry I don't have much food in the house since I just got here this afternoon, but I could probably rustle up some crackers or something." She smiled at Dylan. "Giants must be fed a lot, right?"

"Anyplace around here we could stop for a quick burger?" Reed asked.

He apparently missed her attempt to cajole Dylan. Did this guy ever lighten up? "Oh, sure. Big Bob's, about eight miles down the county road, is good. I'll probably end up there myself tonight."

He cocked his head, and his gaze met hers. "You should join us then."

Kristen cringed. She'd practically invited herself to do just that. "Well…" Valerie's warning clanged in her head. *Don't get involved with fans.* If she'd told her once, she'd told her a hundred times.

"Yes!"

Dylan tugged on Kristen's arm.

"Come with us. Please, Miss Hanover."

Whether his uncle had issued the invitation just to be polite or actually wouldn't mind her company didn't matter at that point. No way could she turn down those big blue, imploring eyes. Besides, this wasn't a book signing or classroom visit. She wasn't on the clock. She couldn't help wondering if the poor kid was starved for attention—or affection. Reed seemed to be taking good care of Dylan but perhaps was light on warm fuzzies. Her heart ached to know Dylan didn't have the spontaneous hugs and kisses of a mom. Kristen looked at Reed.

A slow grin spread across his face.

"What?"

With a chuckle, he leaned toward her, his face only inches from hers. "I think you've been had by the bully blues," he whispered.

She caught her breath at the unexpected closeness but returned the grin. "I think you're right." He'd probably been on the receiving end of those pleading eyes a time or two. She also had the feeling his own smoky blues could be equally persuasive.

A little shiver fluttered up her spine. Dare she explore further?

****

The small diner was old but had an inviting neighborhood feel. And something smelled delicious—freshly baked. "Smells good in here." Reed ushered Dylan and Kristen toward an empty booth. Though early for dinner, a few tables were already filled. "What's the specialty?"

Kristen turned. "Well, the burgers are excellent. But what you're smelling is amazing homemade pie. Marilee, one of the owners, makes them herself."

Reed's mouth watered. He could use some good old-fashioned comfort food. He slid into the faux-leather booth opposite Kristen and his nephew. The metal-trimmed laminate table was a throw-back for sure.

The server, a plump graying woman with a friendly smile, took their orders then placed some crackers on the table in front of Dylan. "A little something to tide you over. Food'll be out real soon, folks."

Dylan ripped into a package of crackers almost before the woman let go.

"Thank you." Reed turned to Kristen. "Back to

your question. The ranch is a couple of hours west of Dallas. It's about thirty-five hundred acres."

"Oh, wow. Did you grow up there?"

"I did. It's a smaller operation than it used to be, but my dad is determined to keep the place running as long as he can."

"I see. But the horses are just for pleasure riding?"

"Yeah. His manager got the idea to have guests come out and stay in some cabins on the land. We'll see how that goes."

"Sounds like a good way to add revenue," Kristen said.

"Maybe. The ranch is a great place to unwind." He leaned back and stretched an arm across the back of the booth. "I try to get out there every couple of weeks." *Or used to.*

"I know what you mean. I thought about keeping the farm for a writer's getaway. Sometimes a change of scenery helps get the creative juices going."

"Makes sense. But that plan fell through?" Her deep intake of a breath hinted he might be treading into sensitive territory. Sam told him the farm was being sold but hadn't given any specifics. Could be a foreclosure situation. She flashed him a wry smile, even as sadness flickered in her eyes.

"It did. My brother wants to cash out."

"Ah. Sorry to hear that. So, you're liquidating?"

She nodded. "Yes. Thank you so much for taking the horses. I hope they're what you're looking for."

"They seem perfect—almost too good to be true." He'd be thrilled to check his dad's horse-buying task off the list so easily.

"They're the best."

Her voice softened, and Reed understood the attachment she must feel.

"I should write up a little bit about each one of them," she said. "You know, some information about their personalities. Would that be helpful?"

"Absolutely." Reed wouldn't mind knowing more, but he couldn't promise his dad's manager, who'd be overseeing the horses, would bother to look at whatever she wrote. He was a stubborn old mule who liked to do things his way. And was almost as bad as his employer. Probably no need to mention that to the horses' current owner, though. "Our manager has a high regard for his horses. They'll be well cared for."

Her cheeks colored. "Oh, I never thought—"

"I know."

The server slid a hamburger and plate full of steaming fries in front of Dylan. "For the starving child." She chuckled then placed a massive meatloaf sandwich in front of Reed. "And pulled pork with slaw for the lady. Y'all enjoy."

All conversation suspended.

Reed bit into his sandwich, hoping the flavor would satisfy his craving. The tangy sauce covering the slab of meat didn't disappoint. "Wow." He wiped a napkin across his mouth then went back for more. "This is great," he said between bites.

"Glad you like it." Kristen smiled and reached for her own plate.

While he chewed, Reed took the opportunity to look at his phone, which had buzzed a couple of times. *Damn.* Three missed calls and a dozen new emails. On Saturday. And probably all had something to do with production—or lack of—in Houston. How would he find time to deal with them?

"Hey, Dylan, you want some french fries with that ketchup?"

Reed looked up to see Kristen grinning at his nephew as she pulled several napkins from the holder and dropped some in Dylan's lap then tucked a few under the plate where the sauce dripped. She was obviously good with kids. Didn't get uptight about little things like spilled ketchup or inconvenient hunger pangs. When she glanced at him, genuine humor lit her face. He saw kindness there, too. Maybe a little on the sentimental side, but was he wrong to discourage Dylan's adoration? So far, she was the one woman he'd met who didn't offer unsolicited parenting advice. Yet, she acted as if she knew what she was doing.

"I can stay with Dylan if you need to make a call," she said.

Her words brought him back to earth. "Oh, thanks. Nothing I need to deal with right now." But his thoughts lingered on her. "You're such a natural with Dylan. Have you…do you have kids?"

Her eyes widened, and she let out an odd cough.

"You all right?"

She held up a hand. "I'm fine. You caught me taking a bite. No kids. Never been married."

"Huh. You just seem so…"

"Childlike? Immature?"

Her eyes sparkled. Reed shook his head. "Uh, no. Not even close."

"I just like kids." She shrugged and popped a chip into her mouth.

"It shows."

"Miss Hanover, you're just cool," Dylan said.

"Well, there you have it." She patted Dylan's head. "From the voice of authority."

Reed laughed out loud. "Dylan, you nailed it."

Tilting his head, Dylan scrunched his nose. "Nailed what?"

"Never mind." Reed reached for his wallet.

"Wait." Kristen held up a hand. "To show you how cool I am, I'm picking up the tab. You're guests in my hometown, after all."

"Not a chance," Reed said. "Anyway, we don't have a check yet. Here's my card if you want to send those horse bios."

"Horse what?" Dylan asked.

"Stories," Kristen said. "I'll tell you and Reed all about my horses. So you get to know them better."

"Okay."

The kid's positive response was encouraging. Maybe he'd get past some of his fears since they were Miss Hanover's horses. Reed watched her scan his business card.

"Viking Oil?"

"Yeah. I'm a petroleum engineer."

"Ah." She nodded.

She drew out the "ah" as if the information cleared something up for her, but she didn't elaborate. Then things quickly wrapped up as the server handed him the check, and Dylan announced he was going to the bathroom. Sliding from the booth, Reed stood. "Be right back." He turned away, ignoring Kristen's protest.

Outside a few minutes later, Kristen hugged Dylan. "You guys be careful out there on the road."

"Will do." Reed was silent a moment but felt as if he needed to say something more. "Don't worry. We'll take good care of the horses."

"Thank you. And thanks for dinner."

"Our pleasure." Then, just because it felt right, he moved closer and brushed her cheek with a light kiss. "You take care."

Smiling, she waved a hand. "Bye, you guys."

Reed waited until Kristen got in her car, then he pulled onto the highway behind her. When they reached the farmhouse, he slowed the car and gave a couple of beeps on the horn.

Dylan waved his arms.

As the vehicle continued down the road toward home, Reed braced for the chatter that always followed their encounters with Kristen Hanover. Instead, a dull silence settled inside the car. He glanced at the back seat to find Dylan's head resting against his hand, his body slumped against the door. Maybe tired. Maybe lost in thought. Or both.

He'd bet he knew exactly what—or who—was on his mind. She stuck in Reed's as well. "Tired, buddy? This would be a good time for a nap." He figured the kid would be asleep in a few minutes whether he wanted to or not.

Dylan leaned forward and glared.

Whoa. He didn't see that coming. "What's wrong?"

"You shouldn't have kissed Miss Hanover."

Oh. This was grumpy, jealous Dylan. Reed spared him another quick glance. "Look, Dylan, I just gave her a friendly little goodbye kiss. That's what grown-ups do sometimes. You know how men shake hands, right? Well, sometimes a gentleman will kiss a lady on the cheek. It's no big deal."

"Miss Hanover is *my* friend."

Reed swiped a hand over his mouth to hide his chuckle. Dylan just proved something every boy should learn—kissing girls can cause trouble. No sense debating this one. "Okay, she can be your special friend. Remember, you got a big hug."

Were they friends with Kristen now? Both of them? He enjoyed her company at dinner. And he didn't think *she* minded the peck on the cheek. With a heavy sigh, he looked out at the long stretch of blacktop ahead—and reminded himself of the distance between Denver and Dallas.

With working out issues at the Houston plant, helping his dad out at the ranch, and raising his nephew, who had time to think about a relationship, anyway?

Chapter Six

Kristen took a sip of wine and tapped the card against the kitchen table. Viking Oil. The guy was an engineer. She shook her head—again. Engineer so did not fit the picture. In fact, the guy pretty much blew the nerdy engineer stereotype right out of the water, though the news did explain his aloof, all-about-business attitude. But for now, she'd have to give him a pass. Given the loss of his family members and becoming a dad overnight, he was probably on emotional overload.

Kind of cool that he used the ranch to decompress. He hadn't mentioned riding, but he was obviously comfortable around horses. She imagined he did just fine in a saddle. And looked pretty fine there, too.

Instead of writing up the horse bios she'd promised, which she wanted to get done before she left the farm, Kristen turned to her computer and did an Internet search for one Reed Armstrong of Dallas. In seconds, dozens of results popped up. *Interesting*. Director of operations for field research. She had no idea what that meant, but the title sounded impressive. Looked like he did an occasional guest-speaking gig, too, and represented his college at career fairs. She'd bet that paid off.

Backing up, she clicked on the profile with Viking Oil and scanned the page. *Huh*. Didn't exactly sound like an office job. How would he manage site visits with Dylan? Who would— Kristen put a palm to her forehead. *Give it a rest.* She nudged back her chair and picked up the wine glass. Stepping outside and into the yard, she looked at the vast night sky filled with stars. She paced the grass before returning to her spot on the porch. Being at the farm this time was making her more restless than refreshed. Her thoughts were scattered.

Pushing off from the railing, Kristen savored the last of her fruity white wine. In three days, she'd be going home—back to real life. Thirteen hours away. Reed Armstrong and his nephew would be way out of radar range.

The wine soured on her tongue.

****

Kristen awoke to sunlight streaming through the windows and by mid-morning was well into the main project for the day. Shovel in hand, and with a little Internet research to guide her, she started with the roses, going for the smallest. Those were most likely to transplant well. She'd filled a couple of buckets when the ideas started flowing. Another story idea. She could show kids what lives in the dirt, like bugs and worms, and what grows there. Did five- and six-year-olds already know things they ate, such as carrots and potatoes, grew in the dirt? That french fries actually started in the dirt? Surely that information would stir up an emotional reaction.

And, of course, the thrill of finding buried treasure was a possibility. In Oklahoma, digging could potentially produce an arrowhead. Playing in the dirt could introduce them to the field of archaeology. Or, they might discover oil—same as a certain petroleum engineer.

Kristen released the shovel, letting it fall to the ground. Wiping her brow, she picked up her mug and headed up the porch stairs. "Good grief," she muttered. She'd gone, what, three hours without thinking of the man? After refilling the mug, she placed it inside the microwave and blew out her breath. What the hell? Reed Armstrong was but a tiny blip, a microscopic dot on the map of her life.

Yet, stranger things had happened. Was there some cosmic reason their paths crossed? After all, odds were slim that out of all the people in Texas and Oklahoma, he'd be the one to show up at the farm wanting to buy her horses. Smiling behind her cup, she relived the brush of his lips across her cheek and gave herself permission to fantasize a bit as she returned to her task. No one else would know. Once he received the write-ups on the horses, he'd have her email address…

The ringing of her phone brought her day-dreaming to an abrupt halt. Glancing at the caller ID, she grimaced. Reality calling. "Hi, John. What's up?"

"Hey. Everything all set for tomorrow?"

Why did he feel the need to check up on her? Everything was 'set for tomorrow' a week ago. "Sure. Nothing's changed."

"You're staying 'til everything's loaded, right?"

"That's the plan. I'm dropping off a key with Diane on my way out." She hoped to get out of town by two o'clock and drive as far as Amarillo. Diane Goldman, their Realtor, would handle details after that.

"You've taken pictures of everything to document what they're taking and the condition? If anything gets broken—"

"It's done." Kristen rolled her eyes. "I'll send you a

flash drive so you'll have all the visuals the day of the auction." She was happy to turn over responsibility for the auction. She wanted no part of that.

"What are you doing now?" John asked.

"Digging up some flowers."

"Why?"

"Because I want to take a few of Mom's flowers with me."

"You mean flowers out in the yard?"

"Um, yeah." She glanced at the pots she'd lined up on the sidewalk.

"Did you ask Diane if taking some was okay?"

"What?" Kristen frowned into the phone. "Why would I need Diane's permission?"

"Because landscaping is part of the property. You don't think someone will notice holes in the yard?"

Oh, boy. If this conversation continued much longer, she'd need surgery to return her eyes to their proper position. "John, get real. No one will notice. I'm not leaving huge, gaping holes in the yard or the beds. In fact, dividing is probably good for the plants, anyway." Kristen heard his heavy sigh.

"Just make sure the spots aren't obvious."

Colorful words danced in her head, but she vowed to remain civil. "The beds are full of flowers, John. The lilies have taken over the ditch. Besides, we agreed we're selling as is. If the new owners want more flowers, they can plant them. I think Mom would love the idea." Nothing else mattered. "Okay, I need to get some water on these, then I'm taking Star out for one last ride. I'll talk to you later." In other circumstances, she'd ask about the kids, keep up some sense of normal family interaction, but she wasn't in the mood. And normal took a leave of absence.

She wrestled the water hose out to the front yard and gave the plants a good dousing, then she unhooked all of the hoses and hauled her saddle out of the barn. At three o'clock, she headed over to the Andersons' place. Inside the barn, she patted each of the horses. "Hey, baby," she crooned to Star. "Let's you and me go for a ride." She took her time saddling the mare and adjusting the halter, all the while reaching out to touch and smooth the horse. At the sound of footsteps, Kristen turned.

"Taking Star for a ride?" Nate asked.

"Yep. Our last rodeo." Kristen infused her voice with a false brightness.

Nate smiled. "Sounds good."

Kristen pointed toward the envelope she'd hung on a nail outside of Star's stall. "I left a key to the barn for Sam so the buyers can go over and collect the tack they're taking."

Nate nodded. "I'll make sure he gets it. You have a good ride."

"Thanks." Her lips trembled, and she silently thanked her neighbor for understanding this was an emotional time. She led Star outside and hopped into the saddle. "Let's go, girl." With a lump in her throat, Kristen turned the mare to the narrow trail that bordered the property line then started a nice, even trot. But at the middle of the field, Kristen let Star pick up the pace to a canter. The cool breeze lifted her hair—and her spirits.

Star had covered this ground countless times, so Kristen just had to stay in the saddle. Star knew where to turn and where not to go.

Now, Kristen wondered if the poor horse was bored to death riding around the fields, pastures, and neighboring properties. Maybe a change of scenery would be good. Could an old horse learn a new trick— or a new trail? She was no animal psychologist, but she hoped so. The horses just might like their new digs and the chance to be ridden more regularly. She'd love to see Reed's ranch and get a visual in which to place the horses, but she didn't have an invitation. West of Dallas, Reed said. On the way to Amarillo by any chance? Her heart skipped a beat. She'd be passing that way in a couple of days. A little stalking of her own, perhaps? Probably not. The ranch could very well have a gate, and the barn might not even be visible from the road.

Still, when she got back to the house, she'd finish the email to Reed. That couldn't hurt, right?

****

At seven o'clock Sunday night, Reed cleared the table, ready to relax in front of the TV. He placed the last plate into the dishwasher then switched off the light and joined Dylan in the living room. "Let's save the ice cream for later, okay?"

"Okay. I'll get my backpack."

Reed frowned. "What for?"

"I have some papers."

Crossing his arms, Reed stared at his nephew. "Papers that I'm supposed to look at?"

Dylan shrugged. "I guess so."

"Bring it on. I hope you weren't supposed to do something this weekend." They'd already missed his turn for show-and-tell once. Masking his annoyance, Reed ran a hand over his face and reached for the wad of papers Dylan pulled out. "Dylan, we gotta remember to do this on Friday from now on." Should he add a backpack check to his calendar, or would that be "helicopter" parenting?

He glanced over the papers. Didn't look like anything significant. Setting them aside, he picked up a blue envelope and ripped it open to find a birthday party invitation inside. For next Friday night.

"Who's Parker Dirks?"

"One of my friends."

"He's having a birthday party on Friday. Do you want to go?"

Dylan hitched his shoulders again. "I guess so."

"Is he a good kid? You like him?" The wheels turned in Reed's head. A sleepover for Dylan might be the answer to his Houston problem. He could get to Houston and back in a long day. He gave a mental fist pump. A sleepover would keep him from having to leave Dylan with Celia or a babysitter. Maybe he could shoot an email to the teacher first and make sure this kid was actually a friend. And he'd have to contact the mom.

Feeling as though he'd been handed a lifeline, Reed clapped his hands. "Time for bed." Silently, he willed Dylan not to remember the ice cream. He set the backpack near the door then headed to Dylan's room for the bedtime routine. "What're we reading tonight?" He figured someday there'd be a change in the menu.

"Miss Hanover's new one."

Reed pulled the book off the shelf and settled beside Dylan. Ten minutes later, Dylan's eyelids drooped. Reed ran a hand gently over the fine hair starting to grow on the boy's head. "Night, buddy."

"Night, Uncle Reed."

Reed was about to return the book to the shelf when he remembered the photo on the inside back cover. He opened it again to see Kristen Hanover's smiling face. He couldn't help wondering if they'd seen her for the last time. Acknowledging the hit of disappointment, he placed the book on the shelf and switched off the light.

Reed snapped the door shut and leaned against it, taking a moment to change gears. The weekend almost over, and he'd barely had an hour to himself. Pushing off, he made his way down the hall, kicked off his shoes, and grabbed his laptop. He settled into the sofa and switched on the TV then turned his attention to the computer, thinking he'd crank out a quick note to Dylan's teacher and get those wheels in motion, then check the availability of a plane. He could go commercial if he had to, but that option would eat up more time.

He opened his email, and his heart bounced. About forty minutes ago, he received a new email—from Kristen Hanover. Subject line: *About the horses.* Setting aside the computer, he padded to the fridge and popped the cap off a bottle of brew.

"Okay, pretty lady." He resumed his place on the sofa with a new purpose. "Tell me about your horses." He scanned the document.

Dear Reed and Dylan,

Wow. I was so surprised to see you two yesterday. Twice. Pleasantly surprised. I'm so happy to know my family's horses are getting a new home on your ranch!

Thanks for the opportunity to tell you a little more about them. I hope it helps you get to know them. Like people, they each have their quirks and temperament.

First, there's Bentley.

She'd written a couple of paragraphs on each horse, detailing their personalities and eating habits. Some helpful stuff that he'd pass along to Roger.

I think they'll benefit from a change of scenery and more interaction with people. If, for any reason, they don't work out, please let me know, and I'll help place them with another owner. I hope you get the chance to work with them and that your guests enjoy them. Sometimes, a horse ride in an open field is all it takes to clear the mind.

Best wishes. I've enjoyed getting to know you. Dylan, I can't wait to hear which horse is your favorite and if you get riding lessons!

Thanks, again.

Kristen

He mulled her words. All pleasant and positive. That last note to Dylan sounded as if she wanted to continue some communication.

An idea took root in Reed's mind. How would she feel about another "surprise?" He took a long draw on his beer, thinking. If he and Dylan picked up the trailer from the ranch, they could get the horses this weekend after he returned from Houston. He'd planned to let Roger handle the transportation, but Reed would bet he'd be fine not doing the hauling. He couldn't remember if he'd mentioned someone else would pick them up but had no doubt Kristen would be more comfortable turning the horses over to him rather than a stranger. And he figured Dylan wouldn't mind a trip to the ranch if he got to see Miss Hanover again.

A meet-up could be a nice end to a crazy week.

Chapter Seven

About an hour from Denver, the rain began, and according to Kristen's dash display, the temperature dropped about fifteen degrees in the last couple of hours. The heavy traffic slowed to a crawl between Colorado Springs and Denver and created tedious driving conditions.

She forgot to check the forecast before she left Amarillo. "Welcome home, right?" she said to Adele on the radio, though she barely heard the music over the rain and windshield wipers. At least the rain would make the ground soft. The first thing on her to-do list was to plant those flowers. The other gazillion errands she faced after being gone for five weeks would probably take several days to accomplish.

All of those things would also have to work around the meeting with the head of the English department for incoming staff members, which promised to be a long session of policies, procedures, and paperwork.

Ready to be home, Kristen exited the highway and, fifteen minutes later, turned onto Cherry Street. Another block and the small, sage-green house with blue shutters and white trim came into view. She blew out a heavy sigh. Two additional cars in the drive indicated one of her roommates had company, meaning she'd have to park curbside. Even though the sale of the farm was pending still, Kristen was tempted to search

Darlene Deluca

for a place of her own. She was ready to move beyond the roommate scene, which made her feel as if she were still in college—or had failed to launch.

Stretching, Kristen stepped out of the car and glanced around. The house looked exactly as she'd left it—except for the bright yellow leaves shimmering like sequins on the aspen in the front yard. She couldn't help but smile. All around her, colorful fall had burst into full swing.

Though water still dripped from the trees and eaves, the rain had stopped. She quickly unloaded the flowers then grabbed her bags and hurried inside.

Allison, one of Kristen's roommates, greeted her, waving a newspaper in the air. "Hey, you!" She wrapped Kristen in a hug. "It's so good to see you." Pulling back, she opened the paper. "Look at this. You're a celebrity. You made the paper on Sunday."

"Ah. So the feature article finally got printed. I thought the editors might've changed their minds." Kristen gave an interview to *The Post* several weeks before she started the tour but hadn't received a definite publication date. She had the feeling the story was on hold as 'canned' material and would be bumped if something better came along. She glanced at the article, which they'd made into a full-page spread that included a photo of her plus two of her book covers.

"This is so amazing." Allison shook the newspaper again.

Her enthusiasm was infectious, and Kristen couldn't help grinning. The piece looked pretty darn good. Did the publication mean she'd actually made Denver celebrity status? Would she be considered guest speaker material now? In demand at dinners and fundraisers? Libraries and independent bookstores were starting to seek her out, but so far, she hadn't broken into wider audiences. Maybe the publicity would make that happen.

The marketing team at the agency encouraged her not simply to write more books but to leverage what she already had in other ways—as if she hadn't been schmoozing, volunteering, and practically begging to be involved in every children's or literary event in town for the past couple of years. Sure, she could climb the celebrity ladder with the people from her hometown or her friend's school, but getting to a similar level of recognition in a large city was harder and became a more significant achievement.

"So, everything okay around here?" She'd only been in contact a few times over the course of the tour.

Allison shrugged. "Same old stuff." She brandished the newspaper again. "This is the only excitement we've had the whole time you were gone."

"Uneventful is good."

"I'm sure your publicist will get copies for you, but I picked up a couple of extras myself." Allison extended a plastic bag toward Kristen.

She thanked her and tossed the newspapers into the basket she'd left for collecting her mail. "Hey, I brought some plants from the farm that need to get in the ground, so I'll be outside for a bit." Might as well get the dirty work done first.

As she passed by the living room, Kristen waved to Morgan and her guests. She'd lived with these two women for a few years, and while they got along fine, she hadn't become close to Morgan. Inside her own room, Kristen dumped her bags then pulled on an old sweatshirt and retreated to the garage for gloves and a shovel.

A few rays of sunshine broke through the clouds, warming Kristen's skin and making the job more pleasant. She finished in less than an hour. As she surveyed her work, a sense of satisfaction wafted over her. Mom would be pleased. Even if the plants weren't in quite the best locations for now, Kristen could move them later. At least they were in the ground and promised to carry on her mother's legacy in the spring.

After a long, steamy shower, Kristen brewed a cup of hot tea and finally opened her computer. Almost two full days offline, and she felt out of touch with the world. Starting with email, she deleted the obvious junk. When she had a stronger attention span, she'd come back to the ones that needed to be read. As she scrolled back to Sunday, she found an unread message from Reed Armstrong. She gasped, her hands stilling on the keypad—a response about the horses. This one she had to read. She scanned the brief words he'd written.

Thanks for the information, Kristen. Really appreciate it. This should be helpful as we work with the horses to get them acclimated to the ranch. I'm hopeful Dylan might show some interest since they belonged to his favorite author. Don't worry. We'll take good care of them.

Reed

All very cordial and polite, but nothing that indicated an interest in keeping in touch. Kristen drummed her fingernails against the keyboard as she mulled the response. So…was that a wrap? Unless a problem came up with the horses, she'd never hear from them again? Though she had no right to attachment, disappointment settled inside her. Somehow, she felt they'd made a connection. That peck on the cheek had been brief, but she'd be lying if she said it hadn't affected her. It…it seemed…affectionate? Friendly?

Oh, well. Friendly didn't mean interested. With a heavy sigh, she closed the computer and headed to the front closet for her guitar. She was no Sheryl Crow, but strumming a few well-known tunes on the guitar relaxed her. Playing also had a way of redirecting her. When she was keyed up, the chords helped her mellow. If she was feeling down, a few minutes alone with the instrument boosted her spirits. Tonight, she could use a little of both.

****

The time was closing in on noon Wednesday when Reed looked up from the design on his computer screen to find Lowell James, Viking's chief operating officer, at his office door.

Standing, Reed beckoned him forward. "Hey, Lowell, come in." He extended his hand to the older man who'd become something of a mentor over the past few years. Only Reed's boss separated he and Lowell in the chain of command. "What brings you 'round these parts?"

Lowell took Reed's hand and patted his shoulder. "Stopped by to see you. How are things going?"

The intensity in Lowell's eyes belied his easygoing tone. Something was up. Reed would find out what soon enough. Lowell didn't beat around the bush. "Great." He gestured toward a chair and wondered if his visitor already knew the statement was a lie. "Have a seat."

Lowell glanced around the office, nodding, before he settled into a chair. "How are you doing with your nephew?"

Taken aback, Reed hesitated a moment. He didn't expect the conversation to be personal. "We…" He adjusted his tie, which suddenly felt tight. "We're doing all right. Thanks for asking."

"How's the boy? Getting along in school?"

Reed nodded. "Seems good. We've got teacher conferences next week. But so far, reports are fine. He's a good kid."

Lowell leaned forward. "Glad to hear it." He ran a hand over his jaw before meeting Reed's eyes. "Reed, I've always been straight with you, and that's not changing."

He attempted a smile. "I appreciate that, Lowell. What's up?"

"We need you in the field. This thing in Houston might be a bigger problem—"

"I'm on it." Reed held up a hand. "Going down Friday morning. The plan's all set." Thankfully, the last piece of that puzzle just fell into place.

Lowell's brows rose. "Yeah?"

"Taking one of the jets."

"Excellent. That's some good news. You've got arrangements for the boy, then?"

What, did he think he was leaving a six-year-old to fend for himself? "Sleepover."

"Sounds good." He leaned forward. "Listen, I don't want to step on any toes here, but I feel like you deserve a heads-up. You've missed a couple of meetings, and I've heard some grumbling."

Reed opened his mouth to object but stopped when

Lowell waved a dismissive hand.

"Don't get worked up. I'm just saying, it'll be good for you to make Houston a priority."

"That's the plan," Reed confirmed again, feeling as if he'd dodged a bullet.

Lowell tapped a hand on Reed's desk. "You know, Reed, you're doing a good deed taking care of your sister's boy. A fine thing. But get some help. Find a nanny, someone who can give you a hand. Don't let the family change affect your work. We need you."

"I understand," Reed said, clenching his jaw. "Not a problem." Didn't he already say he had everything under control?

"Well, the sleepover sounds like a good solution." Grinning, Lowell stood and clapped Reed on the arm. "Maybe time to arrange one of those for yourself, eh?"

Reed gave the expected man-to-man chuckle without any humor. He already received plenty of advice on parenting. The last thing he needed from colleagues was advice on his love life—or reminders his life had become very one-dimensional and did not, in fact, include sleepovers of the grown-up kind.

Lowell glanced at his watch. "Let's grab some lunch."

"Sure." Reed reached for his jacket. *And let's stick to Viking business.*

****

Reed looked at the fuzzy photos of the problem Houston rig again. He couldn't see a crack, and no other issue was visible above ground. Still, numbers didn't lie. Something wasn't right. "Let's shut down this one," he told Marty, the site manager. The decision wouldn't be popular, but he was making the right call.

He'd get his team on a solution back at headquarters and hopefully have the operation up and running again within a week. As he thought about the consequences, he raked a hand through his hair. Probably a few late nights at the office in his future.

For about the hundredth time that day, Reed checked the time and calculated where Dylan would be. By now, the birthday party had started and he was chowing on a couple of slices of cheese pizza. He hoped the food would calm down Dylan. He'd already texted Reed twice. Nothing specific, but obviously the party wasn't holding his attention. Damn, he needed the sleepover to be a success.

The rumbling in his stomach reminded him he needed food, too. "Hey, Marty, let's have some pizzas delivered to the plant and get out of here."

"Sure thing, Reed." He turned to one of his men with instructions.

Since they were working on Friday night, Reed figured the guys were more than ready to be done. Still, free food might keep a few around. They'd earned it. "Tell your crew they can knock off or join us. Pizza is on me."

At ten o'clock, Reed climbed out of Marty's truck at the entrance to the executive airport terminal for the short flight back to Dallas. Inside the plane, Reed settled into his plush leather seat and sent a quick text to Dylan before takeoff.

—Hope you're having fun. Goodnight.—

He planned to pick up Dylan around nine tomorrow morning then head to the ranch to get the trailer. Maybe they'd end up back at the burger joint near Kristen's farm, or maybe they could go someplace a little nicer this time. Though he liked the idea of a surprise, Reed wondered if he should call ahead. Kristen could have plans for the evening. But he decided he'd leave that up to fate.

His phone buzzed, and he pulled it from his pocket. When Dylan's number popped up, Reed's jaw tightened. He debated whether to answer. If something were wrong, Mrs. Dirks would be the one calling. The reality was Reed had to be away sometimes, and besides, he wanted Dylan to do normal things like spending the night with friends. Guilt gnawed at him, but he let the call go to voicemail. A text quickly followed.

—*Can you pick me up?*—

Dylan knew the plan. He'd gone over it step-by-step about a dozen times. He also knew Reed was on an airplane. Hard as it was, Reed tucked away the phone.

At just after eleven, Reed arrived back at his place—his quiet place. How fast things had changed. Without Dylan, the condo seemed empty. Not that Reed spent many Saturday nights hanging around by himself. Lowell was right. He should've scheduled something. Maybe not a sleepover, since he had no prospects in that area at the moment, but at least a beer with some friends. Mitch would probably be out. Reed fished his cell phone from his pocket.

He got a quick response.

—*I'm at Sullivan's. Get down here now.*—

Reed grinned. What more invitation did he need? He changed into jeans and a sport shirt and pulled into the parking lot ten minutes later. Inside the noisy pub, he spotted Mitch and a couple of guys and pulled a chair around from another table. After a round of high-fives, Reed got a beer and fell into conversation with Mitch.

"What the hell is going on?" Mitch asked.

Reed shrugged. "Playing dad and trying to keep my job."

Mitch frowned. "Thought you were on the verge of a promotion, dude."

With a long pull on his beer, Reed nodded. "We'll see. Amazing how fast things can change, you know?"

"This have anything to do with the kid?"

"Everything to do with the kid. Can't travel, can't be at the office late, can't leave him alone." He swore under his breath. "I don't know how people do it."

"Babysitters," Mitch said with an emphatic slap on the table.

"Right." Reed needed help, but he was suspicious of strangers these days. Everyone had an agenda. "I'm tired of people."

Mitch braced an elbow on the table. "What do you mean?"

"Everybody wants something. The other day, a woman called and wanted us to take part in a ten-year study of kids who've lost their parents. Wanted to visit, to interview Dylan, and get in our business once a month." Reed shook his head. "For *ten* years."

"Get out."

"Pretty much what I told her. Maybe they need that kind of research, but I can't see how the constant reminder would do Dylan any good."

With a glance around the room, he noted a couple of groups of women. Without warning, Kristen Hanover's face came to mind. He imagined her at the table, looking at him with that natural, happy smile on her face. Nothing fake or forced. He imagined taking her elbow and moving her away from the crowd and the loud, blaring music, just the two of them. Maybe dancing…maybe just talking.

"So, what are you going to do?" Mitch asked.

Letting go of his hallucination, Reed glanced back at his friend and took another drink of cold brew. "I'm getting some help and doing whatever it takes to get the job done, of course."

Mitch laughed. "Sounds like a plan."

Yeah, but this plan came with some serious implementation issues.

****

Reed opened his eyes to sunshine and immediately shut them again, registering the sharp pounding in his head. The sunshine was a big clue that he'd better get up and get moving. But his body protested. Rubbing his temples, he attempted a sitting position then forced himself upright. *Ouch.* Muscles stiff and uncooperative, he stumbled to the bathroom, glanced in the mirror, and winced. Yeah, maybe Dylan wasn't the only reason he didn't get plowed on the weekends anymore. Man, he felt old.

He reached into the medicine cabinet for an aspirin then stepped into the shower and let the hot water blast his skin. He had to rally. He didn't want to be on the wrong side of the hostess who'd saved his butt. All kids were to be picked up by nine-thirty—which only gave him thirty minutes.

Reed ran a hand through his still-damp hair and hurried up the heavily landscaped walkway of the elegant Dirks home.

"Uncle Reed!" Dylan burst through the front

entrance.

As an unexpected sense of relief rushed through him, Reed grinned. He squeezed Dylan against his side. "Hey, buddy. Good to see you."

"Why didn't you pick me up last night?"

Reed frowned. "I got back late. You know that." He steered Dylan back inside for thank-yous and goodbyes.

"Dylan was a delight," Mrs. Dirks told Reed and beamed at Dylan. "We'd love to have him back for a play date any time."

Score. Reed smiled. "Thanks a lot. We'll make that happen. Maybe Parker can come to our place sometime, too." Even as he said the words, Reed didn't see much chance of the date ever happening. The condo was cramped already. What would he do with two boys? And when would he ever have that kind of time? He put a hand on Dylan's shoulder. "You ready to—"

The kid took off down the stairs.

Reed followed with a last wave toward Mrs. Dirks.

"I don't want a play date," Dylan mumbled.

Reed swore silently. He didn't need an argument. "We'll talk about it later. You remember what's next, right?"

"Yeah. Let's *go.*"

Good. That should help turn things around. Unfortunately, he had to drive to the ranch first. But thanks to his dad's efficient staff, the stop was a quicker in-and-out than Reed expected. Roger had the trailer ready, and Nora, bless her, had lunch plus snacks and drinks to go.

By the time they left, Reed's mood improved, and his head cleared. He admitted looking forward to their rendezvous in Oklahoma. Sam—and more importantly, Kristen—would expect Roger. Reed suspected Kristen would be anxious to meet Roger, the person responsible for the day-to-day care of the horses. He hoped his arrival with Dylan wouldn't disappoint. Smiling, he anticipated the look on her face—a mixture of surprise and delight. Something about her seemed so genuine. Besides being nice and pretty—the words Dylan used to describe her—Reed added real. He pictured her bright smile and fair skin, and heat spread up his neck as a few other terms came to mind as well.

At two-thirty, he pulled the trailer into the Anderson driveway and rumbled to a stop near the barn.

Sam Crenshaw appeared in the doorway.

Reed stepped out of the truck and stretched his legs.

"Mr. Armstrong. Welcome back." Crenshaw peered around Reed. "Did you bring your manager?"

"Nope. Just me and my sidekick." Reed opened the door for Dylan. "We decided to do the job ourselves." He couldn't help glancing around.

"Where's Miss Hanover?" Dylan asked.

Reed looked expectantly at Sam. *Good question.*

"Oh, she's not here." He held up a small envelope. "But don't worry, I've got her barn key so we can get the tack after we load the horses."

Alarm bells rang in Reed's head. Sam sounded as if he didn't expect her to be at her place, either.

"At her house?" Dylan asked.

"That's right." Sam turned to Reed. "Horses first?"

"Fine by me. Hey, Dylan, why don't you wait in the truck while we bring out the horses?" Reed didn't miss the disappointment on his nephew's face, but he couldn't deal with an emotional breakdown now.

Star and Cinnamon complied pretty easily, with some coaxing. Bentley took more effort, but thirty minutes and a bag of oats later, Sam snapped the door into place.

Reed swiped a sleeve across his forehead and locked the trailer.

"Whew," Sam said. "Hopefully, getting them out will be easier. You have help when you get back?"

"Yep. That's not a problem." He reached inside the truck and pulled out an envelope. "We better settle up, too." He handed Sam the signed bill of sale and a check.

"Good deal. I'll meet you at Hanover's."

"*Now* are we going to Miss Hanover's?" Dylan asked.

Reed barely got a foot inside the truck before Dylan pounced. "Hold your horses. We'll be there in one minute." With any luck, she would be, too.

Once again, Reed pulled back to the barn. He opened Dylan's door then opened the side door of the trailer. "The tack should all fit up here," he told Crenshaw, while he kept an eye on Dylan heading toward the house. Still no sign of Kristen.

Focusing on their business, Reed handed Sam one of the saddles.

Dylan reappeared at his side.

"She didn't answer the door."

Sam poked his head out of the trailer. "You need to go to the bathroom, son?"

Scowling, Dylan shook his head. "I want to see Miss Hanover."

"Oh." Crenshaw glanced at Reed then shook his

head. "Well, I sure hate to tell you this, little man, but Miss Hanover went back to Denver. Left earlier in the week."

Dylan turned big blue eyes to Reed.

Oh, boy. Reed sensed a serious meltdown coming. "Why don't you go ahead and hop in the truck, buddy? Maybe we'll stop and get some ice cream."

Dylan jerked his arm. "I don't want ice cream," he yelled. "I want to see Miss Hanover."

Reed's head pounded again. "Keep it together," he said in a low voice behind Dylan. "I know you're disappointed, but this guy's just doing his job. We have to take care of Miss Hanover's horses." Seeing tears well in his nephew's eyes, Reed heaved a deep sigh. The train was about to derail. "I'll be right back."

Reed finished up with Sam then hauled himself into the truck, doing his best not to slam the door—or bang a fist against the steering wheel. *Denver.* So stupid. Why hadn't he thought of that? She never said she'd still be here this weekend. He made an assumption—because he wanted it to be that way.

Chapter Eight

Kristen's cell phone chimed just as she was about to join her roommates for some girl time.

Allison poked her head inside the room. "Hey, I'm popping the cork on a bottle of chardonnay."

Kristen held up a finger. "Be right there." She checked the caller ID and took a deep breath before answering. "Hey, Sam."

"Miss Kristen, how's Denver treating you?"

"Pretty well, thanks."

"Good deal. Just calling to let you know the boys were here to pick up the horses this afternoon, and they're on their way to Texas."

Pushing back her hair from her face, she sank onto the bed. The end of another chapter. "How'd everything go?"

"Not too bad. That Bentley gave us some trouble, but we straightened him out."

She rolled her eyes. Of all the days for Bentley to act up… "Glad he settled down. Thanks, again, for taking care of the loading and for letting me know."

"You bet. That little one sure was disappointed you weren't here."

"Little one?" Kristen frowned into the phone. "What do you mean?"

"The boy. Guess he thought you'd still be at the farm."

Oh, no. As understanding dawned, Kristen's heart sank. Dylan? "Do you mean Reed and his nephew picked up the horses? I thought he was sending someone from the ranch."

"That's what he said before. I don't know what changed, but like I said, the boy wanted to see you."

"Oh, rats. That's too bad. He's such a sweet kid." Kristen groaned inside, hating to add disappointment to Dylan's weekend. She thought back to Reed's email. He didn't give any indication he was driving out again. Maybe something happened at the ranch, and they'd made a last-minute decision. Did their unexpected visit warrant some acknowledgment? She hadn't responded to his earlier note since his language sounded so final. Though she admitted it stung a little, she figured letting go was for the best. What was the point of staying in touch, anyway?

While she talked, she wriggled into cozy slippers. "No worries, Sam. I'm sure he's fine. I actually don't know them well. I only met them a week before at one of my book signings and was completely surprised when they showed up last weekend."

Sam chuckled. "So, he's a fan then. Good deal. Listen, we're all settled up. I'll put the check in the bank on Monday."

Ah, yes—the money part. She was surprised her brother hadn't called about the settlement. "That's perfect. Thanks, Sam." Kristen ended the call and flopped back against her pillow. She felt bad about Dylan, but she was so glad she hadn't been there to see Star loaded into that trailer. Sucking in a deep breath, Kristen pushed off from the bed, determined to put all farm dealings out of her mind and enjoy a glass of wine with her roommates.

"So, how does it feel to be famous?" Morgan asked.

Kristen reached for the bottle of wine on the table. "It feels fabulous," she said in an airy voice.

"Is it paying off?"

Before answering, Kristen took a sip of wine. It was tart and ice-cold—just the way she liked it. "Well, as a matter of fact, I found out yesterday the class I'm teaching at the junior college next semester is filled and has a waiting list." That tidbit of news from the head of the English department kept Kristen going through a tedious three-hour meeting.

Allison lifted her glass in the air. "Nice."

"Seems like you've been gone forever," Morgan said as she wrapped her long, coffee-colored hair into a messy bun.

"I know. Fill me in. What's been going on?"

"You're the one with all the news," Allison said. "How'd your book tour go?"

Earlier, Kristen might have said grueling or exhausting but looking back now, the events had gone incredibly smoothly. Nothing to complain about. "The tour was great. Sold some books and met some fans."

"Meet anyone interesting?" Morgan asked. "I mean anyone over the age of seven?"

Kristen's heart tripped. She should've anticipated that question. They usually started with that one. Did Reed Armstrong count? She met him. He was interesting and over the age of seven. But that might be the end of the story.

Allison's eyes widened.

And Kristen knew she'd hesitated a beat too long.

"Oh, my gosh. Spill."

"So that's a yes?" Morgan asked.

Kristen screwed up her face. "Meeting isn't so hard. But if you'll recall, I was in Texas and Oklahoma, not Denver."

"So what?" Allison demanded. "You can write anywhere. Who is this guy?"

"The story's kind of sad." She gave them the highlights, leaving out the part about him showing up at the farm today. She hadn't had time to process that or decide her next move—if she had one. "Anyway, he's busy with his job and figuring out how to be a dad. And he lives in Dallas."

Morgan held up an index finger. "Hey, don't underestimate the advantages of an online relationship." A marketing analyst, Morgan's job involved delving into the human psyche.

"Might be a good way to start. Takes off the pressure. You know, something about low expectations and commitment."

"Sure, Morgan." Allison elbowed their roommate. "But the sex isn't so great."

Kristen sputtered a laugh.

Grinning, Morgan shot her a wink. "Builds up the anticipation, sweetie."

After the second bottle of wine ran dry, Kristen hauled herself up from the sofa. "That's it for me. Goodnight, girls." She padded to her room with emails still on her mind. Chasing a man wasn't her style, but if she didn't attempt to keep the communication going, would she always wonder if she'd missed an opportunity? If she'd snuffed out a spark before it had a chance to take hold? And in this case, even if nothing romantic developed, what was wrong with keeping tabs on a little boy who could use some TLC?

Maybe late Saturday night after a couple of glasses of wine wasn't the best time to make a decision. Or a move. But after she'd changed into soft pajamas, the tiny light on the computer taunted her. What would be the harm? At least she wasn't drunk-dialing her ex.

Dropping onto the bed, Kristen opened the laptop and toyed with a pen, spinning it while she re-read Reed's email. Technically, it was her turn to respond, so an answer wouldn't be weird. But if he paid attention, he'd see what time she hit Send. Would she seem desperate and lonely, or would he assume she'd been out having a good time and was a night owl?

Kristen shook her head. "Jeez, over-think much?" Hands on the keyboard, she pushed Reply and began typing.

Hello, Reed,

Thanks so much for your care of the horses. Like you, I hope Dylan will soon get over his fears.

She paused, thinking. Keep the conversation firmly on Dylan and the horses or stray a bit into personal territory? She took a deep breath. Nothing to lose, right?

I've always found riding therapeutic. Star was my answer to all things traumatic in high school.

I'm sorry I missed you two today. Heard from Sam that you and Dylan drove out to pick up the horses. I hope you had a good trip back.

She wondered if Dylan had gotten over his disappointment. Had he, as Reed suggested, moved onto something else? Probably. *I'm back in Denver and must get busy writing the next story. You two take care.*

How to sign off? Fondly? Sincerely? Just for fun she typed hugs and kisses, then deleted the silly words. Before she could obsess any longer, she typed *Fondly, Kristen.*

There. Short and sweet. Another quick scan for typos, then she closed her eyes and hit Send. Considering the number of times she'd caught Reed checking his phone, she figured he'd see the email first thing in the morning—if not tonight. How many days would he wait to answer? Or would he? The ball was in his court.

****

Sunday dawned damp and dreary. Low gray clouds hung over the ranch. Careful not to disturb the sleeping boy in the next bed, Reed unplugged his phone from the charger and quietly opened the door. On the stairs, he checked his weather app. Same thing expected in Dallas. Good. Maybe what they had at the ranch would move east soon. Rain would add time to caring for the horses after an introductory workout with Roger—and that Reed could do without. He was ready to put the weekend behind him.

The smell of coffee beckoned from the kitchen, and Reed followed his nose. He glanced around the spacious kitchen but saw no sign of his dad. Probably in the barn inspecting the new animals. Coffee in hand, Reed dropped into a chair at the table and tapped his phone again for the morning's headlines. But before they sprang to life, he noted the blue dots alerting him to new messages. Open or ignore? Remembering his conversation with Lowell, he decided against ignoring. He was, and would remain, on top of things at the office.

Flicking through the messages, he found nothing needing immediate attention. His email inbox also claimed several new memos. He scanned the subject lines. Mostly junk with a couple of— *Wait.* He set down the mug and drummed his fingers against the table. He had a new message from Kristen Hanover. Interesting. Every time he thought he'd heard or seen the last of her, she popped up again.

He clicked on the message.

"Uncle Reed?"

Dylan's sleepy voice startled Reed, and he fumbled the phone as if he'd been caught doing something forbidden.

"In here, Dylan." He'd come back to the email. Standing, he firmly placed the phone on the table and crossed to the refrigerator. "You ready for some breakfast?"

"Uncle Reed, my leg hurts."

Oh, no. That wasn't good. Reed crouched in front of Dylan. Communicating pain was tricky. "Okay, tell me how it feels. Does it only hurt when you put weight on your leg, like when you're walking?" Probably just slept in a bad position, and the kink would work itself out.

Dylan shook his head. "No. It just hurts."

"Like it's sore?" Reed gently massaged and inspected the damaged leg. Didn't see any swelling or bruising. Could be the weather, he supposed. Did the pins absorb the damp chill in the air? The aches and pains could be a lifelong issue.

"Yeah. Like sore."

Okay. Didn't sound like anything to get worked up about. "We'll get you some medicine, and you should probably wear your brace today. Let's see if that helps." Reed set milk and cereal on the table then headed upstairs. He now traveled with a pharmacy of children's meds and first aid items. Back downstairs, Reed opened the packet of chewable tablets.

Dad poked his head inside from the porch. "Roger's here. What's taking you so long?"

Reed's protective defenses went up at his dad's impatient tone. "Dylan's leg is bothering him, Dad. Tell Roger we'll be there in a few minutes." Not long enough for the meds to kick in, but hopefully, Dylan would rally. Reed wanted to get moving, too, but he wouldn't push.

Roger had all three horses in the paddock by the time Reed and Dylan arrived at the barn. "Dylan, you stay on this side of the fence." Reed felt compelled to say, though he knew the kid wouldn't venture in with the horses. "And don't take off your hat. It's chilly." He turned but stopped short at the gate. Man, he sounded— Reed swallowed hard. He sounded like a parent—like a real dad. He kept one eye on Dylan while he, Dad, and Roger worked with each of the horses, putting them through basic moves and commands.

Muttering, Roger took notes as he worked. Finally, he motioned Reed and his dad closer. "All right, keep hold of Cinnamon, and let the other two go for a minute. I think this one is our best leader."

Reed thought so, too. Moving forward, he reached for the reins.

A sharp shriek stopped him mid-stride.

Snapping around, Reed sprinted toward Dylan. He'd gotten too close to the fence. Chest heaving, Reed grabbed Star's reins and pulled the horse away from the rails. "What happened? You okay?" In the next second, he realized the shriek was surprise followed by laughter. At eye level, he could see the smile behind Dylan's hand. Bracing a hand against the railing, Reed blew out his breath.

Dylan rubbed his face. "Star licked me!"

Part of Reed wanted to shake the kid, but his relief at Dylan's laughter was stronger. He ran a hand over Dylan's hat. "Ew, that's gross." Dylan hooted as if Reed had just released a gigantic fart or something.

"No. That means she likes me. That's what Miss Hanover said."

"Then it must be true." Smiling, Reed leaned down to look at Dylan between the fence rails. He pulled the horse closer. "You like Star?"

Dylan looked at Reed.

The surprise in his face made Reed think the kid actually forgot for a minute he didn't like horses.

Dylan shrugged. "She's not mean."

This small admission was a big step. Crouching Reed tugged on Star's halter, pulling her head down toward Dylan. "No, she's really gentle. Want to pet her? Remember how Miss Hanover showed you?"

"Yeah." Dylan slowly held out his hand and touched the horse's forehead.

Star nuzzled closer.

When her tongue came out and brushed against Dylan, he yelped again and stepped backward, nearly losing his balance.

Reed caught his arm. "Easy there, big guy."

"She didn't get me."

"You were fast." He patted Star's saddle. "You want to sit up here for a minute? I'll be right beside you."

Dylan shook his head and looked past Reed to where his grandpa and Roger stood.

Reed got the picture. He didn't blame the kid—those two were an intimidating audience. He let go of Star's reins. "Maybe next time, huh?" Straightening, Reed held up a hand for a high five.

"Are you almost done?" Dylan asked.

The hint of a whine in his nephew's voice was enough for Reed. He couldn't handle whining. Better to quit while they were ahead. "Give me a few minutes to help get the horses dried off, okay?"

An hour later, Reed pulled the SUV onto the road toward Dallas.

True to form, Dylan lasted only a few minutes, his peach-fuzz covered head propped on a pillow against the window behind Reed.

Reed couldn't help a satisfied smile. They'd made some progress today. Should he have praised the kid more in front of his dad, made a bigger deal of the small steps to encourage Dylan more? A deep sadness rolled over him. He'd love to tell his sister about her son's funny belly laugh. She'd think—

Wait, one other person might be interested in the events of the day. His thoughts turned to Kristen and her email, which he hadn't read. Did her message invite further conversation? And was it wrong to involve her more in their lives?

He checked his speed and bumped up his cruise control a notch. Truth was, she'd be the only person interested in the news. Maybe Dylan's reaction didn't qualify as a big news flash, but he felt like sharing the progress. He pumped a fist against the steering wheel.

At least the weekend ended on a high note.

Reed wasn't surprised when Dylan wore out early that evening.

With him in bed and the apartment quiet, Reed finally opened Kristen's email. He nearly choked on his beer. So she knew they'd gone to the farm again. *Great.* Now he felt like a fool. Had Sam called her the minute they left? He heaved a sigh and reread her words. *Sorry I missed you two.* She'd made a point to include them both. That was a positive. *Fondly.* Fondly? What the hell did fondly mean? Was the word equivalent to the generic 'sincerely' in a business memo?

He raked a hand through his hair as her words floated through his head in her voice. Low and soft, with a smile—the perfect smile that lit her face.

Heart hammering, he hit Reply to Sender and began typing. Might as well find out where he stood, even if it was out in the cold.

Chapter Nine

Kristen lifted the paper from the printer on her desk and scanned what she'd written. She wadded the piece into a ball and squeezed it in her fist. The story just didn't flow—sounded stilted and amateurish. Why was she having so much trouble getting this right? At the farm, when the ideas were coming fast, they'd sounded so easy. She'd expected them to practically write themselves. Now, she could hardly craft a well-constructed sentence, let alone a rhyming one.

Her sentences needed to be simple but full of life and energy and color. They had a job to do—to inspire and entertain. Not to mention paying her bills.

No. She had to stop thinking like that. Writing wasn't about the money—her writing was about connecting with kids. She obviously had too many conversations with her brother recently. Pushing back from the desk, Kristen slipped her bare feet into ballet flats and headed to the back door. With a foot, she shoved Allison's laundry basket out of the way. Whatever happened to keeping the common spaces clear of personal clutter? Stepping outside, Kristen pushed back her hair and lifted her face to the cool breeze. She drew in a deep breath, filling her lungs with the chilly evening air—hoping a little air might revive her sluggish brain and infuse her work with a fresh perspective.

She stretched her neck and shoulders and did a few squats to get the circulation moving. Twenty minutes later, she warmed fragrant pomegranate tea and considered knocking off for the day and turning on the television. But vegging in front of the TV would most likely put her to sleep. Instead, she resumed her place in front of her laptop.

Oh, my. This was interesting—a new email from Reed Armstrong. She glanced at the open document she'd been working on. Distracted much? Knowing she couldn't fully concentrate on her work while wondering about the email, Kristen opened the thread.

Hello, again.

Wanted to let you know the horses arrived safely at the ranch yesterday, and we worked with them a little this morning. I think they'll do well. Roger, our ranch manager, was impressed and that doesn't happen easily.

Even better news, though. I think Dylan is starting to like Star, and I'm sure you have something to do with that. Thank you for encouraging him. The horse licked him, and he actually thought it was funny.

Kristen's eyes welled. Great news. That little boy might have some difficulties in years to come if his leg didn't heal properly or he couldn't play sports. Horseback riding could be a therapeutic outlet. Plus riding could give him that tough cowboy image. Of course, he could also grow up to be drop-dead gorgeous like his uncle with those intense blue eyes. Good looks wouldn't hurt his image, either.

With a smile in her heart, she continued reading.

I hope we can go out every couple of weekends. It'd be nice for Dylan to get comfortable around the horses. Anyway, thought you might like to know. Hope all is well back in Denver.

Reed

The smile spread through her body. Wow, that was newsy with a complimentary twist and a dash of enthusiasm. She wished she could hear his voice—the joy and sense of accomplishment she imagined would be there. She'd love to hear Dylan's laughter, too. *Good girl, Star.*

Ignoring the open Word document on the screen, Kristen hit the reply button.

Dear Reed,

That's wonderful news. Thanks for letting me know. I'm so glad Dylan's feeling more comfortable with Star. She's a sweet horse, for sure. At the risk of sending my reader on to "greener pastures," I wonder if Dylan might like some books on famous horses or horse care to help him see horses as helpful or as pets. I know you plan to use them for trail rides, but I always considered Star to be my pet. Maybe he could relate to that. I know a lot of his classmates have pets.

Kristen paused and took a sip of tea. Would that sound like conversation or offering unsolicited advice? The problem with emails was no facial expressions or tone of voice to give clues. She added a disclaimer.

Just thinking out loud here. He might be the type of kid who needs to gradually build up to the unknown or figure out something in his head before giving it a try. I'm sure you two will figure out the best approach! It's great that you're close enough to go to the ranch so often.

It's definitely turned to fall here in Denver. Feels very different from Texas and Oklahoma. While I love summer, sweater weather is nice, too. The air is cool and crisp, and the aspens are gorgeous. Enjoy your time at the ranch. I'm guessing it's beautiful as the landscape changes with the seasons.

Kristen

She reread her note, and a pang of sympathy shot through her. Reed might not have many people with whom to share milestones or worries or information about Dylan. If his friends had children, they probably also had spouses—and much of that kind of conversation would take place among the moms. Maybe the guy needed someone to talk to. She wasn't a mom and might not have words of wisdom to share, but she could listen and be a sounding board, at least. If nothing else, lending an ear to Reed might keep alive her connection to Star.

With thoughts of Reed and his nephew crowding in, Kristen gave up hope of getting any more writing done. Might as well let things simmer overnight and make a fresh start in the morning. Inside her room, she reached for her reading tablet where dozens of unread novels waited for their turn in the spotlight. Maybe she could find something lighthearted or funny. Before she could peruse the possibilities, the low battery warning greeted her. "Great timing." She pulled the cord from the drawer of her bedside table. When she glanced at the computer again, she let the cord slip from her hand.

Already? Staring at the screen, she gaped. Reed Armstrong was turning out to be quite the conversation-alist. Feeling ridiculously pleased, Kristen almost opened the message—but another thought slammed in first. If she'd offended him, she might get a thanks-but-we've-got-this brush off. *Proceed with caution.*

Squinting, she opened the message.

Hey, Kristen, those are great ideas. Thanks.

Kristen blew out her breath. So far, so good.

Maybe he can see what the school library has. I'm busier than usual at work right now and not sure when we can get to the bookstore. I'm in the process of looking for a mature, responsible person who doesn't mind driving to help with Dylan. After-school care charges ten bucks for every five minutes I'm late picking him up. Want to ask how I know this? I don't suppose you'd consider moving to Dallas?!

Kristen laughed out loud and drew her legs under her, settling into the chair.

It sure doesn't sound like you're enjoying the weather there in Denver. And, yes, the ranch is spectacular in the fall. I can't describe it with a writer's skill, but we get a lot of color in the grasses and sumac.

He didn't sign off this time, which made the exchange seem more open-ended, more like a conversation. And kind of fun. But by midnight, her eyelids felt like sandpaper. She hated to be the one to end the—

Hey, looks like time got away from me. I should probably call it a day. Hope I haven't kept you up.

Not at all, she lied. *I've enjoyed our chat.*

Me, too. Goodnight.

She typed *goodnight* but kept the computer open. She grazed her fingers across the keys. Call her crazy, but even without visuals, touch, or a sexy voice, spending a couple of hours exchanging thoughts with Reed Armstrong felt strangely intimate.

****

Kristen dipped her Earl Grey tea bag into the

steaming water and watched the liquid turn to a rich mahogany color. Ah, the color of energy. Monday morning called for a strong cup.

"Okay, Monday, let's see what you've got for me." She moved to her desk. The best thing about starting the new workweek was the quiet it provided. Both her roommates worked eight-to-five jobs requiring them to leave the house early, which gave Kristen the whole place. She sank into her padded chair. Today, she would write amazing, witty words and sentences to entertain and delight young children. But first, email.

Her throat clogged. The first message in her inbox was from the auction company. With a heavy heart, she set down her mug and opened the message. On Saturday, the possessions of her parents' lifetime would be for sale. Strangers would pick through the items and deliberate their condition or usefulness—maybe haggle over how much they were worth. She wondered if her brother would actually go or wait for a report. She'd have to make a plan to be very busy on Saturday. Attached to the email was a copy of the advertisement, which she already knew listed a few specific items along with photos. She wouldn't be opening that file—ever.

Squeezing her eyes closed, Kristen turned away from the computer with a soft sigh. Truth be told, her parents would probably be happy someone else would get some use from their things. Her mother had always been a proponent of reusing and recycling as better options than storage. And certainly more practical. But for Kristen, selling was just so…personal. So final.

She rolled back the chair. That wasn't what she expected to see to start the week. Going through the motions of her morning routine, she struggled to set aside thoughts of her parents and the sale. They clung like a heavy fog.

Thirty minutes later, she headed outside with a pair of scissors. She snipped off the last of the yellow yarrow and a few coral-colored roses then added a small branch of aspen leaves and some other foliage that had turned almost burgundy. Inside, she arranged the plants in an old ceramic vase her mother kept on the entryway sideboard for years. Kristen placed the bouquet on the kitchen table. The combination created a nice effect. She ran a finger over the soft petals and couldn't help but smile. *Very nice.*

After another quick tweak of the arrangement, she dusted her hands on her jeans and reheated her tea. *Okay, time to get to work.* Today, she'd use an old-school method. She pulled some index cards from her desk. Spreading them across the coffee table, she marked each one with a key word or phrase. Sometimes, a visual cue helped figure out the sequence of events or spark a new idea.

Going back through the cards, she added rhyming words. Night. What words would kids relate to? Or find funny or interesting? Fright, of course. And maybe height. Flight. *Oooh, bite was a good one.* Could something bite in the night and give a character a fright? She considered the possibilities. *Hmmm. Maybe not.* Parents wouldn't thank her if she put the idea of being scared at night into their kids' brains. She picked up the next card and wandered the house but found herself uninspired. Her computer beckoned. She should probably get something to Valerie to post on social media. Valerie's words rang in Kristen's head. "Stay in touch. Stay engaged."

Maybe just a quick thank-you on wrapping up the tour. About to compose a message, she found a new, unread message from Valerie—titled "great news." She could go for some of that.

Hey, Kristen, I met with the editorial staff at Warren on Friday. They want to know when to expect the next book! Steph wants to get it in their master schedule.

She caught her breath. Seriously? Her publishing house was actively requesting new material? Her stomach fluttered. Please tell me you didn't promise anything, Kristen implored silently. At this point, she wasn't sure whether a deadline would prompt a full-scale case of writer's block or jump-start the creative juices. Considering her clammy hands, she amended the options to include an anxiety attack.

Nothing would be set in stone, of course, but it'd be great to be on the radar and in their preliminary line-up. It's easier to fall out than to get squeezed in later. Believe me, I know this! So, how are you coming on the new ideas? I know you were excited about a couple of them. Give me a quick update when you get a chance, or call if you want to bounce around some ideas. Happy Monday!

Val

Wow. Kristen rubbed her temples. Sure, falling out of the schedule would be easier. But what were the repercussions if she didn't deliver?

****

The sharp chime of Reed's phone alarm stopped all conversation in the conference room. He jerked his head around to see his vacant place at the table where he'd left his phone. He hadn't tucked the phone into his pocket where the sound might have been muffled. No, it rattled against the hard table surface, in addition to blasting over his voice as he discussed the results of his trip to Houston with colleagues.

"Sorry, folks. That's mine." He lunged for the phone, quickly cancelling the offending alarm. Reed looked at his watch—as if the phone were wrong. *Damn*. He had to get out of here. He felt the stares as he gathered papers. Good thing he'd set the alarm, otherwise, he'd have blown right past Dylan's parent-teacher conference. Why didn't they schedule these things in the evening? He'd taken the latest slot he could get, but the appointment still robbed him of office time.

Reed glanced around the table. Weren't most of these people parents? Surely, they knew the drill. "Sorry," he said again. "You all can keep at it, but I've got to run. I'll be in trouble with the principal if I miss my kid's conference, right?"

"No recess for a week," Ben said.

Light chuckles broke out, but Reed sensed the surprise and judgment behind the thin smiles. Frustration pulled at him—but he had no choice. Twenty minutes later, he pulled into a visitor parking place at Eden Heights Elementary and sprinted to the building, arriving at Dylan's classroom only five minutes past the scheduled conference time. Dylan already sat in front of the teacher's desk.

Smiling, Mrs. Baxter stood and extended a hand.

Reed relaxed, thankful she wasn't annoyed by a slight tardiness.

"Uncle Reed, you're late!"

Something flickered in Dylan's eyes, and Reed realized the person worried he'd be late—or not show up—was Dylan. He wondered if, on some level, Dylan feared Reed would disappear from his life the way his parents had. Guilt washed over him as he squeezed the kid's shoulder. "Hey, buddy."

"Good to see you, Mr. Armstrong. Have a seat, please."

He pulled out a chair and gave a quick nod toward Dylan. "It's okay if he stays, right?"

"Certainly. Student attendance is optional, but we encourage parents to include the children in our discussion."

Mrs. Baxter pushed a stack of papers toward Reed. "These are samples of Dylan's artwork plus language and reasoning skills. He's an excellent student. Gets along well with classmates and generally follows directions."

Thank God. Reed thought so, but he appreciated the affirmation. He wasn't a hundred percent sure what was normal. He'd barely had time to skim the books he'd bought on child development.

The teacher handed Reed another paper. "It's early in the year, of course, but this chart shows Dylan's progress in a number of key areas. The idea is to measure these same skill sets mid-year and again at the end of the school year."

Reed glanced at the paper. The list was long. Kindergarten sure was more serious than it used to be. "Wow. A lot of stuff."

"We want to be as thorough as possible."

"So, I'm wondering…in your opinion, is he doing all right? He's about the same level as the other kids in the class?"

"Absolutely. Dylan appears to be particularly good in language arts."

"We read books every night." Dylan bounced on his chair.

Reed nodded, feeling a little foolish in the pride that swept through him. "That's right," he said. "Probably thanks to your—" He caught himself. Maybe he shouldn't mention Kristen, or at least not her friendship with Dylan's teacher. "To your class," he finished lamely.

"That's great. And reinforcement of what we do here always helps."

"That reminds me, did he go to the library today or ask about getting some books on horses?"

"Library day is Wednesday." She made a note on the paper in front of her then turned to Dylan. "You want books about horses?"

Dylan bobbed his head. "So I can take care of Miss Hanover's horses."

Mrs. Baxter's brows pulled together, and she looked back at Reed.

Guess they couldn't keep the horses a secret. "Right. We bought Kristen Hanover's horses for our ranch, which is a couple of hours west of here."

Her eyes widened. "You mean Kristen Hanover, the author?"

"Yeah. Turns out she was selling some horses the same time we were looking for some."

"Oh, I see. Wow. Such a small world." She stared a moment longer before continuing. "Sure. I'll see if the librarian can help him find some things."

Reed had no idea what to make of the teacher's

reaction. Why would she care? Just unexpected, he supposed.

"But he won't be riding horses, will he? I mean, can he?"

"Not right now."

"That's a good segue into our next subject," Mrs. Baxter said. "Can you update me on Dylan's physical condition? The brace is still necessary at recess?"

"It is. The brace might be necessary for several more months. And definitely still sunscreen and hat for outside."

"Were there any, um…" She glanced at Dylan as she leaned forward. "Dylan's head injury." She cupped a hand at the side of her mouth. "Are there additional symptoms or damage I should be aware of?"

Reed's pulse quickened, and he straightened. "Are you noticing something?"

"Nothing too serious, but sometimes Dylan seems to get lost. He withdraws and misses instructions. I don't want to reprimand him for something he can't control but want you to be aware."

"Don't a lot of six-year-olds do that?" Reed ran a finger along the back of his collar as sweat prickled his neck.

"Of course, to some degree. It's something to watch."

"Absolutely. Thank you. I'll bring it up at his next doctor's appointment." He pulled out his phone to make a few notes of his own, though he couldn't help thinking a little spacing off didn't sound like anything serious. But the thought was sobering. Dylan's head took a sharp blow in the accident, which caused a deep gash and concussion. So far, the scans looked good, but damage still could show up later on. He looked up from the phone to find her steady gaze on him.

"Don't worry. I think you're doing fine."

Reed drew in a deep breath, nodding. "Trying." He took another paper she offered, and he added it to the stack in front of him. Didn't these people believe in modern technology, like email?

"Last thing." She flashed a smile. "Here's a special calendar of events for our classroom that some of the room parents have put together. You'll see from time to time they might ask for help or donations from other parents. Everything is strictly optional, of course."

Optional? Reed glanced at the paper. Classroom events, parties, and contact info for helping with Fun Day, Science Day, and Career Day. With effort, he kept his groan inside. He knew Eden Heights had a good reputation, and people moved to the area specifically to be in this school district. And just as surely, he knew he couldn't do any of those volunteer tasks. He'd probably end up being known as a deadbeat dad.

Chapter Ten

Just before noon on Tuesday, Kristen gave up. She shoved her laptop into her bag. Her quest to find a quiet nook at the library where she could write proved a total bust. She found plenty of nooks—but no quiet. The book carts were squeaky. The kids were cranky. And apparently every house in the neighborhood was under construction.

Enough, already. Might as well be at home.

She headed west out of the parking lot, and the Rockies loomed in the distance, the higher peaks already capped with snow. Thoughts of a cabin in the woods flooded back. She wouldn't have to go far to find one, with Estes Park only an hour and a half away. She could probably find something even closer and get a good, off-season price, too. The more she thought about it, the more she was convinced a short nature getaway was the answer to refilling her creative well. The sooner, the better.

At home, Kristen opened a Word document for notes then opened a new tab and searched for mountain cabins near Denver. *Whoa.* The list was long. She obviously had options.

With only a quick break for dinner, Kristen continued her research into the evening, checking websites and reviews of several possibilities. At almost ten o'clock, she opened her email and found a message from Reed. She smiled. This could be a pleasant end to the day.

Checking to see if you're up and wondering if your ears were burning this afternoon. Maybe you've already heard from Dylan's teacher. We had his parent-teacher conference today, and he told Mrs. Baxter we bought your horses. She seemed surprised.

Oh. Kristen hadn't thought to let Jana know. But did it matter?

We were talking about getting some horse books on library day. Hopefully, Dylan won't start pestering her about you. I don't think he's made the connection about the two of you being friends.

Kristen couldn't imagine Jana minding. She was a great teacher who genuinely cared about her students.

She says he's doing well, so that's a relief. Can't say I'm an expert on six-year-olds. It's been a while. But I've picked up a few books on the subject. Might get those read before he's a teenager.

Kristen heard his voice in her head. He sounded stressed, and she couldn't help wondering whether he was looking for kudos or encouragement—or just talking.

Anyway, hope you had a good day.

Reed

Kristen rolled her neck. Not the best day, but really, what did she have to complain about? A publisher wanted another book. She hit Reply.

Dear Reed,

Haven't heard from Jana, but I'm sure there's no problem. I'm so glad Dylan is excited enough about the horses to mention it. And very happy to hear the conference went well. I'm no expert, either, but I've seen a lot of young kids in the last few weeks, and I'd say you and Dylan are doing great!

My day was a little frustrating. My editor is champing at the bit, so to speak, for a new book, and I've hit a wall. Feeling kind of stuck. I've just been doing some research on going to the mountains for some creative renewal. A getaway to get the juices flowing again. I think a cabin in the woods might do it. The last month or so has been pretty stressful with getting the farm cleaned out and the book tour.

Still, I've made a lot of progress with that and in my business, so I really can't complain. I'm so grateful for enthusiastic kids like Dylan and parents and teachers and uncles who encourage them. I think if I can just get away and clear my head, I can get back on track.

Kristen debated whether to sign off. Would he see the lack of signature as an invitation to keep chatting? Sucking in a deep breath, she hit Send. In the amount of time she took to pour a glass of wine, a response came through.

A getaway sounds great. Hope you find the perfect place and get back your mojo. You have a fan here who's anxiously awaiting the next Kristen Hanover book.

Kristen grinned. Oh, now he was totally sucking up. Or was that his way of encouraging her?

Do it, and enjoy. You're lucky to have a flexible schedule.

Uh-oh. He must be thinking of the freedom and flexibility he'd lost with becoming a parent. Once again, a sharp stab of sympathy hit Kristen. Reed's life had been completely upended. She wondered if he'd missed any guy getaways. Was he skipping golf outings or poker parties that were once regular events in his schedule?

With her thoughts wandering to more personal aspects of Reed's life, Kristen slipped into comfortable leggings and a long-sleeved T-shirt sans bra then returned to the computer.

Thanks. I have some fabulous options. I'm looking forward to it. I'm sure you're feeling the loss of your free time. I remember after my dad died how many events my mom missed because she had to take me or my brother somewhere, or she couldn't find a babysitter, or she was just plain too tired. I hope you find a balance. Taking time for yourself is important, too. Any luck in the nanny search?

When her phone buzzed against the side table, Kristen jumped. She looked at the phone but didn't recognize the number. *Nope.* Not picking that up. When a new message popped up, she did a double-take.

I'm calling you.

What? Wait. Reed was calling her? How—

On the fourth ring, she came to and snatched up the phone. "Hello?" Her voice came out in a breathless rush. She glanced back toward the computer.

"Hi."

Kristen's insides buckled, and she gave a nervous laugh. Definitely him. She recognized the low, silky voice. "Hi. How did you—"

"Find your number? Happened to see it on the papers Sam gave me when we bought the horses."

"Oh." Very observant of him—and convenient for her. Nice going, Sam.

"Do you mind?"

"Of course not."

"Good. I have an idea for you."

"Yeah?"

"This is totally up to you. Just want to toss out something as an option."

"Okay." She drawled the word, wondering where this was going.

"Remember I mentioned the cabins on the ranch? We're renting them and letting people ride?"

"Oh, right." She held her breath.

"Why don't you come out for a few days? The ranch is quiet. Might be a good place to get some writing done."

Blood pounded in Kristen ears. Go to Reed's ranch thirteen hours away when amazing choices beckoned within an hour's drive? Pros and cons pummeled her in rapid succession. She could fly, but that was a lot of money. Plus, she'd have to rent a car to get from the airport to the ranch. She could ride—and see Star again. Would Reed and Dylan be there? If they were, would she really get any writing done?

"You're thinking, I presume?"

Reed's voice broke through Kristen's thoughts. "I am. Wow, that's—that's an idea." Was the suggestion meant to drum up business for the ranch or help her out? Or, was this one of those it-hit-the-brain-so-I-said-it moments? She was familiar with those. "I—yeah, I'll think about it. Thanks. The ranch is a couple hours west of Dallas?"

"Yep. You could fly into DFW. There's also a small airstrip near the ranch, but unless you want to charter a plane…"

"Oh, sure, because that's totally in my budget."

Kristen laughed. *In her dreams*. "I could drive, too, I suppose."

****

Reed ran a hand across his jaw. "That'd make for a long day." *Captain Obvious*. He'd given her an idea, all right. Probably a stupid one. She didn't sound too excited. But he couldn't turn back now. "We could always arrange transportation. If you came on a weekend, maybe Dylan and I could pick you up."

Boom. He put it out there.

"Oh, Reed. That's a very nice offer, but wouldn't the drive be awfully inconvenient?"

Oh, Reed. His name in that soft, low voice of hers sent heat rushing through him. "Don't worry about that. But if you'd rather head to the beach or mountains, that's cool, too."

"All right. I'll add it to my options. Thanks."

An awkward silence filled the air, and Reed wished he could see her face. He imagined a little wrinkle in her forehead as she wondered what would possess him to make the offer. He'd like to know, too. Surely, the Dallas/Fort Worth metropolitan area of more than seven million people was home to at least one interesting, attractive woman he could talk to.

"So, other than travel logistics, what have you got going on this week?" he asked, his voice brisk. He had to change the subject and let her off the hook.

"Several things, actually."

Her voice brightened, and relief washed over Reed. *Moving on.*

"I've got a classroom visit and a couple of writers' meetings, plus I need to get started on my lesson plans for the class I'm teaching in January."

"You teach, too?"

"My first time. I'm giving a writing class at a community college close by. I've done lots of workshops but never a full-semester class."

"On writing children's books?"

"On writing in general. I think I have enough material, but I need to calculate the time. I don't want to assign more than I can read and critique."

"I get it. The more you assign, the more work for you, too."

"True. But the main thing is I have to make sure I have time to be thorough and give good, constructive feedback."

Reed smiled into the phone. Not worried about her time commitment, but worried about doing a good job. Figured. Stupid or not, he wanted her to come to the ranch. In his head, he began planning a strategy for making that happen. How could he entice her without pressuring? Would it be wrong to use her concern for others—concern for his nephew, in particular—to his advantage?

Chapter Eleven

Kristen hitched her carry-on bag over her shoulder and headed toward baggage claim at the DFW airport. She'd tried to stuff everything into one small rolling suitcase but that didn't work. Riding clothes and sweaters took up too much space. According to the forecast, they could expect cool mornings and evenings but warm afternoons. Required more clothes but sounded absolutely perfect.

When she came to the bottom of the escalator and heard the familiar call, "Miss Hanover," she smiled, her heart bouncing. Careful not to catch the tip of her cowboy boots on the edge of the escalator, she stepped off with a wide smile for the boy and man who greeted her, aware that to others the scene would look like a homecoming—a young family reuniting. "Hey, you guys!" She grabbed Dylan's hand and looked at Reed. She hadn't seen him since they'd taken to casual emailing, and Kristen admitted to being a little unsure of their situation.

"Welcome back to Texas." Reed squeezed her shoulder and reached for her carry-on bag.

The tone of his voice was nothing more or less than friendly.

"You look the part."

Of course, he meant her caramel-colored cowboy boots with silver accents. "I'm feeling the cowgirl," she said. "Boots take too much room in a suitcase, so I figured I might as well get on my ranch gear."

"Looks good."

The warm appreciation in his eyes rippled through Kristen.

But before she could respond, Reed ushered them toward the baggage carousel, a hand resting lightly on her back. "Tell me when you see your bag, and I'll grab."

"Okay. Thanks." Blood pounding in her ears, she turned to Dylan and placed a gentle hand on his head. "How are you, big guy? What've you been doing?"

He bounced with an awkward skip. "Reading about horses."

"That's awesome. I can't wait to hear what you learned. Quick, tell me one thing."

"Weeeeell."

He started to speak just as Kristen's belongings appeared. "Oh, hang on, Dylan. There's my bag. The red one."

Reed reached for the bag.

At the same time, Kristen lifted her guitar case from the conveyor.

"Miss Hanover, is that a guitar? Is it yours?"

The awe in his voice made Kristen grin. Maybe he'd take an interest in music. "Sure is." She glanced at Reed. "I figured as long as I was checking a bag, I might as well bring the guitar."

"A woman of many talents, I see."

The words were spoken matter-of-factly but in the more creative region of her brain, she imagined something more suggestive. Was he beginning to see her as a woman and not the horse lady or Dylan's crush? She gave a light laugh. "Well, don't get carried away. I only play for personal enjoyment."

"No performances?"

"Will you play for us?" Dylan asked. "Please?"

She looked into Dylan's bright, hopeful eyes and wondered how many times she'd give in to them. "We'll see."

Reed gave a sharp whoop. "You learn faster than I did. We'll see is always the right answer."

Kristen wasn't entirely sure what he meant, but she took a moment to appreciate the smile in Reed's eyes. She looked forward to seeing him on his home turf— and to seeing the interaction between uncle and nephew. Even though Reed appeared to be a good guardian, she couldn't shake her concern for Dylan. Was it healthy for such a young boy to have no females in his life? Sure, he had Jana, but she'd only be his teacher for a year.

She took Dylan's hand as they made their way to Reed's SUV. After lunch and a stop at the grocery store to pick up food for the week, they finally hit the open road.

By the time Reed turned from the main highway to a blacktop road, Kristen sensed his mood had taken a turn—a wrong turn. His contributions to their conversation became fewer and less enthusiastic. She would've chalked up the silence to an issue with nearing his childhood home except he'd told her that he went to the ranch to relax and decompress. She shot him a sideways glance.

He turned toward her with a wry smile.

"The kid is usually asleep five minutes after we hit the highway."

So that was the problem. Kristen wondered if Reed expected time to talk or quiet time to clear his head and think. He didn't get either one. In a way, Kristen was glad. Dylan's animated chatter might have prevented an awkward car ride. "Ah. Sounds like someone might go to bed a little early tonight, then." She winked at Dylan. "After pizza, of course." They'd purchased half-baked pizzas at the grocery store. To Kristen's surprise, Reed had two coolers in the car—one for them and one for her. A thoughtful touch.

Maybe after Dylan went to bed, Kristen and Reed would have a few minutes to talk. At least then she'd have the option of going to her cabin if things became strained or uncomfortable. Kristen would join them for dinner at the main house tonight, then the two guys would head back to Dallas tomorrow and return the following weekend. "Are we close?"

"'Bout ten minutes," Reed said.

Nodding, Kristen gazed out the window at the passing landscape. She saw nothing but open land broken here and there by craggy red rock and a few scattered trees. "It's beautiful," she murmured. "Looks peaceful." She shifted toward Reed.

He nodded toward the backseat. "Great timing."

Kristen turned to see Dylan asleep, his head falling forward on his chest. "Aw. Poor guy. That doesn't look very comfortable." She swiveled back and fought the urge to rest a hand on Reed's arm. "Hey, sorry Dylan was so keyed up. I obviously bring out the chatterbox in him."

"Not a problem. Like you said, maybe he'll go to bed early and sleep well."

"Does he not always sleep well?" Reed's heavy

sigh was audible.

"Not always. He has his own room at my place, but he won't sleep alone at the ranch."

"Oh."

"Here we are."

An ornate, wrought-iron arbor came into view, announcing the entrance to the Armstrong ranch. *Oh, my*. The ironwork that towered over the road anchored on either side by thick stone pillars that looked like they belonged in an old European village. The vibe was impressive—bordering on intimidating. In another mile or so, a sprawling house appeared on the horizon. Though two-story, the low profile house blended into the landscape with natural stone and earth-tone colors.

Reed brought the car to a stop on the driveway behind the house.

Dylan jerked awake. "Are we here?"

"Sure are." Reed turned to Kristen. "I need to run in and get the cabin key. Hey, Dylan, I want you to stay here while I take Miss Hanover to the cabin."

"I want to go with you."

Reed stepped out of the car and opened the back door. "Not arguing, buddy. Come on. I bet Nora made cookies."

Kristen wondered who Nora was but remained silent. She hadn't heard Reed speak that firmly to Dylan before. And she wondered if she'd been right earlier—the guy needed a short break from parenting.

He returned only moments later and flashed a tired smile as he started the car again.

"Everything okay?"

Like magic, he pulled himself straight and squared

his shoulders.

"Sure. The cabin's just around this curve. Be there in a sec."

Ah. So he wasn't ready to open up in a heart-to-heart. Kristen gazed out the window, taking in the waving red and gold grasses that caught the afternoon sun. Why was talking so much easier online with a thirteen-hour drive between them? What was she expecting, anyway—that a few conversations would break through all Reed's barriers? She already knew he held his feelings in check. Probably compartmentalized every aspect of his life to keep things neat and tidy.

At her first glimpse of the natural log cabin, Kristen gasped. It looked like one of those tiny homes that were all the rage in architectural magazines these days. A couple of steps led to a porch that ran across the front, broken in the middle by the cherry-red front door. Two rocking chairs sat on the porch, which, delightfully, faced west. Visions danced in her head of beautiful sunsets with her guitar and a glass of wine. "Oh, Reed. It's charming." She grabbed her small bag and hopped from the car as soon as it stopped.

Reed unlocked the door then stepped back to allow Kristen in front of him. "I'll get your suitcase."

"Oh, I can—"

He was already headed back to the car.

Inside, Kristen glanced around the small space. The living area and kitchen blended together while a tiny breakfast nook with table sat beside a window. Kristen grinned. She knew where she'd be spending some time. Butt in chair and room with a view.

Reed returned and set the bag of groceries on the kitchen counter. "What about the guitar? Here or leave it for the big house tonight?"

Kristen gave a lopsided smile. She didn't see how she'd get out of that one. "Leave it for now."

"Just in case?"

Kristen saw the teasing light dancing in his eyes. He'd pegged her as a pushover for sure. "We'll see."

He let out a chuckle. "Uh-huh. Want the grand tour?"

"Of course."

Reed opened one door then another. "Bathroom. Bedroom." He pulled her large suitcase behind him then pointed to a small door. "Linen closet here. I put your key and Nora's number on the desk in the living room. Nora's a longtime friend of the family who plays housekeeper for Dad. Call her if you need anything."

Kristen held her breath as she slipped past Reed and peered into the bedroom. Standard size. Nothing elaborate, but the room was nicely decorated in warm beige tones with a few turquoise accents. "It's just perfect," Kristen told him, aware that her voice sounded breathless. She'd never been this close to Reed—alone. And here they were in a bedroom in a small, secluded cabin that might as well be hundreds of miles from humanity. Her cheeks flushed, and she ducked back out of the room. "I love it."

"Great. Do you want to get settled here, then I can run you over to the barn after while? Or you can explore on your own. Up to you. The cabin and grounds are yours for the week so feel free to come and go."

"Let me get stuff situated here, then I'd love to see the horses if you don't mind coming back." She could use a short break to regroup and let her heart rate settle.

"Not at all. An hour?"

"Sure."

"I'll take off then. I don't like to leave Dylan with my dad too long."

Kristen raised her brows.

"He'd probably have the kid sharpening knives or shooting target practice."

"Oh, my."

Reed pulled his keys out of his pocket. "Only half kidding." In the doorway, he stopped then folded his arms and leaned against the casing. "Can I ask you a question?"

Chest pounding, Kristen forced a smile. "Of course." She took a couple of steps toward him and braced a hand against the back of the sofa.

"Is writing your only reason for being here?"

Heavy, charged air closed around her. She wet her lips. How to answer that? Honestly, sure, but…how honestly? "Well, writing is my goal. But—" She glanced around the room before looking at him again. "I'd love to ride my horse, er, Star, and spend some time with…with people I like, too."

As he pushed off from the door, a slow grin spread across his face. "Sounds like an excellent plan." He sauntered closer. About a foot away, he stopped. "You're good with dinner at the main house tonight? Don't let Dylan bully you. You decide."

She gave a shaky laugh. That was the plan, right? She couldn't remember for sure. Her brain was going fuzzy—probably due to lack of oxygen. Reed's proximity robbed her of breath. "I'd love to."

He leaned closer, his breath warm on her cheek. She braced herself for a friendly peck, but when her eyes fluttered shut, his lips grazed hers. Hovered there, and when she thought her legs might give out, Reed caught her arm and pulled her slightly toward him, his lips covering hers again.

He threaded one hand into her hair while the other tipped her chin.

Sparks exploded in her brain, and she grabbed hold of his arm. All of her senses came alive and responded to the unexpected deluge.

A long moment later, he pulled back and brushed a thumb across her cheek. "See you in about an hour."

Kristen couldn't speak but managed a nod. As soon as the door closed behind him, she collapsed against the sofa and ran a finger along her bottom lip. That kiss…Oh, man. The chances of her getting any writing done this weekend just dropped from unlikely to who-said-anything-about-writing?

****

When a car rumbled in the distance, Kristen pushed away from the split-rail fence across the road from the cabin. Surprised to encounter any traffic, she shaded her eyes and squinted at the small jeep that appeared. When one of the occupants began waving, she recognized Reed and Dylan. Her pulse spiked immediately. Smiling, she crossed the road to meet them.

"Hi there!" She couldn't see Reed's eyes behind the sunglasses and wondered if that was by design. Still, she enjoyed the view. His hair was tousled from the open-air vehicle, and the sunglasses gave him a relaxed, beach-bum look. The look suited him. Feeling the annoying heat start in her cheeks, Kristen dusted her hands on her jeans. "So, these are the ranch wheels?"

"Yep. Standard issue," Reed said. "I can get you a set, if you want."

Kristen shook her head. "I'm not planning to go anywhere but here and the barn."

Reed nodded. "You ready to go?"

"Ready." Inside the jeep, she turned to Dylan. "What have you been doing?"

"Working in the garden."

His grimace told her he didn't enjoy the task. "Really? Like pulling out weeds?"

"No. We picked stuff Grandpa likes."

Reed cast a sideways glance. "Things Dylan doesn't like. They're called vegetables."

Kristen chuckled. "I hear that can be a common affliction for kids his age."

"Gross stuff," Dylan said. "Like radishes."

Reaching back, Kristen held up her hand for a high-five. "Have to say I'm with you on that one, kiddo." Belatedly, she realized Reed might not appreciate her sentiment. "But I like lots of other vegetables."

"Nice save," he said under his breath.

"Doing my part."

He brought the jeep to a stop at the side of a barn that looked big enough to hold a dozen horses or more. The rough-hewn doors stood open, and Kristen could tell already this barn was spic and span. Hoses were coiled on their pegs, and the concrete floor was swept clean of hay and debris. "Wow." Swallowing hard, she put a hand against her chest. "This is nice." *Even better than she'd hoped for.* She took Dylan's hand. "Want to show me around?"

"You want to see Star?"

"I sure do."

Only a few yards into the facility, she stopped and

put a hand on Reed's arm. "Oh, my gosh, this is—" Her breath caught in her throat. "This is incredible. So much more than I expected. Thank you," she whispered.

He slid a hand around her shoulders. "You're welcome."

When she reached Star's stall, Kristen's heart bumped.

With a whinny, the horse raised her head over the railing.

"She remembers you," Dylan shouted.

"Yeah, she does." Kristen patted Star, and the familiar tickle of her tongue sent goose bumps up her arm. "Hey, baby."

"Let me get a saddle," Reed said. "I bet Amy's will work."

"Amy's my mom," Dylan said quietly.

Oh. Biting her lip, Kristen knelt and ran her hands up and down Dylan's arms. "Do you think she'd mind if I use her saddle?"

He shook his head.

"Sweetie, do *you* mind?" His solemn eyes looked at Kristen.

"It's okay, Miss Hanover."

"I'll take good care of the saddle." Standing, she gently pulled Dylan from the stall. "I'm letting her out now, okay?"

He took another couple of steps back.

Reed swung a light blanket onto Star's back then added the golden tan saddle. Taking the reins, he walked Star to the barn entrance. With his foot, he nudged over a block for Kristen to step onto.

She ran a hand along the soft leather saddle, her heart aching for the loss. "What a beautiful saddle," she murmured. Then, making sure Dylan was out of the way, she placed a foot in the stirrup and swung up. "This is a great view. Dylan, would you like to sit up here with me?"

Reed stepped closer. "We'd love to join you," he said in a low voice. "But we're not there yet."

"Let's wait then." She rested the reins in her lap and glanced at the step below. "I can ride this week while you guys are back in town."

"No, you go ahead. Have fun."

Kristen debated. Riding alone had its place but wasn't necessarily fun. She took a deep breath. *Fun* wasn't the objective—jumpstarting her creative juices was. And riding was part of that plan. She tapped her heels to signal Star to move forward.

"We'll see you this evening."

"Bye, Miss Hanover!"

"Bye, sweetie." When she reached the road, Kristen turned and waved—and almost went back as a sense of sadness washed over her. They looked rather forlorn watching her ride away. She didn't want to go without them, but Reed went to the trouble of getting Star ready. Just a short ride would be fine. Besides, she'd be with them again soon.

With slight pressure from her knees, she signaled Star to move again. Starting at a slow trot, Kristen set out to enjoy the scenery and get her bearings. She figured that was the main point behind Reed's insistence that she go without them. She could get a better lay of the land on horseback than riding as a passenger in a car.

As the steady clip-clop of Star's hooves lulled her into a familiar rhythm, she let her mind wander. A joint ride would be fun. Too bad Dylan couldn't or wouldn't get on a horse. And what was wrong with his grandpa that he couldn't watch his grandson for an hour or so? She sensed Reed could use a little time to himself. The ranch was his place to work off stress and relax—and he probably hadn't ridden since his sister's death.

Kristen led Star past the cabin then let her pick up the pace. She was amazed at how well Star already knew the road. She'd bet Reed didn't stick to the road or any trail. Well, tomorrow he'd get his chance to ride. She could return the favor. No reason she and Dylan couldn't play for an hour. In fact, she might reap the benefits of a more relaxed Reed as much as Dylan. Who knew what a fresh perspective could bring?

Chapter Twelve

Reed watched horse and rider until they were out of sight behind a whisper of dust. Yeah, a ride with Kristen would've been fun but not if it meant worrying about Dylan the whole time. He didn't need more stress. Reed had never brought a woman to the ranch before. The last person he'd seen on a regular basis didn't ride and wasn't keen on the lack of privacy at the ranch. No get-away cabins were available at the time.

Not that it mattered now, anyway. What would he do…sneak out of the big house at night like a teenager to meet up with Kristen? He imagined how that'd go down. At the first noise, Dylan would be wide-awake and come looking for him.

Didn't keep him from wondering, though, how that scenario might play out. Would she want him to? He recognized a spark. They'd clicked on a couple of levels, no question about that. Reed kicked at the dirt underfoot. Too damned bad he didn't have time for a relationship right now—especially one that required a plane ticket with every visit. Besides, three was a crowd in any relationship.

Still, he hoped for a little time with Kristen after supper.

When Reed pulled up to the cabin a few hours later, he spied their dinner date sitting in a rocking chair on the porch.

With a wave, she rose and came down the steps to meet them.

A smile beamed across her face. She'd left her hair down, and it cascaded around her shoulders, which were covered in a bright gold blouse. She replaced the cowboy boots with some short boots that sported higher heels. The package made a pretty picture that sent a hum through his veins. How the hell was he supposed to keep his hands off her around Dylan?

"Hey, guys!"

"How was your ride?" Reed asked.

"Lovely. It's beautiful out here. More so than I realized."

"See anyone else?"

She gestured toward the road. "I waved to someone in front of one of the houses I passed, and I saw a bunch of cows."

"Miss Hanover, Uncle Reed brought your guitar into the house."

Reed glanced at her. "Didn't think it should sit in the sun."

"Thanks. I forgot it was still in the car." She turned toward Dylan. "We'll play the guitar later, okay?"

Reed looked forward to that, too. With a little luck, she'd serenade Dylan off to la-la land. As Reed brought the jeep to a stop, he saw his dad sitting on the wide porch that ran across the back of the house. He regretted he didn't have a chance to expand on his earlier remarks to Kristen. Probably should've given her some background. He'd have to rely on her class to handle any awkward comments his dad might make.

As Reed made introductions, he spotted the look on his dad's face change from surprise to confusion. Yeah, he might not have mentioned Miss Hanover was not some elderly spinster.

"You're the teacher?"

"No. I'm a friend of Dylan's teacher. I'm an author. I write children's books."

"She's my special friend." Dylan put a thumb to his chest.

Reed's dad gave a sharp chortle and shot him a sideways glance. "Is that right?"

Both the tone of voice and look called B.S. on that statement—and Reed wondered how fast he could put his hands on a roll of duct tape. The next question was whose mouth to use it on. "Kristen, what can I get you to drink?" he asked. "Glass of wine? Cocktail?"

"A glass of wine would be nice. Thanks. White if you have it."

"She might like that Sauvignon Blanc Amy liked," Dad suggested. "We've still got a whole case."

"Yes. That would be lovely."

When Reed saw the flash of sympathy in Kristen's eyes as she took a step toward his father, he hesitated.

"Mr. Armstrong, I've enjoyed getting to know Reed and Dylan, but I'm so sorry about the tragedy in your family. What a terrible loss."

"Thank you. Call me Jack." His glance shifted toward his son. "Reed? You gonna get this lady her wine?"

"Coming right up." She'll probably need a whole damn bottle, he muttered to himself. Reed grabbed a beer and brought three bottles of the wine for Kristen. If she liked it, she might as well take some back to the cabin. By the time he returned, his dad refilled his glass, and Dylan helped himself to a juice box. "Okay, everybody. Here we go." He handed Kristen her glass then tapped his bottle to it. "Cheers to new friends."

"Uncle Reed, what about the pizza?"

"I'm on it, buddy." He rested a hand on Dylan's shoulder. "Just need to let the oven heat up."

"What can I do?" Kristen asked. "How about some veggies to go with that, Dylan?"

He wrinkled his nose and shook his head with more vigor than necessary.

The sound of Kristen's soft laughter made Reed wish he could keep up some clever banter to keep her entertained. He'd never met a woman whose voice conveyed so much warmth. Reaching for his beer, Reed cleared his throat. "We've got a great-looking salad in there, thanks to our housekeeper, Nora."

"Perfect," Kristen said.

Twenty minutes later, the heavy scent of spicy pepperoni and melted cheese filled the kitchen, and they gathered around the table. True to form, Dylan chattered through the meal. Jack kept a keen eye on Kristen, observing the interaction as though he were watching a movie. When his father abruptly pushed back his chair and announced he was going to his room to watch TV, relief flowed through Reed.

"Miss Hanover's going to play the guitar," Dylan said.

Ah, that duct tape would sure come in handy. Reed held his breath, hoping his dad wouldn't say anything to reveal his disdain for people in "soft" occupations such as artists, musicians, and writers.

His dad nodded. "Good to meet you, Kristen. Let us know if you need anything at the cabin."

As soon as Reed helped Kristen clear away the

dishes, he refilled her glass then retrieved her guitar from the front room. "Why don't we go outside?"

Kristen took a seat on one of the doublewide cushioned chairs.

Light sparkled in Dylan's eyes, and he scooted a stool right smack in front of her.

Happy to be a bystander, Reed sat farther back.

Kristen ran a hand across the strings, tuning the instrument, then leaned toward Dylan. "I might not know how to play any songs you like. Tell me some songs you know."

"The dancing dog!" Dylan shouted.

" 'Dancing Without a Collar On'?"

"Yeah!"

In seconds, Dylan shot from the stool and shook his booty.

Reed couldn't help laughing at the scene. The moves seemed so natural he wondered if Amy and Brian held similar jam sessions with the kids. So many reminders of his sister today. He took a long pull on his beer. How would he ever replace what Dylan lost? Sometimes, he thought the weight of the responsibility would crush him.

"Let's see, do you know "The Happy Song" or "I'm A Believer"? Did you see *Shrek*?" Kristen asked.

Dylan put a hand to his face, partially hiding a grin. "I know those."

When he finally collapsed on the stool several minutes later, Reed scooped up the kid and settled him between his legs. "Okay, sport, let's listen to Miss Hanover for a while." What he meant was, go to sleep now.

Kristen flashed Reed a soft smile and began

humming another song—a slow one this time. The slower rhythm did the trick. A few moments later, Dylan slumped against Reed, his slack weight proof he'd given in. Reed motioned to Kristen to keep playing while he carefully lifted Dylan. "Be right back," he whispered.

In the dark, Reed slipped off Dylan's boots and jeans, but that was as far as he was willing to push his luck. One night without brushing his teeth wouldn't send the kid into "cavity arrest." He pulled a light blanket over him and quietly shut the door. He returned to the porch to find Kristen backlit against the low yellow light.

She hummed softly while running her fingers across the guitar strings.

The private concert stirred something inside Reed. Though he hated to break the mood, he wanted to be closer. "Mind if I join you?" He tilted his head toward the empty space beside her.

****

Kristen looked up to see Reed saunter toward her. Finally, just the two of them. A warm glow spread over her. She tucked the guitar under her arm and pulled up her legs. "Of course not."

Reed sank onto the cushion and ran a hand across the back of his neck.

"Did he stay asleep?"

Reed offered a tired smile.

"He did."

"You look like you could turn in early, too."

"Nah. I'm good." But when his glance met hers, he blew out his breath with a shake of his head. "That was a lie. I'm beat." He leaned forward and rested his forearms on his thighs.

"I should go then." She straightened.

But Reed stretched an arm in front of her. "No. You should stay. This is nice."

"Are you sure?"

"Absolutely. You're very talented."

"Well, thanks, but—"

Reed put a finger across her lips. "Shhh. You are."

Kristen gave a shaky smile. "Listen, you have every right to be exhausted. With no preparation or warning, you were handed the responsibility of raising an energetic kid, and it's a demanding, twenty-four-seven job. I want you to go for a ride tomorrow. All by yourself. Or you and your dad. Whatever. I'll keep Dylan for a couple of hours."

Reed propped his head against a hand. "Thank you. I appreciate the offer, but you're not here to babysit."

"I don't mind at all. If I didn't want to, I wouldn't offer. You never know, maybe Dylan can help with my book. The set-up is perfect, really—my target audience in a one-on-one focus group. Besides, remember what I told you when you asked if I came here only to write?"

He lifted her hand and gave it a squeeze. "I remember."

A jolt of electricity shot up her arm, and she wondered if he could sense it. Was he looking for a reaction? She left her hand where it was. "So, there you go. I'll have fun hanging out with Dylan."

"Hmm. We'll see."

Kristen chuckled. "That, by the way, is not the right answer in this case. Come on, have you even ridden once since the accident?" When he hesitated, she nudged. "The truth."

"No, I haven't."

"Because you can't leave Dylan with your dad?" She swiveled to face him. "What's that all about?"

Reed toyed with her fingers in the silence. Finally, he stretched an arm along the back of the chair and looked at her. "You sure you want to get into the Armstrong family dynamics?"

In a way, Kristen already felt as if she were involved. "Well, I'm sitting here with you. I'm spending a week on your father's ranch. I'm drinking your sister's wine. And your nephew is one of my biggest fans. It might actually be a little late for that question." *Oh, boy.* Would she get an earful if Valerie only knew the extent to which Kristen was involved. Her agent's warning gave her pause, but she pushed aside the concern.

"Okay, here goes," Reed said. "My dad's a little rough around the edges. And that's the way he likes it. He thinks boys should be tough. He has an irrational fear of sissies, and he's been pushing Dylan to get on a horse, even though he knows the kid is scared. If he did get him on a horse, my dad would let Dylan ride without a helmet, which is expressly forbidden by his doctors and probably his mother."

Kristen sucked in her breath. "Oh. That's not just an opinion. We're talking about safety." She couldn't imagine her parents taking that kind of risk.

"Exactly. So I feel like I can't trust him not to do something stupid."

"I get it. Wow." She shook her head. "That's too bad. He really doesn't see the safety aspect?"

With a heavy sigh, Reed stretched his legs and readjusted. "Boys get scrapes and bruises. Getting hurt makes 'em stronger. You fall off a horse, you get right back on."

"And you know this from personal experience." Her comment was a statement, not a question.

"I do." He gave a wry smile and lifted a hand to the air. "Hey, I turned out okay, right?"

Kristen returned the smile. "Looks that way on the surface, at least."

Reed chuckled and moved closer.

Her pulse went crazy.

"Never even been to therapy," he whispered a second before his lips met hers.

His body heat was in such contrast to the cool air around her, Kristen shivered. Or maybe the shiver had nothing to do with the air at all. Maybe his touch just sent shockwaves over her skin. Feeling his right arm slide around her shoulder, pulling her closer, she was vaguely aware his left hand gently pried the guitar from her hand.

Unencumbered, she lost herself in his kiss, enjoying the sensation of floating and the warm tingles shooting through her.

"Mmm," Reed murmured against her lips. "Pretty sure this is the only therapy I need."

They were tossing the term around in a lighthearted way, but Kristen's thoughts circled back to Dylan, and she pulled back. "What about Dylan? Is he doing all right? Do you think he'll need counseling?" Wincing, she clamped a hand over her mouth. "I'm sorry. That was terrible timing. I have a bad habit of blurting out something when it hits my brain."

He smiled.

But the damage was done. Her words dampened

the mood like water on fire.

Reed continued sifting his fingers through her hair.

His gaze shifted somewhere behind her, and she wished she could take back her words.

He blew out his breath. "Probably. Eventually. I don't think he can fully process what happened now, but when he's older, he might be confused or angry about what he lost."

When he glanced back at Kristen, worry flickered across his face. The future he and Dylan faced could be as volatile as a minefield. She rested a hand on Reed's thigh. "All you can do is love him. Just be there. From what I can see, you're doing a great job."

"Thanks." He brushed a thumb over her hand. "Have I told you how glad I am I let Dylan drag me to a book signing a few weeks ago?"

Kristen let out a whoop and nudged him with an elbow. "I knew it. You didn't want to go, did you?"

He winced in his turn. "Was it that obvious?"

"Oh, yeah. Your body language screamed, get me out of here. Plus, you were still in your suit. I figured you came straight from work and were probably a little *hangry*."

Chuckling, Reed crossed his arms and rested his head along the back of the chair. "I knew you were Miss Observant. Goes with the territory, I guess."

"Exactly. People-watching is my favorite sport."

Covering a yawn, Reed straightened again. "Well, watching me sleep won't be very interesting. Know any more songs?"

"I can manage a couple of others." Kristen reached for the guitar. She should probably go back to the cabin and let Reed get some rest, but he seemed reluctant to end the evening—and she wasn't putting up a fight over that. She moved her hand across the strings and hummed a few notes, too nervous to break into song. Performance wasn't her strong suit.

"You have a beautiful voice."

Her cheeks warmed, and she cleared her throat. "Thanks."

"Did you ever play in a band?"

Kristen grinned. "Would the seventh-grade talent show count?"

"Hey, if you got on stage and sang or played a musical instrument in front of people, it counts."

"The performance was even recorded."

Reed shot her a sideways glance, brows raised. "My mother was in a close relationship with her video camera for a few years."

"Ah. I can see why. Play her favorite song."

At the unexpected request, Kristen sucked in her breath. How could he know her mother had a special song she loved to hear Kristen play? She memorized the tune years ago and played it probably hundreds of times. She began softly singing the words to John Denver's "Country Roads."

By the time she came to the closing lines, she saw Reed's eyes had fallen shut. She continued humming a bit longer to keep from waking him abruptly. It'd make a funny story later—how on the first night they had some time alone she put him to sleep with her music. She'd like to learn more about his family and the accident, but that could wait. He might not be ready talk about the wreck.

For several minutes, Kristen quietly watched the even rise and fall of his chest. She exercised great restraint to resist running her hands through his hair. Turned out he was wrong—watching him sleep was indeed interesting.

She hated to wake him, but the temperature was dropping, and she needed to get back to the cabin. Walking in the dark wasn't an option. She glanced toward the driveway, wondering if she could take a jeep. Sure, but the chances of starting it without waking Reed were slim. With no alternative, Kristen rested a hand lightly on Reed's arm. The hard muscles underneath his shirt offered proof of hard work outside a swanky office. When he still didn't wake, she scooted closer. Heart pounding, she touched his forehead and trailed a couple of fingers along his temple.

His eyes fluttered open.

"Hey," she whispered.

A lazy smile spread across his face. "Morning, gorgeous."

"Not quite, handsome. You want to drive me to the cabin or hand over the car keys?"

Reed sat up and glanced around. "Oh, damn. I fell asleep, didn't I?"

She linked an arm through his. "Only for a few minutes. No big deal."

He kissed the top of her head then took her hand, pulling her up with him. "You're way too nice."

Chuckling, Kristen tucked the guitar into its case.

Reed took the case then slipped his other arm around Kristen's shoulders and steered her to the jeep.

"Don't get out," Kristen said moments later at the cabin.

But without comment, he pulled out the guitar and followed her to the door.

Kristen fumbled with the lock.

"Need a light?" Reed held up his cell phone.

Really? Did he think light was the problem? "No. I've got it," she managed to say without breaking into hysterical laughter.

When the door finally swung in, Reed took a step forward and set the guitar on the floor. Then he stepped back over the threshold and put a hand under her chin.

She could hardly breathe in the charged air. "What time do you want to go tomorrow?"

"Totally up to you."

His gentle caress across her jawline made focus difficult. "Nine? Ten? What time does Dylan get up?"

"Too damned early. He tends to wake earlier on weekends than school days."

"Ooo. That's a bad habit."

"Uh-huh. Why don't I drop him here around ten?"

"Sounds good." She leaned against the woodwork for support. In the next instant Reed's arms came around her, and she lifted her face for the kiss she'd anticipated.

Warm lips met hers, and the blood whooshed in her ears. Then she was oblivious to anything except Reed and the heat shooting through her. With a soft murmur, Kristen wound her arms around his neck, and the kiss continued until she thought it would consume her.

Long moments later, Reed sighed against her lips. "I should probably get back," he whispered, though he made no move to do so.

She remembered they weren't really alone. If Dylan woke up... Nodding, she let her arms fall.

He brushed a thumb across her lips. "Goodnight."

"Night." The sweet dreams were sure to follow.

****

Kristen rose early the next morning—something she did only under duress—and felt surprisingly rested. After filling a travel mug with steaming tea, she slipped into jeans and boots then stepped into the soft morning light, which cast a pinkish glow on the fields around her. A light breeze whispered across her face.

Crossing the road, Kristen braced against the fence and looked behind the cabin where a ridge of rock that looked as if it belonged in New Mexico stood against the sky. If the ridge were accessible, it'd be a great place to watch the sun set. She'd have to ask Reed about getting there. *Reed.* Her thoughts easily drifted his direction. She took a sip of tea but knew more than the hot beverage warmed her insides. What she didn't know was how she felt about that. Was she crazy to start a long-distance relationship? Did she want a relationship with everything else on her plate? And the question that niggled in her brain, but she didn't really want to consider—how much of Reed's attraction had to do with Dylan?

She pushed off from the fence and began walking. Boots weren't the ideal walking shoes, but she meandered slowly, letting the scenery help clear her head. *Take it a day at a time and don't overanalyze.* Besides, she couldn't control feelings any more than she could control events. The only thing she needed to think about today was getting some direction on her next book.

With that goal in mind, she headed back to the cabin to get ready. When the jeep rumbled to a stop outside, Kristen hurried to the door. "Good morning, you two."

"Hi, Miss Hanover." Dylan hauled his backpack and another bag out of the backseat.

"What've you got there?"

Reed came up the stairs. "Morning. He insisted on bringing books and snacks." He leaned in and planted a platonic kiss on Kristen's cheek.

She swallowed her disappointment and couldn't help wondering why he was so cautious around Dylan. Surely he'd seen kissing before. "That's great." Kristen smiled at Dylan. She'd have to address the other question with Reed privately. She pulled Dylan to her side. "We might work up an appetite and need snacks. I don't know if I bought anything he'd like."

Reed took a step back and braced a hand against the doorframe "You guys have fun, okay?"

"That's the idea," Kristen said brightly. "You, too."

She held his gaze, and her breath caught at the warm appreciation in his eyes. The look went a long way toward restoring the positive vibes.

He reached out and pushed a strand of hair from her face. "I will. Thank you."

Smiling inside and out, Kristen gave a last wave as Reed climbed into the jeep, then she turned to Dylan. "Okay, kiddo, let's get this party started."

Behind the cabin a small yard was outfitted with a gravel fire pit, a couple of chairs, and a picnic table with benches. Kristen set her computer on the table then picked up her pen and notebook. "Want to play a new game?"

"Like in one of your books?"

"Something like that. How would you like to help me work on a new book?"

His eyes widened, and his mouth dropped open.

"Really? Can I?"

"Yes, really. I want you to be my helper. Now, here's what you do. Look at the house for a minute, then I want you to turn toward me and tell me as many things as you can remember." She'd planted a few small details, but what she really wanted to know was whether the game held his interest. If he found it dumb or boring, she'd have to scrap the concept and move on. Either one would be the kiss of death. "I'll count to ten, then you can turn around." She counted softly. "Okay, tell me what you saw."

"A door."

"One door or two?"

"Umm…" He started to turn back.

Kristen gently took his arm. "Nope. No peeking."

"I don't know."

"What color is the door?"

He screwed up his face.

Laughing, Kristen turned him around. She didn't want him to feel as if he'd messed up. "One, two, three." She clapped as she spoke. "What do you see?"

"A window. Steps. Shoes. Chairs." Shouting, he danced from one foot to the other.

"Excellent. What kind of chairs? What are they made of?"

Dylan turned toward her, eyes bulging. "Miss Hanover! That's so much stuff."

"I know. I want you to look at something and really see it. See what it's made of and what color it is and whether it's shiny or dull or old or new. Understand?"

He nodded.

"So, what do you think? Is the game fun?"

"Uh-huh. Let's do some more."

Kristen checked her watch. She'd give her ideas another thirty minutes then switch gears. When time was up, she allowed a short break before heading back to the picnic table. "Okay, Dylan, now I want you to tell me some stories."

She ran a hand over the soft fuzz on his head. "As you get older, you'll forget a lot of things that happened when you were little. You might only remember a few important things." Hoping she wasn't making a mistake, she stopped and swallowed hard. "If you want to tell me some stories about your mom and dad and baby sister, I'll write them down so you'll always have them and can read the stories when you're older. Would you like to do that?" As tears welled, she pressed her lips to keep them from trembling.

Dylan bobbed his head.

"Okay, let's start with your little sister. What was her name?"

"Hannah." A toothy smile widened across his face. "Daddy called her Hannah Banana."

"Oh, that's funny." Kristen began typing. "What do you remember most about her?"

"She always wanted her dirty dog."

"Her dirty dog? Like a toy?"

"A toy dog." Dylan gestured with his hands and became more animated as he spoke. "She wanted it all the time. Mommy said that dog was dirty and disgusting." Twisting his face, he hit the air with his fist. "But she didn't care. She liked to suck the ears!"

Laughing, Kristen typed Dylan's words and wondered if Reed still had the toy. Sounded as if its loss would've been traumatic. *Oh, no.* She groaned inside. It'd probably been in the car with them. She would not ask about the toy dog. "Did your dad have a funny name for you, too?"

Dylan thought a moment and shrugged. "No. He just called me his main man." He held up his palm. "Dylan, my main man, gimme five."

Oh, hell. Whose idea was this? Good thing she could type without seeing the keys. She brushed a sleeve across her cheeks and took a deep breath before continuing. "Okay, sweetie, tell me something about your mommy."

He folded his hands against the table and went quiet.

"Can you remember her favorite color?" Kristen prompted.

"Red," he shouted. "She wanted a red door and red flowers."

"Yeah? At your house? You had a red door?"

He nodded.

"So, your mom liked flowers. Did she have a garden?"

"Yesss. And she put my footprints in it."

Kristen slid an arm across Dylan's shoulders and gave an internal fist pump. These were the kinds of details she wanted to document. "That sounds cool. Tell me how she did that. Did she trace around your feet?"

"No. I stepped in the cement. Hannah did, too."

"So she made stepping stones for her garden?" Those should probably come to the ranch.

"Yeah, and we put beads and stuff all around." He pinched his fingers in the air as if sprinkling glitter.

Once again, Kristen wondered about family pictures. Sounded as if making those stones could've been a fun photo opportunity. Maybe she should steer

Dylan away from photo ops and talk more about feelings or rituals and routines. *Whew*. She knew which one of them would be exhausted tonight. "Tell me about one of the silliest things you ever did with your mom or dad. Can you think of anything?"

"Burned the waffles!"

"Yeah?"

Bouncing, Dylan rocked the bench. "Daddy was supposed to watch them, but Hannah started crying, and he forgot so the waffles were a little bit burned."

"Just a little bit?" she asked.

His head bobbed up and down. "So, Mommy said I could put the whipped cream on my waffle. Then Daddy put on some more." Dylan pinched his fingers close together. "And a little bit more. Then he gave me the can, and I squirted on a whole bunch like a big tower."

One of Dylan's hands went over his head for emphasis, and a huge smile covered his face.

"Then Mommy got out the chocolate chips and the sprinkles she puts on cookies. And I covered all the whipped cream with sprinkles, too."

Picturing what he described, Kristen couldn't help wincing. "Did you eat it?"

"Sure did."

"Was it good?"

"It was awesome." Laughing, Dylan rubbed his belly.

Kristen laughed with him. "I don't know, kiddo, that sounds like an awful waffle to me." As soon as the words left her mouth, a story idea hit her brain. "Hey, maybe we should write a book called *The Awful Waffle*."

The light sparkled in Dylan's eyes. "Yeah!"

"I might have a lot of books to write."

"I can help."

"Well, let's write these memory stories first. Sounds like your mommy and daddy were a lot of fun."

As his grin faded, Dylan looked up with big, solemn eyes and nodded.

Kristen's breath caught in her throat, and she folded him into a tight hug, squeezing her eyes shut and willing herself not to cry. She was so glad she thought of the journal. If she could capture even a fraction of the excitement and emotion she heard in Dylan's voice, the journal would prove a treasure—and maybe a tool of healing in years to come.

****

Reed didn't plan to spy on them, but he wasn't in any hurry to alert Kristen and Dylan to his presence, either, when he could tell they hadn't heard him come around the back of the cabin. They were apparently deep in thought. Dylan sat in front of Kristen at the picnic table, and they were both focused on her computer screen.

When Dylan looked up at Kristen and she rested her cheek on his head, Reed's heart skipped a beat. The picture was profoundly touching. The two had clearly made a connection, and he was grateful to Kristen. But at the same time, a heavy sadness hit his gut. This was his sister's child. And she was missing out. God, Amy was missing her kid's whole life. The pain of that—

Kristen looked up.

The quick smile and wave tripped his heart again. Swallowing hard, he moved forward.

Kristen closed the computer and swung Dylan

around. "Hey, there," she called. "How was the ride?"

As she walked toward him, her pale yellow sweater clung to her slim figure. Heat shot up the back of his neck, and his thoughts went another direction. To a different kind of ride. His mouth went dry as day-old bread, and he could hardly muster a response. "Great," he croaked.

Good thing he and Dylan were heading home this afternoon, or he'd be thinking seriously of locking Dylan in a room in front of a television for a while. Recovering his composure, Reed offered a wide smile and a more appropriate response. "Ride was good. I met up with Randy, one of the hands who lives on site, and we went around the back property line where we could let the horses run a little."

Free rein on an open stretch was exhilarating. Something about the rhythmic dance of the horse's hooves against the ground released his own restless energy and pent-up frustrations. He met Kristen's gaze. "Thank you."

She started to speak, then her glance shifted to Dylan, who'd followed them inside.

Reed had the distinct impression that she, too, would've liked a moment in private.

But she simply smiled. "You're welcome. I didn't hear the jeep pull up."

He jerked a thumb over his shoulder. "Left Thunder tied to the porch post out front. He's pretty happy munching all the grass within reach."

"What about water?"

"I'll get it." Passing Kristen, he'd swear he felt an electrical charge.

She took a small step back and looked away.

"Speaking of munching, who's ready for some lunch?"

"Me!" Dylan shouted.

"That'd be great," Reed said.

"Coming right up. Dylan, why don't you wash your hands then get your sandwich, okay?"

Reed stopped in his tracks. As soon as the bathroom door swung shut, he stepped toward Kristen. "Thank you." He tipped her chin. This time, her lips met his, and that was the only answer he needed. He pulled her close but reluctantly let go seconds later when the water stopped running. Blowing out his breath, he pressed another quick kiss to her lips, but it didn't nearly scratch the itch.

When Reed returned from giving water to Thunder, he saw Dylan was already seated at the small square table inside, and Kristen was at the kitchen counter. The cozy domestic scene seemed surreal.

"Have a seat." She tipped her head toward the table. "Be ready in a sec."

"Let me wash up, and I'll give you a hand." In an attempt to clear his head and re-set, Reed splashed cool water on his face. He and Dylan soon would be on the road back to Dallas. Back to reality. Reed headed for the kitchen. "What can I do?"

Kristen handed him a glass of iced tea. "Really, nothing."

"Uncle Reed, guess what?"

Reed pulled out a chair and turned his attention to his nephew. "What?"

"Me and Miss Hanover wrote stories while you were gone."

"Yeah? That's great. That's why she's here, you know. To write stories."

"I told her about Mommy and Daddy."

Reed went still, his hand halfway to his mouth. He set the glass back on the table and glanced at Kristen, who slowly turned. He struggled to understand her expression while thoughts tumbled through his brain. He looked back at Dylan. "What do you mean?"

"Stories," Dylan said with a shrug.

As if that explained anything.

Kristen set a plate piled with fresh spinach salad and sliced grilled chicken in front of Reed. "I thought talking about his parents might help him remember them," she said softly. "I typed while he talked, so it's like a little journal."

"Oh. I thought you were working on books."

"We did that, too." She placed her plate on the table and pulled out a chair.

"But the journal is just for him," Reed pressed.

Her brows pulled together.

"I told her about the waffles Daddy burned." Dylan paused and slurped his juice. "So we're writing a new book called *The Awful Waffle*."

"Maybe," Kristen said. "I'll have to spend some time playing around with the concept. It's a cute idea, anyway."

Reed frowned. He thought she was testing her own ideas on Dylan. But Dylan told family stories? Not for the first time, he wondered if he should consult a child psychologist. Would talking about his parents help Dylan, or would that increase the pain and trauma? Was it better to simply let them go? Everything happened so quickly...the accident...the funeral...dealing with Dylan's injuries and recovery. They'd jumped into action with hardly any time to think at all.

He nodded toward Kristen, as she seemed to be waiting for some kind of response. "Yeah," he said. "I, uh, I'd like to read that." Reed ate his salad on autopilot, nodding while Dylan talked about his day with Kristen. Sounded like they easily filled the time. When the ice cubes rattled in his glass, he stood and carried his dishes to the sink. Then he glanced at his watch—time to face the inevitable. He and Dylan had to go. "Can you bring him down in the jeep?" Reed asked Kristen.

"Absolutely. We'll let you get a little head start then meet you at the house."

"That'd be great. Thanks." Reed unhitched Thunder and rode back to the barn, still mulling the lunch conversation in his head. He couldn't quite put his finger on what was bothering him, but a nagging voice wouldn't be silenced.

He swung the saddle back onto its rack, and the obvious hit him front and center. Kristen wrote books for a living. If she published a book based on Dylan's stories, she'd make money from it. Her agent and editor and publisher and bookstores everywhere would profit from his sister's death—from their family's trauma and heartache.

His stomach clenched. Cute story or not, how could he allow that?

Chapter Thirteen

Chill air surrounded Kristen as she returned to the cabin alone. The temperature had taken a sudden dip—but the feeling was more than the gray clouds rolling in. Reed's goodbye was unquestionably cool, and his eyes were missing the warmth from this morning. The pathetic peck he gave her barely skimmed her cheek.

She pulled on a sweater and pondered the change. Something obviously bothered him, but she'd have to wait until tonight, after Dylan went to bed, to get the details.

Wandering into the living area, Kristen sank onto an arm of the sofa. She wanted to talk to Reed and clear the air, but oh, man, she didn't need any more stress in her life. Was he jealous that Dylan opened up? Concerned he might tell something too personal? Just thinking about dealing with an issue made her tired—and sad. She admitted an attraction to the man. In fact, the way she flushed and overheated in his presence was embarrassing. Good grief, she'd had relationships. Maybe the mood swing, whatever the cause, was a sign that this one came with too many complications.

Or, he could've received a message from work that preoccupied him and had nothing to do with her at all. With a shake of her head, she pushed those thoughts to the back burner and glanced at her watch. Too late in the day for a nap. Instead, she brewed a cup of herbal tea and picked up her sketchbook and a pencil. Even though she didn't create the illustrations for her books, she always sketched the scenes page by page, matching words with the proposed action. The rough drawings helped bring the story to life.

She didn't have a storyline thought out yet for *The Awful Waffle*, but the wheels turned in her head. She loved the title and was sure the idea would lend itself to some fun illustrations. Bonus points if it could be a source of happiness for Dylan. Another thought merged in and tugged at her heartstrings. She caught her breath. She could dedicate the book to the memory of his parents and little sister. That was reason enough to make it happen.

After a light dinner, Kristen dug her phone out of her purse. She hadn't used it since yesterday morning and didn't want to run out of battery when Reed called. As soon as she plugged in the phone to charge, a notification popped up that she'd missed a call from her brother. *Yesterday.*

Her chest went cold, and Kristen sank into the nearest chair at the breakfast nook. She looked out the window at the evening shadows stretching across the fields. The getaway already accomplished one goal—it kept her mind off the auction of her parents' belongings yesterday. So, why was her brother calling? Surely they wouldn't have results already.

Debating whether to return the call, Kristen released a long, slow breath. She didn't care about the results of the sale, and she didn't like her brother's attitude, but being around Dylan and Reed had certainly reminded her of the value of family. Her brother was the only family she had. Kristen picked up her phone and hit the callback button.

"Hello?" John's voice came on the line.

"Hey, it's me."

"Hi. Did you hear from the auction house?"

"No. Why?"

"I talked to them last night. They said the sale went well. Sold most of the big stuff, and only a few small things are left to go in their retail shop."

Kristen sucked in a deep breath and rolled her shoulders. So the ordeal was almost over. Only the sale of the farm remained. "Oh, that's great." She feigned an upbeat response.

"I'll give Matthews a call tomorrow and see about getting the proceeds dispersed as soon as the check comes in."

Jim Matthews, their mother's longtime attorney, was handling the details of the estate. Kristen wasn't sure he wanted to be bothered with incremental payouts but whatever. "That's up to you," she said. "I'm not in a big hurry for the money."

"Might be nice to have before Christmas."

John's comment reminded Kristen he had more financial obligations than she did. Maybe he could use the extra cash.

"Speaking of holidays," John said. "Ellen wanted me to remind you this year is our turn to visit her family for Christmas, so we'll be going to Minneapolis. You're welcome to join us."

Like a rock dropped from a bridge, Kristen's stomach fell hard. She'd deliberately avoided thinking about holiday plans this year—the first Christmas without Mom. John and his family never traveled for Thanksgiving and after they had kids, they split every other Christmas between the two families. Tears stung her eyes. No way could she spend this Christmas with her sister-in-law's family. The atmosphere would be all hustle and bustle and kids with no time to reflect or remember her mother.

"Oh. Well—" Kristen stalled to give herself time to react calmly. "Thanks, John. Please tell Ellen I appreciate the offer, but I'll probably stay close to home." She pressed her lips and took a deep breath. *Home.* She'd never missed a Christmas at the farm.

"By yourself?"

"No, I've always got invitations from friends." She had standing invitations from Allison and Jana, but she'd always made the holidays about family. Looked like that was about to change. "Honestly, I'd rather have a quiet holiday this year."

The distance yawned between them, and Kristen knew each year it'd be harder to get together and would take more effort to prevent them from simply slipping away.

"Well, you can always let us know later if you change your mind," John said.

"Sure."

"Also, I talked to Diane Goldman yesterday. She hasn't had much interest in the farm yet."

"No surprise there." Kristen kept her voice light and upbeat. "It's only been a couple of weeks. I'm sure she's still working on getting the information in front of the right people." And that fast she knew she wouldn't be changing her mind about the holidays. Her brother's impatience about the farm gnawed at her. "We knew we were heading into a tough selling season. We might not see much activity before spring." *Ugh.* Kristen groaned inside. She'd opened the door and practically welcomed him to berate her again for dragging her feet on closing out the estate.

Her brother's heavy sigh came across the line loud and clear.

"Listen, thanks for the update." Kristen hurried to cut him off. "I'd better let you go. Tell everyone hi from Aunt Kristen, okay?" She ended the call before he could respond and then let her head drop. Christmas would be tough, no doubt about it.

If not for Reed's promise of a phone call, Kristen would've crawled into bed. She was lounging on the small sofa, barely awake, when her phone finally buzzed again at nine forty-five. Scrambling upright, she confirmed Reed's number before answering. "Hey."

"Hi, not too late, is it?"

She released the breath she'd been holding. He sounded perfectly normal. "Of course not. How was the drive?"

"Good. Guess who fell asleep five minutes from the ranch?"

Kristen sputtered a laugh. "Figures. And then he wanted to stay up later tonight?"

"Only a little. I think he was pretty worn out."

"You know, I think that kid's mind goes so fast it's over-compensating for him not physically running."

"You might be right." He paused a moment. "Listen, there's something I want to talk to you about."

Kristen's heart skipped a beat. She didn't miss the serious tone in his voice. "All right. I wondered if something bothered you when you left this afternoon. What's up?" She began pacing the tiny quarters.

"This morning, when you were talking to Dylan.

170

Were you looking for new story ideas?"

Kristen had trouble making a connection. What did that have to do with anything? "Um...actually, I'm always looking for new story ideas. That's—"

"I thought you wanted Dylan's reaction to ideas you were already working on."

"I did. Having his input was great to gauge his level of interest and engagement." She struggled to get at the issue. "Reed, I don't understand. Are you upset that Dylan talked to me about his parents?"

"Here's the deal. I don't like the thought of anyone making money from our family's tragedy."

Kristen heard the edge in his voice and sucked in her breath. "What are you talking about?"

"If you publish a book based on Dylan's memories about his parents, a lot of people make money, and that feels wrong."

Conflicting thoughts rushed in, and she put a hand to her chest. *Oh, man.* She hadn't considered recording Dylan's memories might look as if—

"Just tell me that wasn't part of the plan."

"Oh, Reed. Of course—" She stopped short, and her face flushed hot. Did she hear that right? "Wait. I have to tell you I'm not a mercenary out to take advantage of a six-year-old child who's lost his parents and little sister? Are you serious?" Her voice pitched up, though she kept inside the expletive dancing on the tip of her tongue.

Deafening silence filled the air.

"Wow," Kristen said. "You thought that was my plan? That I came out here with the goal of—"

"That's not what I meant."

"What did you mean?"

"I guess—I just need you to know Dylan's story isn't up for sale."

Kristen shook her head, trying to clear it. "Um. Okay."

"I'm sorry," he said at the same time. "Look, that thought was stupid of me. The story caught me by surprise, that's all. I thought you two were talking about your books and horses. Dylan said you didn't talk at all about the horse books he's been looking at."

Kristen closed her eyes. *Damn.* She forgot about those. She was supposed to help Dylan get more comfortable with horses. He'd been excited to tell her at the airport, and they'd never circled back to the topic. So, that was a *fail*. But did being forgetful make her an insensitive opportunist?

She opened the back door and stepped outside to let the breeze cool her over-heated skin. "I— No. I'm sorry. We didn't get around to talking about horses. We got sidetracked with the journal." In her mind, that didn't quite explain his ridiculous conclusion she'd been pumping Dylan for story ideas, but it did remind her how little they really knew each other. How could he kiss her or look at her the way he did and ever think something so negative? "Reed, you—you really thought I might be deliberately using Dylan? I'm still wrapping my head around that. I mean, I thought we…" They *what?* "That sounds like you don't trust me, and I don't understand that."

"Look, I'm with you. I can't believe that even occurred to me. After the accident, people couldn't get enough of the story. Magazines and newspapers wanted interviews and information. Like the accident was a show of some kind. The whole thing turned my stomach. I'm still getting calls for interviews, and Dylan's aunt wants to sue the guy's estate and insurance company. So, the talk about a book based on one of Dylan's memories hit me wrong."

Oh, wow. She had no idea. People could be so self-absorbed and thoughtless. "I understand," Kristen said softly. "But you can look at the idea in other ways. From Dylan's standpoint, a book with ties to his family could be a special keepsake. I can't promise the book would even get sold, and I can't say people won't want to get paid to produce it, but maybe royalties could fund a scholarship for Dylan or some kind of memorial for his family." When he didn't immediately respond, she felt obligated to fill the pause. "Just thinking out loud here."

"I am such an idiot."

At the regret in his voice, Kristen's heart bounced. "I won't argue with you there."

"Feel free to give me a good punch next weekend."

She let out a shaky laugh. "I just might." Her thoughts did a quick rewind to the past weekend. Where was this thing between them going, anyway? She took a deep breath and forced herself to bring up the topic. Might as well get it all on the table. "You know, Reed, maybe there's something else we need to talk about—like what's going on between us."

Oh, how she wished she could see his face. When only silence greeted her, she wondered if the call had dropped. "Reed?"

"I'm here. Not sure I know how to answer that. I guess I feel like we're kindling right now."

"Kindling?"

"Say you're building a fire in the pit at the ranch.

You've got kindling to get things started, right?"

"Uh-huh."

"You start with a spark."

Ah. She saw where this analogy was going.

"Some will catch fire real fast then fade out. Some won't do anything. Maybe a little smoke and smolder. And some will start a slow, steady fire that burns a long time."

Peering into the darkness surrounding the cabin, Kristen shivered. A fire would be nice. "Okaaay," she said. "Let's say there's a spark."

"I think we could say that."

She'd swear she could feel the warmth in his words. It wrapped around her like a down-filled blanket—and went a long way toward soothing the abrasion of his earlier comment. Her heart pounded like crazy, and she had to wet her lips before she could speak again. "So what's…what's next?"

He let out a soft chuckle. "I guess we see what happens."

"Reed, tell me this. Why won't you touch me in front of Dylan?"

He blew out a long breath. "The truth? Because I'm afraid of a kindergartner."

Wait. Mr. Oil Executive was afraid of a little kid? Kristen sputtered a laugh. "What?"

"Remember the first time I kissed you goodbye at the burger joint in Oklahoma?"

"Yeah." A flush rose in her cheeks. How could she forget the first warm graze of his lips?

"I caught hell from Dylan over it. He wants to be your special friend."

"Oh." That was something she hadn't considered.

It was a little weird but sweet at the same time. "Did you talk about it?"

"Nothing heavy. Just told him that was how adults greeted each other sometimes. At the time, I wasn't sure we'd ever see Miss Hanover again. So, I agreed."

"I see. So how do we fix that?"

"I'm thinking."

"Hmmm. Me, too. Would you be off the hook if I made the first move?" She gave a light chuckle. "You know, threw myself at you?"

"I wouldn't object."

Humor danced in his voice, and Kristen laughed. "Well, we'll see."

"I'll look forward to that. What time on Saturday would you like to get started? Or should we make it Friday night?"

"Now don't pressure me. Haven't made a plan yet."

"All right. But think about it."

"I already am." She wasn't quite sure whether to call the sound he made a groan or a choke, but she sensed fire crackling through the line.

"You going for a ride tomorrow?"

At his sudden change of subjects, she grinned. "Yeah. I think so." Absolutely. After this conversation, she'd need one to clear her head.

"Oh, hey, back up a sec," Reed said. "We can't get there on Friday night. There's some kind of program at Dylan's school. We'll head out first thing Saturday morning."

"I'll be waiting." Kristen ended the call with Reed's fire analogy still on her mind. They'd agreed to test fate and see what happened to the spark, but she couldn't help wondering—if they moved forward, would they flame or fizzle? And would someone get burned in the process?

****

The next morning, Kristen tugged her boots over her jeans, about to head down to the stables. She hoped an invigorating ride would get the creative juices flowing. Now that she had solid concepts confirmed, she had a lot of writing to do.

A soft knock at the door startled her. Kristen opened the cabin door to find a salt-and-pepper-haired woman wearing hot pink eyeglasses holding a covered basket.

A smile widened across the woman's face, and she waved a hand. "Morning, dear. I'm Nora Wheaton, housekeeper, cook and all-around general assistant at the big house."

"Nora, it's so nice to meet you." Kristen returned the friendly smile and took a step back. "I'm Kristen Hanover. Please, come in." She wondered if Nora made house calls bearing gifts to all visitors or whether Reed arranged this.

Nora stepped inside, headed straight to the kitchen, and reached into her basket. "Did some baking last night. I've got pumpkin bread, sunflower seed rolls, and my amazing homemade apricot preserves."

Kristen blinked. *Wowza.* This woman could add welcome wagon and angel to her long list of roles at the big house. "Oh, my gosh. Thank you so much. Those all sound wonderful." Belatedly remembering her manners, she moved toward the table. "Do you have time for a cup of tea?"

Nora's eyes sparkled behind the glasses. "I'd love

it. As long as I'm not keeping you from something else."

"Not at all." She could ride later and write all night if necessary. No schedules. No commitments. Kristen put the kettle on the stove—a more civilized way to brew tea for company.

"I've heard a lot about you, Miss Hanover. And I've read your charming books. That little Dylan just loves them." She selected a tea bag from the box Kristen offered and pulled out a chair. "Thank you."

"Thank *you*. Please, call me Kristen." She dropped into a chair across from her visitor. "You've spent some time with Dylan then."

"Oh, yes. He's a doll. I thank the lord every day he survived that terrible crash."

"He's a sweet kid. So young to deal with such a tragedy."

"Heartbreaking," Nora said. "That precious little girl. Well, they were all precious. Mr. Jack loved his girls. To lose them after losing darling Rosalyn...I suppose heartbreaking is the only word for it."

"Rosalyn was his wife?"

"That's right—and my dearest friend."

And Reed's mother. Kristen hated to pry, but she wanted more information. "You've known the family a long time?"

"Forever. I first met Rosalyn when Roger, my husband, came to work for Jack. My word, I was only twenty-five. Roger was twenty-seven, and we've been here ever since." A wistful smile turned Nora's lips. "Can you believe that?"

"There must've been good chemistry."

Nora lifted her hands in the air. "Oh, we had so

much fun. Rosalyn and I took to each other right away. And even though Jack was the boss, he and Roger were as close as brothers." She leaned forward, and the light in her eyes sparkled again. "Sometimes fought like 'em, too. Still do."

"Nora." Kristen spoke softly. "What happened to Rosalyn?"

The light and smile faded immediately, and Nora's gaze shifted behind Kristen. When she looked back at Kristen, she let out a long sigh. "Sudden heart attack. Got up one night and just dropped. Gone before Jack could even get to her side. I think that's what haunts him most. He never got to tell her goodbye."

Kristen swallowed hard, her throat tightening with unshed tears, and she pushed back her chair to get the kettle. "It's so sad," she murmured as she poured hot water into their cups.

"Honestly, I don't know how Jack's still standing. Works himself to oblivion, I suppose. Thankfully, he hasn't taken to the bottle to nurse his sorrow. To bury a wife, a child, plus her husband, and a grandchild. No one should have to bear so much grief."

"You're right." Kristen took a sip of the soothing lemon tea.

"After Rosalyn passed three years ago, I stepped in to help Jack with meals and housekeeping. And I'm still at it. The kids are grown so only Roger and I are left at our place. Figure I might as well put myself to good use. If I'm cooking for the two of us, what's another one or two, you know?"

"I'm sure your help has made a huge difference. Especially these past few months."

"It's been hard, but life goes on. You sure have

brightened life for that little boy." Lifting her cup, Nora tipped her head down and eyed Kristen over the rim of her glasses. "And perhaps for his uncle, as well?" She paused. "Am I reading that right?"

Kristen knew her face must be all shades of pink. The conversation turned personal before she saw it coming. How would Nora even know that? And would anything Kristen said circle back to the family? She couldn't think of a coherent answer on the fly.

Nora waved a hand. "You don't have to answer. I probably sound like a nosy old biddy."

Kristen couldn't help but laugh at the description. Nothing could be farther from the truth. She sensed the loyalty in this woman. And probably protectiveness, given what her friends had gone through. Who could blame her?

"Not at all. And I'm thrilled I might be a positive influence for Dylan. I'd love nothing more than to help him through this awful time." She didn't add that she was not, in fact, using the kid for her own selfish purposes. "As for his uncle..." Kristen smiled and shrugged. "Well, you could say there might be a spark." Hey, if that got back to him, they were his own words.

"I suspected as much. That young man sure has his hands full. Having someone special in his life right now would be such a comfort."

A warm flush spread to Kristen's face again. She wondered where "someone special" fell in the spark-to-steady-burn spectrum.

"Anyhow," Nora said. "Reed doesn't know a thing about being a daddy, but he'll do all right. He's got a good heart and does anything he sets his mind to. Always has."

Scrambling to keep up with Nora, Kristen nodded. If she'd been that close to Reed's mother, she must know a lot about him, as well. Kristen considered pummeling her with questions. But before she could craft a question that wouldn't sound blatantly obvious, another thought struck—Dylan wasn't completely without female influence after all. He had this lovely woman to look out for him. Relief washed over her.

She reached out and touched Nora's arm. "I'm so glad to know Dylan has you in his life. I've been worried about him being surrounded by men and not having enough...oh, I don't know...tenderness and affection."

Nora squeezed her hand. "Well, sweetie, one thing I know is worrying doesn't help. I don't see him often, but let me tell you, when I do, I hug on that boy as much as I can."

The smile returned to Nora's eyes.

She pushed back her chair. "I'd do anything for Rosalyn's little ones. Now, I should be getting back. I'm so happy to meet you, Kristen. Thank you for the tea. Just holler if you need anything."

As unexpectedly as she'd arrived, Nora waved and disappeared in the cloud of dust the jeep left behind. And left Kristen to rein in her train of thought. She shook her head. How could she concentrate on writing when her mind swirled with questions about Reed and his family?

Chapter Fourteen

At the sound of tires rumbling in the distance, Kristen jumped. She'd kept busy helping Nora prepare meals for the weekend while her husband and Jack were out doing whatever ranch work they tended to on a Saturday morning. But mostly, she'd been waiting for Reed and Dylan to arrive.

A productive week was coming to a close. The combination of beautiful scenery, quiet solitude, and a relaxed schedule proved fruitful. Every time she thought about her new stories Kristen went almost giddy. Finally, the words flowed, and the stories came to life. With that progress made, she was ready to enjoy a fun weekend with Reed and Dylan.

"Sounds like they're here," Nora said with a broad smile.

Kristen stepped into the dim front room with an answering grin. But as she peeked out the massive picture windows of the living room, disappointment replaced excitement. "I don't think so, Nora. It's a red car."

Nora was beside her in a moment. Wiping her hands on a tea towel, she let out a sigh. "That would be Celia, Dylan's aunt. She calls a lot but never lets us know when she's coming."

"Oh. Does she live close by?"

"Not as far as I know. I haven't quite figured her

out. She's from Dylan's dad's side. None of us know much about her. She keeps saying Dylan is the only family she has now, and she doesn't want to lose him. If you ask me, she seems kind of lost herself."

Kristen's heart sank, and she followed Nora back to the kitchen. She selfishly wanted Reed and Dylan to herself today. Entertaining Dylan's aunt wasn't in the plan. Besides that, she already felt biased against the woman based on Reed's comments.

"Obviously you have nothing to worry about," Nora said. "But I'd bet my last dollar she's not just interested in Dylan."

"What do you mean?" Kristen asked.

"Reed is an attractive man, as you know."

Ugh. Though the two weren't related by blood that sounded a little weird to Kristen. She was wondering if Reed had any inkling when a car door slammed near the back entrance. Shelving those thoughts for now, she pasted on a smile.

"Knock-knock," a high-pitched voice sang out at the same time the French door opened. "Jack? Nora? Anybody home?"

"In the kitchen, Celia," Nora hollered. "Come on in."

A thin woman with white-blonde hair appeared in the doorway. Her mouth formed an 'O' when she made eye contact with Kristen. Her glance darted to Nora. "Oh, dear me, you've got company."

Nora gestured toward Kristen. "Celia, this is Kristen Hanover, a friend of Reed's and Dylan's."

Kristen extended a hand. "Good to meet you."

At the same time, Celia turned to Nora. "Are they here? I didn't see a car."

182

Celia glanced back at Kristen and briefly touched her hand. "Pleasure."

Seeing Celia turn to Nora again with an expression that came close to a pout, Kristen struggled to keep her eyes from bulging at the silly reaction.

"Where is that darling nephew of mine?"

"On their way," Nora said. "What would you like to drink?"

"Coffee with a little cream if you've got it."

"Always." She poured a cup and handed it to Celia. "I'll let you add the cream."

"Looks like y'all are getting ready for a feast."

"No one goes hungry around here," Nora said. "Can you stay for lunch, Celia?"

Kristen held her breath. Though she vowed to be friendly, she hoped this wouldn't be an extended stay for Dylan's aunt. Unfortunately, the queasiness in her stomach warned her of just the opposite.

"Well, thank you, Nora. I'd love to." With a bright smile, Celia picked up her mug and perched on a barstool.

Kristen felt Celia's eyes on her in the silence, and when she looked up, the woman gave her a cool speculative gaze.

"Are you visiting for the weekend, Kristen?"

"Heading home tomorrow." She wasn't inclined to get into the details with Celia. They planned to leave mid-afternoon to get to the airport in time for Kristen's six o'clock flight. Denver suddenly seemed a cruel distance—and she had no idea when she'd see Reed and Dylan next.

"Uh-huh. And where's—"

Wheels crunched on the gravel outside.

"Must be our boys." Celia hopped from the stool and made a beeline for the back door.

Our boys? Kristen washed her hands and followed, regretting Celia's presence even more. She'd hoped for a private greeting with Reed, and while throwing herself at him was an exaggeration, she'd planned to at least take his hand or arm after she hugged Dylan. Would the additional audience make a difference to Reed?

Celia stepped down the stairs, waving both hands. As soon as Reed opened the car door for Dylan, Celia crouched with outstretched arms. "Dylan," she hollered. "How's my Bumblebee?"

Dylan stopped short of his aunt but was still close enough for Kristen to observe them.

"Hi, Aunt Celia."

He accepted her hug, but when he looked up and saw Kristen, he pushed back from Celia and made for the porch. "Miss Hanover!"

Grinning, Kristen waved and caught him against her. "Hey there, Dylan. How are you, sweetie?" She looked toward the driveway to see Celia fall into step beside Reed.

"Hey, Reed."

"Hello, Celia. What brings you out here today?"

"Just visiting." She gave a little shrug. "Hoping I'd catch you two."

Kristen opened the door for Dylan then turned back to greet Reed. The warm light that bounced in his eyes ricocheted through her. She reconsidered the possibility of throwing herself into his arms, but restraint won out, and she lifted her face for a kiss on the cheek. She stayed close beside him, though, as he dropped one of the bags to hold open the door for Celia.

"I'll get the door." As she spoke, Kristen noted the sour line of Celia's lips. "Is there anything else in the car?"

"Nah. We didn't bring much for just one night." He leaned in and gave her a quick kiss. "Sorry we couldn't get here last night."

"Me, too," she whispered.

Inside, the noise skyrocketed with greetings and conversation. True to her word, Nora held Dylan in her arms. She set him down and a moment later placed a platter of cinnamon rolls on the table. "This should tide everyone over until lunch."

Or at least take off the edge, Kristen thought, sensing some nervous energy in the air.

The plate emptied in seconds.

"Kristen, did Nora give you the grand tour of the house?"

Kristen was about to pull out a chair when Reed's voice stopped her. She silently thanked her new friend for not taking that initiative. "No. No exploring."

He nodded toward the hallway. "Come on. I'll show you around."

She stepped forward and tossed a quick glance Nora's direction.

"Dylan," Nora said. "Why don't you tell me and Aunt Celia about the program at school last night? I want to hear all about it."

Kristen smiled inside. She found an ally in Nora.

"You might enjoy the library." Reed spoke in a loud tone as he steered Kristen from the room. As soon as they were out of sight and hearing range, Reed stopped and pulled her into his arms.

She muffled her laughter against his shoulder—until he tipped her chin and looked into her eyes.

"Hey."

Her throat constricted. "Hi, there," she whispered a second before his lips covered hers. Then, words were impossible...and unnecessary. Reed's warm hands traveled across her back, and the spark ignited, sending fire through her veins as the kiss deepened. Kristen barely registered time or place—until Celia's high-pitched giggle broke the spell.

Kristen let her hands drift down Reed's solid chest. "I suppose I should see that library," she said with a soft sigh.

"In a minute," Reed whispered against her skin.

He trailed kisses along her jawline. A long moment later, he buried his face in her hair and blew out his breath. "You were saying?"

Kristen linked an arm through his. "Tour?"

"Ah, right. This way."

Inside the library, Kristen gasped. "Wow." She expected something much different. Clean, bright white bookcases lined the walls, and light streamed through tall windows that framed a window seat lined with pillows. In one corner, an overstuffed chair with side table and reading lamp invited a cozy read. "Oh, my gosh. This is fabulous."

When her gaze landed on a pink enameled framed photo sitting on the small desk, she realized the room belonged to Reed's mother. Kristen lifted the frame and ran a finger across the glass, staring at the family portrait. "Your mother and sister were stunning," she whispered. Then she could hardly make out individual faces as tears welled in her eyes. But she recognized happiness. She saw the smiles and the love shining in the photo. As Kristen's shoulder shook, Reed's arms enfolded her again.

He rocked her gently for a few minutes then took the frame from her hand and steered her to the window seat. "You okay?"

"It's just so sad. What a beautiful family. I feel bad that Dylan won't remember his grandmother and had so few years with his mother." Reed remained silent before sitting beside her.

He slid an arm across her shoulders. "This was my mother's favorite room. Amy used to do homework here, but I mostly messed around in the window seat. I don't know if Dad ever comes here anymore."

"I bet Nora does." Reed looked at her with surprise in his wide eyes, as if he'd never considered that before.

Then he nodded. "I bet you're right. This is where she'd feel Mom's presence most."

"Maybe I can read to Dylan in here tonight."

"An excellent idea, sweetheart." Reed squeezed her hand. "Thank you."

His low voice was laced with sincerity. Kristen cocked her head, brows raised. "For what?"

"For caring."

****

As soon as Jack and Roger returned, Nora declared it lunchtime.

Kristen helped Dylan load his plate with a couple of tacos then she filled her own plate and slid into a chair beside Reed. Inside, she still glowed from her few minutes alone with him. Well, maybe she wasn't doing a good job of hiding the glow. As she glanced across the table, she caught curious looks from both Roger and

Jack.

Squirming under the scrutiny, Kristen turned to Dylan. "Hey, Dylan, after lunch let's go over to the barn. You can show me some of the things you've learned in the books you've been reading. How's that sound?"

In a sideways glance, she saw Jack's eyes narrow. Even if Dylan never conquered his fear of horses, Kristen hoped his grandfather would at least appreciate his efforts. She smiled in Jack's direction. "Dylan's been learning about horses so he can understand them better and be more comfortable around them." She specifically avoided any mention of actual riding.

Jack nodded. "That's fine, but to learn to ride, you gotta get on a horse."

Kristen groaned inside. Damn it, was the man a perpetual grump? Based on his recent loss, she was inclined to give him a little break, but, seriously, would offering some encouragement kill him? "Well, different people learn in different ways." She forced a cheery tone.

"Hey, y'all, guess what I did last week?" Celia suddenly spoke up and turned heads around the table. "I did a presentation at a high school in Dallas talking about the dangers of distracted driving. Isn't that cool? I'm helping teach students to be more responsible."

"You mean based on Amy's and Brian's accident?"

Reed's voice dropped to a low timbre. *Oh, no.* Kristen thought through that scenario. Was it cool or self-serving? A one-time thing or a road show? Holding her breath, she watched Reed slowly lower his fork.

"Yeah. To help keep other people from going through such a horrible experience the way we have,"

Celia said. "Like the gal at the PTA said, personalizing the message makes it more real to the kids 'cause they never think such a bad thing could happen to them."

"Did they pay you for the talk?" Reed asked.

Celia jutted her chin, and her lips pinched as she looked at Reed. "Of course. They paid for my time and expenses."

"What expenses?"

Kristen heard the exasperation in Celia's sigh.

"Travel and presentation expenses." She tossed back her hair and glanced around the table. "The program was very well received, y'all. The PTA president thought others would be interested, too."

"So, you're selling the program to other schools? Like a business?"

Reed's voice hardened, and his words dripped with disdain. Under the table, Kristen rested a hand on his thigh as a gentle reminder to stay calm.

"People share true stories all the time," Celia said. "Haven't you ever read a book or watched a movie based on a true story?"

Ugh. Celia's comment grazed a little too close to home. Kristen pushed back her chair. "Can I take any plates?" If this turned into a family drama, she didn't need to be part of it, and neither did an impressionable child. "Grab your books, and let's go to the barn," she whispered to Dylan. "We can take some cookies."

In the kitchen, Kristen scraped plates and placed them in the dishwasher, then put a handful of oatmeal raisin cookies into a plastic bag. Nora joined her.

"I'll get the rest of this cleaned. You and Dylan run on." She stepped forward and wrapped her arms around Kristen. "Roger and I will need to leave soon. So nice getting to know you this week. I'll email you that cookie recipe. Come back soon, okay? And stay in touch."

Kristen nodded, hugging her back. "I will. Thanks for everything, Nora." On the way out the door, Kristen gave a quick wave to Roger. "Great to meet you, Roger. See you later."

Outside, she drew in a deep breath of fresh air. As far as she was concerned, they could spend the rest of the day outdoors. The clear skies and warm temps might help keep—or restore—a sunny mood. She glanced up the road toward the cabin, wondering if the possibility of a sunset watch party on the ridge had bitten the dust. Probably.

"Ready?" She took Dylan's hand as they walked down the stairs and away from the conversation inside. Unfortunately, the physical distance couldn't keep her mind off it. Kristen wasn't one to encourage family strife, but she wouldn't be sorry if things got heated and Celia decided to leave.

Heading toward the barn entrance, Dylan shouted facts and figures about horses.

He was clearly taking his task seriously.

"Guess what kind of horse has spots?"

"Oh, let's see." Kristen pretended to think about her answer. "What's that word?" She suspected the name itself prompted Dylan's interest. He liked the funny words she made up in her books as well.

"Appa-loooooo-sa."

Grinning, Kristen smacked a hand against her forehead. "That's right. Have you ever seen one?"

"Grandpa has one."

"Really? I haven't seen it. Do you want to show

190

me?" Inside the barn, Kristen stopped to pet Cinnamon. "Hey, pretty girl."

Dylan kept hold of her hand but also hung back.

"Do you know why she's named Cinnamon?" Kristen asked.

Dylan bobbed his head. "Because the color."

"Uh-huh. Have you learned another name for that color?"

He thought a minute then nodded again. "Sorrel."

Laughing, Kristen pulled him against her. "That's right. Wow. You're really good at remembering things. Do you know the Appaloosa's name?"

"Charlie."

"Let's go find Charlie."

They walked past the front stalls that were home to Kristen's horses and turned the corner to another row of stalls. Kristen ventured back there once during the week but saw only one other horse at the time. Jack must like to ride Charlie.

Charlie greeted them with a deep neigh.

"Oh, my. He's really pretty, isn't he?" Kristen patted the horse's head.

"See his spots?" Dylan asked.

"Sure do."

With a loud flourish, Dylan began naming the various parts of the horse.

Then Celia appeared. "Hey, you guys."

"Where's Uncle Reed?" Dylan asked.

Celia glanced back over her shoulder. "I don't know. I think he's talking to your grandpa. Do you want to go for a ride?"

Dylan stepped back. "No."

Celia pursed her lips. "Well, why not? Why is

everyone being so grouchy today?"

A flush warmed Kristen's face, and she understood why Dylan's parents chose Reed as guardian. Dylan's aunt had an edge. "Dylan hasn't been cleared for horseback riding. A fall could re-injure his leg, and we certainly don't want another bang to his head."

Celia put her hands on her hips. "Well, I wouldn't let him fall."

Kristen gently pulled Dylan against her. She wouldn't let Celia badger the poor kid. "Which horse do you usually ride, Celia?"

She ran a hand through her hair and glanced around. "I don't get to ride very often. I guess I won't today, either."

The pout again.

Celia crouched in front of Dylan. "Which horse do you like best, Bumblebee?"

Dylan looked up at Kristen.

She offered an encouraging smile. He knew Star was the gentlest horse at the ranch.

"Star is nice," he said.

"Great. Maybe next time I come, I'll ride Star." She grabbed hold of his hand. "And in the spring, maybe we can all go for a ride."

Kristen couldn't help frowning. How was she not picking up on Dylan's less-than-enthusiastic responses?

When the sound of heavy boots on pavement signaled the arrival of one of the men, Kristen turned. She recognized fatigue in Reed's eyes. But he quickly masked it behind a smile.

"What's going on back here?"

"Horse talk," Kristen said. "Dylan is our expert speaker, and today he's telling us about ranch horses."

Glancing around, she pulled a hoof pick from a hook on the wall and held it in front of her mouth. "What good are horses, anyway?"

She handed Dylan the "microphone" then took several steps back, giving him center stage. The kid's face lit up. He held the pick close to his lips and began listing the ways in which the horses helped around the ranch, hamming it up with gestures and a loud voice for his audience.

"And on a ranch, you need horses for the cowboys so they can catch the cows." As if riding a stick pony, Dylan skipped around, his arms circling in the air as he pretended to twirl a rope that would lasso a cow.

Laughing, Kristen glanced at Reed. When she looked back at Dylan, he grasped at the air.

In slow motion, he teetered, caught himself, then lost his balance.

Kristen gasped and lunged forward.

In the same instant, the hoof pick clattered to the ground, and Dylan's face connected with the cement floor.

"Dylan!"

Blood covered his face when he stood, crying.

"Oh, hell." Kristen got to him first. Looked as if he had a busted lip and a cut— Oh, no. A cut along his eyebrow, on the same side as the scar from the accident.

Reed knelt beside her and reached for Dylan.

Kristen turned to see a wide-eyed Celia cowering near one of the stalls. "Celia, run inside and find a bag of peas or corn or something in the freezer. Quick."

"Let's take a look," Reed said.

"Hang on a sec." Kristen shifted the boy in her arms. "Shhh, Dylan. It's okay, sweetie. Let me see. I need to make sure you didn't damage any teeth." She peered inside his mouth, but with the dim lighting and mixture of blood and saliva, she couldn't be sure. "Yeah, let's get him inside where the light's better."

Reed scooped Dylan into his arms. "You're okay, big guy. Probably looks worse than it really is." Inside the house, he settled Dylan onto the table. "I'll get a towel."

Nodding, Kristen patted the still-sobbing Dylan. "Hey, sweetie, we'll get you all fixed up, okay?"

Reed returned with a wet washcloth.

"Thanks." Carefully, Kristen wiped Dylan's face.

Celia finally came back with a package of frozen corn. "Here. Will this work?"

"Perfect." Kristen dabbed at the cut above Dylan's eye while he sniffled, clinging to her arm. "Hmmm. This might need stitches. Is there anyone close by who could do it?"

"Thirty minutes. You sure that's necessary?"

She looked sharply at Reed. Taking hold of his arm, she held his gaze. They would do what was best for Dylan—even if best meant rushing him to a hospital and calling in a plastic surgeon. "Getting hurt doesn't make you a sissy," she said under her breath.

He held up a hand. "Got it, Boss."

Kristen turned to inspect the wound again. The bleeding subsided, allowing her a better assessment. "You know, I really think a couple of butterfly bandages would work." Uncertainty shaded Reed's eyes.

"You sure? Do you have any experience with this kind of thing?"

"First aid. Lifeguarding."

"Good enough for me. Give me a second to check the bathrooms. I know we used to keep stuff like that around here."

She sent him a soft smile, glad her first-aid training could be of some use. "Maybe some children's pain med, too." Kristen pressed the frozen bag to Dylan's face and pulled him into her lap, gently rocking him. "Just hold that to your face, sweetheart."

Celia sidled up next to them and patted Dylan's head. "Poor baby."

"He'll have some bruising for sure," Kristen said.

"Yes, and he was just starting to look better."

"Still a cutie-pie. What about your leg, Dylan?" Kristen asked. "Did you bang your knee or anything?"

Dylan nodded. "My knee."

Kristen pulled off his boots and pushed up his jeans. Sure enough, the skin was scraped there, too. "Just a little bit." She lifted the washcloth again and gently washed the area, dabbing at the already distressed skin that scarred his leg. An ugly pink line of stitching ran the length of Dylan's calf and up above the knee where she couldn't see. The leg seemed thin, probably because it hadn't recovered the muscle. No wonder he walked with a slight limp. She only hoped the injury would get better as he grew.

Reed returned and spread the contents of a first aid kit onto the table.

Looked like it had a little bit of everything. Kristen selected a tube of antiseptic and a cotton ball.

Reed opened the box of chewable tablets.

"I'll get a glass of water," Celia said. "That'll help the medicine go down."

Kristen touched Dylan's scarred leg. "He banged

his knee, too," she said quietly to Reed. "Maybe when you get back to Dallas, you can take him in to see his pediatrician." A hint of impatience flickered in Reed's eyes. He didn't disagree, but Kristen figured he worried about the time he didn't have for a trip to the doctor's office. She let out a long, slow sigh. Reed needed a Nora in Dallas.

After Dylan took the pain tablets and some water, Kristen carefully applied the bandages to his wounds. The result might not be pretty, but she felt confident they'd done all the right things. "Do you want to lie down now?" Kristen searched his splotched face and heavy eyes.

Dylan shook his head.

"Hey, Bumblebee," Celia said. "How about if Aunt Celia reads one of your favorite books? Did you bring some?"

"In my backpack," he mumbled.

Well, rats. Kristen swallowed her disappointment. She planned to read her new book with Dylan in the library's cozy window seat. But so far nothing had gone according to plan. Maybe tomorrow. Was there any chance of salvaging the weekend? Of spending time alone with Reed and Dylan?

"Let's sit in the living room and in some more comfortable chairs," Reed suggested.

With the rush of adrenaline wearing off, Kristen dropped into one of the soft sofas, thinking a nap was an excellent idea.

"I'll get the book," Reed said. A moment later, he returned with Kristen's book and two wine glasses.

"Good call," Kristen whispered.

He gave her a wry smile. "Thought so. Celia, glass

of wine?"

"Yes, please." She reached for the glass before picking up the book Reed placed on the coffee table.

"*What Will You Be?*" Celia read the book cover. "By Krist—" Her mouth dropped open, and her head snapped up. "Kristen Hanover. Oh, my gosh. Is that *you*?" Celia stared at Kristen.

The expression on her face changed from surprise to accusation—as if Kristen had been keeping a secret. "Yes. I'm a children's book author."

"Well, my goodness. A celebrity. How in the world did you—"

"Aunt Celia," Dylan groaned. "Are you going to read?"

Celia repositioned on the sofa. "Just a minute, Bumblebee. It's not polite to interrupt."

The scolding in her voice caught Kristen by surprise, and she couldn't help wondering about Celia's story. Was she looking for something, or did she truly want to stay connected with Dylan? Did she enjoy spending time with him? Getting to the ranch on a regular basis took no small amount of effort. If Kristen was to be part of Dylan's and Reed's lives, maybe she should get to know Celia.

Kristen smiled at the bruised and battered Dylan who'd flopped back against the sofa. "I met these guys at a book signing in Dallas. No reason you'd know that." She kept her tone light and friendly. "What do you do, Celia?"

"I work in a shop. A boutique, actually."

Her voice took on a defensive edge, making Kristen wonder about Celia's employment history.

"It's very trendy and upscale."

Reed entered the room with a bottle of wine and a beer, the elixirs to help soothe the nerves of the grown-ups. He filled the glasses, then sat beside Kristen and blew out a long breath. "Never a dull moment, right?"

"I wouldn't mind bringing down the excitement a notch." She lifted the glass to her lips. Over the glass, she caught Celia's hard stare.

"Well, you two look very cozy."

The sweet voice didn't match the pinched look on her face, and Kristen recalled Nora's warning. Maybe now Celia would give up any romantic fantasies for Reed.

"I didn't realize we had a little romance—"

"Aunt Celia." Dylan groaned again.

Kristen sucked in a deep breath and declined to comment.

Finally, Celia began reading.

And Kristen's thoughts drifted back to the scene in the barn. A wave of guilt rolled through her. By handing him the hoof pick, she'd encouraged Dylan's play in the barn. In her mind's eye, she relived the incident, thankful the heavy brass pick hit the floor first and spun away from Dylan. She shuddered inside. The injury could've been worse.

****

Jack strolled into the kitchen about five-thirty—whistling.

Kristen couldn't help wondering just how removed his quarters were from the main living space that he could avoid all the commotion. Was it deliberate? And what did he do when he withdrew from everyone? Sleep? Turn up the volume on the TV to drown out the rest of the world? She recalled Nora's relief that Jack hadn't turned to drinking to deal with the blows he'd been dealt. His face was drawn and tight, but he was lean and muscular. Seemed quite healthy on the outside.

He nodded at Kristen and Celia. "Smells good in here, ladies."

She and Celia were, without much enthusiasm, uncovering the dishes Saint Nora prepared for supper.

Kristen watched Jack grab a glass, add some ice, and open a bottle of whiskey from the bar cabinet before heading toward the door where, outside, Reed manned the grill while a worn-out Dylan colored quietly.

"What the heck happened here?" Jack's voice carried through the open door.

As Dylan's grandfather learned he'd missed the drama, Kristen hoped he'd realize they probably could've used his help, and he could be more attentive to his grandson. Placing the medley of vegetables in the oven, she checked her judgment. Maybe the man simply had nothing to give—or didn't know how. Again, she wondered what she could—or should—do to help this family heal. To help Dylan feel loved and secure. Or was she butting in her nose where it didn't belong?

She glanced toward the porch. The evening hadn't provided her much opportunity to explore Reed's spark-fizzle-flame theory—though sitting next to him on the sofa, thighs and arms touching, sent a warm simmer through her. Considering the circumstances, she'd dipped into willpower reserves to resist resting her head on his shoulder.

After supper, Kristen finally had a moment alone with him—the bright side of offering to handle cleanup.

Standing at the kitchen sink, she pulled out the lower rack of the dishwasher then handed Reed a plate. "How about I rinse and you load?"

"Yes, ma'am. Any specific order I should follow?"

She heard the teasing in his voice—a much-needed change from the subdued dinner. "Hmm. Why don't you give it a try first?"

"Am I being evaluated?"

Kristen laughed. "Maybe. Let's say I appreciate men who have some skills in the kitchen."

He leaned across the appliance.

A wicked glint danced in his eyes, and her heart skipped a beat.

"Oh, I have skills, sweetheart. Let's just say they might be put to better use in other rooms."

The flutters in her chest made it difficult for Kristen to breathe. But then Reed's lips covered hers, and breathing was no longer a priority. When the dishes in the sink shifted, the kiss ended abruptly.

"Oh, shoot!" Kristen lunged toward the faucet as water cascaded over the tower of plates. She turned off the water and sagged against the counter. "Oh, my gosh. That was close."

"Who's schooling whom on kitchen skills?" Reed asked.

Grinning, Kristen shoved a plate at him. "Here. Do your thing." She went on auto-pilot while they finished rinsing dishes and clearing the counter—and wondering if they'd ever get beyond stolen kisses in a few minutes of privacy. More than that, though, she yearned to curl up together on a comfy chair for a long talk. Video on a tiny screen and email just weren't the same. She seriously wished Celia hadn't shown up.

Kristen placed the dish soap under the counter and closed the door with a little more vigor than necessary. She pushed the handle on the dishwasher a few minutes later.

Reed stopped her. "Whoa, Boss. What do you think?" He crossed his arms and waited. "Did I pass the test?"

Dumb it may be, but curiosity won out. Kristen pulled out the lower rack again. With the exception of one pan turned the "wrong" way, he'd filled it exactly as she would have, including knives and forks with prongs down. "Wow!" Kristen whooped. "Nicely done. You get a gold star." Stepping closer, she lifted her face and was rewarded with another quick kiss. "Don't ever let anyone say you don't have skills."

With fresh drinks in hand, Kristen moved in front of Reed and joined Dylan and Celia in the family room. Someone had started a cozy fire, and Dylan was sprawled across a huge pillow in front of the television. Celia filed her nails in a chair behind him.

"So, what are we watching?" Reed asked.

Dylan swung around. "A movie." His eyes widened. "Aunt Celia's never seen this one."

"Oh, the horrors."

Humor laced Reed's words, and Kristen hoped the tone signaled a more relaxed mood.

"How has she survived?"

Celia rolled her eyes. "I've seen almost all the other animated shows."

Reed and Kristen sank onto the sofa partially facing the TV. Kristen glanced out the picture window beside them. The night sky was clear, and probably hundreds of stars would be visible if they went—

"Uncle Reed, can we go to Sunnypoint? Mommy and Daddy said we were going."

Kristen snapped back to the present. Watching Reed, she held her breath. *Please don't say, "we'll see."* She willed Reed to give the only right answer. If he couldn't manage the travel, she'd take Dylan to Sunnypoint herself. In fact, she'd love to. Lord knew he deserved a fun vacation, and the popular theme park was sure to be a good time for a kid. Looking from Reed to Dylan and back again, she was surprised to see pain flicker across Reed's face.

He nodded. "You bet, buddy. Maybe we can when school's out."

Kristen shot Dylan a reassuring smile before turning back to Reed. "What's wrong?"

He was silent for a moment then put a hand over hers and squeezed. "He's right. They were thinking about going on a cruise. Or some kind of big trip. One of the saddest things we found after the accident was inside Amy's and Brian's safe deposit box."

Reed's voice was strained, and Kristen's held her breath, bracing for his next words.

"Passports for all four of them." He shook his head. "A passport for little Hannah. That one, man, that hit hard."

"Oh, Reed." Kristen twined her fingers through his, and she didn't care that Celia watched. "How awful."

"Brian loved to travel," Celia chimed in. "He always said he wanted the children to have more experiences than things."

Reed ran a hand over his jaw. "I suppose I should find Dylan's and have it with me."

"What'd you do with it?" Kristen asked softly.

"I'm sure Dad's got the passport somewhere around here. Probably exactly where we left it." He reached for his beer and took a long pull. "It's been almost four months, and just this week, he finally talked to an agent to start work on selling the house in Amarillo."

"Oh. I didn't realize..." Kristen remembered her own inertia after her mother's death. 'Dragging her feet,' her brother called it. She understood Jack's immobility—and the gut-wrenching emotion that went with it.

"Looks like the only trip in our immediate future is to Amarillo," Reed added wryly.

Disappointment hit Kristen's chest with a thud. Swallowing hard, she reached for her own glass.

She hoped they might take a trip to Denver.

Chapter Fifteen

Reed's cell phone buzzed inside the shallow drawer of his desk Monday afternoon. He hit Send on the email he'd just finished then checked the number on the phone. Not one he recognized. But scrolling through his missed calls, he realized he'd had three attempts from a different number. Who was— Heart racing, he looked again. Except for the last digit, the number matched the school's.

Damn. He meant to call or send an email to Dylan's teacher about the weekend's accident and suggest no recess, but Monday at work demanded his attention and focus. He'd hit the ground running this morning and forgot. He pressed Redial and tapped his foot while he listened to the ring—and got no answer. Swearing under his breath again, Reed shoved his laptop into his bag. Five-fifteen was close enough.

Twenty minutes later, he pulled into the school's parking lot and jogged to the after-care room just off the gymnasium. He was surprised to find Dylan's teacher in the room, talking to a woman Reed didn't recognize. Dylan sat at a table and didn't get up the way he normally did when Reed arrived.

Instead, Dylan looked at Mrs. Baxter.

Was he asking permission? Frowning, Reed caught the slight shake of her head before she stepped toward him.

Dylan remained seated.

"Hey, buddy." Reed turned raised brows to Dylan's teacher.

"Mr. Armstrong. We've been attempting to reach you this afternoon."

Reed braced a hand on his hip. "I'm sorry. I only saw the calls a few minutes ago. When I tried to call back, I didn't get an answer. I didn't recognize the num—"

"Mr. Armstrong."

The other woman, older with piercing dark eyes, took a step forward.

"I'm Alice Johnson from Child Protective Services. If I could have a few minutes of your time?"

He shook his head. "I'm sorry. You're who?"

"I'm with Child Protective Services. We received a call this morning concerning your nephew."

Stunned, Reed held up a hand. "Whoa. Time out. You got a call from whom?"

The woman glanced at the floor before meeting Reed's gaze. "The call came in as anonymous, but that's not really important. We have an obligation to investigate every report we receive."

"Report? What kind of report?" Blood pounded in his ears.

"The caller expressed concern about the nature of your nephew's injuries." She gestured toward Dylan.

White-hot anger ripped through Reed. Some busybody who didn't know anything about him or Dylan or what happened at the ranch had called Child Services? Thought he was abusing Dylan? Using his nephew as a punching bag? The idea was so ludicrous, Reed gaped at the woman. "You have got to be kidding me." He barely managed to speak. The woman, Alice whatever-the-hell-her-name-was, held up a hand.

"Before you get too upset, you should know we get hundreds of anonymous tips, many of which turn out to be completely unfounded. But as I said, our job is to follow up. We want to protect the children in our community. If we could visit for a few minutes, we might be able to clear up this whole issue." She gestured toward a table in the corner of the room and began walking.

Reed assumed he was supposed to follow. He glanced at Dylan first. "I'll be right back, buddy." Questions pounded his brain. Had they already talked to Dylan? Was that legal? With his jaw tight and muscles clenched, Reed forced himself to stay calm.

"Let's start with some basic information."

Reed went through the mundane details of his relationship with Dylan.

"Mr. Armstrong, I have to ask this. Have you ever struck your nephew?"

"Absolutely not." Reed was surprised flames weren't shooting from his lips with every syllable.

"Very good. Now, I want you to know we've already spoken to Dylan and his teacher. The concern could all be a simple mistake. Mr. Armstrong, could you tell me about the injuries your nephew sustained recently?"

With as much patience as he could muster, Reed relayed the story of the weekend's incident at the ranch while the woman took notes. Notes, he presumed, for a file—on a potential child abuse case. Reed clenched his fists. *Unbelievable.*

"He was in your care the whole time?"

"Yes." The memory flashed in Reed's mind. Three adults had stood only feet away from Dylan, and the fall happened so fast not one could prevent it.

"And were witnesses present?"

"Yes."

"Anyone not related to you or Dylan?"

Reed cringed. No way did he want to drag Kristen into this nonsense. He cleared his throat. "Yes. A friend."

The woman picked up her pen again. "Name and contact information, please."

"Why is that necessary?" He couldn't disguise the defensive tone to his voice.

Alice leaned toward him. "Mr. Armstrong, these questions are all routine. At this time, I see no reason to contact anyone else or open an investigation. Your story corroborates what Dylan told us. The information is simply for the file."

With great reluctance, Reed gave her Kristen's name and number.

Closing the notebook, Alice stood and faced Reed.

He nearly shot from his chair.

"I'm sorry to put you through this, but I'm sure you understand our duty is to ensure your nephew's safety. It sounds as though someone noticed Dylan's bruises and became concerned. No harm done."

The woman had the nerve to offer a smile, and Reed ground his jaw.

"Better safe than sorry in our line of work, Mr. Armstrong."

"Now what?"

The woman spread her hands. "We're finished here. You're free to go."

"Great." In a few quick strides, Reed covered the space back to Dylan. "You ready, sport?"

Dylan nodded.

When her gaze met Reed's, Mrs. Baxter had the grace to look embarrassed. He wondered about her role in the ordeal.

"I'm so sorry," she said quietly. "I want you to know I believed Dylan when he told me what happened."

"Thank you." Reed checked his temper. He had no reason to distrust or blame her. At this point, he didn't even care what moron made the call. But he did care about the worry in Dylan's eyes. No harm done? Looked like he faced some damage control. *Damn it.* He needed to concentrate on work and not have to worry about Dylan while he was at school. Reed took Dylan's hand and headed for the parking lot, still shaking his head.

"Who was that lady?"

Reed waited for the sound of the seatbelt clicking into place. He blew out a breath. How much should he say about the ordeal? "We'll talk about her when we get home. But you don't need to worry, okay?" Getting no response from Dylan, Reed turned and nudged his leg. "How was school today? Everybody think you got in a fight?" He glanced in the mirror. The purple bruise around Dylan's eye had deepened in color, and Reed admitted the injury looked as if someone punched him square-on.

"Yeah, but I told the truth. I said I just tripped."

"Good. That's best. Hey, what sounds good for supper?" After today's events Reed was loathe to stop for fast food, but they just got home from the ranch last night, and he hadn't had time to go to the grocery store. If he'd had a chance to think straight, he could've called ahead for carry out. At this rate—*Oh, damn.* He glanced at his watch. They had less than an hour before Chelsea Malone, a junior at Southern Methodist University, was due at his place for an interview—the first of two babysitting interviews he scheduled for this week. He hoped she could cook or at least go to the grocery store. Oh, yeah, and she also needed to be a competent driver, reliable, trustworthy, and like kids.

Reed tugged on his tie to loosen it. A few minutes later, he pulled the car into the parking lot of a Mexican place not far from home. Not his favorite, but the service was quick. Tonight, it would have to do. He ordered a beef burrito and a beer then faced Dylan. "Listen, buddy, about that lady at the school today. I want you to know that everything's okay. Somebody, probably one of the moms at school this morning, saw your eye and got worried. The moms didn't know you fell at the ranch, and they thought someone might've hurt you."

"Did they think you hurt me?"

Setting aside his anger that he even had to have this conversation, Reed leaned forward. "Dylan, I would never hurt you. You know that, right?"

Dylan nodded, but his eyes shifted from Reed to the table in front of him. "You're not going away, are you?"

Though his soft voice was almost a whisper, Reed heard the fear it carried. "Dylan, look at me." Round eyes looked up, and Reed held his nephew's gaze. "I'm not going anywhere. You're my family. My job is to keep you safe and take care of you, just the way your mom and dad would've wanted, and that's what I'm doing. Got that?"

All of a sudden, Dylan scrambled out of the booth and flung himself at Reed.

"Easy there, big guy." Reed caught his nephew close then held up his hand for a high five. And wondered if the reassuring words were true.

They were the words Dylan needed to hear, but sometimes, in the dark corners of Reed's mind, doubt crept in, and he questioned himself. Could he do what Amy and Brian asked of him? Was he really up to this challenge?

****

Reed tucked Dylan in for the night then closed the bedroom door and released a long breath, ready to put this day behind him. Or turn it around. He smiled at the thought and pushed off from the door. He could do that with one phone call. Kristen picked up immediately.

"Hi," she said.

Her cheery and expectant voice was a welcome sound to Reed's ears.

"How was your Monday?"

He gave a short, humorless laugh. "Had quite a day."

"Uh-oh. By the tone of your voice, I'm thinking you don't mean that in a good way."

"You're right. You won't believe what happened." Her responses as he told the story of the surprise visit from Child Protective Services were gratifyingly indignant.

"No. Way. Oh, Reed. That's absurd. How's Dylan? I'm sure he didn't really understand."

"He knew something was wrong."

"Was he scared?"

He remembered the quiver of his nephew's lips. "A little."

"Oh, that hurts my heart. Do you want me to talk to him?"

Reed sank onto the sofa and stretched his legs across to the coffee table, relaxing for the first time in more hours than he cared to count. "Nah. He's okay. And probably already asleep."

"Good. Obviously whoever made the call hasn't seen you interact with Dylan."

"Thanks. That's the funny thing. Most of the other parents have been friendly and helpful. Almost to a fault. I mean, I've gotten notes in his backpack from moms telling me the best places for birthday parties and which clothes and toys are in or out."

"What?"

Kristen's warm laugh came over the line, and Reed found himself chuckling.

"You've got to be joking."

"Nope. A typed list. I kid you not. So, clearly, they think I'm incompetent. I can handle that. But violent? Gotta say that one shocks a bit."

"Don't worry about it. Someone got a little carried away with her imagination."

"Yeah." He ran a hand over his jaw. "The whole ordeal makes me wonder, though."

"Wonder what?"

Reed hesitated. "If this really makes the most sense for Dylan. I mean, would he be better off with a family? Or a mom? Instead of—"

"What? Reed, come on. You can't be serious."

"I know this is what Amy and Brian set up, but you

have to admit, it's not ideal."

"Life isn't always ideal," Kristen said. "Besides, who else will love him the way you will? You're family. What else would you do? Foster care?"

"I don't know. There's Celia."

"Who was deliberately *not* chosen as his guardian."

"Okay, but they also had some really good friends in Amarillo who I met a couple of times. He'd be in a family and in a familiar environment. That might—"

"Reed, don't. Don't let one crazy incident mess with your head. I know it's not easy. Becoming Dylan's guardian completely disrupted your life. But you're doing a great job. One of these days, you'll look back, and raising Dylan will be one of the best, most fulfilling accomplishments of your whole life."

"I appreciate the confidence, but there's always a chance I could screw up. Screw up Dylan."

"Every parent's nightmare."

Reed let his head fall back. *Parent.* That word still rocked his system. "I suppose so."

"What you need is some help. Did you end up cancelling the interview with the college girl today?"

"No. She was here. Wish you could've wired in."

"Why?"

"A second opinion would be nice." Hearing the doubt in his own voice, Reed straightened. Jeez, what was his problem? He sounded like a whiny wimp. Kristen was right. He was giving today's event way too much play in his head.

"Well, what was she like?"

"Twenty-one," Reed told her dryly. "Very twenty-one." Kristen's giggle was infectious, and he found himself laughing as well. "I suppose she's all right. She seems to know her way around the city and isn't afraid to drive. Willing to work some Saturday mornings."

As he spoke, Reed made his way toward his bedroom and the elliptical he'd crammed in there when the second bedroom went to Dylan. Even if he couldn't lift weights, he had to get some exercise.

"Why Saturdays?"

"Because I am seriously out of shape. Haven't been to the gym since I've had Dylan. Can't believe I'm still paying for the membership."

"Hmm. I think you might be exaggerating the dire consequences."

That she'd spent enough time evaluating or thinking about his body to render an opinion sent a warm humming through Reed's veins—and another thought lodged in his brain. Sure, he might have solved his gym dilemma, but how would he ever get some time with Kristen? Alone.

Pushing those thoughts to the back burner was getting harder and harder. Reed tossed a towel around his neck and put the phone in speaker mode.

"Anyway, did she and Dylan hit it off?"

Reed reluctantly went back to the primary topic of conversation. "Hard to say. Seems like Dylan is slow to warm up to people. Except for you. She talked to him and asked a couple of questions, but I could tell his injuries spooked her. Doesn't want to be responsible for meds and that kind of thing. I'll be glad when his hair grows out enough to hide the scar."

"For sure. So, you giving her a try or waiting for the other interview?"

"I'm all for a trial run. Even if she's not the best fit, I don't think he'd be in any danger. How will we know for sure if we don't try?"

****

Considering Reed's predicament, Kristen paced the floor. She agreed with giving the girl a try. Dylan was old enough to help with questions that might come up and, more importantly, to report back to Reed. Plus, Reed clearly needed a little time to himself. She didn't think for a minute he was serious about giving up his guardianship of Dylan, but the fact that he'd even thought about it proved the guy needed a break.

She pressed the phone closer to her ear as a dull hum rumbled in the background, muffling Reed's words. "Hey, you sound funny all of a sudden."

"Sorry, I put you on speaker phone while I'm working out. You know, multi-tasking."

"Ah." Interesting visions danced in Kristen's head. Had he stripped down while they talked? As much as she enjoyed listening to his voice, she wouldn't mind an image as well. "So, open the video chat."

"What, you're looking for proof of my need to hit the gym?"

"Yes, I believe a personal assessment is in order." His low chuckle sent goose bumps over her skin.

"Will do."

A moment later, Kristen switched from phone to computer and caught her breath as Reed's face filled the screen.

"Hi," he said.

Kristen heard the humor in that one word. "Hi." She covered her disappointment at the black T-shirt by pretending excessive scrutiny of Reed. "Yep. Better get Chelsea scheduled quick."

"Ouch. That's brutal."

"You asked for it."

"Unfortunately, she's not available *this* Saturday," Reed said,

"Oh, for Pete's sake."

Reed laughed. "That's a nice way to say what I was thinking. Don't you ever cuss? Do you have any bad habits? Tell me one bad thing you've ever done."

Kristen rolled her eyes. "Aren't we getting a little off topic, here?"

"You, sweetheart, are a much more interesting topic than Chelsea-the-babysitter. Come on. Humor me. I had a rough day, remember?"

"Okay, fine. Poor baby." One silly but memorable incident came to mind. "In sixth grade, a boy who had a crush on me started bringing me packages of bubble gum, which I thought was totally cool. A couple of weeks into this, a friend told me the guy had been stealing the gum from a local convenience store. I didn't want to believe it. I liked the attention, so I kept accepting the gum. Then one day I overheard him bragging about the stealing, and I felt sick and guilty, as if I were an accomplice. Could never chew bubble gum again."

Reed burst out laughing. "You have to be kidding. That's it? Chewed stolen gum. That's classic."

Cheeks flushing, Kristen reconsidered the video call. "I'm sure I could think of others, like lying to my mom about going somewhere, but, hey, I'm basically a nice, boring person, okay?"

Grinning, Reed held up his hands. "Hey, nothing wrong with being nice."

"What about you? Are you some kind of reformed juvenile delinquent, or what?"

"What makes you think I'm reformed?"

She laughed in her turn. "Because you're a decent person. Because you take in young children. You visit your dad. You care about your work." And, she swallowed hard, you show interest in other people. She couldn't remember any of the other guys she'd dated asking that kind of question.

"My bad side manifested itself in high school pranks. For which, I was almost always punished. You've met my dad, right? The man was a firm believer in corporal punishment."

"Ah, yes. Parenting by fear." An awkward silence took over as Kristen, and probably Reed, too, realized the conversation had come full circle with a heavy thud. Of course he hadn't caused Dylan's black eye, but...spanking? Like father, like son? Plenty of reports documented that people who were abused as children often grew up to continue the cycle.

"Kristen."

His deep voice startled her, and she took a moment to realize Reed had turned off the machine and moved closer to the camera. Feeling guilty over her own thoughts, she cautiously looked at the screen.

"Remember those parenting books I bought at your book signing? Don't worry. I know all about time out. Redirecting. Things like loss of privileges. Grounding. Alternatives to hitting."

"No one's worried." Smiling inside and out, Kristen spoke softly. In that moment, an idea formed. Why couldn't she help them out? She mulled the possibilities. Jana lived near the school and obviously Reed did, too. She could crash at Jana's place, maybe give her and Adam a date night, and also give Reed some flexibility. She hadn't been home much in the last six weeks, but she didn't really have to be. Her teaching commitment didn't start until after Christmas break. Yeah, she had blog posts to write and lesson plans to finish, but she could do those anywhere. What was one more week?

Her roommates wouldn't mind one fewer body in the house and another week of not sharing bathrooms. If nothing else, going back to Dallas would keep Kristen busy—keep her from restlessly watching book sales or thinking about the sale of the farm or how her new manuscripts were being received. Her mother always told her the best way to take your mind off your own troubles was to help someone else. She had the time. If she had the opportunity to make a difference for Dylan, it'd be wrong not to. "Hey, Reed. Go ahead and plan on spending some time at the gym Saturday. Chelsea might be busy, but I can be there."

His brows drew together. "What?"

"I've got the time. I'll see if I can stay with Jana for a week or so until you find someone competent to help with Dylan."

"I couldn't ask you to do that."

"You didn't ask. I offered."

A slow grin spread across his face. "You know what, Kristen Hanover? I like you."

The words were nice, but the look in his eyes took away Kristen's breath.

****

"Hey, Stranger," Jana answered Kristen's call.

Still floating from her conversation with Reed, Kristen smiled into the phone, ready to put her idea into action. "Sorry I've been out of touch. How's everything there?"

"Same as always. Not a second to myself. I'm in the closet right now."

Kristen chuckled sympathetically. Probably only a slight exaggeration, considering Jana's full-time job and busy toddler. "In that case, I think you'll like my proposition."

"Oh, yeah?"

"How would you feel about a guest, a night out, and a little help around the house for maybe a week?"

"I like the sound of that," Jana said. "Keep talking."

"So here's the deal. I'm wondering if I could crash at your place and take turns helping out you and Reed Armstrong. He's having some trouble even finding the time to interview people to give him a hand with Dylan. I don't have any special reason I have to be tethered to my place right now, so—"

"Wait a minute. Back up. You mean Dylan in my class and his uncle?"

"Those would be the ones." As if she knew others by the same names?

"What is going on?" Jana demanded. "Last time we talked, you were renting a cabin on his dad's ranch. Now you're coming to babysit? What gives?"

"Well, I— We've become friends, I guess."

"*We* as in you and Reed or you and Dylan?"

Kristen and Jana went way back. They talked guys, boyfriends, dates—shared advice and opinions on the subjects. But for some reason, Kristen hadn't told her best friend about her relationship with Reed. Why not? Thoughts warred inside her, and doubt crashed in. Was it too good to be true? Was it laughable that someone as gorgeous as Reed would be interested in her?

She'd always been relatively popular in their small high school but never the girl all the guys clamored to be with. She doubted she'd ever been the subject of anyone's dreams. But surely as people grew up and matured, those things changed. After all, she'd had a few boyfriends. "Both." She hated the defensive tone of her voice.

"Wow. Okay, I need a minute to get my head around this. You're interested in Reed Armstrong? As in…dating?"

Kristen resented the pause and the surprise in Jana's voice. "Yeah. Is that so hard to believe?"

"Easy there. I'm just surprised, that's all. It's weird to think about."

"Why?"

"Because he's the parent of one of my students. That's T-M-I. I mean, I shouldn't know dating kinds of things about him."

Grinning into the phone, Kristen curled into the sofa. "You mean like whether he's a good kisser?"

"Oh, get out. Are you freaking kidding me? You've kissed him?"

Laughter bubbled to the surface. "I have."

"Oh, my."

"Is that awful?"

"Honestly, he doesn't strike me as your type. He's so…so buttoned up and serious."

"You know, when I first met him, I thought so, too, but he's really not. He's a nice guy. And he's good with Dylan." Kristen gasped, remembering the day's earlier events. "Oh, my gosh. Dylan—at school today." She lurched from the sofa.

"You know what happened at school today?"

Kristen heard the caution in Jana's voice. "I just got off the phone with Reed before I called you. You know, I was there. I saw the whole thing."

"Wait. You mean you were with Dylan and Reed at the ranch?"

"Yes."

"I thought you were writing in a cabin."

"I did that, too." Kristen let out heavy sigh. Was Jana being deliberately dense? "I can't believe someone actually thought Reed hit Dylan. So ridiculous."

"Well, I have to say, his eye looked really bad, as if—"

"What?"

"Kristen, I can't have this conversation. I can't talk to you about Dylan. That's confidential information."

"Jana, get real." Kristen blew a strand of hair from her face and leaned against the kitchen counter. "How can it be confidential when the whole class saw him with a black eye?"

"Right, but they don't know about Child Protective Services. I'm not—"

"You aren't telling me anything I don't already know."

"Okay, but it's still weird. Listen, let's skip that part and go back to your visit. You want to come to Dallas for a week? And stay with me?"

"Yeah, if that works for you. I'd love to see Kayla, and I could watch her one night while you guys go out. Be honest. When was the last time you had a date night with your hubby?"

"Probably a few months ago."

Kristen grinned. "So, it's about time, right?"

Chapter Sixteen

By the time Kristen heard Jana's garage door open, her darling playmate had been down and out for nearly two hours. The glow on her friend's face when she walked inside was worth every minute of the thirteen-hour drive from Denver. Grinning, Kristen unfolded her legs and set down her magazine.

Jana tiptoed into the living room, her glance darting around the room. "How'd everything go?" she whispered.

"Fine," Kristen told her in a regular grown-up voice. "You don't have to whisper. She's sound asleep. How was your date?"

Adam moved in behind Jana and placed his hands on her shoulders. "Date was great," he said. "Thanks for watching the mini, Kristen."

"My pleasure."

"Think I'm ready to call it a night." He moved around Jana.

"Me, too. I'll be there in a few minutes," Jana said.

Adam headed down the hallway.

Jana sank onto the sofa and patted the seat beside her. "Sit down for a sec. You want anything to drink? A nightcap?"

"You mean an adult beverage that doesn't involve grape juice, apple juice, or orange juice?" Jana's fridge was well-stocked—for a toddler.

"I could rustle up a glass of wine. But, hey, don't underestimate what can be done with fruit juices."

"That's okay. I'm good." And she was pretty sure Jana's husband was waiting.

But Jana curled up and leaned toward her. "Hey, I've been thinking."

Kristen raised her brows. "Uh-huh."

Jana started to speak, but stopped.

"Spit it out."

"Okay, I don't want to assume anything, but I was thinking maybe you and Reed…that you might like to go out with Reed. Without Dylan."

Kristen sputtered a laugh. "Well, I have to say, that'd be one benefit of finding a nanny."

Jana cocked her head. "Well, maybe I can help with that. Why don't I take Dylan tomorrow night so you and Reed can go out?"

Kristen raised her brows and stared at Jana. "Can you do that? I mean, does the school district allow teachers to babysit a student?"

"It happens. I wouldn't advertise it, but I know a few teachers who babysit on a regular basis."

Thoughts tumbled through Kristen's brain. She hadn't packed for going out, but she could probably make something work. Taking Jana's offer would basically mean arranging a date with Reed. Would he be okay with that? Or, should she casually mention that Jana offered? But that would tell Reed she'd been talking about him—about them. If she—

Jana waved a hand in front of Kristen's face. "Hellooooo. Wow, you blasted off to la-la land fast."

"Oh. Sorry." Kristen offered a sheepish smile.

"So?" Jana pressed.

The smile widened as Kristen nodded. "That's pretty good thinking, girlfriend." She could work out the details in the morning. So, there'd be a surprise for Dylan. And a surprise for Reed. They'd agreed that Kristen would show up at Reed's place unannounced. She couldn't wait to see the big grin light up Dylan's face. His spontaneous delight warmed her heart every time.

She glanced at her watch. If she wanted to get a good night's sleep, she should probably turn in. From the many conversations with Kayla's mother, Kristen knew that sleeping in was a foreign concept in this household. Besides, she was due at Reed's at eight thirty. "Curtain call for me, my dear."

"For sure." With a yawn, Jana got up and began turning off lights. "But let's peek at the princess first."

Tiptoeing, Kristen followed Jana into the small, dim room and stood beside the white wooden crib. The peaceful rise and fall of her little chest was captivating. And running a finger along those chubby pink cheeks was hard to resist. "She's so precious, Jana," Kristen whispered. She hugged her friend's arm. "Goodnight, Mommy."

Kristen was about to switch off the bathroom light when an unwelcome thought stopped her. Kids took so much time and energy. Maybe the date thing with Reed was all wrong. She slowly crossed the room and sank onto the bed, hugging a pillow to her chest. As much as she'd like to go out with Reed and spend some time alone, right now might not be the best time to show him he could have more fun if Dylan weren't around.

****

Her own anticipation of the surprises on schedule

for the day pushed Kristen out of bed early enough for a cup of coffee with Jana before heading to Reed's.

"Want a to-go cup?"

"No, but thanks for the offer. I should get moving." Kristen drained the last sip of eye-opening liquid in her mug and savored the bold flavor. Jana brewed a strong cup. Though Kristen preferred tea, she enjoyed an occasional cup of coffee, as well.

Jana squeezed her arm. "Keep me posted. Anytime is fine. We'll probably order in a pizza."

"Sounds good. I'll text you as soon as I know the plan." She blew another quick kiss to Kayla in her high chair.

Outside, sunshine flooded the crisp fall air and matched Kristen's lighthearted mood. After tossing the issue around with Jana, she decided the date was a priority—as was showing Reed that people with children could still go out and have fun. He didn't have to choose one or the other.

She dropped her denim jacket into the passenger's seat. The day promised to warm up, and she hoped to find a nearby park where she and Dylan could spend some time. Even though they had to be careful with his leg, she'd love to see him out doing normal kid activities.

Turning down a residential street, she wondered if other children lived in the neighborhood for Dylan to play with. Surely some of the other kids from school lived close by. It was a nice area with large houses and beautiful landscaping. From her visits to the school, she already knew the district had upscale residents. Top sports brand and designer backpacks lined the hooks at the back of the classrooms.

Three more turns, and she came to a small group of tidy-looking, multi-family units in traditional white clapboard and red brick that served as a buffer between the larger homes and a quaint office and retail area just off the expressway. She found Reed's unit and pulled into the drive.

Leaving her guitar and computer bag in the car for now, Kristen hurried to the small front porch and rang the doorbell. She adjusted the loose, autumn-green tunic over her khaki skinny jeans while she waited. Her grin was automatic when Dylan opened the door. "Hey, Dylan! I guess I found the right house."

"Miss Hanover!" His eyes bulged. "What are you doing here?"

"I'm here to visit you and your uncle, silly." She swallowed past the lump that formed in her throat as she saw the lingering bruise under the boy's eye. "Are you too busy for visitors today?"

Shaking his head, Dylan grinned and opened the door. "No. You can come in."

"Why, thank you, sir."

"Uncle Reed," Dylan hollered over his shoulder. "It's Miss Hanover!"

Kristen looked past Dylan and saw Reed saunter toward them. If Dylan's enthusiastic greeting wasn't enough to ensure her welcome, the light sparkling in Reed's eyes sealed the deal.

"I was hoping it would be."

Warm humor danced in his voice, sending a soft humming through her veins.

Dylan spun around. "You knew she was coming?"

Reed ruffled the growing curls on Dylan's head. "Wanted to surprise you."

Heart hammering, Kristen took a step forward and raised her face. "Hey," she said softly.

He brushed her lips with a light kiss just before Dylan tugged on her arm.

"Come on. You can be on my team."

"Your team?" She raised her eyebrows and looked back at Reed.

"We're seeing who can build the tallest tower," Dylan said.

Kristen rolled her eyes. "Of course, it has to be a competition."

"More fun that way," Reed said. "Blame it on the chromosome. Hey, Dylan, I'm letting Miss Hanover take my spot while I go to the gym."

"Okay."

He leaned close to Kristen. "Thanks. Won't be gone long. The rest of the day is wide open."

"Take your time." Kristen surveyed the kitchen table covered with colorful plastic blocks. Looked like thousands of pieces. "Wow. This should keep us busy." As the door closed behind Reed, Kristen began sorting blocks. "Do you especially want to build more towers, Dylan? Or we could work on something together, like a fort or a castle."

"Yeah! Let's make a castle."

"Okay." She began clearing a space in the center of the table then she helped Dylan construct a large base, watching as he created a pattern by alternating the colors. The kid definitely had a creative side. She glanced around the living area, wondering if Dylan had access to a computer. It'd be fun to see what kind of stories he could come up with on his own. "Hey, Dylan, want to show me your room when we're finished here?" She hadn't thought to ask either of them about how they'd done his room, and now she was curious to know.

He shrugged but stayed focused on his project. "Sure."

"Did you have your own room at your old house?"

He looked up. "Yeah."

"What was it like?"

"Really cool. It had a big rocket on the wall and space stuff on the ceiling."

"That does sound cool. Did your mom paint the rocket?"

"Nope. Some other lady did." Dylan turned wide blue eyes on Kristen. "Hey, maybe we could paint on my walls. Like you did at your house. With those lines to show how tall I am?"

"Maybe we could. We'll have to ask Uncle Reed." She was touched he even remembered the primitive drawings she and her brother made at the farmhouse. Painting at this place seemed unlikely, though. And even if they did, their art would be covered over for the next tenant. When she and her brother painted their wall, they knew they were in their "forever" home. Kristen was about to give him the standard "we'll see" when inspiration struck.

Leaning across the table, she squeezed Dylan's arm. "You know what? If we can't paint on these walls, we'll go to the craft store and get a giant roll of paper and paint it instead. That way, even if you guys move, you can always take the chart with you." The smile that lit up Dylan's face was nothing short of energizing.

"Can we?"

"You bet."

Dylan scrambled off his chair. "Let's go now."

Laughing, Kristen scooped him into her arms. "Let me look at your room first." She twirled Dylan then followed him down the hallway.

"This one."

Just inside, Kristen stopped short. *Aw, man.* She'd seen hospital rooms with more color and character. The walls were basic beige, and the bedspread was a camel color with a simple geometric design. Tasteful, sure, but nothing said boy or kid. No dinosaurs, robots, spaceships, superheroes, or theme of any kind. This had to be fixed.

"It's okay, Miss Hanover."

Her face must've shown her dismay. Shooting him a quick smile, Kristen rallied. "What would you think about shopping for new things for your room?" She couldn't help wondering if Reed simply hadn't thought about the room, didn't have time to deal with it, or was just plain clueless. But at the same time, a pang of sympathy hit hard—for both of them. Fortunately, a little online shopping could solve the problem.

"Can we do the painting?" Dylan asked.

"Tell you what. Let's get on my computer and see if we can find some things you like, then we'll get paper, and we'll paint a chart to match. How's that sound?"

The suggestion got a rapid nod of approval.

After they dumped the blocks back into a large plastic tub, Kristen retrieved her things from her car and opened her laptop at the coffee table. She patted the seat beside her. "Let's take a look, kiddo."

A wide variety of options for boys' bedding and wall decorations filled the screen, and Dylan was quick to give thumbs up or down on the selections. After several minutes, he wavered between space and music themes. But then a shark bedspread appeared on the screen.

"That one's cool," he said.

"Yeah? You like sharks?"

"I like that."

Graphic navy and gray sharks created a pattern across a medium sea-blue background. The choice would probably last a while, and the simple design would be easy to duplicate on a wall chart.

"Looks awesome to me." She took a screen shot of the page then continued scrolling.

Ten minutes later, the garage door rumbled open, and Dylan bounced off the sofa. So much for easing into the conversation. But surely, Reed wouldn't have any objections.

****

Reed stepped inside and dropped his duffle on the floor. The workout was good. He needed to push himself and use his muscles. But his concentration was zilch because he was anxious to see his guest. Or, more correctly, *their* guest. The question churning over and over in his mind the past few days was how much Kristen wanted to see him and how much she wanted to see Dylan. Some of both, he supposed, was best. At this point, they were a package deal. He also was anxious to see her on their home turf.

"Uncle Reed!"

Reed was surprised to hear Dylan shout with excitement in his voice. "Hey, buddy, you guys have fun?"

Dylan moved toward him, flailing his arms. "Yeah.

We're picking out stuff for my room, and Miss Hanover said we can paint a chart. It's gonna be cool."

Reed glanced from his nephew to the woman who appeared in the entryway.

Kristen smiled but with a hint of hesitation. "We're looking at some options."

Reed nodded. The room. He should've expected this. Knew he should've done something about it before now. More proof that he was in over his head. But, hey, he was trying to be a dad, not a decorator. And for that matter, Dylan never mentioned changing the room. Never complained about it. Did he really care that much? Crossing his arms, Reed raised his brows. "You want to change your room?"

When Dylan pulled back and shrank into himself, Kristen bit her lip. She offered an encouraging nod.

He gave Kristen a quick look before turning back to Reed. "Can we? We found some shark stuff on the computer…"

His voice waivered before it trailed off, and it bothered Reed. Was Dylan afraid to ask for something?

"If it's okay with you," Kristen said.

"Sure. Sharks sound cool to me." He held up a hand to Dylan and received an energetic high-five as the kid came back to life. "Whoa," Reed said. "You're going to knock me over." He nudged Dylan toward the living room.

Kristen fell into step. "You don't mind, do you? I didn't promise anything."

"No. His room is one of the things we just haven't gotten to yet. Let's do it. Does online mean I don't have to go shopping?"

"It sure does." She cocked her head and shot him a

smile. "All it requires is your credit card."

Reed laughed out loud at her sassy smile. "Ah, now I understand. You're here to spend my money."

"And it's only day one."

Reed stopped. He had half a mind to kiss that smirk right off her face. He would, if Dylan wasn't only a few steps away. "Thanks for the warning."

He headed for the kitchen and a glass of cold water. When he turned back, he found Kristen perched on one of the barstools at the black granite counter and studying him. He took a long, slow drink of the water, and locked his gaze with hers. "Something else on your mind? Wait." He gestured around the room. "Don't tell me. The color's all wrong? I need new wallpaper? Appliances? Black towels stunt intelligence in kids?"

"Haha. Okay, smarty pants, something else is on my mind."

He crossed his arms. "Uh-huh. How much will this cost me?"

"The price of dinner. Maybe a movie."

"Who's smarty pants?" Dylan demanded from the other room.

"Me," Reed said. "Who has ears as big as an elephant's?" He responded to Dylan while Kristen's words rang in his head. Dinner and a movie? What did that mean? While he was gone, did the two of them cook up a plan that involved dragging him to a new animated release? Please, no, he implored silently. He wondered if these two weren't to be trusted alone together.

Pushing off from the counter, he reached into his pocket and retrieved his wallet. With a flip of his wrist, he removed his credit card and held it out to Kristen.

"Will this do?"

She plucked the card from his hand. "Very nicely." Hopping down from the stool, she motioned for him to follow. "Come see what you're buying."

"I trust your judgment." But he followed, anyway.

"Dylan, are you sure about the sharks? Should we buy them?"

"Yes. I want them."

"Okay. Here goes."

From behind the sofa, Reed peered at the image on the computer screen, happy to see the designs weren't completely juvenile or cartoon-like. "Do the two-day shipping," he said as Kristen began the purchase process.

While the page refreshed, she opened a Word document and began typing.

So big ears can't hear. Jana has offered to keep Dylan this evening if you'd like to go out.

Questioning eyes met his gaze. Dylan's teacher? He frowned, re-reading the sentence. Why would—?

Kristen moistened her lips and turned back to the keyboard. *Just the two of us.*

When understanding dawned, it hit him square in the chest. "Really?" he croaked in a hoarse whisper.

Smiling, she nodded. "Yeah. What do you think?"

Heat roared through Reed, and his first thought was to suggest a night *in* for just the two of them. Probably not what she had in mind, but that didn't stop him from wondering how she'd react to the idea. He settled for slipping a hand across Kristen's shoulder. His heart bounced as her silky hair brushed against his bare arm. "Absolutely."

With a smile, she placed her hand over his. "I

haven't mentioned the idea to Dylan, but I do need to let Jana know for sure," she whispered.

"What are you guys talking about?" Dylan asked.

Reed rolled his eyes. Nothing like a whisper to get someone's attention.

****

At six-thirty that evening, Reed told Dylan goodbye then hovered near the door while Kristen lingered. She gave Dylan a second hug and spoke to Jana in hushed tones.

"You two have fun." Jana waved toward Reed.

"Bye, Uncle Reed," Dylan shouted.

"Bye," he said again as Kristen joined him at the door. He held the car door for Kristen then slid into the driver's seat beside her, realizing they hadn't decided on a destination.

"Dylan seemed happy enough when we were leaving," Kristen murmured. "I think he'll have fun with Kayla. It'll probably be like playing with his little sister. I hope that doesn't make him sad, though."

Shifting the car into reverse, Reed glanced her direction. "He'll be fine. I bet they have a grand time."

"I hope so. I'm so glad he was okay with—"

"Kristen."

She twisted around. "What?"

"Dylan will be fine tonight. Can we please not spend the evening worrying about him?"

"Oh, my gosh." She clamped a hand over her mouth, shaking her head. "I'm sorry. You're right. He's in a great place with awesome people. That's the whole point."

Reed reached for her hand and twined his fingers with hers. "So, where we headed? You have someplace in mind?"

She turned wide eyes his way. "You live here," she said, laughter in her voice. "Don't you know any good restaurants in Dallas?"

He hadn't taken a woman on a date in so long, he actually might not. "Maybe, but I have another idea. What would you think about going to the art museum first? Believe it or not, I wouldn't mind seeing its current exhibit."

"Yeah? Exhibit of what?"

He understood the surprise in her eyes. A lot of people thought engineers and culture didn't mix. He gave her a lopsided grin. "Cowboys. Photos of ranch life. From what I understand, they're black and white and pretty damn good."

"Mmmm, cowboys. Works for me."

"Unless you'd rather see a movie instead."

"The photo display sounds great. I'd rather be able to talk."

So would he. Reed turned the car to move onto the expressway, still silently thanking Dylan's teacher for the night of parental leave. Heavy Saturday night traffic made the drive about thirty minutes to the museum downtown.

"Wow. I think this traffic might be worse than Denver's," Kristen said. "I wonder if a big event is going on."

"The traffic is always like this. At least there's no snow."

"Oh, no kidding. One of the perks of working at home is that on snow days I can watch the weather from inside while I stay warm and cozy."

Reed already knew she'd originally gone to Denver

for a job opportunity, and she didn't ski much, which begged the question of why she stayed there now that she made her living from writing. "Dallas would be happy to have you." He pulled into a parking place and gave her a pointed look.

When her only response was a smile, Reed let the suggestion go. Oh, how he wished she'd consider moving. Outside, he rested his hand against Kristen's lower back. Her long blouse fluttered with the breeze, hinting at the curves underneath. She looked amazing. Appearance was only a small part of the equation. The combination of personality, poise, and the soft floral scent of her perfume made for an intoxicating package, and he struggled to keep his mind on the task and attendant in front of him. He didn't know the time of their curfew, but already, he wanted the night to slow down.

Tickets in hand, Reed guided Kristen through the main lobby to the exhibition area. A life-size cowboy cut-out greeted them outside the exhibit entrance. Not the kind you'd see on the cover of a romance novel, all buff and built, but a weathered old face, full of knowledge and experience on the land, with scuffed boots and a sweaty brow.

"Oh, look at this guy." She turned a wide smile on Reed. "This is going to be fabulous."

Several other people milled around the multi-room display area, and dozens of photos in all sizes dotted the walls. A close-up of a man leaning against a porch rail caught Reed's attention. The camera had vividly captured the man's laughter and light dancing in his eyes. "Wow," Reed said. "For a minute, I thought that was my dad."

"Really?"

Reed heard the surprise—or doubt—in Kristen's voice, and he blew out a long breath. "You probably haven't seen him smile like that, but he used to. My mom knew how to make that man laugh."

Kristen hooked her arm through his. "Yeah? Tell me about your mother."

As they moved to the next photo, Reed took her hand. As poignant memories assailed him, he slowed his pace. "She had a dry wit. Well-versed in sarcasm with a little irony on the side." He looked down at Kristen. "She was strong. Had to be for life on the ranch, I suppose. But she was also fun—the easy-going one. Together, I guess she and Dad had a yin and yang thing going. You could always tell she loved life and her family."

"I'm sure you miss her."

"I do. Everything changed when she died."

Kristen squeezed his hand. "I know what you mean."

Reed pressed a quick kiss to her hair. "I know you do. Your mother was obviously a wonderful person. I want to hear about her sometime."

They stopped in front of a picture of two young boys roping a calf. With a chuckle, Reed pointed. "Now that brings back a few memories."

"Did you do that?"

"Sure. Every boy on a ranch ropes."

Kristen shook her head. "It's a miracle any of you survive."

"Can't argue with you."

As Reed wandered through the room holding Kristen's hand, the ebb and flow of life weighed on his mind—how in one crazy moment someone is gone from your life and in another someone else appears. No one could make sense of it.

He was enjoying the photos and the trip down memory lane, but the pictures also reminded him he'd rejected that life. He had a solid career, and he'd worked hard to get where he was. After this little hiatus, he had to double-down the rest of the week and take advantage of Kristen's presence. He'd be stupid to blow this promotion opportunity now. Not many people in their thirties rose to the executive suite.

Looking around, he found Kristen had drifted to another group of photos featuring horses. He moved behind her and ran a hand possessively across her back. "The cowboys not holding your attention?" She leaned into him, sending his pulse jumping.

"I like these guys. Just look at them—the artist really captured their personalities." She pointed at the images. "You can tell this one's gentle, and this guy's feisty."

Reed couldn't help chuckling. "Feisty? Do people really use that word?" Her elbow gently connected with his side.

"Horse people do."

"Is that right? Pretty sure my dad would yank me out of the saddle and make me do hard labor if he heard that word come out of my mouth."

"Haha!" Kristen clapped her hands. "I love real-life experiments. Let's give it a try next time I'm at the ranch."

Reed wasn't sure whether the *feisty* sparkle in her eyes or the assumption there'd be another visit to the ranch made his heart skip a beat. But he was sure he'd never experienced this easy, light-hearted contentment simply being with a woman before. He swung an arm around her shoulder. "I'm in."

Reed's watch showed nearly eight-thirty when they left the exhibition hall. As he guided Kristen toward the parking garage, Reed mulled their options. Should he take her somewhere swanky? Popular? Quiet?

"What'd you have in mind for dinner?"

She interrupted his thoughts with his own question. He went with his hunch. "Something close by?"

"Please."

Grinning, Reed opened her car door. "Okay. I know a little Italian place not too far that shouldn't have a long wait. Would that work?"

"Perfect." She stepped forward to get inside the car.

But Reed didn't budge...couldn't budge. He gazed down, the mellow light casting highlights on her hair. All he could think about was running his hands through the thick mass. Every muscle in his body tensed, strained to feel her against him.

She looked up with arched brows. "What's the—"

Reed placed a finger over her lips. "In a minute." Pulling her forward, he bent his head and slowly moved his lips across hers. Food could wait.

****

Kristen closed her eyes and melted into the warmth surrounding her. Finally, some time alone with Reed and a chance to stoke the kindling—or at least have an adult conversation. Pulse hammering, she wound her arms around Reed's neck and let her fingers slip inside his collar, reveling in his caresses.

When a car engine roared to life nearby, Reed

tightened his grip for a moment before ending the kiss. "Guess that's our cue," he whispered. He pulled back and ran a thumb across her cheek.

Kristen let out a shaky breath. That simple gesture, his gentle touch on her face, seemed so…affectionate. She ran a hand down his arm and glanced around the parking lot. Against the deep blue sky, the streetlights twinkled. "Guess so. Pretty soon my stomach will be making as much noise as that car."

The restaurant was only a few minutes away, tucked into a small strip of older brick buildings.

"It's not much to look at, but the food's good." Reed opened the door and ushered Kristen inside.

Based on Reed's description, she expected a hole in the wall. Instead, the restaurant had a quiet, refined atmosphere filled with savory scents of bread and spices. So far, the man proved to have excellent taste.

She slipped into a chair.

A server who introduced himself as Corbin arrived with ice water and a basket of bread, for which Kristen's grumbling stomach was grateful. She ordered a glass of wine and reached for the Italian loaf. "Instant gratification," she said. "My kind of place."

"Didn't mean to starve you."

Kristen grinned. She wasn't complaining. "I think I'll make it. I'm glad we went to the museum."

"Me, too. Thanks for indulging me."

Corbin interrupted with their drinks.

After placing dinner orders, Kristen took a sip of her wine then leaned forward. "So, the exhibit featured a lot of pictures of men and boys and a few women, but not many girls. While you were playing cowboy and roping steers, what was your sister doing?"

"Unfortunately, while there is the rare exception, on a ranch boys and girls get segregated into traditional roles. I remember Amy spending a lot of time in the kitchen with Mom." He paused a moment then chuckled. "I can tell you for sure that Dylan gets his imagination from his mother. Dad used to tease her about having tea parties with chickens and goats."

"Did she, really? Ha! That's great. Have you ever mentioned it to Dylan? He might get a kick out of that." Ever on the lookout for story ideas, Kristen tucked it away in her head—a barnyard tea party would make a cute visual. She refrained from mentioning the fact, but at the same time, she wondered if keeping quiet was deceitful. Should she have an honest conversation with Reed about her story ideas? Tell him that she picked up ideas and inspiration all around her—from a casual comment, a newspaper story, a billboard, an overheard conversation, a walk, anything, really. Would he clam up and be afraid to speak freely?

She was glad when their salads arrived, giving her something to focus on besides Reed's intent gaze, which tended to send an embarrassing flush to her face. She popped a fork full of lettuce, olives and mozzarella cheese into her mouth.

"How is it?" Reed asked.

The house-made Italian dressing was billed as 'famous' in the menu. "It's delish," she said. "You're doing great—two for two."

"I'll call that a winning streak." He held his glass toward her. "Speaking of winning, here's a late toast to your local celebrity status."

Kristen's heart fluttered. She tapped her glass to his, touched that he remembered the newspaper story she'd mentioned several days ago. "Thank you."

"I looked it up online. They wrote a nice article."

The tone of his voice caught Kristen by surprise. It hinted at something...that he was impressed? Did the positive publicity somehow validate her success for him? "Yes, my agent is thrilled, as you can imagine. She has visions of grandeur for me."

"As she should. And what does that look like? Fame and fortune?"

Kristen shrugged. "More book tours, probably. And maybe some speaking engagements." She gave him a pointed look. "How many rich and famous children's authors do you know?" As much as she played down the article, she got goose bumps every time she read the words. She couldn't help feeling as if she were on her way to realizing her dreams. Would she sound silly and juvenile to say so?

Kristen mentally berated herself. She'd wanted to sit and talk to Reed, so why did she feel self-conscious every time the conversation turned to her work?

"Okay, you got me there," Reed said. "But I'm not exactly a connoisseur."

"Here we are, folks." Corbin appeared with plates of steaming pasta.

Kristen inhaled the zesty scent of marinara sauce that generously covered the house-made penne noodles. "Anyway, I'm loving the upward swing." Kristen lifted her fork, ready to dig in. "Right now I just need to keep the momentum going."

"You deserve the recognition. You're very talented and have a knack for connecting with kids."

"Thanks. That's always my goal." His praise enveloped her in soft warmth, and at that moment the connection with him felt so tangible she could almost touch it, see it in his eyes, hear it in his voice.

"Even if you never wrote another book, you could have a whole new audience every year with more kids coming into your age level, right?"

"True. Just remember not every kid is like Dylan. They don't *all* love my books."

"So we know which ones will be total failures."

She swatted his arm. "That is so bad." This would be a good opportunity to mention she'd sent drafts of *The Awful Waffle* and another story to her agent and was waiting to get some initial response. But again, she held back. If Valerie didn't love the story, or didn't think she could sell it, why open a potential can of worms?

Anyway, that was enough about her books for now. She'd cross that bridge if and when she came to it. She met his eyes. "Can I ask you a personal question?"

Her heart somersaulted at his slow grin—as usual.

He spread his hands above the table. "You can ask me anything."

"How do you happen to be unattached? Have you ever been married?"

"Two questions."

"Well, you said *anything*."

"So I did. Never been married or engaged. A few relationships, sure." He leaned forward. "Honestly, my focus for a long time has been work. After I graduated from the University of Texas, I just wanted to get out there and prove myself."

Kristen frowned. "To whom?"

"Me—and my dad, of course. He would've liked for me to take over the ranch."

"Ah. Was the decision contentious?"

"Not too much. I think on some level he knew the ranching business wasn't a good fit for me."

"Why's that?"

"Ranching is a slow, solitary business. Manual labor. I wanted to do more, to contribute something that seemed more relevant."

"But aren't petroleum engineers a dying breed?"

"Maybe long-term, but not in my lifetime. Besides, I'm a new breed. Viking is on the cutting edge of engineers looking to extract oil in ways that are more environmentally friendly."

"You mean like fracking?"

Reed shook his head. "Not at all. We're retrofitting old pumps to manage them better. Our technology allows us to better monitor every pump and refinery at every step in the process."

"Really? I admit, I'm reluctant to completely trust an oil company."

"Yeah, I can see that on your face."

"Sorry. I mean, to a big business—it's all about profits, right?"

"You aren't alone in your thinking, believe me. We definitely have an image problem to deal with as well."

In which case they should be using *his* image. Who wouldn't trust that face? Kristen's thoughts veered as she conjured an entire promotional campaign featuring the handsome rancher who cared about the land giving a spiel about satisfying energy needs while also protecting the environment.

A sense of pride washed over Kristen. His integrity was nothing short of sexy.

"We're about ready to launch a new leak detection

system," Reed told her. "The company wants a patent first, and we're still doing some tweaking, which is why I'm getting pressure to spend more time in the office right now."

"Is the system something you're in charge of?" Kristen took a sip of wine. Now they were getting somewhere.

"Pretty much. My team, anyway. The thing is, I used to practically live at the office, so everyone got used to me being there all the time. With Dylan, I can't work as much."

"No way that could last, though. Those hours are unrealistic for anyone."

He shrugged. "Maybe. For people with families, for sure. That brings me back to your original question. I was seeing someone before the accident."

Kristen did some quick math. Not so long before she met him.

"What happened?"

"In a word, Dylan."

"What?" Indignation ignited inside Kristen. "Are you serious?"

"Yep. Early on I couldn't leave him, and she didn't want to put going out on hold. I guess she figured out before I did there'd be a long adjustment period." He reached for her hand. "Just as well."

The server's timely appearance kept Kristen from going off about the insensitive woman who'd rejected Dylan.

Corbin slid a small card onto the table. "Dessert tonight, folks?"

Reed handed the card to Kristen. "Up to you."

Dessert already? Kristen smiled at Corbin. "Why

don't you give us a few minutes?"

"Of course. No rush."

Kristen glanced at the menu. She didn't need dessert, but she wasn't in a hurry to end their evening, either.

"When is Jana expecting us back?" Reed asked.

"About eleven."

He peered over his wine glass. "I don't suppose she mentioned a sleepover."

Kristen sucked in her breath. The idea certainly crossed her mind and probably Jana's and obviously Reed's. Just the mention of a sleepover with the handsome, sexy man sitting across from her turned her insides to mush. She let out a choked laugh. "I think that might've been a little awkward." She willed a normal, lighthearted tone to her voice.

Reed reached across the table and caressed her hand with his thumb.

As shivers shot through Kristen's body, she looked into Reed's deep, smoky eyes.

"How do we do this long distance?"

His voice dropped to a husky timbre.

Well, okay, who needed oxygen anyway? "I—I don't know." She searched his face. "I guess the bigger question is do we want to do this, given the long distance?"

A charged silence filled the air and time seemed to stop as her question hung in the space between them.

Finally, Reed squeezed her hand. "The distance complicates things, but I'm not ready to let you go."

The look in his eyes nearly scorched her skin, and his words held her in awe as they pounded in her head.

"You don't realize how addictive you are, do you?"

She stared, her foggy brain unable to keep up. Addictive? Turning, Kristen looked behind her, then back to Reed. "*Who* are you talking to?"

A slow, lazy grin spread across his face.

"Oh, it's you, sweetheart. So many times in the last six weeks I've thought that's the last we'll see or hear from her. And every time I didn't want it to be."

"Same," she said softly.

He folded his arms against the table. "Do you know how many boarding schools are in Texas?"

Kristen gasped. "What?"

"*I* know." He adjusted his glass and tapped a fist against the tablecloth. "I know the names and where they're located. But you know how long it's been since I've looked at one of their websites?"

She had an idea, but she shook her head.

"About six weeks. I see your beautiful smile. I hear your lovely voice saying 'Oh, Reed,' and everything snaps into place. Everything is better."

He was being serious, Kristen knew. But maybe things turned a little too serious. She couldn't help herself. She picked up her glass and glanced at him over the rim. "Oh, Reed."

His sharp laughter cracked through the air.

Kristen joined in, but the original question remained unanswered. How could they do this long distance?

Chapter Seventeen

Reality hit hard Monday morning. Kristen left Jana's house early to pick up Dylan and get him to school so Reed could get to the office earlier than usual. She was barely functioning when she and her travel mug of strong Earl Grey pressed the doorbell at Reed's place.

When Reed greeted her at the door, she had enough awareness to notice he wore a perfectly fit charcoal gray suit with crisp white shirt—and looked delicious. A morning pick-me-up for sure.

He planted a quick kiss on her lips. "Morning, gorgeous."

Ha. Really? That was a stretch. "Hey," she said. At seven a.m. she didn't do perky.

A moment later, Reed grabbed his briefcase. "I'm out of here. I'll move Dylan's booster seat to your car before I leave. You're cleared for pick-up at the school. I'm sure everyone will be happy to see Dylan with a responsible adult."

Kristen offered a sad smile at the reminder of last week's crazy events. She'd have to remember not to glare suspiciously at the moms, though she couldn't help wondering who was the culprit.

"Hopefully, that's all over." She glanced toward Dylan at the kitchen table. Almost all signs of his injuries from the fall at the ranch were gone. Only a slight greenish tint remained in the skin around his eye.

"I'll let you know when I can get away tonight," Reed said. "If I can't be here by seven, you two go ahead and eat without me."

"Sounds good," Kristen said, though she hoped he could join them. She had visions of having a meal on the table for him when he arrived home. But without knowing a specific time, that wouldn't be do-able. At least she could put a few things in the freezer for future busy nights.

"You two have a good day," Reed said. "Text me if you need anything." He tipped Kristen's chin. "Thank you."

Her throat tightened. "You're welcome."

Another quick kiss, and he was gone.

Kristen joined Dylan at the table. "Good morning, Dylan." She pressed a kiss to the top of his head.

"Miss Hanover, you're taking me to school today."

"Yes, I am. I'll pick you up, too."

"That's cool. The other kids will—"

Kristen held up a hand to stop him. "Hey, Dylan, let's don't tell the other kids, okay? Driving you isn't a secret, but we don't need to advertise it, either." She had no idea if any of the other kids would be jealous since they saw her as a celebrity, but she didn't want to hurt any feelings. "Can you try not to make a big deal of me being here with you?"

"Okay, Miss Hanover." He slurped the last of the milk in his cereal bowl.

"What else do you want to eat? Fruit? Toast?"

A puzzled gaze met hers.

"I just have cereal."

Hmm. Looked like her shopping list was growing.

"Okay, buddy, go rinse your bowl and put it in the dishwasher, then let's get ready to go."

Dish in hand, he scrambled off the chair. "You want me to?"

"To what?"

"Put my bowl in the dishwasher."

Careful not to show any criticism of Reed or the way they'd been doing things, Kristen smiled and nodded toward the kitchen. "Um, yeah. You're big enough." She could see Reed doing cleanup just to make it faster and easier, but the kid might as well learn now to pick up after himself.

"Good job," she told him when he finished the task. "Brush your teeth then grab your backpack."

Kristen wandered into the kitchen to reheat her tea while Dylan collected his things. "I need sixty seconds," she called. She stopped short when her gaze landed on two boxes of her favorite teas sitting on the counter. She couldn't imagine when Reed had time to get those, but she appreciated the gesture. What a thoughtful thing to do. It was just a little thing, but it showed...She squeezed her eyes shut. It showed consideration—that he paid attention and thought of her. Kristen sagged against the counter, emotions pummeling her. Was this for real? She drew in a shaky breath. The gift reminded her of the simple things her parents used to do for each other. And they were two people she knew to be deeply in love.

"I'm ready." Dylan appeared in the kitchen, backpack dangling from his shoulder.

Straightening, Kristen added more water to her mug and slipped it into the microwave. "Okay. Just a sec." She'd been seriously sidetracked.

The drop-off line moved more efficiently than Kristen expected, and within minutes Dylan hopped out of the car. She hesitated a moment, watching as he made his way to the open double-doors. When he turned and waved, his face lit with a happy grin, her heart bounced. Kristen returned the grin. As far as mornings went, this one was turning out to be… She shook her head as the word *fun* popped in. Surely she was still in bed dreaming.

Well, a trip to the grocery store would most likely take care of that. In the parking lot, she reviewed her list and added a few items. She was about to open the car door when her phone buzzed. Fishing it out of her purse, she checked the number. Wasn't from any of her contacts, but she recognized the Denver area code.

"Hello, this is Kristen."

"Ms. Hanover, this is Cheryl Weston calling from the Friends of the Denver Ballet. How are you?"

Regretting I answered, Kristen thought, sure she was about to hear a fundraising pitch. "Excellent, thanks. What can I do for you, Cheryl?"

"I know this is extremely short notice, but we've had a cancellation for one of the tables at our annual ball this weekend, and the Ballet would like to invite you to join us."

Kristen's heart sank. Oh, no, she groaned silently. Not this weekend. *Why this weekend*?

"The idea," Cheryl went on, "is for each guest table to include a local celebrity. One of our board members saw the article about you in *The Post* recently, and we'd love to have you."

Kristen knew of the ball—always a big event among Denver movers-and-shakers and would be great exposure to that community. She'd love to be one of the featured guests. It'd be perfect, visiting with the public but in small groups. She bit her lip, thinking. Were the advantages worth cutting her trip short and bailing on Reed and Dylan? They didn't have specific plans, but Jana had mentioned the possibility of a get-together at her place Friday night.

"Ms. Hanover?"

"Yes. I'm sorry, I'm trying to think if there's any way I can be there. You see, I'm out of town this week."

"Well, as you can imagine, we're in a time crunch on this, so I'm afraid we do need a response right away."

"Of course. I understand." She drew in a deep breath. "Thank you so much for the invitation. I'm very honored to be asked, and I hope you'll consider me for next year, but I'm afraid I'll have to decline this time." Kristen winced even as she gave her answer. She'd been hoping for this exact kind of call. Was turning it down a mistake? Maybe this call proved she was on the radar—and more opportunities would follow.

"We'll keep you on our list of candidates," Cheryl said. "You have a great day."

"Thank you." Slumping against the seat, Kristen ended the call. Way to burst her morning bubble.

****

The scent of lemon-pepper chicken sizzling in the oven wafted through Reed's apartment by the time Kristen finally sat down with her computer and cell phone. The day passed so fast she had only an hour before picking up Dylan, and a check-in call to Valerie was still on the agenda. That her agent hadn't called to say she'd received the manuscripts was unusual.

"Hey, you!" Valerie picked up enthusiastically. "You must have some kind of ESP psychic thing going on. I just talked to Steph at Warren about you."

"Oh, yeah? Fill me in."

"Love the stuff you sent. Really nice. The *What Can You See?* follow-up is a no-brainer. She'll get that into the system. Might have a few minor tweaks."

"Wow. That's great."

"The waffle one is special, Kristen. With the right illustrator, it could be a total classic. The next big thing. Seriously."

Chest pounding, Kristen gasped and laughed at the same time. "Oh, my gosh. They've already accepted the book?" That would have to set a world record.

"Well, no commitment or offer, but she loves it. Loves the side story about the kid. In fact, she asked me a lot of questions about him. I'm thinking she might want to add his story to the back flap or something. Maybe a cute picture of him eating a waffle?"

Kristen's stomach dropped. *No. Way.* Reed would flip out. "Wait. Valerie, how does she even know about Dylan?" Nothing about Dylan was included in the manuscript or the proposal. Holding in a scream, she put a hand to her forehead. She'd mentioned it in her memo to Valerie. And Valerie had been with her on the tour when she first met Dylan and Reed. *Damn.*

"Oh, I told her the story. Is that a problem?"

"Actually, it could be. His uncle, who's also his guardian, isn't keen on any publicity or profit from the accident."

"It wouldn't be from the accident." She gave a little laugh. "And no one will publish a book if they can't make any money from it."

"I know. I agree. But I see his point, too. Making the kid a celebrity because he lost his parents? Does that make the loss seem like a good thing?"

"The story is cute regardless of losing his parents," Valerie pushed back. "Their deaths didn't have anything to do with the waffle incident, right?"

"True, but I only know about the story because his parents died. I asked him memories about them." Flopping back into the chair, Kristen massaged her temples. "I don't know. I guess it's a gray area."

"Listen, we aren't even sure exactly what they'll want. No reason to freak out yet. We'll wait for an offer and see what happens. Who knows? I might be able to shop the book around and get a bidding war going. Then *we* call the shots."

Her excitement came through loud and clear, and Kristen had to admit the idea of a bidding war and auction made her lightheaded.

"All right, I've got to run, Kristen. I'll be in touch as soon as I hear anything. Nice job, hon."

With that, Valerie left Kristen holding her phone and for the second time that day, wishing she'd kept it turned off and tucked inside her purse. If the guys asked about her day, she'd have to regale them with adventures in grocery shopping.

She responded to a couple of emails then grabbed her keys. She couldn't be late to pick up Dylan.

This time, Kristen pulled into the parking lot and got out of the car. Following Reed's directions, she made her way to the after-school room and introduced herself to Caroline and Abby, the women in charge, while Dylan bounced around her.

"Okay, buddy, let's go," Kristen said. "Great to meet you both." With a wide smile, she took Dylan's hand. "Where to, kiddo? We can go home, go to a park, the library? What sounds good?"

"We can go to the library now?"

"Sure. Do you have your card?"

"In my backpack."

"Done deal." She located the ~~nearest library~~ on her GPS then pulled out of the parking lot. An hour later, she turned the car into Reed's driveway and helped Dylan carry his haul of books.

"Is there a show you like to watch after school, Dylan? You could get a snack then turn on the TV or look at your books while I work on supper."

Kristen slipped her phone into her pocket, though she hoped Reed would simply show up. She was washing fresh green beans when the phone buzzed. Her hopes sank. Reed said he'd call if he couldn't get home in time for supper. She dried her hands and looked at the text.

—Leaving now—

Grinning, Kristen held the phone against her chest then happily set the table for three. Rummaging through Reed's cabinets, she found a few colorful cloth napkins and a small pitcher she'd filled with mixed flowers from the grocery store. Nothing fancy, but maybe a step up from the ordinary. Those details probably wouldn't matter to the guys, but they mattered to her. In fact, Kristen realized, she wanted things to feel better—to *be* better—when she was around.

At six-thirty, the garage door went up.

A moment later, Reed's smiling face peeked into the kitchen. He dropped his bag on the counter and shrugged out of his suit coat.

"Hey, there," Kristen said.

He moved forward and planted a kiss on her lips. "Hi."

"Hi, Uncle Reed," Dylan called from the front room.

He seemed to have gotten used to the idea of Reed kissing Kristen.

Reed turned. "Hey, buddy. How was your day?"

"Okay. We went to the library after school."

"Yeah? Cool."

He turned back to Kristen and loosened his tie. "Wow. Something smells great in here."

"It's almost ready. What would you like to drink?"

He opened the refrigerator and took out a bottle of beer, which Kristen promptly removed from his hand. Opening the freezer, she pulled out a frosty mug and expertly poured the beer into the glass.

"Very nice," Reed murmured.

The appreciation in his eyes matched the tone of his voice, and Kristen felt the warmth all the way up her spine. "Hey, there are several papers from Dylan's backpack on the desk."

"Okay. Thanks."

Reed turned to the desk and rifled through the papers then waved one in the air. "Holiday program. Guess I better get that on the calendar."

"Dylan, do you have a part in the program?" Kristen placed a tray on the table.

He nodded. "Singing. We all sing. And I get to play the tambourine."

"You do?" Kristen grinned, glad to know the school encouraged participation in music and the arts.

"That's awesome."

"Yeah, and get this," Reed said. "He's out of school for two weeks for Christmas." Reed shook his head. "Two full weeks. I think one of those might end up being take-your-kid-to-work week."

"Isn't the day care center open?"

"Nope. Whole place shuts down."

"Oh, Reed. What a hassle." What did they expect working parents to do? She wanted to help, but she couldn't keep running to Dallas every couple of weeks. The benefits of moving to Dallas weighed on her mind.

Reed wandered back into the kitchen. "How can I help?"

She handed him a bowl of fruit. "Put this on the table. Dylan, time to wash your hands. Supper's ready."

While Dylan was occupied, Kristen leaned against the table close to Reed. "I have an idea."

Taking her hand, he met her eyes.

"What would you think about sending Dylan to Denver after Christmas? I'll have about two weeks before my class starts."

"You mean put him on a plane?"

"Sure. The airlines help with kids traveling alone all the time."

"Huh. You think he'd be up for it?"

"Not sure, but—" Another thought popped in, and she waved her hand. "No. Never mind. The weather's better here."

Reed pulled her in front of him. "I wasn't looking for a volunteer. You're already doing a lot."

"I know you weren't. But what about the ranch? Maybe Dylan would like to stay in one of the cabins with me? He might think that was fun. Going there would be less stressful than worrying about him flying alone."

Reed ran his hands up and down her arms. "It's an idea, but why don't you take a few days to give it some more thought?"

"You know, I think Dylan might be getting less fearful of the horses. He's really excited about the new horse books we got at the library. Maybe I could work with him if the two of us were at the ranch alone. Less pressure."

Reed shook his head. "How did we ever get lucky enough to find you?" He brushed his lips across hers again.

Dinner was exactly what Kristen imagined—just the three of them talking and laughing. No rush and no interruptions. Even Reed seemed relaxed. And not once did his cell phone make an appearance during the meal.

"Who likes apple cobbler and ice cream?" Kristen asked. She'd lingered at the table, talking with the guys long after all their plates were empty.

Reed's brows rose.

"I wouldn't turn any down."

"I do!" Dylan shouted.

The kid's eyes sparkled.

Kristen pushed back her chair. "Now, I didn't make this, but it looks delicious. That grocery store has an amazing bakery. Dylan, you want to help clean up the big plates?"

She waited while he stacked his own plate on top of Reed's then followed him to the kitchen.

A moment later, Reed joined them holding Kristen's wine glass. He refilled it then took the dessert she handed him.

"Thanks."

A lopsided smile lit his face.

"I think I could get used to this."

A wave of heat spread through Kristen, and she refrained from reminding him she'd be there only for a few more days. Sure, she'd had fun today, but could she get used to it? Playing housewife? Mom? With her career taking off? Maybe not full-time, but she admitted she enjoyed a quiet night in with these two.

"What's the plan for tomorrow?" Reed asked.

"Pretty much same as today. I'll spend the day here, do a little more cooking, and then I'll do the same at Mrs. Baxter's house Wednesday and Thursday." She cleared dishes as she spoke. The days flashed in her mind. A week could go by so fast.

Reed pushed back his chair and reached for the plates. "Let me do this. The cook doesn't clean up."

"Miss Hanover, do you have to go to Mrs. Baxter's house tonight? Why can't you stay with us?"

Kristen flicked a quick glance at Reed. How to tackle this? As simply as possible, for sure. "I do, sweetie. Mrs. Baxter is expecting me."

"You could call her."

"Dylan," Reed said. "You know we don't have an extra bedroom."

"I'll sleep on the floor, and you can have my bed," Dylan pleaded.

His eyes implored Kristen.

She sucked in her breath. No way to cave on this one. "That's very sweet of you, Dylan, but all my stuff is there—my clothes, my toothbrush, my special pillow. I'll be back in the morning."

His shoulders slumped, and he kicked at the rug

before he looked at her again. "Miss, Hanover, if you and Uncle Reed get married, you can come live with us and be my mom."

The air whooshed from Kristen's lungs.

"That's what Annabelle in my class said."

Thanks a lot, Annabelle. Kristen recovered before Reed did. "Well, sweetie, those are things for grown-ups to talk about. Right now, I live in Denver, and it's kind of far away. I hope you and Reed can come visit me sometime and see our pretty mountains." She took Dylan's hand. "Anyway, we have some books to read tonight. You ready?"

She looked at Reed and almost laughed at the relief on his face. "Are you joining us?"

"Yeah, for a few minutes." Leaning toward her, he spoke under his breath. "Nice save."

Kristen grinned in return. "Thanks." The awkward moment passed, but she would pay big money to know what was going through Reed's mind.

She curled up beside Dylan. "What are we reading tonight? You choose."

"This one about musical instruments." He pushed back the others.

Reed picked up the scattered books. "Looks like a good one," he said. "I think I'll let you two do this without me tonight." He ran a hand over Dylan's head. "Night, buddy. Sleep tight."

Swallowing her disappointment, Kristen reminded herself that her job was to give Reed a break. She smiled at Dylan. "I like this one, too. And after we read it a few times, I bet you'll be able to identify every one of those instruments."

His head bobbed. "You can test me."

Laughing, she squeezed him close. She loved his enthusiasm for learning. What kid wanted to be tested? When his bright blue eyes looked up, Kristen's chest tightened. She'd never imagined loving someone else's child so much.

Minutes later, Dylan yawned, and his shoulders slumped.

Kristen closed the book. "That's enough for tonight." She kissed his forehead and turned out the light. "Goodnight, sweetie. See you in the morning."

She returned to the living room and found Reed sitting on the sofa, his laptop on the coffee table in front of him. A teasing comment about cyber withdrawals was on the tip of her tongue when he closed the lid. Instead, she happily sank onto the sofa beside him. "That is one adorable kid."

Leaning back, Reed slid an arm around her shoulders. "Speaking of, guess who called today."

Kristen cocked her head. She didn't plan to tell him about her calls today. "Who?"

"Celia."

"What did she want? Besides you, I mean."

Reed swiveled to look at her, his eyes wide.

"Oh, come on. Don't tell me you didn't notice her pouting when she saw we were together at the ranch. I don't think she came out just to see Dylan."

He blew out his breath. "I noticed," he said grimly. He nuzzled into Kristen's hair. "Thank you for saving me."

"Anytime. So what was the call about?"

"Nothing really. Checking to make sure Dylan was doing all right, she said. I don't know, I always feel like she wants something."

Kristen let her head fall against his shoulder. "I know you're maxed out right now, but when things settle a little, you might want to try and get to know her better. She *is* Dylan's aunt."

"I'm sure you're right, but yeah, the to-do list is kind of full."

She grazed a hand across his. "Hey, it's about time for me to get going."

Reed groaned and looked at his watch. "Guess Dylan was up later than I realized."

"Time flies," Kristen murmured. "And the Baxter household is early-to-bed, early-to-rise."

Standing, Reed pulled Kristen up and against his chest. "Do you have to go to Mrs. Baxter's tonight?"

Her heart somersaulted. "Didn't we already cover this?"

"Didn't like the answer."

"Yeah, me either."

His lips met hers, and his hands began exploration across her back, moving slowly to her waist and hips as he pressed her closer.

"I've been thinking," he said against her lips.

"Uh-huh?" How could he think right now?

"If you and Dylan go to the ranch at Christmas?"

"Yeah?"

Reed lifted his head and twined his fingers through her hair. "Maybe we get Nora to keep Dylan for a night and we do a grown-up getaway."

Kristen stood mesmerized, her throat constricting at the same time her heart swelled. Slowly, she nodded.

"It's been on my mind a while," he said.

She let out a soft laugh that turned into a giggle as Reed pulled her into his arms. "Mine, too."

No doubt Nora would be happy to help implement the plan. But Christmas was a month away. When she went back to Denver in a few days, would she still be on his mind?

Chapter Eighteen

Like a kid waiting for Santa, Kristen kept an eye on Reed's front door, looking and listening for signs of the delivery truck. She was anxious to get the bedroom project finished before she left. Already she'd devoted half the morning to taping off the main wall, hoping that a brighter color on one wall would be enough to make the room pop when they added the new bedspread and other elements.

She had paper and paints for the chart ready as well, but would wait for Dylan to start on that project.

At the table, she continued sifting through ideas on websites for writers. She needed at least thirty writing prompts for her students to match her lesson topics, and they were harder to come up with than she'd expected. So far, she had about twenty. Finally, she got up and went outside for a short break. Reed's place included a small patio and patch of yard—good for the breath of fresh air Kristen needed, but not near enough room for a young boy to run and play. Would she be pushing her luck, especially considering the bedroom renovation, to suggest they move to a larger house? She wondered if on some level the decision to stay put was Reed's way of hanging on to a small part of his old life.

She snagged a long piece of grass near the fence and waved it across her hand. She was shedding her old life as well—or her life was morphing into something new. Her mother's death left a vacant spot for sure, but then Dylan and Reed rocked her world. In fact, they were suddenly front and center. Just thinking of the upcoming night away with Reed turned Kristen's insides to mush. That he would feel the same made her positively giddy.

She sank into a patio chair, and his words played in her head as they had all night. *"It's been on my mind a while."* She smiled at the memory. Once she got all the lesson plans, assignments, and writing prompts put together for this class, she could always repeat the curriculum somewhere else—somewhere like Dallas. The Dallas area had to be home to a dozen community colleges. She'd miss the mountains, but, hey, that's what vacations were for.

A rumbling in the street snapped her back to the present, and she sat up straight before bolting inside. *Finally.*

The boxes sitting on the front porch were bulky but not heavy, and Kristen maneuvered them into the front room. She grabbed scissors and opened the boxes to check the contents. With the exception of the sheets, which needed to be washed first, she'd let Dylan be the one to pull it all out. It'd probably feel like Christmas Day. She'd have to remember to snap a picture— possibly the first picture of Dylan's new life.

She'd just closed the lid on the washing machine when her phone lit up with a call. "Hello?"

"Do you have a few minutes to talk?" Valerie asked.

"Sure."

"Okay, I've got some news."

Kristen glanced around. She'd already shut down

her laptop, so she grabbed a pen and pad of paper from Reed's desk and almost skipped back to the patio. If she read Valerie's tone correctly, the news could be big. "Tell me."

"All right. Listen, and please let me finish before you freak out."

Oh. Kristen's stomach dropped. That didn't sound good. "Okay, go."

"Warren wants both books. They really want the waffle one. And they've offered an amazing advance."

Kristen stilled her hand above the paper. "Really?" The sound of her heartbeat pounded in her ears.

"This is all verbal right now, but Stephanie's writing an official offer. I'll email you as soon as I get it."

Kristen flipped a couple of pages and began writing, her hand shaking as she scribbled the details Valerie spelled out. She was right. This news was big—happy dance ahead.

"Now, here's the deal. They're offering you an additional bonus for an exclusive piece about the boy. Maybe a short non-fiction. If the uncle has a problem, she thought they might settle for a long introduction in your words about your inspiration for the story."

A cold blast swept through Kristen. Talk about a burst bubble. "Valerie." She squeezed her eyes shut and said the words her agent wouldn't love. "I can't do that." The line went deathly silent for a moment.

"Damn it, Kristen. Do you want to launch or not? You need to take some time and think about this. We're talking about a whole new level in your career."

Alarm bells clanged inside her brain. "What does that mean? Did she say they wouldn't publish it without

Dylan's story? What about *What Can You See?* That book is completely separate." Valerie's heavy sigh came across the line.

"I don't know. I didn't ask. But Steph acted like the waffle book hinged on having the kid, too. And you sure won't get that kind of advance for the other story. I can guarantee that."

Kristen tapped the pen against the table, tempted to bang her head as well. "You have to push back, Val. Threaten to take it to another publishing house. Tell her I can maybe mention Dylan in interviews, but I can't have his story as part of the book. I just can't."

She wondered, though, what would happen if she presented the offer to Reed. Would he understand? Change his mind? Compromise? Could she stand to see the disappointment in his eyes? Val was right—she needed to think this through.

"I'll hedge for now, Kristen, but I can tell you a new house won't be as generous. Give the idea a couple of days. Sleep on it. At least tell me you'll think about it, okay?"

Right. As if she could *not* think about it. "I will. I promise."

"Let's touch base next Monday."

In a daze, Kristen picked up the pad, though she didn't need to look at the numbers again. They were permanently seared on her brain. The washing machine beeped, and Kristen responded on autopilot. In the kitchen, she took a long drink of cold water. As tempting as screaming and throwing things might be, she had to push aside those thoughts. She couldn't let Valerie's call cast a shadow on her week.

Kristen left the sheets in the dryer and went to buy

paint. Once they got home from school, she wanted to get started and not have to go back out. No after-school care today. Instead, she pulled into the line of cars waiting at the school's curb.

Ten minutes later, Dylan hopped into the car.

"Hey, there. How was your day?"

"Okay."

"What'd you learn?" She pulled the car away from the curb.

Dylan put a hand to his head. "I learned...I learned that sharks are fish, but whales aren't."

"That's cool. What—"

"Can we go to the park today?"

Kristen shook her head. "Nope." She glanced in the mirror and saw Dylan's wide eyes.

The kid probably didn't hear "no" often. She smiled. "We've got a busy night ahead of us."

"How come?" Dylan slumped against the seat.

"Just a lot to do." Apparently, he'd forgotten about today's delivery.

Back at Reed's, Dylan picked up his backpack and trudged up the steps.

"All righty, kiddo, pick up the pace. We've got work to do." She unlocked the door and stepped aside, knowing that the boxes were front-and-center. As Kristen suspected, it took only a second for memory to click.

"Miss Hanover," Dylan shouted. "It's here!"

Laughing, Kristen opened the camera app on her cell phone. "I know. I've been waiting all afternoon for you. Okay, hold the pillow under your chin."

He tucked the shark-shaped pillow under his chin and posed with an ear-to-ear grin.

Kristen reached out and smoothed his haphazard hair to the side. The wisps didn't quite cover the scar on his forehead, but they inched closer. "So darned cute." One for the scrapbook, for sure. "Let's get started."

Inside the bedroom, Kristen moved back the furniture and covered the carpet with drop cloths then opened the windows. "You might have to sleep on the sofa tonight. Once we start painting, it'll be stinky in here."

"That's okay."

Kristen poured paint into a shallow pan and handed Dylan a roller brush.

His eyes widened as he gaped.

"You can do this," she said. "I'll paint the edges and all the high places, but I want you to work on the big part right in the middle."

With a laugh that came from deep in his throat, Dylan dipped the roller and swiped paint across the wall with a flourish.

While they worked, Kristen mentally planned the growth chart. She'd probably have to spread everything on the driveway to find enough room to work. Maybe she'd take the rest of the roll and paints out to the ranch, and they could do some kind of mural or— Oh, yeah, Dylan didn't get the memo. "Hey, Dylan, guess what?"

"What?"

"You know how your Christmas break is more days than Reed can take off work? Well, we talked about you and me spending a week or so at one of the cabins on the ranch. What do you think about that?"

Dylan stopped painting. "You mean just us?"

"Yeah."

"And not with Grandpa?"

Oh, boy. She'd have to navigate this one carefully. "Well, we'd be at the ranch, so I'm sure we'd say hello to Grandpa. But we'd stay in the cabin instead of the big house." The kid's eyes lit up.

"Yeah! That'd be awesome."

Kristen smiled as she carefully smoothed paint along the edge of the window. "Maybe we could invite your grandpa to our cabin for dinner one night. That'd be a nice thing to do, right?"

Dylan resumed painting. "Okay."

Kristen added cooking and painting to the list of things they could do at the ranch. Of course she'd have her guitar, and they had the horses and books. She'd need all of those things to keep a six-year-old boy entertained for a solid week. The prospect might be a challenge, but it'd be fun. Amazing how things worked out. Before this week, she'd been dreading Christmas and New Year's. Now, she could hardly wait.

****

Reed's smile lingered after he got Dylan to bed Friday night. Kristen would be back in town for Christmas. They'd spent the evening with Jana and a few other families, and Reed had been standing nearby when Jana issued the invitation. The look in Kristen's eyes when she glanced his direction acknowledged she had extra incentive.

"I'd love to," she told Jana.

"Come a few days early, and we can do some last-minute shopping and baking," Jana suggested.

"Sounds great," Kristen said. "I'll bring the wine."

"Deal." Jana lifted her glass to Kristen's while she, too, glanced at Reed.

With Kristen already in town, they might have an extra day or two at the ranch before Reed had to return to the office. Sounded like a win-win deal.

When Kristen arrived Saturday morning, Christmas together was still on Reed's mind. As soon as the doorbell rang, he put a cup of water in the microwave and let Dylan open the door.

"Morning, you guys."

Dylan waved a ruler and black marker. "Can we do it now, before Uncle Reed leaves?"

Grinning, Kristen stepped inside. "Absolutely." She glanced at Reed. "You don't mind, do you?"

He already knew he wasn't getting out of the house before the finishing touch—the growth chart Dylan and Kristen painted to match the new bedroom—was installed.

Reed held up his hands in surrender. "Tell me what to do." He tacked the chart to the wall in line with Kristen's pencil mark.

Her phone clicked as she rapidly snapped photos. "Looks great."

"It's awesome," Dylan said.

Reed admitted the room was a vast improvement. Kristen took care of all the details down to the big poster of about a dozen sharks hanging above the desk. Nothing silly or cartoonish, but a chart with facts about the different species. Educational and cool at the same time. "I sure like that poster. The Tiger shark is cool."

Brows raised, Kristen cocked her head. "You know about sharks?"

"I know a little something about sharks. I was an Earth Sciences major in college before I switched to Engineering. I watched about twenty hours of television during the last *Shark Week*."

"I want to watch *Shark Week*," Dylan shouted.

"We'll have to find out when the next one is. Okay, Dylan. Step over here, and let's see how tall you are." He rested the ruler on Dylan's head and marked the spot on the paper. "Did you get that?" Reed asked Kristen. When she peeked out from behind her phone, luminous eyes met his.

"Got it."

"You know, you're good at this. Maybe I should have you redo my room, too."

"Great idea," she said. "I'm thinking a cowboy theme would be just the thing."

Dylan hooted. "Yeah, Uncle Reed!"

"That's it." Grinning, he gave a playful tug on Dylan's chin. "I'm out of here before I get myself in trouble."

"Have fun. We'll meet you at the park at eleven," Kristen said.

Her words were soft, and her eyes looked everywhere but at him. Reed had the feeling the day could become emotional. He'd probably better brace himself for a cranky kid on his hands for the next few days. He was more than a little tense himself. The week was coming to a close—and they had no plan to see Kristen again before Christmas.

Pulling out of the drive, Reed tapped his fist against the steering wheel. If this patent would hurry up and come through, maybe he could squeeze in a long weekend in Denver. They should probably reciprocate a trip. Had Dylan ever been to the mountains? To Colorado? Reed didn't know the answers to those questions, but he figured he could easily get his buy-in.

Ten minutes later, he turned into the center's parking lot and didn't even remember the drive. He grabbed his duffle and jogged up the sidewalk, ready for a good workout. The sounds and scents of people and equipment in motion greeted him in the entryway.

"Holy hell. Look who's here."

When a familiar voice reached him over the din of machinery, Reed stopped short.

"Beginning to think I'd never see you again."

With a wry grin, Reed met his friend at the door to the weight room and punched him on the shoulder. "Hey."

"Where's the kid?" Mitch glanced behind Reed.

"Someone's watching him for a couple of hours."

"That's great, so you finally got some babysitters lined up. That means you'll start coming to basketball again? Can you get someone tomorrow? We've got people coming over to watch the Cowboys game. You in?"

Mitch's questions hit in rapid succession. But the last one hit hard. *Tomorrow*. They had no plans. Tomorrow, Kristen would be gone. "Not sure I could get someone on short notice."

"So, plan on next weekend. I mean it. Bring Dylan along if you have to." He swung a towel across his shoulders.

"You on your way out?" Reed asked.

"Nah, think I'll do some running." He hitched a thumb. "You coming?"

Reed hesitated. Did he want some company and conversation, or would he rather get lost in his own thoughts?

"Come on," Mitch pressed. "How's the job? They

promote you yet?"

They claimed side-by-side treadmills and hollered over the low humming of the machinery.

"Don't have an official offer. Wassmer retires end of the year. I don't want to jinx it, but I'm thinking right before Christmas, and we get a fresh start January one." Assuming he could stay on top of things until then. He couldn't wait for his current boss, Dan Wassmer, to retire. The man was a chauvinistic, good-ol'-boy, throwback from earlier days, who'd been biding his time for a couple of years. He did little around the office except get in the way and annoy the hell out of the people, especially the women, around him. Reed suspected all along that Wassmer was transferred to his area as a stopgap between being useful and retiring.

He increased the resistance on the machine, though it probably wasn't necessary since thinking of the situation at work easily increased his heart rate—or blood pressure.

With Kristen around all week, he figured his heart rate was already elevated. He probably should've made some special plans for today. Some little surprise. He glanced at his watch. Could he still pull off something? What could he do?

"So, you free all day?" Mitch asked. "We could grab some guys for a pick-up game."

"Nope. Just a couple of hours." He thought about the offer, though. He couldn't remember the last time he'd hung with the guys. Weekends with the guys fell into the *before-Dylan* timeframe. But he couldn't ask Kristen for more time—not today. Check. He wasn't giving up any more time that he could be spending with Kristen today. Twenty minutes later,

Reed parted ways with Mitch. "I gotta do some weights. I'll catch up with you later."

Mitch nodded. "Sounds good. Remember, my place next weekend."

Reed gave a tentative thumbs-up. He spent another twenty minutes lifting weights then headed for the shower. Couldn't stop thinking about doing something for Kristen. She appreciated the tea he left the first day she came to his place. Maybe she liked surprise gifts. Or flowers. Didn't every woman like flowers? Or chocolate? Raking a hand through his hair, Reed laughed at himself. He really was not this inept. But something about Kristen made him want to make sure he got it right. He wanted the smile that lit up her whole face to be because of him.

Not far from home, Reed pulled into a parking spot at a retail strip center. Inside the small jewelry shop, he found just the thing. Knew it immediately. A flower made of orange glass breaking out from a background of silver with orange beads dangling from the bottom. Fun and colorful—very Kristen.

While the sales clerk wrapped the gift, Reed shifted his glance to the other display cases where diamond rings sparkled under the lights. Heat unexpectedly shot up the back of his neck. He looked down at his bare hands. He'd never worn any jewelry. Had never spent much time contemplating the significance of these rings—the sign of being claimed by one woman. It crossed his mind now.

Maybe he should ask Kristen to marry him. He had feelings for her, no doubt. But was it too soon? Was their spark the real deal? This week had proven one thing for sure—life was a hell of a lot easier with

Kristen around. But even if he asked, and even if she said yes, she'd want an engagement and time to plan a wedding. She'd want to complete her obligations in Denver. They couldn't be together immediately. Hell, he probably couldn't even find a good time to ask. Maybe he wasn't a romantic, but he knew a marriage proposal should be special. A memorable proposal required some set-up. How could he—

"Can I show you anything else?" The saleswoman gestured toward the case.

Her question hung in the air a moment then Reed shook his head. "Just the necklace, thanks."

He tucked the small package into his glove box for later and drove the short distance to the park, where he found Kristen pushing Dylan on a swing, both laughing and obviously having fun. As if they didn't have a care in the world. He watched for a few minutes, in awe of their easy attachment. Reed swallowed hard and opened the car door, hoping his presence would be a welcome addition and not an intrusion.

****

The day passed in nanoseconds. Waiting until Kristen made one last trip to the grocery store late in the afternoon, Reed found some paper and markers for Dylan to make her a card. "I got her a nice present." The kid's face fell.

"I want to get her a present, too."

"I think we're out of time, buddy."

"Can it be from me, too?" His bottom lip slipped over the top.

Uh-oh. A pout often turned into something else. Reed brushed a hand over his nephew's head. "You bet." Any other response would be immature. "It's a necklace with a big orange flower. Maybe you could make the card match."

"Okay."

When the kid's eyes brightened, Reed breathed a sigh of relief.

Dylan grabbed for the orange marker on the table. "She likes orange."

"I know."

Reed chose the restaurant for their last night with Kristen—a nearby American bistro serving "upscale comfort food." That meant the menu featured fried chicken Dylan liked.

As dinner wound down, Dylan leaned across the table, almost upsetting the glass of water in front of him. "Can we do it now?" he asked in a loud whisper.

Nodding, Reed pulled the card and package from the pocket of his jacket.

"Miss Hanover, we got you a present."

Kristen's glance shot from Dylan to Reed. "Oh, you guys that's so nice, but you didn't need to."

"I made a card, too," Dylan said.

"Well, thank you, sweetie." She squeezed Dylan's hand and sent him a wide smile. "Hey, I've been thinking about something. How about when just the three of us are together, you call me Kristen instead of Miss Hanover?" She looked at Reed, brows arched. "What do you think?"

"Sure." Miss Hanover did seem a little formal, but why did everything she said remind him they wouldn't be together much longer?

Kristen slid the card from the envelope and smiled immediately. She pulled Dylan into a quick hug. "You drew all this? What a cute picture." She turned the card for Reed to see the two stick ponies surrounded by orange flowers.

"Nice job." He gave Dylan a thumbs-up and turned his attention back to Kristen. Her mouth dropped open before wide eyes met his.

"Oh, my gosh. This is absolutely gorgeous."

"Miss—Kristen, why do you like the color orange so much?"

"Because it's a bright, happy color." She lifted the necklace from the box, and a smile lit her face.

Reed's chest tightened. Man, he'd need a cold shower tonight.

She clasped the necklace behind her then patted it against her chest as she put an arm around Dylan. "I love it. Thank you, sweetie." Then she turned to Reed. "It's beautiful."

In the next instant, her foot grazed his calf under the table, and electricity shot up his spine. Tongue tied by the soft message in her eyes, he could only nod.

As Reed drove back to his place, tension hung in the air inside the car. The goodbyes loomed ahead. Kristen already mentioned heading back to Jana's early to pack and spend a little time with the family—before her morning departure.

Reed's cell phone broke the silence, but in keeping with current protocol, he ignored it. Inside the apartment, he noted Kristen draped her jacket over the back of a chair instead of hanging it up—another reminder she wouldn't be staying long.

"Miss Hanover, can—I mean, Kristen, can we read now?"

Reed glanced up from his phone to find her focused on him. "Sure. Go ahead." Damn, the missed call was from his boss. Why would he be calling on a Saturday night? Probably not a good thing. No, probably something inane and completely unnecessary. And could wait. Instead, he turned his attention to the two people on the sofa and listened to the soft lilt of Kristen's voice as she read out loud.

Looking up, she stopped reading. "We can go to the bedroom if you need to make a call."

Reed waved it off. "Nope. You're good." Knowing she wouldn't drink another glass of wine, he got up and made her a cup of tea.

"Thanks," she whispered.

Her gorgeous eyes held his gaze for a long beat. He'd swear only seconds had passed when she closed the book. Reed checked his watch. Almost ten. When his phone rang, vibrating against the table, he started.

"Take it," Kristen said. "I'll tuck in this guy."

Nodding, Reed picked up but still watched the retreating figures holding hands down the hallway. He blew out a long breath. "Hey, Dan. What's up?"

"Hello, Reed, sorry about calling on a Saturday night. But I figured it's too early to interrupt anything real exciting, right?"

Reed winced. *Spare me the not-funny stuff.* "No problem. What can I do for you?"

"Well, I'm looking at your Black Magic report and missing some numbers."

"Really?" The guy couldn't find the broad side of a barn in daylight. Reed reached for his laptop and made room on the coffee table. "What are you looking for?"

"Numbers, of course." He laughed. "Always gotta go over the financials."

"Uh-huh. Let me put you on speaker while I look at

my computer." Not that he wanted to look at his computer screen when he had a much more interesting subject just down the hall.

****

Kristen waited for Dylan to brush his teeth then pulled the covers down. "In you go." She tucked the blanket under his chin and let her hand slide down his arm as she leaned in to brush a kiss across his cheek. "Goodnight, sweetie. I had a fun time this week."

"Kristen, can't you come back tomorrow?"

The sadness in his sweet voice stole Kristen's breath, but she forced an upbeat tone. "Nope. I need to get home. But I'll see you in a few weeks, okay?"

He reached out and grabbed her hand. "Okay. Bye-not-good."

Furrowing her brow, Kristen tilted her head.

"That's what Mommy used to say when she had to leave but didn't want to."

Fighting tears, she turned his small, pudgy hand inside of hers and gave a squeeze. "Bye-not-good. Sweet dreams, kiddo." Switching off the light, Kristen closed the door and leaned against it for a minute. She'd just thought of a fun Christmas gift. She could record herself reading a couple of her books, and even when she wasn't there, Dylan could follow along. Pushing off from the door, she walked softly toward the front room. Sounded like Reed was still on his call. As she moved closer, Kristen couldn't help but overhear.

"Heard you finally found a babysitter for the boy," the caller said.

"She's not really a babysitter," Reed told the man. "She's a friend."

Oh. Kristen stopped, surprised to be the subject of

the conversation.

The man laughed. "Is that right? As in girlfriend? Even better."

Kristen frowned. What was that supposed to mean? She stepped to the side and leaned against the wall, careful to remain out of sight.

"Okay, now look on page nine of the report, there's another chart," Reed said. "Under the chart are the averages. There's also a breakdown for each location and cost of installation that corresponds to those numbers at the back. Starts on page seventeen."

"Great. Ah, I see them now."

"Let me know if—"

"Okay, here's what you need to do, pal. Put a ring on that finger and get your head back in the office."

"Excuse me?"

"Reed, men aren't meant to be single parents."

"Got that right," Reed muttered.

His words were muffled but discernable. Kristen stifled a gasp. *Who the hell is this guy?*

"Listen, it's none of my business, but I know you want my spot, so let me give you some advice. Leave the home stuff to the ladies. I guarantee you this little gal you're talking about is looking for more than a babysitting gig. You're a great catch, buddy—looks, money, the whole package."

Reed's laughter filled the air.

Heat flushed Kristen's face. He thought that was funny?

"I've thought about it," Reed said.

Whoa. He'd thought about what, exactly? That he was a great catch or that "home stuff was meant for the ladies?" A low simmer grew inside Kristen. This conversation became more interesting—make that more *outrageous*—by the second.

"Stop thinking and do it so you can get back to concentrating on the Black Magic system and your career."

"Not a problem, Dan. Believe me, it's on the brain twenty-four-seven."

Kristen tasted disappointment as her ego took a hit. Was that true?

"Trust me on this," Dan went on. "The wife and I've been going a solid thirty-six years. She gets the credit card, and I get…Well"—he gave a hearty laugh—"I get whatever I want."

What. A. Douchebag. Kristen clenched her fists at her sides, fuming. Why wasn't Reed telling this moron where he could shove his "advice?"

"Thanks, Dan. I'll see you on Monday."

Kristen stood frozen in the hallway, yet her ears burned. Was that conversation for real? *Wow.* Leaning against the wall, she rubbed her temples. She could not believe Reed would even allow the man's comments one synapse of a brain cell. Besides, how arrogant would you have to be to assume a woman would marry you for your looks and a credit card?

Indignation swelled inside Kristen. Not this "little gal." Surely, Reed knew her better than that. She pushed off from the wall, and the new necklace bounced against her chest. Swallowing hard, she took hold of it, brushing her thumb across the smooth glass. Was the gift any more than a nice gesture given out of affection? Old doubts crept in. Or could it be payment for services rendered? A dangling carrot meant to entice her with promises of a well-endowed bank account?

No, she couldn't, *wouldn't*, believe that.

When she entered the room, Kristen found Reed propped against the back of the sofa with a beer in hand. "Who in the world was that?"

He shook his head and grabbed her hand. "That was the dinosaur I hope to replace next year. Unfortunately, he also happens to be my boss at the moment."

"Sounds like a great guy." Sarcasm dripped from her words, and she gave Reed a pointed look. "I feel sorry for his wife."

"Same. Anyway, forget him." He propelled her forward.

That was it? She'd hoped for a little stronger criticism, maybe outright denouncing of the man's archaic comments. Much as she'd like to melt against Reed's chest and feel his arms around her, she couldn't do it. Maybe the call was well-timed. She probably needed to put a little distance between her and Reed. She needed time to think and sort out her feelings— especially if they were planning a grown-up getaway.

"I think Dylan's already asleep." She moved toward the table where she'd left her purse and jacket.

Reed put a hand on Kristen's arm to stop her from picking up her things. "Not so fast."

With a deep breath, she glanced up but couldn't hold a steady gaze. "I should probably get going."

Frowning, he tipped her chin. "You okay?"

She nodded, but her throat clogged. "Sure."

Reed threaded his fingers through hers. "It's not fair that Dylan gets to be tucked in, and I don't."

The playful, suggestive timbre of his voice was almost her undoing. She offered a halfhearted smile.

Then, before she could even think of anything else, Reed's lips crushed hers. But Kristen had trouble responding. She felt numb, unsure, her foggy brain unable to reconcile the man pressing against her with the man she'd heard on the phone. Did her feelings run deeper than his? And how much of his feelings had to do with Dylan? She shook her head and took a step sideways. "Sorry, I just— I should go." But Reed's grip tightened.

"Hey."

Tears welled in her eyes, and in the next second, Reed gathered her into his arms, his warm hands circling her back.

"I'll miss you," he whispered against her hair.

Kristen held onto him for a moment before pulling back. Swiping at her eyes, she turned away. "Bye." He probably expected something more, but her thoughts were jumbled, and her emotions were all over the place. She couldn't help wondering…what, exactly, would he miss?

Chapter Nineteen

—Safe travels. Call me when you get there.—

That text message from Reed greeted Kristen at eight a.m.—five minutes after she shoved her suitcase into the hatch of her car and left Jana's house.

That fast, the doubts, the call, and the confusion came roaring back. Was she being a fool? Was he playing her...using her because of Dylan's attachment?

So much for putting Dallas in the rearview mirror. Memories burned her face. She'd outright told him she wanted to sleep with him when she agreed to a New Year's getaway.

Leave the home stuff to the ladies? "Oh, sure, and who do I leave the home stuff to when I'm on a book tour or teaching?" Kristen spoke to the empty car. She specifically told Reed she'd have more tours as her books took off. Did he think she'd set aside her own career aspirations?

Maybe she was reading way too much into the call, but the tiny voice in her head kept telling her to question—to be on guard. Sadly, she admitted respect for him had taken a hit. If his affections were genuine, if he really cared for her—or respected women at all— why didn't he tell that douchebag he was out of line?

At her first stop to gas up, Kristen bought a large iced tea and a 'share' size peanut M&Ms that she had no intention of sharing. When she returned to the car, she checked her phone, and the missed text from Reed sent her pulse skyrocketing.

—*Miss you already. Give me a call if you want some company along the way.*—

Ha. No, that wasn't happening. She'd probably end up in a ditch. Kristen shoved the car into gear and cranked up the volume on her playlist, hoping for some relief from her own thoughts.

As the miles passed, the landscape changed, and the shadows deepened. She'd barely crossed the Colorado state line when the first patches of snow appeared. Although the roads were clear for now, she straightened and turned down the music to give driving her full attention. Long hours after she'd left the Dallas fairy-tale life behind, Kristen pulled into her snow-free driveway and rested her head against the steering wheel. She was in no hurry to make that drive again.

With the hour difference, the time was only nine o'clock in Denver. But Kristen didn't care. She just wanted to disconnect. But she had one thing to do first. She dug her cell phone out of her purse. She'd love to hear his voice—to get some assurances. But she was determined to put some space between them—at least for a little while. Would distance make him miss *her*? She needed to find out. She tapped out a quick text.

—*Made it. Heading to bed now.*—

She knew she couldn't sleep right away, but she didn't want to talk, either. Tucking the phone in her purse, she rolled her suitcase down the hallway. But thoughts of upcoming conversations with Reed lingered like a bad taste in her mouth. What would he have to say for himself? Would the next call be their last?

****

No mistaking that Monday vibe. At the dining room table Monday morning, Kristen pushed away the mug and massaged her temples. She seriously considered going back to bed. She couldn't decide whether she really felt sick or had anxiety from expecting calls from both her agent and Reed today. Picking up the mug again, she wandered to the back door. The sky was a bright, crisp blue that made the frozen grass sparkle. Any other day, she would've found it pretty.

Leaning against a sunny spot on the wall, Kristen glanced around, already missing the more spacious feel of Reed's condo. Closing her eyes, she sipped her tea and let the warm sunlight wash over her—soothe her. Long moments later, she took a deep breath and pushed off from the wall. Might as well face her fate. "Stop stewing," her mother used to say. "You're not a potato." With renewed energy, Kristen showered and dressed. Hair clipped up and fresh tea in hand, she punched Valerie's number.

"Well, hello there. You've been on my mind. And on my list of people to touch base with today. What'd you decide?"

Kristen squared her shoulders. Only one answer was right. "Val, I need you to push back on the personal stuff and present the waffle book as a stand-alone children's concept. Simple as that. I can't agree to any mention of Dylan, except maybe as a dedication."

"Which would mean nothing to anyone who didn't already know the story," Valerie countered.

"I know, but I honestly believe the book doesn't need it to sell. Dylan's story isn't mine to tell, and I can't betray the family." In spite of her annoyance with

Reed over the work-related phone call, she wouldn't deliberately provoke him or use Dylan to further her career. Integrity meant more than money. "If they say no, we can shop it around and not mention the origins of the idea at all."

In the silence that followed, Kristen wondered if Valerie took offense to her comment, as though Kristen blamed her for tipping off their editor about Dylan. "Listen, Val, I understand Dylan's story is compelling. We just can't use the little boy as a selling point. I should've made that clear from the beginning."

Valerie sighed. "I hate to see that advance and bonus slip away, but I get it. I'll counter with Steph and let you know."

"Thanks, friend."

"I sure hope you aren't making a mistake that could affect your career."

Her words settled like frost in Kristen's chest. Would the publisher decide she was too difficult to work with? Not serious enough about her career? She'd just have to take that chance. "Me, too," she said softly. Kristen ended the call and vowed to put the book out of her mind. She couldn't do any more to influence the publisher. She gave them a solid concept, and if they didn't grab it, she had to believe someone else would.

She spent the rest of the day working on visuals to go with her lesson plans—and checking her cell phone. Much as she wanted to ignore it, the call she knew was coming loomed like a thundercloud. Maybe she just needed to remind Reed how much she valued her career. Could she do that and not mention the interest in *The Awful Waffle*?

By two o'clock, a dull throb at the base of her neck

made concentration harder. When no call came by four, she resigned herself to waiting until Dylan went to bed—and that was a long time to wait.

****

The lie Reed told his boss on Saturday haunted him all morning. Not only was he not concentrating on his work, he was reliving Kristen's lackluster departure on an endless loop. That soft "bye" as she turned for the door confused him. He fought the itch in his fingers to pick up his phone and call her. Why hadn't she wanted to talk during her drive yesterday? He couldn't shake the feeling that something was off.

Late afternoon when the office began to clear out, Reed closed his door and yanked open his desk drawer. He needed to pick up Dylan in thirty minutes. That gave him enough time to touch base at least.

Kristen picked up on the second ring.

"Hey, angel, how's your Monday going? Did you catch up on some sleep?"

"Oh, I guess so. Re-acclimating always takes a little time."

"How was the drive?"

"Fine. Didn't get any shorter, that's for sure."

The distance in her voice came through loud and clear, as well. Frowning, he braced against his desk. "You didn't want to talk."

"Well, I had some things on my mind, and talking can be distracting."

Reed smiled into the phone, hoping the distraction and one of the 'things' on her mind was him—that she was as unhappy about being separated from them as he was. "We sure missed you this morning." He'd missed seeing her smile before starting the workday.

"But getting back to the regular routine is probably good. I really think if you talk to some of the moms, Dylan could hitch a ride in the mornings."

He paused a beat at her matter-of-fact tone mixed with…indifference?…impatience? "That's not what I meant. We missed *you* this morning." Silence filled the air as he waited for a response. Had she missed them, or was she happy to be back in her own place and her other world?

"Me, Reed? Or my services?"

Blood pounded in Reed's ears as he tried to make sense of that odd question. "What? Kristen, what's the matter?"

"I need you to know something, Reed."

He took a deep breath. "Okay, shoot."

"I need you to understand my career is very important to me. I love spending time with you and Dylan, but I…"

As her voice trailed off, Reed wondered if she'd decided she couldn't afford to spend the week after Christmas with Dylan and needed to let him down. "Go on."

"Oh, I don't know."

Reed frowned at the exasperation in her voice. Was he missing something here?

"I guess that's all."

"Kristen, are you saying you need to work and not spend the week after Christmas with Dylan?" At this point, a schedule conflict would be one huge problem.

"No, of course not. That's a definite. Really."

Reed glanced at his watch. "Okay, well, I need to pick up Dylan. I'll call you tonight. In the meantime, I'll be thinking about you. How's that?"

"Sure."

He placed the phone on his desk, still feeling as if something wasn't quite right. That was weird...*wait*. Her services? She'd done a lot, but surely, she knew he appreciated her help. In his head, he went back over the events of Saturday but couldn't pinpoint a potential issue.

Had spending a week with the two of them scared the hell out of her? Disappointed her? Or had she gotten cold feet over his suggestion of a New Year's getaway? Maybe she wasn't ready after all.

Reed shoved his laptop into its case and headed for the door. He had plenty of ways to stay busy until the call with Kristen, but his thoughts lingered on her. He admitted coming home to Kristen after work was nice. Thinking about the possibility of waking up to her, as well, sent a warm humming through his veins. The waking up part would be nice, though getting out of bed every morning might be more difficult. As he pulled onto the freeway, he let a slow smile spread across his face. He could have worse problems.

****

Two weeks later, the getaway was on Reed's mind again. Conversations with Kristen seemed normal...but she hadn't mentioned making a plan. With a few minutes to kill in his office, he debated whether to bring it up or make arrangements and surprise her. His last attempt to surprise her had been a disaster. Either way, he'd better at least see if Nora was available.

He glanced at his watch. That call would have to wait until after his meeting with Lowell. Slipping into his suit coat, Reed made his way to the executive suite.

Lowell ushered him into his office and shut the

door. "Have a seat, Reed." He gestured to the sitting area in front of his desk.

Adjusting his tie, Reed perched on the edge of a wingback leather chair.

"Congratulations, Reed. Effective January one, you're our new vice president of operations."

Blood rushed to Reed's head as he extended his hand and received a hearty shake in return. "Thank you, Lowell. I appreciate your confidence."

"An announcement and press release will go out Monday."

"Sounds good." Perfect timing. After the first of the year, things should slow down, and maybe he could catch his breath. Hopefully, one of the people he was interviewing would work out for part-time and summer care for Dylan. In the back of his mind, a hope burned Kristen would move to Dallas when her class finished in May. But even if she did, he remembered her comment about her career. He figured he understood her concern and knew he couldn't ask her to be his child-care backup. Thankfully, school was in session from January until spring break. Things were coming together.

Thinking the meeting was over, Reed was about to push back his chair when Lowell handed him an envelope. "These are documents from Travel. We want you with us at the Petroleum Summit in Brussels. The arrangements are already made."

And things just got more complicated. Panic welled inside of Reed. "Wait. Lowell, do you mean this year's conference? As in right before Christmas?"

Lowell's brows arched. "That's the one. Not a problem, is it?"

Stalling, Reed cleared his throat. "Um, I wasn't—"

"You've got care for the boy now, right? Some of the guys extend the trip and turn it into a holiday vacation for their families."

The colorful words pounding in Reed's head didn't do justice to his feelings.

"It's a great opportunity to meet some international players." Lowell tapped his knuckles against the desk. "We're not presenting this year, but Ben is on one of the panels."

Ben was Viking's CEO, and the summit was a bi-annual big deal. Attending would be an honor. As a member of the executive team now, Reed had to make this happen.

Lowell stood and clapped him on the shoulder. "Let me know whether you want to bring up your secretary or transition to a new assistant. You can move into Dan's office right after the holiday."

"Great. Yeah, let's bring Shannon on board. She can handle the work and deserves the promotion." And might have to take on some babysitting duties. None of the nanny services she'd contacted on his behalf wanted to schedule interviews before Christmas. But this crunch was his own fault. He'd been completely distracted by Kristen and let alternate care for Dylan go unresolved too long.

Reed left Lowell's office riding the exhilarating wave of being named an officer in the company but also feeling as if he were only one rogue wave away from drowning.

Chapter Twenty

Reed passed by the other offices on the executive floor, nodding.

Andrew Cuthbert, Viking's CFO, gave a thumbs-up.

The gesture confirmed the others knew what just happened.

Back in his own office, Reed quietly shut the door and blew out his breath. Talk about good news/bad news. So now what? Share the news or face the next hurdle? Visions of sharing a bottle of champagne with Kristen came to mind. He could wait until this evening and do a video call so he could see the sparkle in those gorgeous green eyes. Or, he could settle for a quick call and the smile in her voice.

What he really wanted was to fly to Denver, whisk her off to the mountains of Aspen, and have a private, romantic celebration for just the two of them. Did people do that sort of thing anymore? If he didn't have Dylan to consider, would he? Would he ever again have that kind of freedom and spontaneity?

He picked up his phone but stopped short. Would she be excited for him, or would she worry the promotion would mean more time away from Dylan? He wondered, too. Or, would she think he hinted for help? Could he tell her about the promotion and skip mentioning the conference? He raked a hand through his hair. How could he not tell her he'd be out of the country? Maybe if he nailed down a plan first...

Reed sank into his office chair and looked through the travel documents Lowell gave him. The return flight arrived home late on the twenty-third, so they could still get to the ranch for Christmas Eve. The schedule would be a whirlwind with some intense jetlag, but it'd work. Unfortunately, that scenario also meant they probably wouldn't see Kristen until she arrived at the ranch after Christmas.

As the news of his promotion spread through the office like a flash flood, Reed had to put aside the scheduling issues. For the next two hours, he did nothing but answer the phone and greet the associates who stopped by his office. What happened to an announcement on Monday? He didn't mind, though. The commotion kept him busy—and gave him a temporary reprieve.

But at the end of the day, the problem persisted like a dead weight on his shoulders. He figured his best option was to get Dylan to the ranch early and hope Nora could pitch in and lend a hand. Surely between the two of them, his dad and Nora could keep Dylan alive and entertained for a few days. He needed to talk to Nora, anyway. Feeling the time crunch, he punched the ranch number and paced the room.

"Hello there, Reed."

Nora's familiar and soul-comforting voice came on the line, and Reed let his shoulders relax.

"I've been meaning to contact you about our Christmas," she said. "I know this will be a hard time without your sweet sister and her family. Really hard. But I want you, Dylan, and your father to come to our place for dinner."

"Have you talked to Dad?" Her heavy sigh was audible.

"I have. He's leaving the decision up to you."

Thanks, Dad. It'd be nice if he'd weigh in on this one. Not that Reed saw many choices. They couldn't ignore Christmas, and Dylan was still young enough to need a visit from Santa. "Sounds good to me, Nora. Thanks for taking care of us. Spending the day with friends is just what we need."

"Excellent. Now, can we plan on any other guests? You're welcome to invite Kristen, too. I'd love to see her."

Her lighthearted hopefulness squeezed Reed's chest. Nora and Kristen had formed an easy friendship in Kristen's short time at the ranch. He'd love to have Kristen there, but this wasn't a good year for guests. Anyway, she already made plans to be with Jana's family. "Just the two of us this time, Nora."

"Oh, I'm sorry to hear that. What about Celia? Do you know if she has a place to go?"

While he held the phone to his ear, Reed rolled his neck. How the hell would he know Celia's holiday plans? He had zero desire to interact with her and—

"We could at least extend an invitation. It'd be the nice thing to do."

Of course, it would. Not that he cared much about being on Santa's 'nice' list this year. "I leave that up to you, Nora."

"All right, I'll take care of it. Don't worry about bringing a thing. We'll keep it low-key with turkey and the usual fixings."

"Perfect." He knew from experience that Nora's

"low-key" meant the spread would rival any four-star restaurant.

"I'll talk to Jack, but let's plan on y'all being here about eleven."

"Sure. That sounds good. Listen, Nora. Is my dad around?"

"Hasn't come in yet. Want me to have him give you a call?"

"Yeah, that'd be great. Let me run this by you first." He dropped into his desk chair and pinched the bridge of his nose. "I'm really in a bind. Got the promotion I've been hoping for today, and the top brass want me to attend a conference. Looks like I have to ask Dad to keep Dylan for a few days before Christmas. The school's closed, and I can't take the week off. Was thinking if you could check in on them occasionally, it might be okay." Reed held his breath, waiting for her reaction.

"Oh, Reed, congratulations, hon. I'd absolutely love to pitch in. In fact, I'd be happy to have him at my place, but Roger and I are heading to Albuquerque to visit my sister before Christmas. We'll be home the day before, if that helps. And then, guess what?"

The excitement in her voice was unmistakable. "Sounds like something good."

"Oh, my gosh. It is. We're going to Mexico right after Christmas."

With a heavy thud, Reed's stomach dropped. She had to be kidding. Had they ever gone away at Christmas? Not in his memory. He swallowed his disappointment. "No problem, Nora. That sounds like a great time, and you guys deserve a vacation." There went his getaway with Kristen. "What about Dad?

Think he can handle it?"

"I don't know, Reed. It wouldn't be ideal."

To say the least.

"His back's been bothering him. He seems to be off his schedule. Sleeping in a bit. And you know he's always been such a morning person."

As was Dylan. Would that leave Dylan unattended in the mornings while his grandfather slept? Or all day, for that matter? Reed groaned inside. Without Roger around, Dad would have more work to do on the ranch. Mild panic settled in Reed's chest.

They talked for a few more minutes until Reed could politely duck out. "It's about time for me to get Dylan, Nora, so I better let you go. We'll see you soon."

He ended the call and used every ounce of self-control not to fling the phone against the wall.

****

With her lesson plans in good shape, Kristen turned to Christmas prep. She and her roommates didn't do a lot of holiday decorating because the small house was already on the cluttered side. But this year, she wanted to use some of her mother's decorations. From the storage area downstairs, she retrieved several of her mother's favorite glass ornaments and placed them in a shallow tray on the dining room table. Then she added a few twigs and evergreen sprigs to make a simple but elegant centerpiece. "Very nice," she murmured. The scent of the evergreen made the whole room smell like Christmas.

When her phone chimed from the counter, she turned. The smile was automatic. "Hey, Nora. How are you?"

"Great, sweetie. Did I catch you at a good time?"

"Sure. You know what's next on my list? Making your German chocolate brownies to take to a friend's house for Christmas."

"Excellent. I sure was hoping to see you over the holiday, but it sounds like we'll miss each other."

"Well, I'll be out there the whole week after Christmas. I'll see you then."

"No, honey, believe it or not, Roger and I will be basking on a beach in Mexico. First time ever."

"Wow. That sounds fabulous, Nora, but I'll miss seeing you." Kristen forced an upbeat tone to her voice, but her heart sank. No Nora meant no one to keep Dylan for a night. As disappointment settled inside her, she swallowed hard. Did Reed know?

Unwelcome thoughts crowded in. He hadn't mentioned their night away for a while. Was it no longer a priority since he had Dylan's after-Christmas childcare arranged? Oh, how she wished she hadn't overheard that conversation. That damned call made her question Reed's every move.

"I think I'll get started on some almond bark and peanut brittle this weekend." Nora's voice broke in.

"Sounds heavenly." Kristen remembered how much fun she had cooking for the holidays with her mother. Doing the same with Nora would've been fun, too.

"Now, you've got real butter for the filling?"

"Yes, ma'am. And real vanilla."

"Perfect. Makes all the difference. I guess I'll cut down my quantities for this year. We'll be such a small group."

At the reminder, Kristen's heart clenched. "It'll be

a tough one, Nora," she said softly. "I'm glad you're getting some time away." And she meant it. She and Reed could figure out something else for another time—if they still wanted to.

****

At nine o'clock, Kristen retreated to her room, anticipating the call from Reed, which had become a routine every night after Dylan went to bed. Her phone rang at five after. "Hey, there."

"Hey, angel. How was your day?"

"Pretty uneventful." She'd wait to mention her conversation with Nora. "How about you?"

"Which do you want first? The good news or bad news?"

Kristen's heart pounded. She didn't want any bad news. Or at least none worse than having to postpone their night alone. She let out a heavy sigh. "I'd prefer to skip the bad news altogether."

"I know. But, hey, you're speaking to the new vice president of operations for Viking Oil."

The unmistakable pride in his voice was her clue—this announcement was supposed to be the good news. But was it? A higher rank might mean more money and prestige, but would the promotion also mean less time at home and less time for Dylan? She did her best to react with excitement. "Congratulations! Wow, that's great." And then she remembered the *real* good news—he'd be replacing the old geezer who expected the little wife to take care of the kids and have a hot meal on the table every night. *Good riddance.* "So that means bye-bye old boss, right?"

Reed chuckled. "It does, indeed."

"Soooo," Kristen drawled. "I guess I better hear the

bad news."

"This is terrible news, babe. I talked to Nora today. She can't keep Dylan that last night after Christmas."

Kristen felt like laughing and crying at the same time. He sounded as disappointed as she was. "That *is* terrible news."

"Any ideas for Plan B?"

"Oh, gosh, not off the top of my head." But the gears turned in her mind. Jana again? Or a trip to Denver? Couldn't Dylan hang out with her roommates for a night once he got to know them?

"Here's the other thing. We'll probably miss you before Christmas. The promotion comes with a ticket to an international conference held in Brussels three days before Christmas."

"What?" She nearly shrieked. "Are you serious? Oh, Reed, how in the world will you manage that?" As soon as the words left her lips, her blood went cold. He wasn't. Surely, he wasn't asking her to take care of Dylan before Christmas, too. Was he?

The pause in the conversation didn't reassure. Waiting, Kristen held her breath.

"I'll manage. I'm getting overnight help lined up for Dylan."

"Yeah? You've already got it covered?" Don't do it, she told herself. Don't do it. *You have to set boundaries.* If she didn't, she had no one but herself to blame if she felt used.

"Looks like one of the day care gals can pitch in."

"Oh, that'd be perfect. He already knows them well."

She breathed a sigh of relief—and hoped that was the end of the news.

****

After a restless night, Kristen got out of bed early—a battle still raged inside her as she wavered between holding her ground and being helpful to Reed and Dylan. Setting aside the guilt, she brewed a strong cup of tea then opened her laptop, hoping work would keep her mind occupied. She scrolled past the ads that popped up to see if she had any emails that needed her attention before turning to...*Wait.* Her heart pounded. A message to Kristen and her brother from Gloria, the real estate agent handling the farm. The subject line read *Potential Buyer.* Slowly, Kristen lowered her cup, noting John hadn't responded yet. Pulse hammering, she clicked on the message.

Confused, she stopped reading and started over. *What?* Someone wanted to buy the land but not the house? Why would... Oh. A commercial operation. They owned land all over the state and didn't need the house.

As she read Gloria's personal opinion, Kristen swallowed past the lump in her throat. "This is a fantastic offer, but I have to say I think selling the house by itself could be difficult."

No duh. Who would—

Kristen bolted upright, adrenalin pumping through her veins. Oh. My. Gosh. *She* would. With the advance from her new books, she could manage...No, she might not receive an advance—at least not a big one. Standing, she sagged against the table, thinking through the options. Would it be worth giving a little bit on the Dylan story to keep the farmhouse? Perhaps just a mention that the book was based on a true story? She hugged herself around the middle, her conscience gnawing.

Kristen paced the room, debating in her head—until the obvious hit her like a water balloon to the face. Laughing out loud, she clapped her hands. *For Pete's sake*. She didn't need the advance. Her half of the land sale would more than cover the cost of the house and an acre or two—with plenty left over for new furnishings and maintenance.

Ideas tumbled through her brain and gave shape to her dream of creating a writer's retreat. If she furnished the house with daybeds and bunk beds and pullout sofas, she could hold regular events for aspiring writers. When she was there, she'd be closer to Jana and—

Kristen's breath caught in her throat. She'd also be closer to Reed and Dylan.

Chapter Twenty-One

Early on the morning of the Brussels trip, Reed confidently slipped his favorite red-and-gold tie through the knot at his neck then shrugged into a perfectly tailored, charcoal gray suit coat. At the school, he told Dylan goodbye and dropped his duffle with the staff in the after-care room.

While Reed was gone, Dylan would spend a night or two with each of the directors and a night with his administrative assistant—all responsible adults who were familiar to Dylan. To Reed's great relief, that plan came together pretty easily. The only snag was Tuesday was the last day the center was open. Mitch would have to pick up Dylan at the end of the day and keep him for an hour or so until Reed got home. For the hundredth time, he begged for smooth travels. On Wednesday morning, Mitch would drive to Kansas City to be with his family.

Reed had done the best he could to satisfy his commitments to Viking and to arrange competent care for Dylan.

Those arrangements could've worked—*should've* worked.

Reed raged silently, slamming his laptop bag onto a chair at London's Heathrow airport. Due to a major storm on the last day of the conference, he was delayed several hours just getting to London. The good news, according to the airline, was that because of the huge backup, he hadn't missed his connecting flight. The bad news was that all afternoon flights were in danger of being cancelled. If the heavy snow continued, the chances of getting out were slim to none.

He calculated the time again. If he could get a red-eye, he still could be in Dallas by the time Mitch had to leave tomorrow morning. He stood in line for a cup of coffee then texted Shannon with an update. Then he called Mitch.

"Hey, you on the plane?" he asked.

"Nope. Hit a snag, bro."

"Damn. What do you need?"

"Not sure yet. Just wanted you to know I won't be there on time. Maybe not until morning. Can you keep Dylan overnight? If I can't get there, I'll have someone else pick him up." Who the hell could he bother on Christmas Eve? Of course, he knew who. He just didn't want to go there.

"Not a problem," Mitch told him.

"Thanks." He sagged into the chair. "I owe you." Reed glanced at the television screen in the seating area. All the news coverage focused on the blizzard.

"Worst storm in nearly a hundred years," the announcer said.

Yeah, that's great. Glad to be part of this historic moment. Reed's frustration mixed with heavy sarcasm.

The hours crept by until at almost midnight the airport announced it would close for the night. Reed ran a hand over his jaw, considering his next move. He did the math. Six p.m. in Dallas. No way would he be there by nine o'clock in the morning. Defeat hit him square in the chest, and he squeezed his eyes shut. With

Shannon and Mitch both leaving town for the holiday, Reed had only one choice.

****

Kristen quickly rinsed her hands then picked up a towel as she swiveled to look at her ringing cell phone. With a catch in her throat, she glanced at Jana. "It's Reed. I'd better take it."

"Sure. I'll watch the cookies."

Hurrying to the living room, Kristen answered the call. "Hey, how's it going? I heard on the news a big storm hit London. Can you get out?" A heavy sigh came through loud and clear.

"Not looking good. I hate to do this, but I need a favor. Are you at Jana's?"

"Yeah. Where are you?"

"Still at Heathrow. No one's going anywhere. Long story short, I can't get home tonight, and I need someone to pick up Dylan from a friend's house in the morning. Any chance you could do that and keep him for the day?"

Kristen couldn't help shaking her head. What were these people thinking to schedule a business trip so close to Christmas? What if she couldn't pick up Dylan? What if she hadn't been at Jana's for the holiday? Tamping down her frustration, she took a deep breath. "Of course. Let me get something to write on." She dug out of her purse a pen and paper. "Okay, what's the address?" She wrote as he gave her the information and refrained from asking the dozen questions buzzing in her head.

"Mitch needs to leave his place at nine. Can you get there by then?"

"Sure. Should I stop by your place and get fresh

clothes for Dylan?"

"I'm hoping to be there by the end of the day, so that's not necessary. I'll keep you posted."

Kristen couldn't stop shaking her head. "What if that doesn't happen? What about Christmas Eve? Santa for Dylan?"

"Santa's supposed to go to the ranch."

"And you were *supposed* to be home today, right?" She couldn't help the edge that crept into her voice.

"It'll be fine. We'll tell him Santa left his stuff at the ranch."

A chill swept through her chest. "Oh, Reed, that would be awful for him to wake up Christmas morning and not have Christmas. Why don't I get his things? If you're delayed again, he can stay here, and I'll take care of Santa." The key to his condo still dangled on her key ring.

"I suppose that'd be the safe thing. You'll find a bag of presents in my bedroom closet."

"Okay. Hope things get moving."

"Thanks," he said. "Hey, Kristen?"

"Hmm?"

"Sorry about this. I really appreciate your help."

She swallowed hard as her emotions veered all over the place, and guilt threatened to envelope her. "It's not a problem," she told him softly. Ending the call, Kristen returned to the kitchen and Jana's curious gaze.

"Everything okay?"

Kristen sputtered. "Um, no. He needs a favor."

Jana's hands went to her hips. "Another one?"

"Yeah, apparently that promotion didn't come with child care."

****

Kristen keyed the address to Mitch's apartment into her cell phone and twenty minutes later pulled into the parking lot. When the door opened, Dylan pushed past a good-looking man sporting a dark, trimmed beard and launched himself into Kristen's arms.

"Kristen!"

Crouching, she caught Dylan against her and gave him a good, long hug before standing and introducing herself to Reed's friend.

He extended his hand. "I'm Mitch. Pleasure to meet you, Kristen. Sorry to get you out early this morning, but I need to hit the road pretty soon."

"Not a problem, Mitch. I'm glad to help. Are Dylan's things ready?" She needed to get moving to tackle her to-do list, as well.

"You bet. Let me grab those."

Mitch tossed Dylan's bag into the car.

Kristen shot him a speculative glance, wondering, if Reed had ever mentioned her to his friend. Did he know they were in a relationship? If so, he wasn't giving anything away.

"Good to see you, kid," Mitch said. "Hope Santa brings you some good stuff." He gave Dylan a little bump on his shoulder. "I better get going. See you later."

"Safe travels." Kristen gave a quick wave then climbed inside the car. Once they were both buckled, she pulled the car out of the drive and moved into traffic while she stewed over the sequence of events unfolding.

"Kristen, where are we going?"

She glanced at Dylan in the rearview mirror. She'd

practically ignored him since they'd been in the car. Switching gears in her head, she flashed him a wide smile. "We'll spend the day at Mrs. Baxter's, but first, we have to stop by your house to get you some clean clothes in case Reed doesn't get home tonight."

When she brought the car to a stop in Reed's driveway, she sat still a moment and ran a thumb across the key. Lucky she hadn't taken it off her key ring. Inside, Kristen flipped on lights and headed to Reed's room where Dylan's 'Santa' gifts were stashed.

"Dylan, I need to do something for Reed. You find some clean clothes to take, okay?" Keeping her gaze from landing on Reed's bed, she headed for the closet and found the loaded plastic bag. Turning, she couldn't help but notice the photos on Reed's dresser—the same family photo she'd seen at the ranch and another one of just Reed and his mother. She lifted the frame for a closer look. He must've been in his early twenties. Their smiles were about a mile wide. Kristen brushed a hand across his handsome face as heat pooled in her center. At least this way she'd see him before he left for the ranch. They hadn't talked about when they'd do their own Christmas. She'd bought him a rich silk tie in deep tone-on-tone orange—a functional gift for a new executive that she hoped would also serve as a reminder of her.

Kristen replaced the photo of Reed and hurried back outside to hide the gifts before Dylan saw anything. Thankfully, she could make sure he had Christmas. She glanced around the living room—no sign of a stocking or Christmas tree. Reed probably banked on Nora taking care of all that at the ranch.

Getting a stocking jumped to the top of Kristen's

list of last-minute errands. Hopefully, she could still find something. "Hey, Dylan," she called. "You about ready?"

"I don't know what to take."

She entered the room to find he'd dumped the entire contents from his bag onto the bed.

"Oh, boy. Let's start over." Kristen turned toward the dresser drawers. "Did you have a fun week with Mitch?" She wasn't sure how many days he'd been with Mitch and how many with the gal from day care.

Dylan mumbled something.

Kristen swiveled. "What?"

"One night at Mitch's house."

Kristen lifted a stack of shirts from a drawer. "What do you mean?"

"I stayed with Miss Abby, too. And Miss Caroline from school. And the lady that works with Uncle Reed."

Frowning, Kristen stopped mid-stride. "You mean you stayed with all those different people while Uncle Reed was gone this week?" Reed hadn't mentioned all those names. That's what he meant by having everything "under control?" Hands on her hips, she stared at Dylan.

"Yeah. But I think I got all my stuff. I didn't leave anything behind."

A deep ache squeezed Kristen's heart. This poor kid had been schlepped around from house to house, and he was responsible for keeping track of everything? She wanted to drop to her knees, pull him close, and hold him tight. Instead, she forced a smile and held out her hand for a high-five. "Good for you, kiddo."

She didn't trust herself to say more without

showing emotion, so she focused on helping Dylan repack his duffle with clean clothes. But she couldn't help wondering if anyone had taken him shopping, to visit Santa, or out to see Christmas light displays. Had they sung Christmas carols or read the Christmas story? Might be time for a heart-to-heart with Reed. With a heavy sigh, Kristen zipped the bag. "There you go, big guy. I think that's it."

She texted Reed.

—I've got Dylan.—

Then she dropped the packages, along with Dylan, at Jana's house. "Hey," she whispered to Jana. "I need to go pick up a few things. Can I leave him with you?"

"Of course. Here, let me get you an iced tea to go. I just poured one for myself. It's that tropical kind you like."

"Sounds fabulous." She took a sip from the cup Jana handed her. "Mmm, that's delish. I can taste the mango. Just what I need to help me fight the crowds. Thanks. Do you need anything while I'm out?"

"Nope. I'm good."

"Okay, I won't be long." Of course, Christmas Eve was the worst day to shop, but she could probably take care of everything with a quick visit to a hardware store and a drug store. Not that it mattered. She'd go to the mall if that's what it took to give Dylan a good Christmas—to keep him from feeling abandoned. A quick Internet search located a bookstore in a strip center only a couple of miles away. *Even better.*

Humming along to the cheery holiday tunes in the store, Kristen dropped items into her basket—and she didn't stop until she was sure the stocking would be properly stuffed, regardless of where Santa found it. As thoughts of her own family's traditions assailed her, she blinked rapidly and swiped a hand over her eyes. Her mother had always been creative and generous with "Santa" gifts, and digging into the stocking was always the highlight of Christmas morning. No surprise that stuffing stockings was one of Kristen's favorite holiday traditions, and she was glad to do it for Dylan. She'd shipped a box of gifts to her nieces, but a mailed package wasn't the same.

At Jana's, Kristen shoved the gifts in a closet for safekeeping and hung the simple red stocking on the fireplace. She'd barely hung it in place when her phone buzzed. As she suspected, another flight delay. No way Reed would be home by morning.

After a Christmas Eve dinner of cornbread with chili and a beautiful fruit salad, the group settled in front of the TV for a marathon of Christmas shows. Dylan curled up in front of Kristen, and she wrapped her arms around his waist. This was how Christmas was supposed to be. And Reed was missing out.

As the credits rolled on *Frosty The Snowman* a few hours later, Jana clapped her hands. "Okay, everybody. Bedtime for kiddos who want a visit from Santa."

Kristen tucked Dylan into the sleeping bag in Kayla's room. "Sweet dreams, Dylan."

"Kristen, are you sure Santa will find me here?"

She gently ran a hand across Dylan's furrowed forehead. "Don't worry, sweetie. He'll find you. Now, you better get to sleep so he can work on that."

With a sleepy smile, he snuggled in. "'Night, Kristen. I love you."

Kristen thought the lump in her throat might choke her. *This kid.* "Goodnight, Dylan. I love you, too."

Just before midnight, a cup of lemon chamomile tea in hand, Kristen tiptoed to the living room to join Jana in filling stockings.

"Ooo, that smells good," Jana said.

The lemony aroma rose with the steam. "Tastes good, too. Want me to make you a cup?"

"No, thanks. Don't want to be up in the middle of the night." She gestured toward the pile of gifts spread on the floor. "Wow, you found some great stuff in a time crunch."

Grinning, Kristen tucked a package of football-themed pencils into Dylan's stocking. "And I only had to go to two stores. I love that hardware store over by the hospital. It has a little bit of everything." She added candy, a few toys, a harmonica, and the flash drive of her narrating her books, then topped the whole thing with a pair of silly slippers. She hung the stocking on the mantel and placed the wrapped books and art supplies under the tree.

She couldn't wait to see Dylan's face tomorrow morning. When her phone buzzed, she lunged for it. Another update from Reed.

—I have a new flight assignment. Should be home by one.—

Kristen squeezed her eyes closed, still torn between reassuring him that things were fine and laying into him for not being honest with her and nearly ruining Dylan's Christmas.

****

Kristen wasn't sure what woke her—the scent of homemade cinnamon rolls or the sound of Dylan's excited voice. Either one was enough to launch her out of bed Christmas morning. She slipped into her robe and headed to the kitchen to discover she was the last one up.

After a cheery round of "Good morning!" and "Merry Christmas!" greetings, Jana handed her a steaming mug.

"Thanks. Smells amazing in here."

"Kristen!" Dylan tugged on Kristen's hand. "You were right," he said in a loud whisper.

"You peeked?"

His head bobbed. "Yeah."

Laughing, Kristen pulled him against her. She loved Christmas morning. "Well, I want to see, too." She joined the bustle into the living room where packages crowded the Christmas tree and five assorted stockings bulged from the mantel.

"Kids first." Jana lifted Dylan's stocking from its hook.

Kristen dashed for her cell phone. "Hang on. We need pictures." She snapped dozens—and wondered if missing this event bothered Reed. She'd be devastated if she missed her child's Christmas. And waking up on an airplane on Christmas morning? No, thanks.

****

Squaring his shoulders, Reed approached Jana's quaint bungalow-style home. He rang the doorbell and waited, unable to quell the churning in his stomach—which could be due to the lack of a decent meal in the past thirty-six hours or facing the disappointment of the people inside.

When Kristen appeared at the door, he drew a deep breath, his heart tripping.

"You made it!"

The smile on her face didn't quite reach her eyes,

which seemed to challenge him. "Finally." Reed stepped inside and brushed a kiss across her lips. "Merry Christmas. You're a sight for sore eyes." He glanced behind her, expecting to see Dylan, but he could only hear laughter and conversation from the other rooms. Probably having fun with his Christmas presents—and hadn't missed him at all. He looked at Kristen again when she took hold of his arm.

"You missed the best part of Christmas."

At the sad tone in her voice, Reed exhaled slowly. He hadn't missed on purpose. "I know. Thanks for stepping in. At least we'll still have Christmas at the ranch."

"Come on in."

He followed her into the main living area.

"Dylan," Kristen said. "Look who's here."

"Hi, Uncle Reed." Dylan barely glanced up.

"Reed, so glad you made it," Jana sang out. "What an ordeal. I bet you could use a drink."

Adam stepped up to Reed and extended his hand. "Good to see you again. What can I get you?"

A quiet hotel room and time alone with Kristen, Reed thought. But he kept the idea to himself. "I'd love a beer. Thanks."

"Dinner should be ready in a few minutes," Jana said.

"Hope you didn't wait on my account." Reed rubbed a hand along the back of his neck, and let his shoulders relax—finally. He was glad to be back in a normal environment.

"Perfect timing."

She offered a reassuring smile. Reed figured that was a lie, but he appreciated the hospitality of her words. "Thanks. Something sure smells good."

"Classic turkey and pumpkin pie. Seems like Kristen and I've been baking for days. We've got pies, cookies, cranberry-walnut bread…"

"Sounds amazing. I'll just take a minute to wash up."

Jana nodded and gestured toward the hallway. "Of course."

When he returned, he took the beer Adam handed him and made his way into the cozy living space where Dylan sat on the floor playing with Jana's young daughter. Reed ran a hand across Dylan's back. "Hey, sport. How you doing?"

"Good. Look! Santa came."

Reed admitted some disappointment in Dylan's lack of interest in his return. But, hey, who could compete with Santa? "Awesome. What'd you get?"

"Books and more blocks, the racing game for my video player, and a new hat. And Kristen gave me some cool art supplies."

"Nice." Reed cleared his throat and glanced at the stack of gifts. And a stocking. More reminders that Saint Kristen had bailed him out of trouble. God, how he wanted to wrap her in his arms and lose himself. Wearily, he shoved a hand in his pocket and listened to the sounds from the kitchen—listening for her voice.

A moment later, Jana appeared in the room and scooped up Kayla. "Okay, you guys. Come on in."

"Wow." Reed surveyed the table in the dining room. "This looks great. Have to say I'm a little tired of airport granola bars, bananas, and peanuts."

"Was it worth it?" Kristen asked.

Reed looked across the table but couldn't read

anything in her expression.

"The conference, I mean. Was it worth all the travel hassles?"

"Well, the conference part was good." *No.* All the worry and stress and hassle made the trip a huge pain in the neck. But under other circumstances, the conference would've been great. Being with the team was part of the job. Did she think he had a choice? They'd had no time to talk about it. Watching her now, he had the feeling she was holding back—and not exactly on board with his promotion.

With a slight nod, Kristen lifted her wine glass.

Taking advantage of the pause, Reed turned to Adam and changed the subject.

An hour later, after they were stuffed with dessert and had a to-go bag for the road, Reed started the process of winding down the festivities. He knew gathering Dylan's things and saying goodbyes would take a while. He couldn't help but wonder if Kristen would pack her bags and come with them if he asked.

She caught him in the hallway.

"Hey," Reed said. "I—"

"Wow, sounds like Dylan's had a whirlwind week. Lots of stopovers."

At the censure in her voice, his thoughts stuttered. He sucked in a deep breath. "Yeah. A lot of people helped out."

In the next second, Dylan appeared and flung himself at Kristen. "Kristen. I don't want to go." He clung to her leg.

Reed caught the warning look she shot him.

Bending, Kristen faced Dylan. "Sweetie. You'll have a lot more fun at the ranch. Another whole

Christmas!"

His arms went around her neck.

At the same time, Reed stepped forward to peel him off. "That's right," he said. "Everyone's waiting on us."

Dylan buried his face in Kristen's neck. "I want to stay here."

Kristen put up a hand.

Reed stopped and shoved his free hand into his pocket, waiting and reminding himself to be patient. He understood Dylan might have some anxiety about him being gone for several days, but what was he supposed to do—not work?

Slowly, Kristen stood. "I'll see you again in a few days, kiddo." She gave him a wide, encouraging smile. "You remember all the things we're going to do, right?"

Dylan nodded against her leg.

Reed shifted and spoke to Kristen as he gently attempted to pry Dylan away. "Listen, don't worry about bringing groceries next weekend. We'll have the cabin stocked. See you on Sunday. Come whenever it's convenient."

"I'll text you."

Reed lifted Dylan into his arms then pulled Kristen into a side hug and kissed the top of her head. Then he headed for the kitchen to say goodbye to his hosts. "Jana, Adam, thanks again for everything. I really appreciate all you've done."

With three sets of eyes staring at him, heat warmed his collar, and Reed felt as though he were under surveillance. Or maybe he was getting a glimpse into his future—constantly asking for favors, juggling too many balls, and feeling like he'd let down someone no matter what.

Was his life now one big juggling act? Did the frenetic balancing make him a skilled multi-tasker or a two-bit clown in a three-ring circus?

Chapter Twenty-Two

Reed put gas in the SUV and got himself a large, black coffee. He needed a caffeine kick. He and Dylan both needed a nap, but only one of them would get it. Pulling onto the highway, Reed let his mind drift. Of course, his thoughts went right to Kristen. She looked amazing—soft and soothing in a long green sweater and a scarf that sparkled with silver threads woven through it. Reminded him of the silver tinsel they used to put on Christmas trees.

How he wished he'd invited her to Christmas at the ranch. He'd wanted to spare her the potentially grim "celebration," but now, he just wanted her beside him. He shook his head. How ironic that she'd been in his bedroom while he was gone. He'd imagined her there on a number of occasions, but in his mind, the scenario was very different.

That train of thought derailed as Dylan shifted in the backseat, and Reed looked ahead to the weekend. He hadn't actually missed Christmas. Okay, so he missed the whole Santa thing, but Christmas round two was about to commence. Nora texted she'd prepared plenty of food for an evening dinner, so they'd still go to their place, still have a meal together, and still open presents. Maybe he could recapture a little holiday cheer.

He stopped briefly at the big house, picked up his

dad and a few gifts, and got right back in the car.

"Where's the fire?" Dad asked.

Reed forced down his shoulders and took a deep breath. The rushing and busy-ness of the last few days had him wound tight. He felt like a rubber band stretched too far—and about to snap. "Sorry," he said. "Been in a hurry for three straight days."

Minutes later, he pulled the car into the drive of their friends' house—another reminder of how far from normal this Christmas was. Reed never went anywhere but home for Christmas. Roger and Nora had a nice house that they'd added on to and renovated a couple of times. The interior was comfortable and inviting—but not the same as the big house. It wasn't home.

He grabbed a bag from the back seat and scooted Dylan ahead of him. Bright holiday lights twinkled across the porch—a hopeful sign of holiday cheer. This year, Reed put Christmas in the force-it-until-you-feel-it category. Next year would be easier. Next year all the "firsts" without Amy and Brian and Hannah would be behind them. They would always have a gaping hole in the family, but in a year, maybe the pain wouldn't feel quite so raw. "Ho, ho, ho," Reed called out, his arms full of packages.

Nora greeted them at the door. "Merry Christmas! So good to see you. Go ahead and put those in the family room. I thought we could open presents first and eat a little later."

"Whatever's easiest for you, Nora," Reed said. "I know you guys are heading out tomorrow."

"No worries. Our flight's not until four o'clock."

"Besides, she's had her bags packed for a week," Roger said.

"Yes." Nora elbowed her husband. "Some of us plan ahead. Come on, let's get you something to drink. What'll you have?"

"How 'bout a good ol' fashioned Christmas beer?"

"Coming right up."

They wandered into the main living area dominated by a large Christmas tree and fireplace. Reed glanced around, feeling the emptiness of the room. "The guys already gone?" He hoped Nora's sons and their families would help fill some of the vacant spaces.

"Yes. Joe has to work tomorrow, and Drew is splitting time with his wife's family."

"Sorry we missed them."

"Me, too." She pulled Dylan against her side. "But I can't wait to see this guy open his gifts."

"Well, *there* you are." Celia's voice rang through the room. "My goodness, that took just about forever."

Turning, Reed cringed inside. He'd completely forgotten about Celia. Had she been there all day? He glanced at Nora. She smiled, but her eyes gave the answer. *Aw, man.* Her presence must've been awkward.

"Merry Christmas, sweet Bumblebee." Celia took Dylan's hand. "Come here. I have something for you."

The rest of them followed her lead and began the gift exchange with Dylan front and center.

The package Celia pushed toward Dylan was almost as big as him. Reed had to chuckle as the kid's eyes bulged.

"Is that for me?" Dylan asked.

"Sure is. Open it."

He tore into the wrapping like a human shredding machine to reveal an enormous stuffed shark. Grinning, Dylan threw a leg over the back of the shark. "Look! I can ride it."

"Pretty cool," Reed said. The big, impractical gift wouldn't hold Dylan's attention for long, but he couldn't argue with that smile. The shark would fit right in with the room Kristen pulled together.

"Isn't that fun?" Clapping her hands, Celia crouched in front of Dylan. "I'm so glad you like it."

Reed glanced at Dylan's aunt and realized they'd brought no gifts for her. Hopefully, she didn't expect any. Christmas was about the kids, right? Not for the first time he wished his sister was here to navigate. With a silent groan, he realized Dylan should've given Jana a gift, too. And Kristen. Holy hell, he hadn't even bought anything for Kristen. He'd have to fix that oversight—and fast. He could have something for her next weekend and pretend he'd planned their own private celebration. "Wow. Looks like the Christmas of big boxes."

He reached for the stack he and his dad brought. This time, the tower stood taller than Dylan. Reed handed him the top box. His grandpa had insisted on these, and Reed hoped Dylan wouldn't show any disappointment.

Inside the first box was a top-of-the-line cowboy hat. "Let's see how it fits." Reed placed the hat on Dylan's head. "Looks mighty swanky, Cowboy."

Dylan gave a hesitant smile. "Thanks, Grandpa."

The second box held a matching pair of leather cowboy boots, and Dylan's smile got bigger.

"Whoa. These are cool."

Reed breathed a sigh of relief.

"Try 'em on," Grandpa told Dylan.

Reed knew they'd fit, because he'd given his dad

the measurements.

"Oh, look at that." Nora clapped her hands. "So handsome. You look like a real cowboy."

The third box contained a new helmet. "You'll need this if you and Miss Hanover work with the horses this week," Reed said.

"Where is Miss Hanover?" Celia's brows rose.

Reed saw the challenge in her eyes.

"She's at my teacher's house," Dylan said.

Reed wasn't interested in discussing Kristen with Celia. He moved past her and pulled out the package for Nora and Roger. At least he'd remembered them. He and his dad weren't exchanging. Neither one needed anything or had a desire to shop.

"Thank you, Reed." Nora tucked the package under the tree. "Let me check on those rolls."

He figured that was her way of glossing over the fact that he had no other packages to give. While his dad and Roger resumed their earlier conversation, Reed gathered shredded wrapping paper scattered across the floor. During the transition from gift opening to dinner, he stared into the darkness from the large picture window in the front room. He'd be glad to put this Christmas behind them.

Celia sidled up beside him. "No Kristen, huh?"

He squared his shoulders. "She's coming Sunday to stay with Dylan while school's out."

"Don't play dumb." Celia took a sip of her wine. "I mean no more Kristen for you? Why isn't she here? I thought you two were a thing." Bracing an arm against a chair, Celia leaned forward.

The stance afforded Reed a clear view of exposed cleavage—an old and worn tactic he'd seen before. He turned, ready to make his escape.

"It's really sad," Celia murmured.

"What's that?" Reed snapped.

"I wonder how many women poor Dylan will get attached to then miss when you split up with them."

Reed clenched his jaw. *Damn.* She'd probably been drinking, probably bored out of her mind all day. Maybe annoyed at receiving no notice and no gifts, but he was not in any mood to put up with criticism from Celia. What made her jump to the conclusion he and Kristen were no longer "a thing?"

Didn't matter. He wasn't explaining his private life to Celia, anyway. Reed held up a hand and lowered his voice. "I never said no more Kristen. Anyway, it's nothing you need to worry about."

"Well, I am worried." Celia's voice pitched up. "My nephew is my concern, you know. Ever since the accident, you've been pushing me away and acting like I don't have a say in anything. It's not right."

Hands on his hips, Reed faced her. "What's this all about? Dylan is fine. He just needs to be doing ordinary six-year-old stuff. It's not about me or you." When her nostrils flared, Reed knew he'd only stoked the flames.

Nora poked her head into the room. "You two joining us?"

"We are," Reed said. "We're done here," he added quietly under his breath.

Celia's face flushed pink, and she twisted her hands, glaring at Reed. "You know, I could petition for custody of Dylan. And I'd probably win."

Reed braced a hand against the window casing, his head spinning. Was she kidding? "Celia, the will spells out everything."

"Well, still, I— You know, judges, they look at lots of things," Celia stammered as she passed him. "Things like women sleeping over and…and child abuse investigations."

"Reed, I'm making your father a gin and tonic," Nora called from the other room. "Would you like one?"

"Sounds great." He moved to the bar area and took the glass Nora handed him, practically guzzling the lime-infused liquid. Then he fumed through the dinner prayer. He hadn't had a woman sleep over in months. And that— *Wait a minute*. He snapped up his head and stared at Celia. How the hell did she know about the call to Protective Services? He never told her. Or Nora. The only people who knew…Celia was there. She'd seen the whole thing. She could've provided details. She made that call.

White-hot fury roared through Reed. He pushed back his chair and stood, pointing an accusatory finger at Celia. "You called Social Services, didn't you?"

Celia's eyes widened.

"Didn't you?" he demanded.

Celia stood, too, wringing her hands as her glance darted wildly around the table.

"You think that will win you points with a judge? Get you some money?" Reed thundered.

Stunned eyes stared from around the table.

"It's your own fault," Celia cried. "You—You want to control everything. You want to keep Dylan away from me. You keep—keep pushing me away!"

"Why do you want custody of Dylan?" He hadn't seen her interact with Dylan enough over the years to be sure. According to his sister, Celia flitted in and out of their lives at her own convenience—or when she needed cash.

"Because he's my nephew, and I have as much right to him as you do. I want to know if you're acting in his best interest, the way Brian would've wanted." Her face twisted, and her hands flailed in the air. "I should have some say in how he's raised and how you spend his inheritance."

"Boom!" Reed shook a finger. "Exactly what I thought. You want in on the money. You made that call to Social Services after Dylan got hurt to build a case against me to get hold of Dylan's trust. Do you honestly think a judge would decide in favor of a liar?"

Celia's lips trembled, and her chest heaved. "Why do you want Dylan, Mr. Big-Shot Businessman too busy to get home on time for Christmas?"

Reed struggled to keep from shouting that he hadn't asked for this role. He'd been given Dylan whether he wanted him or not. Taking on the guardianship was hard enough without facing constant roadblocks from people around him. "I want him because I want him raised properly. I want him protected from money-grabbers—from people who would use him. I want him because that's what his parents wanted."

"Reed," Nora cut in.

Her normally cheery face was chalk white. Reed braced his hands against the table. Here he was, in an argument at someone else's house on Christmas. "I'm sorry, Nora. I'm as surprised by this behavior as you are. You've made us this nice meal and now—"

"I'm not trying to get Dylan's money." Celia's voice broke. She gestured around, her hands flailing.

"He's—he's my nephew, too. Look at you all. You still have a family. You have each other," she cried. "I don't. I lost my brother, you know. You keep pushing me away, and I—I don't have anyone else." Her voice dropped to a tearful whisper. "He's—He's all the family I have."

A deafening silence descended on the room.

"Celia." Nora put a hand to her chest.

"Aunt Celia, you just need to get a life," Dylan piped up.

"What?!" Celia gasped.

"Oh, Dylan," Nora said.

"You!" Celia lashed out at Reed. "You've turned him against—"

"That's what Daddy said."

Celia's face crumpled, and she burst into tears.

Aw, man. Reed shook his head.

"Now, Celia, honey." Glancing Reed's direction, Nora put an arm around Dylan's aunt. "Calm down. Of course, Dylan's still your family."

"Family?" Reed countered, scorn in his voice. "Is this how you think family treats—"

Standing, Jack held up a hand. "That's enough." Frowning, he looked from Reed to Celia. "I don't know what this fighting is all about, but we're not tearing into each other. Let's just try to get along with what we've got left."

"Dad." Sadness flickered in his eyes.

"It's Christmas, son. Your mom— She wouldn't have wanted this arguing."

His words chilled Reed, and he could see the muscles working in his dad's jaw. Knew the absence of his mother and sister weighed on him. He should've known the family wouldn't get through the holiday without some kind of meltdown. Their emotions were just too raw.

"Celia, you're the boy's aunt and no one wants to take that away," Dad continued. "But let's get one thing straight." He wagged a finger between Reed and Celia. "No one is getting any of Dylan's money except Dylan." He cleared his throat and addressed Celia. "We don't cause trouble for each other. You got a problem with something concerning the boy, you talk to Reed about it. We don't go behind each other's back. You're one of the few people Dylan has left to give a damn about him. Remember that."

Reed's thoughts immediately went to Kristen. He had no doubt she cared more for Dylan than his aunt did. His throat tightened. Kristen counseled him to be more considerate of Celia. What would she think of Celia's betrayal? Was it his fault?

He flung himself back into his chair at the table, ready for this ordeal to be over—and still burning inside. After she'd pulled a stunt like that call, how could he accept Celia as family? He stole a glance in her direction. Her face was pale and splotchy, and he had to admit she looked chastised. Thinking back on the incident at the ranch, Reed figured Celia had been mad as hell that weekend and lashed out as a result of seeing both Reed and Dylan had obviously become close to Kristen. He'd bet money that had something to do with Celia's outrageous behavior. *'Hell hath no fury like a woman scorned.'* So, yeah, his rejection had probably fueled her anger. But he wouldn't apologize for his feelings.

In the quiet tension, Reed picked his way through

the meal, tasting nothing and leaving Nora and Dylan to keep a conversation going.

"Okay, everybody, time for dessert." Nora stood and gathered plates.

Relief flooded through Reed. *Please. Let's move on*, he implored silently.

"We've got apple pie and German chocolate cake. Take your pick."

"Apple pie," Dylan shouted.

At least the kid was unaware of the tension and lingering awkwardness.

"Let me help," Celia said quietly. Eyes downcast, she pushed back from the table.

Reed tracked her as she followed Nora to the kitchen. Was it all an act, or was she serious? Did she truly care about Dylan? Was she capable of being a responsible, stable influence? Feeling emotionally drained, he took a gulp of water.

As Reed went through the motions of eating the sweets, Celia's words reverberated in his head. They would probably haunt him—or at least keep him up at night.

Why did he want Dylan? Was he acting in the kid's best interest?

And the question that hammered him constantly— was he Dylan's best option?

****

Kristen waited until evening to call her brother, hoping the Christmas commotion had died down enough that the girls would be willing to break away and say hello to their auntie. She wanted to keep that connection.

"Hey," her brother's voice came on the line.

"Merry Christmas."

"Merry Christmas. Did you have a good day?" She made a point to keep a lighthearted tone.

"Yeah, good but different."

Kristen swallowed hard. Having Dylan changed things. She hadn't spent time quietly reflecting on her mother's absence as she'd planned. Not until now, anyway. "Very. I wish we could've been together and spent some time remembering Mom." Her brother's heavy sigh was audible.

"That's why you didn't come, isn't it? Because you figured we'd forget about this being the first Christmas without her? We didn't forget, Kristen. Ellen wore a necklace Mom bought her, and the girls both wore clothes she gave them. I said a few words during the dinner prayer. It'd be nice if you could give me a little credit instead of always accusing me of only being interested in the money. I miss her, too, you know."

Kristen ran the chain of her mother's diamond necklace across her bottom lip. "That's nice to hear. I haven't heard you say that, John. Whenever we talk, you only ask about the estate and the money."

"And you assume the worst. Just because I'm not sentimental about all the physical stuff doesn't mean I don't miss Mom."

"I don't want to argue on Christmas." Kristen swiped at hot tears running down her cheeks. "Those were…those were nice things you did. I hope the girls will remember her."

"It'll get harder, but we'll try. At least we've got lots of pictures of her with them."

"Can I talk to them?"

"Sure. Hang on."

Excited voices filled the air, and Kristen couldn't help smiling. She asked about their gifts and heard sheer happiness as her nieces talked over each other. Kristen's heart lifted. "I'm coming to visit you as soon as I can." And she meant it. She didn't want to lose touch with these girls.

"When, Aunt Kristen? When can you come?"

Kristen grinned into the phone. "Maybe for spring break. I'll talk to your dad and see what we can work out." She talked for a few more minutes, then Kristen told the girls goodbye. But the conversation stuck with her—and went a long way toward reviving the relationship with her brother. That he'd included their mother in his in-laws' celebration soothed the ache inside Kristen. *There it was...the magic of Christmas.*

She didn't love the idea of spending spring break in Chicago, though. With a little money loosening up from the sale of the farm, she wondered if her brother could afford a trip—if they could meet up somewhere warm. Visions of a sunny day at the beach came to mind. It'd be great to escape the winter. She and— Another thought sprang up, and her heart stuttered. Reed probably would be in a pickle again at spring break.

She remembered Dylan's wish to visit Sunnypoint. Wasn't that on every kid's list? Spring break in California sounded perfect. Could she pull off a vacation? As quickly as her anticipation spiked, it fizzled again. Would it be fun or would she spend the whole time missing Reed, who most likely would not have time off for spring break? Would that bring her right back to being a convenient babysitter?

Chapter Twenty-Three

As soon as the ranch house came into view, butterflies took flight in Kristen's stomach. She was running about an hour late, and she knew Reed needed to get going. He still had a lot of catching up to do after being gone from home for a week. But she wanted a little time with him. She longed to clear her mind—to exorcise this constant niggling that buzzed in the back of her mind like a pesky mosquito. What she really wanted was some assurance that Reed missed her as much as she missed him. That the spark was alive and crackling—and had nothing to do with Dylan and everything to do with his feelings for her.

By Texas standards, the temperature outside was cold. The air nipped at Kristen's face as she stepped out of the car. But she warmed immediately when the door opened, and Reed jogged down the steps to greet her. She hesitated a second to gauge his reaction, but the wide smile quickly propelled her into his arms. Wrapping her arms around his waist, she snuggled in, reveling in this moment just for them. "Sorry I'm late."

"I've been waiting." He lowered his lips to hers. "For this." His hand pushed into her hair at the back of her neck, gently pressing her closer.

Eyes closed, Kristen melted into him as the kiss deepened, every nerve ending buzzing.

"Would you guys stop kissing and come in?"

Sputtering a laugh, Kristen pulled back and peeked around Reed to find Dylan holding the door open on the porch. She grinned at Reed. "Looks like we're busted."

Turning, he put an arm around her shoulders and started up the walk. "I'm surprised it didn't happen sooner."

"How's he doing? He was awfully clingy when you guys left Jana's."

"He's good. I'm sure he'll be even better now that you're here."

Kristen moved ahead of him and stretched out her arms to Dylan. He'd gotten through that little rough patch. No sense raking Reed over the coals about it now. Like Jana said, kids bounced back. Still, she was determined to make this week something special. "Hey, Dylan. You ready for a fun week?"

"Yeah! Let's go to the cabin."

Kristen laughed, hugging him to her again. "Okay, in a minute." She greeted Jack and noticed the stack of bags near the door. "Wow, Dylan, is this all your stuff?"

He nodded, practically bouncing up and down.

"And we already took a load over this morning," Reed said.

"Looks like we'll have everything we need. And, Jack?" She turned to look at him. "Dylan and I want to fix dinner for you one night over at the cabin. Let us know which day would work best for you."

"Ah, that's not necessary." Jack shook his head and gave a brief swat of his hand.

"Well, we'd like to, but we don't have to decide right now." She couldn't be on the premises with Dylan and ignore his grandpa.

He nodded and picked up a bag.

Reed took another. "Dylan, grab your backpack."

Kristen supervised the loading and waved goodbye to Jack.

With Reed following them, Kristen kept an eye on the rearview mirror. She hadn't expected to be whisked straight to the cabin so soon but didn't mind. She unloaded groceries as Reed brought in bags. "Hey, can you stay for supper?" she asked when he finally settled against the counter in the kitchen.

He pushed a strand of hair behind her ear. "I'd love to, but I should get on the road pretty soon. I could use a good night's sleep before I head to the office in the morning."

"Right. You'll probably have a lot of catching up to do." If he was tired and distracted, he shouldn't be driving at night. "Be sure to text me when you get there."

"Will do."

Kristen wished the weather was warm enough to sit outside where they could talk while Dylan played. The tiny cabin quarters didn't offer the chance for private conversation. Would they ever have a chance to sit down with a bottle of wine or cup of coffee and just relax? Who would've thought something so simple would be so difficult to achieve? Kristen waited while Reed told Dylan goodbye, then she walked with him to the front door.

"You guys have fun." Reed brushed a thumb across her cheek then pulled her close. "I don't know what I would've done without you this week."

Not exactly what Kristen wanted to hear. She longed for "sweet nothings" in her ear. His lips brushed against her cheek and then her lips, sending tingles over her skin.

"Kristen, I—" He went still for a moment, resting his forehead against hers, then planted another quick kiss on her lips. "I'll call you."

She caught her breath and watched him jog down the cabin's two steps. Two-stepping—that just about summed up things. She couldn't help feeling as if she and Reed were going 'round and 'round in some kind of dance. Sometimes, they swayed together in easy rhythm. Other times, she wasn't sure their steps were in sync.

****

With great reluctance, Reed climbed into his car and left the ranch—and Kristen—behind. But out of sight was definitely not out of mind. Already, he looked forward to calling her after Dylan's bedtime.

Yeah, he had a lot of catching up to do back in the office, but he wasn't giving up on the idea of a night away with Kristen. He'd also spend the week putting together some options and schedule some time to find a nice Christmas gift for her. He wished he'd thought to pick up a few things in Europe, but the last-minute scheduling and bad weather overshadowed everything else. Okay, those inconveniences and maybe a huge brain cramp on his part.

He ran a hand across the knotted muscles at back of his neck, wondering if she'd even noticed the oversight. Fortunately, Kristen had an easy-going personality. With a little luck, he could make his blunder right.

****

The next morning, Kristen awoke with Reed's kiss

still on her mind. What did he start to say before he stopped himself? His kiss had been warm and tender—and she let her imagination run wild, thinking of ways that sentence could've ended. Certainly with more than, "I'll call you."

Shaking her head, she pushed herself upright. She'd probably never know. Anyway, she heard Dylan rustling around from the other room. Time to refocus. This week was about Dylan.

Kristen wanted to make the week a lot of fun but also to help Dylan become as self-sufficient as possible. In his circumstances, the kid needed life skills. She started in the kitchen, where she taught him how to use the microwave and peel potatoes—anything she could think of to make life easier for these two guys.

Every day they read books and played games, and with afternoon temperatures warming to the low sixties, they also went down to the stable. Each time they went, Dylan helped feed and groom the horses. Kristen quizzed him on safety procedures and riding commands and watched his confidence grow.

In the evenings, after Dylan went to bed, Kristen curled up in front of the fire with a cup of tea and talked to Reed. Just the rich timbre of his voice warmed her, lulling her into their own little fantasy world away from work and worries.

She'd set the wheels in motion for buying the farmhouse and two acres of land and daydreamed ahead to the summer that loomed with possibilities. But she kept the news to herself for now. With so many variables at play, she didn't want to make a premature announcement. She admitted she also wasn't ready to let Reed know she might be available for future scheduling snags. She wanted to let him go through the interview process with these nanny services and see what he could arrange on his own.

As her dream of owning the farmhouse inched closer, so did her goal of getting Dylan comfortable enough to ride a horse. Though she'd never taught horseback riding lessons, she knew the basics and hoped she could competently pass them on.

On Wednesday, despite a chill in the light breeze, Kristen drove Dylan to the barn. She saddled Star then turned to her reluctant pupil. "Okay, big guy, let's take our favorite, four-legged friend out for some exercise. Help me put on the halter." She kept her voice matter-of-fact. Time for the next step. His grandpa was right—books offered volumes of instruction but to really learn to ride and conquer his fears, Dylan had to get on a horse. They were running out of time. Tonight, they were having Jack over for dinner, and she hoped to have some good news to report on Dylan's progress.

She helped Dylan pull the straps over Star's ears. "Good job. We're ready. Now, you'll get on first then I'll get right behind you."

Dylan's eyes widened. "Do I have to?"

Kristen bent to his eye level. "No, but you're missing out. How will you know you don't like to ride if you don't try?" When he didn't answer, Kristen raised her brows. "You and Star are friends now, right?"

Dylan nodded.

"You know I wouldn't want you to do something that wasn't safe, right?" She squeezed his hand and smiled. "Let's give it a try."

He took a tiny step forward.

But doubt lingered in his eyes. She crouched again. "I promise I won't let go of you, sweetie. All you have to do is sit upright and hold on." Though she didn't always wear one, today Kristen would ride with the protection of a helmet. She snapped hers on first then reached for Dylan's and gently adjusted it on his head. "This fits perfectly." She fastened the strap under his chin. "You look like a professional rider."

She lifted him onto Star's back. Then, in one fluid motion, she slid a foot into the stirrup and swung her leg over the saddle behind him. One arm securely around the boy in front of her, Kristen held her breath and carefully led the horse from the barn.

When Star moved into the sunshine, Dylan let out a long "Whoooaaa."

Hearing the awe in his voice, Kristen leaned around him. "Pretty cool, huh? Everything looks different from up here, doesn't it?" Star wasn't a large horse, but she was tall enough to provide a different vantage point, especially for a young kid.

Nodding, Dylan turned his head.

His wide smile warmed Kristen's heart, and she squeezed him tighter. "You're doing great, sweetie. We're just walking over to the corral." Kristen hoped the fenced enclosure, only a dozen yards from the barn entrance, would make Dylan feel more protected.

Kristen circled five times, careful to keep Star at a steady walk. All she wanted to accomplish today was for Dylan to keep his balance and get a feel for the saddle. As they approached the gate for the last time, she slowly loosened her grip on Dylan. By the time they got to the latch, he didn't even realize he was sitting on his own. Kristen cheered inside, but she had to play it cool.

With one hand resting lightly on Dylan's waist, she guided Star to the barn. "Hold onto the railing. I'll get off first then help you down."

Back on the ground, he whirled toward Kristen.

"You did it!" She held up a hand. "Wow. I'm so proud of you."

Dylan's eyes shone.

He promptly smacked her hand with his own. "Can we go again?"

Kristen laughed. "I think that's enough for today, but we'll practice again tomorrow, okay?" She didn't want to risk even a tiny setback in today's success.

For the rest of the day, Dylan talked about nothing except his ride on Star. His excitement had Kristen veering back and forth between happiness over his progress and sadness that none of his family members were there to witness his accomplishment. She texted Reed right away.

—Oh, my gosh. You won't believe this. Dylan rode Star with me today! We'll tell you all about it tonight!—

As soon as his grandpa walked through the cabin doorway to join them for supper, Dylan rushed toward him. "Grandpa, guess what? I rode Star today. I did it!"

Jack flicked a glance at Kristen, then he tipped his chin at Dylan. "Good deal."

Kristen tried to look on the positive side. At least he hadn't said, "It's about time." Dinner conversation was stiff and shallow, and Kristen silently cheered when Jack took his leave after only an hour.

She couldn't wait to get Reed on the phone and let Dylan boast about his big day.

****

Reed pushed through the door at seven-thirty. He'd worked late every night this week and still brought reading material home. Tonight, he hoped to get in a podcast before his call with Kristen and Dylan. Sounded like they had a great day—momentous. He looked forward to hearing the details.

After dropping his briefcase on the sofa, he plugged in his phone then set the packages for Kristen on the table. He couldn't help smiling. He'd done well. The orange leather journal would be from Dylan, and the etched glass vase—to be filled regularly with flowers—would be from him.

Reed opened his laptop on the coffee table. Podcasts were a great invention. He could listen in a comfortable chair, wear sweats and a T-shirt, and drink a cold brew at the same time. After a quick change of clothes, he twisted the cap from a bottle of his favorite IPA and grabbed a legal pad from his desk, just in case he wanted to take notes.

Reaching to adjust the angle of the monitor, he ended up knocking the paper onto the floor. Reed glanced down to find the pad on its side and open to a page of writing. He did a double-take. The handwriting looked like Kristen's. As he scanned the page, a slow burn ignited in his chest.

The numbers blurred in front of him. She was selling Dylan's story? *She was selling Dylan's story.* If the numbers on the pad were any indication, she'd done a damn good sales pitch, too. Slamming the paper onto the table, he shot to his feet.

Shock rooted him to the floor. Memories tumbled through his brain in rapid-fire succession. Kristen's strange hot-and-cold behavior over the past few weeks.

He'd chalked up her occasional distance to sadness or disappointment at having to leave him and Dylan. In reality, she was hiding something.

He raked a hand through his hair. *The pictures.* She'd taken so many pictures of Dylan in his room and at the park and Christmas morning. Why all those photos? To go with the story? For promotion? What an idiot he'd been—he'd left Dylan in her care again.

Blood pounded in Reed's head as he paced the room. What was she doing right now? Getting material for more stories from Dylan? Using him? Her words rang in his ears. *We'll tell you all about it tonight.*

Like hell. How could he stand that? How could he look into her eyes and see her betrayal? God, he'd trusted her…and she turned out no better than Celia. Or the ambulance chasers. Or any stranger eager to make a buck. He flung the notepad across the room. Apparently, he was the only one who had a problem with profiting from a tragedy.

Should he go get Dylan? Right now? He sank onto the sofa again, head in his hands. What good would that do? With an ache deep inside, Reed pulled out his cell phone and sent a text.

—*Can't do a call tonight.*—

****

Kristen stared at the text message from Reed. What? What in the world was going on?

She texted back.

—*Hey, are you okay? I'll tell Dylan, but call me when you can.*—

—*Won't have time. I'll see you on Saturday.*—

Kristen gasped. What the hell? He wasn't planning to talk over the next two days? Something was very wrong.

"Is that Uncle Reed?" Dylan pulled on her arm. "I want to talk to him, too."

Kristen set the phone on the table and pulled Dylan against her. Though her chest pounded with worry over Reed's cryptic message, she couldn't let it show. She gave Dylan a wry smile. "Sorry, kiddo, looks like Uncle Reed is busy tonight. Maybe you can catch him tomorrow. Anyway, great job today. How about we read some books now?"

She let Dylan do most of the reading while she mulled Reed's strange text. Had he been pulled out of town again and didn't want to tell her? What if he was too busy to respond to Dylan's accomplishment—or respond with proper enthusiasm and praise? Would he burst Dylan's bubble? He'd taken a huge step forward and deserved some recognition.

Kristen tucked in Dylan then curled up in her own bed, chilled inside and out. She picked up a magazine and turned a few pages, but she couldn't even say what any of the articles were about. Finally, Kristen sat up. She pulled the phone from the charger and opened messaging.

—*Hi, again. Hey, sounds like you're super-busy, but if you get a minute, maybe you could check in with Dylan and give him a digital high five.*—

She threw aside the covers and wandered into the living area. Staring into the darkness outside from the back window, Kristen heard the long, mournful sound of a coyote howl in the distance, and a sense of loneliness stole over her.

Turning away, she checked the lock on the back door then pulled a throw blanket from the sofa and wrapped it around her shoulders.

Several dark-chocolate-almond candies later, she paced the cabin floor. Waiting and wondering, she wrapped her arms over her chest. What was going on?

Chapter Twenty-Four

The next morning, Kristen was happy to have a few minutes alone before Dylan woke. Picking up her cell phone, she quietly slipped into the kitchen for her first cup of tea. Sucking in a deep breath, she checked messages and found a response from Reed—a brief response.

—I'll touch base with him in the morning.—

She swallowed hard. Okay, that would be great. But what about her?

"Morning, Kristen."

She looked at sleepy-eyed Dylan and knew she had to rally. "Good morning, sweetie. Ready for some breakfast?"

He nodded and moved toward the kitchen.

"I'll make some toast. You get the milk." Helping with meals and cleanup, Dylan was now her sidekick in the kitchen. "Hey, have you heard from Uncle Reed?"

A smile lit Dylan's face. "Yeah. He wants us to send a picture of me riding Star."

Kristen forced a grin. "That's an awesome idea." She kept private the fact she'd probably have to let go of him to get that kind of picture. "We'll do it this afternoon."

They spent the morning making bird feeders for the small yard and patio behind the cabin, then watched from inside as several sparrows and warblers came to visit. Kristen continued to watch her phone—even though Reed told her in no uncertain terms that she wouldn't hear from him until Saturday.

At lunchtime, Kristen barely touched her egg salad sandwich, one of her favorite lunchtime meals. With anxiety gnawing at her, the pungent smell turned her stomach. She gave up after a few bites. "Let me put on my boots and let's head to the barn. Are you ready to take that picture?"

Kristen thought she saw a passing flicker of doubt in Dylan's eyes. She figured the kid was excited and scared at the same time. Inhaling a deep breath of fresh air, Kristen pulled the small portable platform into the staging area then led Star from her stall so Dylan could help with the saddle. He'd already gained so much confidence. Tomorrow, she might consider a short ride along the road, but today, she led them to the corral again. She absolutely could not, *would not*, let her consternation about Reed interfere with Dylan's progress.

They circled for thirty minutes at a walk before Kristen signaled Star to pick up the pace to a slow trot. Then she helped Dylan take the reins and put the horse through some commands. After that, Kristen brought Star to a halt. She swung down from the horse but instead of reaching for Dylan, she took hold of the lead rope. "Want to go around again?"

Grinning, Dylan nodded. "Yeah!"

"Okay, I'll walk beside you like this."

The smile faltered. "You're not getting on?"

"Nope. I'll be right here. This way, I can be the teacher and watch you." She took two steps back, pulling her cell phone from her jacket. "Okay. Let me get a picture first." She snapped several then retrieved a carrot from her pocket and held it out to Star. "Good girl," she murmured. She was just as proud of Star as she was Dylan. No doubt the easy temperament of the horse factored into Dylan's comfort level and success. "All right, kiddo, let's do this. Just hold on and remember to look up. You don't have to watch your hands. Concentrate on your balance. That's the trick, remember?"

"Okay."

Kristen patted Star and slowly began walking. For now, she kept one arm on the saddle, ready to grab Dylan in case he started to slip. "You're doing great," Kristen said as they hit the halfway mark.

"Can we go faster?"

Kristen blew out her breath with a nervous laugh. The kid sure went from scared to confident in a hurry, but she didn't want to rush things. "Not today, buddy. Let's keep it nice and easy." Dylan might be relaxing, but Kristen wasn't. Her tense muscles were on high alert, ready to spring into action in a nanosecond.

"Let's go around again," Dylan said as they neared the gate.

"One more time. Then we'll take a break." She needed a break, even if he didn't. A long soak in the tub might be on her agenda after Dylan went to bed tonight. She led Star and Dylan around the perimeter of the arena one more time then reached for Dylan. At the sound of clapping, Kristen whirled to see Jack striding toward them. Apparently, he'd seen Dylan on the horse. As she set her student on the ground, relief rushed through her. Excellent timing.

"Grandpa, did you see me?" Dylan shouted.

The excitement in his voice was unmistakable. Holding her breath, Kristen opened the gate. Jack wasn't jumping up and down with enthusiasm, but he wasn't scowling, either.

"Sure did." He held his hand toward his grandson. "Good job." His glance flickered to Kristen.

She'd swear appreciation lit in his eyes.

"You're good with him," Jack said quietly.

Feeling ridiculously pleased, Kristen flushed. "Thanks. He's definitely not ready to ride on his own, but he's getting more comfortable. Needs time to figure it out." She looked pointedly at Dylan's grandfather.

Jack nodded. "Reed's got his hands full. It'll be helpful if we don't have to worry about the boy so much."

And that fast, a low simmer ignited inside of Kristen. She was done feeling sorry for Reed. Who didn't have their hands full? Their plates full? Busy lives? Too many things to do and too little time? Life threw curves at everyone. And for that matter, why couldn't Jack pitch in?

Kristen glanced sideways at Dylan, glad to see him preoccupied with picking grass. She took a step toward Jack. "You know, Mr. Armstrong, you could help in that area. Did you know Reed won't go for a ride while he's here? He's afraid to leave Dylan alone with you for even an hour."

The creases between Jack's brows deepened. "He told you that?"

"He did. Because he can't be sure Dylan will be safe. I don't understand. Who would want him safe more than his own family, including his grandpa? Especially now?" Kristen didn't want to hurt the man,

347

but he and his son were testing her patience. Might as well lay it on the line.

Jack's stare turned hard. "You telling me how to take care of my family, miss?"

"I'm telling you this might be a good time to put your grief into something productive and work with Reed and Dylan. Figure out what they need and do your part to help. You might have to change your tactics or reprioritize your time."

The man's jaw flexed.

She should probably shut up now, but she was on a roll. "I know you're grieving, but withdrawing into this hard, stoic shell doesn't help. It doesn't make Dylan feel loved and secure—and that's what he needs most right now. Let me ask you something. Have you ever hugged Dylan?"

Jack pressed his lips, and silence stretched between them.

Kristen followed his glance toward Dylan, and turned. "Hey, Dylan, why don't you grab a juice box out of the cooler?"

When Dylan was out of earshot, Jack took off his hat, and his gaze drifted to a place behind Kristen. "I don't remember."

Tears pricked Kristen's eyes. That was just about the saddest thing she'd ever heard. "Even when he was little? Did you play pat-a-cake? Bounce him on your knee? What about—"

Jack held up a hand. "Kids don't need to be coddled and held all the time. I don't believe in praising someone for doing ordinary things that are—"

"Ordinary?" Kristen shook her head and flailed a hand in the air. "What in this situation could possibly be ordinary except a grandpa loving his grandson? Showing affection isn't the same as praising, Jack."

He cleared his throat. "It's—It's not how we do things on the ranch. My wife, she was the affectionate one. She did all that kind of—"

"Yeah, I get it. Leave that to the ladies," Kristen muttered.

Jack frowned, his eyes narrowing.

"You and Reed have some kind of spat?"

Kristen removed her helmet and shook out her hair. Not yet, but one loomed on the horizon. Whether Reed wanted to talk or not, she would get an explanation for his abrupt checkout. But she certainly wouldn't discuss the problem with Jack. "Not at all," she said. "Listen, we'd better take care of Star."

Jack nodded again but didn't move out of her way or offer to help with horse duties. "He keeps things pretty close to his chest. Might be hard to know what he thinks," Jack said. "He never brought a woman to the ranch before you."

Kristen swallowed hard, her throat suddenly clogged. Reed hadn't actually *brought* her to the ranch. Not as his guest. The first time she'd been there to write and see Star's new home. This time, she was simply child care.

Now he'd shut down on her. With a flutter in her stomach, she wondered if the spark had been snuffed out. When the night away didn't come to fruition, had he decided babysitting was really all he needed from her?

****

By Friday night, Kristen admitted to being out of gas. Keeping an active six-year-old boy fed, cleaned, and entertained twenty-four/seven for a week took a lot of energy and creative juices. Though she'd enjoyed the week with Dylan, she was ready to be done with the full-time babysitting gig.

After dinner, Kristen sent Dylan to pack his things, and she tackled the cleaning with vengeance. She wasn't about to leave a mess for Nora to come home to. Kristen finished the job then tossed the rubber gloves under the sink as her cell phone buzzed.

A new text message from Reed.

—*If it's easier, go ahead and leave Dylan with my dad, and I'll pick him up there. Thanks.*—

Kristen crumpled at the sink. He didn't want to talk to her or see her. Why not? How ridiculous. She would not abandon Dylan. She'd drive him home as planned, and she'd find out what exactly was going on with Reed. Huffing, she picked up the phone again.

—*No worries. I'll drop him at your place.*—

On Saturday morning, Kristen took one last look around the bedroom to make sure she hadn't forgotten anything.

Dylan appeared in the doorway. "Kristen? I can't find my big shark."

"A big shark?"

"The one from Aunt Celia."

"I don't know, sweetie. Maybe Reed took it back to Dallas with the other stuff." He hadn't mentioned the gift before.

Dylan flopped onto the bed. "Oh."

"What kind of shark are we talking about?"

He spread his arms wide in the air. "A big one. I bet it's a Great White."

"A stuffed toy?"

"Yeah, I can ride it."

"Oh. Cool. Well, I bet it's already in your room, waiting for you."

"Uncle Reed says we can go see real sharks at Sea World when we go to Sunnypoint."

Kristen stood still, staring. Were they actually making plans? She couldn't imagine how Reed would pull off that absence from work. "With Aunt Celia?"

Dylan shook his head. "No. Uncle Reed got mad at Aunt Celia."

Uh-oh. That didn't sound good. Reed hadn't mentioned an argument. For heaven's sake. Was he deliberately alienating everyone? She squeezed Dylan's hand. "Well, it's nothing you need to worry about. Come on, big guy, we better load up."

Kristen shoved the last bag into her car and glanced toward the main house. She wasn't sure whether Jack would be there or out in the fields. Should she stop for one last goodbye? Would he even notice if they didn't? The man's emotional constipation kept him so distant from others—even the people he loved. Not that she believed her calling him out would cause a significant change. Earlier conversations with her brother echoed in Kristen's head. *People show feelings in different ways.* She let out a heavy sigh. Maybe Jack couldn't relate to small children, and he'd come through when Dylan was older.

"In you go, kiddo," Kristen said. Waiting for Dylan to climb inside the car, she debated her next move. As soon as his seatbelt clicked into place, she pulled onto the gravel road. Jack probably wouldn't care either way, but she'd feel guilty if—

The house came into view, and the choice was

made. Kristen saw Jack sitting in a chair on the wide porch, cup of coffee in hand. Though a little cold for breakfast outside, the morning shone with one of those crisp, cloudless blue skies. She pulled the car to a stop and glanced at Dylan. "Just a quick stop here to tell Grandpa bye."

Jack stood and moved down the steps. "You two out of here?"

Unsure of her welcome, Kristen offered a tentative smile. She didn't want any animosity with Jack, but she might have burned that bridge.

"Yep. That's a wrap for us," Kristen said in a friendly, upbeat voice. "Maybe next time he's here, Dylan can show you some of the things he learned about horses." Please be patient with him, she implored silently.

Jack nodded, and he rested a hand on Dylan's shoulder. "Sounds good."

Dylan twisted and grabbed hold of Jack's arm. "Bye, Grandpa."

As she watched the scene, Kristen choked back a gasp.

Jack leaned down and patted his grandson's back.

Dylan wrapped his arms around his grandpa.

Hand at her mouth, Kristen blinked back tears. Relief rushed through her, and she cheered inside. This first step was exactly what she'd hoped for. She moved forward and reached for Jack's hand.

He covered her hand with both of his. "Drive safe, now."

"Will do. You take care." She gave him a shaky smile and wondered if she'd ever see him again.

****

At the sound of a car door slamming, Reed looked up from his computer. Standing, he squeezed his fists at his sides, hoping for strained cordiality. Surely Kristen wouldn't make a scene in front of Dylan. With any luck, she wouldn't even come inside.

He opened the door to find her coming up the steps right behind Dylan. His heart ached a little when she flashed a smile—a brittle smile that didn't light her face.

"Here we are," she sang out.

"Hey, buddy." Reed ran a hand across Dylan's shoulder. "You have a good time?" He searched the kid's face but saw no indication he knew of any trouble. In fact, with more color in his cheeks than usual, he looked healthy—as if the time spent outside with Kristen had relaxed him.

"Yeah. We did lots of stuff."

"Here, let me take the bag." He lifted Dylan's duffle from Kristen's hands. "What's left?"

"Just some odds and ends. In the shopping bag."

He tossed the duffle inside then turned toward the car. "I'll grab it." He hoped she'd follow him.

Instead, she stepped inside the apartment.

Reed blew out a breath. He supposed he owed her a pit stop at least.

"Hey, Uncle Reed, can I open my new racing game now?" Dylan poked his head outside.

"Just a minute." Unwired for a week and he couldn't wait ten more minutes to get on his game system? "You might want to tell Miss Hanover bye."

Reed bounded back up the stairs and into the house, closing the outer glass door but leaving the main door open.

Kristen sent him a cool stare. "Mind if I stretch a minute?"

"Of course not." Don't play games with me, he added silently.

She took a step toward him. "A video game sounds like a great idea." She cupped a hand around her mouth. "I'm not leaving until we talk."

As weariness settled in his bones, he slumped against the back of the sofa. "Listen, Kristen. I owe you. I know. I appreciate what you've done. Let's just let the rest of it go, okay? I knew letting Dylan get attached to you was a mistake from the very beginning. You got what you wanted, so let's move on."

Her eyes went round.

The fake innocence twisted his stomach.

"Excuse me? Got what I wanted?" she repeated in a loud whisper. "What are you talking about?"

Reed looked away from Kristen. "Hey, Dylan, if the new game needs set up, play something else for a few minutes, okay?" He turned back to her furious glare.

She stood with her hands on her hips. "I want some answers," she said. "What is going on with you? Why are you avoiding me? You're not being honest with me, Reed."

He straightened and faced her. "I think we both understand the situation."

"Situation? What does that mean? You found other help for Dylan, and you no longer need my services? I hope it's better than last time. Remember how you said you had everything under control then you tossed him from house to house for five days? Yeah, Dylan told me."

Reed struggled with the pained look that distorted her face. Was the outrage all an act? He crossed his arms, ready to defend himself. "Look, the arrangements weren't ideal, but he was with responsible adults. You don't need to worry about Dylan. He's fine."

"Right. Never mind that he hardly left my side at Jana's or that you had to peel him off my leg to go to the ranch. All of this trouble so you can be a big-shot executive for an oil company? Can you not see how self-centered and pathetic that is?"

Her words scraped like sandpaper, and Reed's face burned as he recalled Celia also using the 'big-shot' term. "Let me tell you what's self-centered and pathetic," he countered. "Using a kid's tragedy to make a name for yourself and line the pockets of an agent and publisher." He gave a harsh laugh, ignoring her shaking head and stunned expression. "God, you fooled me. I trusted you, and you handed Dylan over like a prize."

"No, Reed. I didn't. Why would you think that? Why are you accusing me of using Dylan again? What trust?"

Reed held up a hand. "Stop. Please. I really can't take more of this act. I saw the proof. I saw the numbers. Have to say, looks like a sweet deal. For *you*."

****

Mind reeling, Kristen stood rooted to the floor as Reed strode to his desk and pulled out a sheet of paper that looked as if it'd been wadded into a ball then smoothed flat again.

He waved it in the air—then began reading out loud the terms the publishing house offered Kristen for Dylan's story.

She groaned inside. She left the notes in the legal

pad, and he found them. That's why he shut down. To keep her cool, Kristen briefly closed her eyes. "Where's the contract, Reed?" she asked softly. "Do you see my signature on an agreement?" When he was slow to answer, she tapped the paper in his hand. "Just so you know, that sweet deal is what I *turned down* to protect Dylan."

Reed straightened, legs slightly apart, one hand on his hip, and stared. "Why didn't you tell me?"

"What's to tell? I turned it down." Kristen's voice rose along with her temper. "Why would I even bring it up? How could I tell you anything when you refuse to talk to me?"

Reed pinched his brows.

"These questions are not difficult." Acid laced Kristen's words.

He waved the paper. "This deal didn't happen in the last couple of days. This is why you were acting weird that last day you were here. Why you couldn't get out of here fast enough."

Tears burned Kristen's eyes. Why in the world did he refuse to trust her? She'd been well on her way to falling in love with Reed Armstrong. But they were done. She couldn't have a relationship with someone who didn't trust her—who misjudged her so badly.

"You've been stringing me along. Making me believe you wanted a relationship, but I'm really just convenient childcare, isn't that right?"

"No, it's not right." He clenched his jaw. "How could I be in a relationship with someone who would use a kid—"

"Oh, give me a break." Kristen's voice rose again. "You know some scribbled notes on a piece of paper prove nothing. That's an excuse. You used me."

"It looked bad," Reed shot back, practically yelling. He broke off, and his gaze shifted behind Kristen.

She whirled to find a wide-eyed Dylan in the hallway. She swiped at the tears dampening her cheeks. "Hey, sweetie, did you get your game to work?"

"Kristen, what's the matter? Why are you crying?" With fists clenched, Dylan looked from Kristen to Reed.

"Uncle Reed, why are you yelling at Kristen?"

Kristen hurried toward him. "It's all right, Dylan. Listen, it's time for me to go." She pulled him close. "I had so much fun this week." She couldn't help the tremble in her words. Pulling back, she gave him a bright smile. "I'll miss you." Her chest tightened as she squeezed his hand. Who would've thought caring for this sweet kid would cause so much heartache? *Valerie.* Valerie would've thought so from the beginning.

Was a broken heart the price for not heeding her agent's warnings? Kristen straightened, ready to get away and put Reed Armstrong in the past. She turned toward the door.

But Reed blocked her path. "Kristen."

Shaking her head, Kristen yanked back her arm to avoid any contact and skirted around him. "I'm so disappointed in you."

"Kristen, wait."

She stepped onto the small porch and let the door click into place.

What would be the point of looking back?

Chapter Twenty-Five

I'm so disappointed in you.

A blunt object to the head couldn't have hit harder than those words. And they'd hammered Reed since the moment Kristen spoke them and walked out of his life. That one sentence made him feel like a disgraced lowlife, as if he were one of those popular personalities who'd taken a nosedive from fame and fortune to ruin and scandal, wrecking people's lives in the process.

He climbed out of bed early on Sunday—the effort of trying to sleep was wearing him out. He brewed his coffee extra strong and ignored his laptop while he waited for Dylan to wake.

Stepping outside, Reed shrugged into a light pullover. A dim, pinkish light and cool breeze greeted him. Usually, a new year energized him. He was ready to tackle the new goals and projects outlined for the company and his team—to do something noteworthy. This year, he'd lost some zeal, and he knew it. He blamed the lack of excitement not only on becoming Dylan's guardian, but everything that happened since then. Meeting Kristen Hanover had shaken him.

He braced against the patio door. Past protocol for moving on would've been to dive headlong into work. This time, things were more complicated. First, he didn't have the option of spending day and night at the office. Second, his head just wasn't there. What he really needed was for Dylan to outgrow Kristen's books and move on to something else. How could Reed move on when the nightly reading ritual almost always included one of Kristen's books, which always ended with Kristen's photo? The photo that showed her gentle smile—the one seared on his brain.

He'd been wrong. So damn wrong. She hadn't sold Dylan's story but had, in fact, given up a nice offer to protect Dylan. He shook his head. How did things get so fouled up? She was the best thing he had going and thanks to him, the entire relationship was one big mess.

He pushed the info button on his phone and Kristen's face popped onto his screen—the picture he'd taken that day at the park. As he ran a thumb across the screen, his chest tightened. For about the hundredth time, Reed considered calling her. Or testing the waters with a text. Flowers? He thought of the Christmas gifts shoved into the far reaches of his closet—the vase he'd expected to fill with flowers. Hell, he didn't even know her address. No doubt he owed her an apology. But he figured no amount of apologizing would matter right now. He'd have to force himself to be patient and give her time to calm down.

Reminders of her were everywhere…he thought of their day at the park and the shark-themed bedroom that had her fingerprints all over it. So much to process.

At seven-thirty, sounds of movement from inside signaled the real beginning of the day. Reed pushed off from the door and took a gulp of coffee. Grimacing, he swallowed the lukewarm liquid and opened the door.

Dylan appeared, still wearing pajamas.

"Morning, buddy."

"Uncle Reed, I thought of something to do today!"

To close out a cold, dreary week, Reed promised to spend Sunday doing something with Dylan. Just the two of them. Hopefully, they could find something that wouldn't remind Reed of Kristen every minute of the day. "Yeah? Me, too." He and Dylan were each supposed to come up with at least one idea. Reed figured he had the kid beat but wanted to hear his ideas anyway. Maybe they could do more than one. "Okay, you go first."

Dylan put a fist into his palm. "Let's go see the sharks at the aquarium."

Reed dropped his jaw then he broke into laughter and caught Dylan in a chest hold. "Are you kidding me? You stole my idea!"

Dylan's eyes bulged.

"You want to go?"

"You bet I do. Let's get you some breakfast first." Reed headed toward the kitchen. "Hey, how'd you know about the aquarium?" He didn't remember ever mentioning the place.

"Mrs. Baxter talked about it at school."

"Cool. I think you're gonna like it." At ten o'clock, he steered Dylan into line at the aquarium and minutes later they were inside. Reed stopped in the lobby area to study the map of exhibits.

"Let's go to the sharks first," Dylan said.

"Sure thing. This way, sport."

Dylan took hold of Reed's hand, swinging their arms back and forth.

Reed smiled down and gave Dylan's hand a quick squeeze, catching the kid's contagious enthusiasm.

The hand-lock ended as soon as they entered the glass tunnel and Dylan spotted the first shark in the tank surrounding them. "Look," he shouted. "There's one. Wow! Hey, Kristen, look at—" Dylan quickly turned back to the tank. "I mean Uncle Reed," he mumbled.

Reed couldn't count the number of times he'd done the same thing—turned to tell Kristen something or picked up the phone ready to give her a call. Until he remembered. Letting the awkward moment pass, Reed crouched for another angle at the sea life swimming around them.

Dylan chattered on, pointing and naming several of the creatures.

The excitement in his voice made Reed wonder if he had a budding scientist on his hands. The kid seemed to like nature and animals as much as he did making up stories and reading. Watching his interests unfold would be fun. Reed glanced up in time to see a large gray shark swimming right toward them.

"Whoa!" Dylan shouted. When the shark bumped the glass, he ducked. "Did you see that?"

Reed couldn't help laughing at the awe on his nephew's face. He ran a hand across Dylan's shoulders. "Did you think he was going to get you?"

"No. I knew he couldn't, but he was a big one."

"He sure was." Reed followed Dylan through the tunnel going as slow as possible without getting in the way of other people. Finally, Dylan agreed to take a look at some other exhibits, and they left the shark tank. When his stomach growled, Reed checked his watch. No wonder—already past their normal lunchtime. "Hey, buddy, I'm getting hungry. Let's check out the restaurant."

After he carried their tray to a table and got Dylan settled, Reed took the opportunity to study the map again.

Between bites of chicken-fingers, Dylan insisted Reed list all the exhibits they hadn't been to. "Okay, let's go to the rain forest, but we still have to go back to the sharks again."

"Aye, aye, Captain," Reed said. "You're the boss." He allowed another hour and a half touring the museum. Reed watched as Dylan listened to the staff members and soaked up new information at each display. He could almost see the wheels turning in Dylan's head as he processed the facts and figures. The kid was smart.

Not that Reed was surprised. His parents were smart, too. Amy was an excellent student, always at the top of her class, curious, involved in lots of extra-curricular activities. Dylan probably would be the same. Reed followed Dylan through another loop of the shark tunnel then opened the door to exit for the last time. Dylan tugged on his arm.

"Look!" He pointed toward a set of glass doors.

Ah. He spied the gift shop.

"Can we get something, Uncle Reed?"

Never mind all the Christmas gifts he'd received only a couple of weeks ago. "Maybe. Let's check it out. Maybe something for your room?" Thirty minutes and much debating later, they left the store with two books about sharks and ocean creatures, a "sea monkey" kit, and a ceramic dish in the shape of a fish—a belated Christmas gift for Mrs. Baxter.

"That was awesome, Uncle Reed. Can we come back?"

"I bet we can. Hey, how 'bout a ride to the car?" He knelt so Dylan could climb onto his back, and a sense of accomplishment rushed through him. The day was a definite success. He enjoyed the displays and had more fun watching Dylan have fun than he'd imagined.

If only he didn't have the urge to tell Kristen about every single detail…

****

Stuck inside due to the cold, rainy weather, Reed and Dylan spent the next three nights at home playing board games and watching all the science and nature shows Reed could find on television. Unfortunately, the rain didn't coincide with *Shark Week*.

On Wednesday night, Reed caught Dylan putting the harmonica Kristen gave him into his backpack. "What are you doing with that?"

"Taking it for show-and-tell."

"Tomorrow is your day for show-and-tell?"

"Mrs. Baxter said everybody could bring one Christmas present."

Reed nodded. Sounded like good thinking on her part. The kids probably needed to ease back into school.

"But I'm wearing my new boots, too."

Reed couldn't help laughing at Dylan's impish grin. He'd bet every kid in class would test those limits. "Okay, get them out of the closet now so we don't have to look for them in the morning. It's about bedtime." He picked up game pieces and tossed them into the box. Then he reached for the empty popcorn bowls. As he moved toward the kitchen, the closed laptop he'd left on the table caught his attention. He had plenty of work to do but not a lot of interest in doing it. Every time his mind wandered, it reminded him he was still in the doghouse with Kristen, and he still didn't know what to do about that.

"I'm ready," Dylan called from his room a few minutes later.

"Be right there," Reed hollered back. He closed the dishwasher and switched off the lights. Now to get through the nightly reading routine that he considered nothing short of torture.

Reed entered the room and found Dylan sitting on the bed, holding one of Kristen's books.

"All right, sport, let's—"

"I miss Kristen."

Something snapped inside Reed—could've been his own frustration or one too many mentions of Kristen. He couldn't remember Dylan ever saying he missed his mom or dad. "What about your mom, Dylan? Don't you miss your mommy?"

Dylan's eyes went round, and his bottom lip quivered. "Yes, I miss her and Daddy, too," he yelled. His face turned red, and he glared, clenching his fists. "But they're in heaven. Mommy can't come back. Ever."

Reed raked a hand through his hair. Moving forward, he knelt in front of his nephew. "Okay, buddy. I know. I'm sorry. I—"

"Why won't anybody stay?" he cried. "What did I do?"

Reed's heart pounded as he tried to console Dylan. "Nothing. You didn't do anything wrong. I shouldn't have said that."

Suddenly, Dylan went white and silent. He stared at Reed.

Reed caught his breath. Had he caused a flashback? "What?"

"Where's Kristen?" Tears streamed down the kid's

face. "Why did she leave? Did she die, too?"

Oh, hell. He pulled Dylan into a fast, hard hug. "No, buddy, she didn't die. She's fine. I promise."

Dylan punched Reed's shoulder. "How do you know?"

Damn, damn, damn. He deserved this meltdown. And he had to fix it. With Dylan's tears wet on his jaw, Reed drew in a deep breath. "Let's call her."

Sniffling, Dylan lifted his head. "Can we?"

Reed took Dylan's hand and helped him out of the bed. "Absolutely." Please pick up, he begged Kristen silently.

"Can we do the video?"

Of course, he wanted visual proof. "Sure." Resigned to his fate, he checked his computer, but she didn't have her app open. He'd have to send a text.

—Hey. Would you mind a quick video call from Dylan?—

He figured that's the only way she'd take the call.

The call came through, and a moment later, Kristen's face appeared on the screen. Reed's heart tripped.

Dylan rushed toward the computer, waving his hands in front of him. "Kristen! Can you see me?"

"Hi! I could if you'd move your hands, silly."

Though she smiled, Reed saw concern in her eyes.

"What's the matter, sweetie?"

No doubt her words were meant for Dylan, Reed thought grimly.

Dylan swiped an arm across his face and sniffled.

Reed knew Kristen would see the tears. Man, the night had taken a fast, furious nosedive.

"Can you come for a visit?" Dylan asked.

At the sound of Dylan's voice, Reed winced. Funny how tears could be heard, too.

"Oh, honey, I'm sorry I can't. I'm teaching a class, remember? Hey, have you read any good books lately?"

Reed had to smile at her easy re-direction. He stood to the side so he had a view of the screen, but he couldn't tell whether he was in her line of sight. Her warm voice had an easy calming effect on Dylan but had the opposite effect on Reed. He hitched a thigh on the chair and listened, knowing a cold shower loomed in his future.

"You can call me anytime," Kristen said.

As the call wrapped up, Reed snapped back to reality. Seconds later, his phone chimed indicating a text message.

—Want to tell me what that was all about?—

Reed gave Dylan a little prod. "Hey, buddy, why don't you head back to bed?"

—That was you saving my ignorant hide. Again.—

Reed bet his response would put a smile on her face. He wondered if she'd take a call instead of texting. He missed talking to her. Check that. Same as Dylan, he missed *her*. Plain and simple.

He read her next comment and did a double-take.

—Listen, Reed, I'm considering taking my nieces to Sunnypoint Park over spring break. What would you think of letting Dylan join us? Does he get time off for spring break?—

Reed's pulse hammered. The invitation was only for Dylan, but at least it kept the door open and kept her in their lives. They'd have to talk and work out arrangements. He didn't know the dates off-hand, but he didn't care. He fist-pumped the air before coming

back to earth and answering her. Absolutely.
—*We could make that happen.*—

Chapter Twenty-Six

By mid-January, Kristen launched into a new routine that included school days once again. Her own writing was temporarily on hold while she balanced her schedule and waited for publication of the new books.

Today, she had a couple of hours before class to meet Valerie. Inside one of her favorite coffee shops, Kristen slid into the booth opposite her agent. "Hey, stranger."

Valerie grinned and waved both hands. "Hey, lady. So good to see you."

"You, too."

Frowning, Valerie cocked her head. "You look tired."

Kristen shrugged. "I'm fine. Just busy." Even though she was determined to re-focus, she admitted Dylan and Reed still occupied a good deal of time in her thoughts. That teary phone call from Dylan didn't help. But telling Valerie would get Kristen the see-what-happens-when-you-get-involved-with-a-fan speech. In her head, Kristen pulled an imaginary zipper across her lips. She could do without a re-run of that speech. She would never regret her time with them or caring for Dylan.

"How's the class going?" Valerie asked. "You like teaching?"

She took a sip of her signature strong, black coffee

then, placing her elbows on the table, she leaned forward and gave Kristen her full attention.

"Great so far. We've only met twice." She checked her watch. "Next session is at eleven. I think there's some talent. They seem interested, at least."

"Sounds promising."

"It is. I've got students ranging from right out of high school to a couple of moms returning after being out of school for several years. Should be fun to see how they all do."

Unfortunately, the roster included that one guy sitting right up front, as if he'd been sent specifically to distract her. His intense eyes and curly dark hair reminded her of a younger Reed Armstrong and pulled at her every second of the class period.

"Fun to have a mix." Turning, Valerie plucked an envelope from her bag and handed it to Kristen. "Got a little something for you." Eyes sparkling, a wide smile spread across Valerie's face. "Your signing bonus."

Kristen took the envelope but didn't open it. Her first payment for *The Awful Waffle*. Valerie could've just mailed the check, but since she was in town for another author's tour, she'd insisted on getting together. Kristen swallowed hard, unable to shake the irrational feeling that the money was dirty. *It wasn't.* She'd taken a simple incident and created a story that made sense, entertained, and rhymed. Without her, the story remained only a memory in a little boy's head—one that soon would be lost to time.

"You don't seem too excited," Valerie said.

"Oh, I am." Straightening, she forced a smile. "I love the book, but it's caused some problems."

"With the little boy?"

"Well, not really. The boy's dad—guardian."

Kristen's thoughts on where they stood weren't clear anymore. Was Reed okay with the book without Dylan's story? Stupid or not, she'd feel better if she actually had his blessing.

Valerie frowned. "Do you think he could cause trouble? Don't hold out on me, Kristen. Do we need to run this by legal counsel?"

"No. It's fine." Besides, the contract already went through Legal. She'd signed it, clearly stating she owned creative license to the content. Since she didn't include any pictures or references to Dylan, no releases were needed.

"Good. They've signed Randi as the illustrator. She's agreed to the fast track, so we have a target release date this summer. Nothing is definite, but Steph mentioned the Seattle Expo." She grinned and bobbed her head. "Clear your calendar, and make sure you've got flexibility. They'll want you on tour."

Kristen picked at the almond croissant on the plate in front of her. "You think I'm good until July, though?"

"Yes, I could see a couple of pre-interviews but nothing that'll take a lot of time."

"I'm thinking about hosting my first writers' retreat at the farmhouse in June." She took a sip of her soothing chai latte then smiled. The plans were coming together—in her head, at least.

"That sounds great." Valerie held up her cup. "Cheers to you, my friend." She tapped her mug to Kristen's.

To moving on, Kristen added silently.

"Congratulations. Things are taking off for you.

Kristen's smile became a little laugh, and a current of excitement surged through her. "Thanks. I guess they are. Just need to make some updates to the house and buy new furniture—bunk beds, day beds, sofa beds. I'm hiring an electrician to install outlet strips and make sure we're set up to handle all the phone chargers and computers."

"Good idea. Hey—"

Valerie's voice turned back to a business tone.

"Do you especially want beginning writers? What about an agency event? Could you handle ten or twelve people?"

Kristen couldn't help letting her mouth drop open. Goosebumps erupted on her skin "Sure. That'd be the perfect size."

"Let me talk to the group. We're due for a getaway with some of our top producers."

"Just let me know." Ideas pummeled Kristen as she and Valerie parted ways in the parking lot. Professional groups would be perfect. She planned to contact writing groups, librarians, and colleges, and she hoped to host enough events to cover the cost of insurance and taxes on the property. Though she'd lost some enthusiasm for spending time in Oklahoma, she did her best to keep her eye on the prize. Every day she reminded herself the hard work was about the house and achieving her goal. The farmhouse would be hers. Already, scenes danced in her head of Christmas back at her childhood home.

This weekend, she'd start putting her plan into action. Jana agreed to spend Saturday at the farm helping Kristen with her vision for rearranging and furnishing the inside spaces. Now that her spring schedule included a trip to California, she needed to make long weekends count. And keeping busy would keep her mind off her broken heart...right?

****

Reed stared at his boss, and a cold blast swept through his chest. Kuwait? Was he serious?

Ben waved a hand Reed's direction. "Black Magic is your baby. Get started on an installation manual. Global has a lot of rigs, and we'll need to figure out how to cost this. Once they've got the technology, it's theirs. Doesn't matter how many units they have. We know they're interested, so let's be sure we're ready."

Around the table, people scrambled with notes and calendars.

But Reed glanced toward the conference room door. All he could think of was finding a way out.

"Even if they sign in the next few weeks," Ben added, "we're probably a good six months away from implementation. Reed, make sure you're ready to go. We'll need a team on site to train them and make sure installation goes smoothly. You'll head up the process."

Global was a huge outfit headquartered in Kuwait. A sale to them would undoubtedly mean a multi-million-dollar contract. But mentoring them on their turf? No way. A sense of dread settled in Reed's gut. Going to Kuwait, at least for an extended period of time, was not in his plans—or anywhere near the realm of possibility. As soon as the meeting ended, Reed bolted to his office. He hadn't been there ten minutes when Lowell appeared in the doorway.

"Got a minute?"

"Lowell, sure. Come on in."

He stepped inside and shut the door. "Looked like

you were surprised by Ben's announcement."

Reed rose from his chair. "Which one?"

"You heading up implementation in Kuwait."

"Yeah, I guess I was."

"Reed, don't take this wrong, but I don't see you excited about much we've got cooking right now. Something's not right."

Boom. He hit the nail on the head. Everything was off. His life was heading in a direction that didn't interest him—and moving away from the two people who mattered most.

"I've been thinking." Lowell toyed with a business card in his hands. "Rich Showalter, a headhunter with Diamond Services, came to see me a couple weeks ago. He heard about the staff changes we've made and came sniffing around. He's a good guy. We've worked with him before."

Frowning, Reed stared at his friend and mentor. "Lowell, I—"

Lowell handed him the card. "What you do with this information is up to you. I would never push you out or suggest you leave, but I wonder if we're the right fit for you now. You like R&D, figuring out stuff, and the thrill of the breakthrough. You won't get much of that in the executive suite. I should've realized before but selfishly wanted you up here. This Showalter guy's looking for someone to design new oil delivery systems. You might want to give him a call."

Reed studied the card then looked at Lowell. "Are people talking around the office?"

Lowell shook his head. "Not at all. This is between you and me, and I intend to keep it that way."

As a weight lifted from Reed's shoulders, he

nodded and drew in a deep, calming breath. When the door closed behind Lowell, Reed glanced around his spacious new office—the window view, art on the walls, and large mahogany desk screamed status. Every day they congratulated him on his achievement. He walked to the window and looked out. Bracing against the glass, he took in the surrounding buildings and the Dallas skyline in the distance. Truth was, status was the last thing he needed right now. He needed flexibility—maybe a place with a younger workforce with people more used to single parents, two parents working outside the home, and the concept of live video conferencing and distance working. Consulting came to mind, as did research. He could go back to his Earth Sciences background.

Reed studied the business card in his hand again. Whether or not this place turned out to be a solid lead, Reed needed to make a change. His bank account could handle the hit for a while—hopefully until the right opportunity came along. The point was, he had options, and he owed it to his sister—and Dylan—to explore them.

****

On Friday afternoon, Reed waited just long enough to let Dylan get to after-school care. He wanted a minute with Jana alone. Outside the classroom, he tapped on the open door.

Seated at her desk, Jana looked up. "Hey, Reed. Come on in. How are you?"

Her pleasant greeting carried a tone of wariness. "Great. Listen, I have a favor to ask. I know, I sound like a broken record, right?"

She stood and tilted her head.

Reed sensed her hesitation. Yeah, she was Dylan's teacher, but she was also a loyal friend of Kristen's. He figured she knew all about the waffle book and his break-up with Kristen.

"How can I help?"

Her all-about-business tone wasn't encouraging. "I need Kristen's address."

She furrowed her brow. "You don't have her address?"

"Nope. Never needed it."

"In Denver?"

"Yeah."

Jana toyed with a pen from her desk.

Reed kept his focus on her face, assessing her response. How could he convince her to give him the benefit of a doubt? He could practically see the gears turning in her head.

"Why?" she asked, eyes narrowed.

Reed shifted his stance. "Because I want to see her."

"You're going to Denver?"

He crossed his arms in a show of determination. "I am."

"When?"

"Now. Bags are packed and in the car."

"Oh."

Her eyes widened, and her voice pitched up.

"Well, I guess I'd better tell you she's not there."

Reed stared hard. "You're sure?"

"Yep."

"Do you know where she is?"

"Tell me why you want to see her."

Reed rubbed the knotted muscles at the back of his

neck. "Because I—I need to talk to her."

Jana's brows arched, but she remained silent.

"Look, I don't know if she'll even see me, but I have to try. I want to—" He heaved a sigh. "I'm in love with her, and I—"

"Okay, okay." Jana held up a hand. "You know you dug yourself a pretty big hole, right?"

"Yeah, I know. I'd like to dig myself out." He noted Jana didn't elaborate or offer an opinion on the likelihood of his success.

"She's at the farm."

"The farm? In Oklahoma?"

"That would be the one."

Reed frowned. "What's she doing there? I thought the farm was sold and shut down."

"She bought it."

Shoving his hands into his pockets, he shook his head. "Wait. Kristen bought her family's farm?" How did she pull that off? Did the publishing house offer a decent advance after all? Guilt rushed through him. He knew what she'd turned down.

"Just the house. The buyer wanted the land but not the house, so Kristen's keeping it."

"I see." *Interesting news*. Only the house—and only a two-hour drive away. His pulse quickened. "Okay, well, I know where the farm is. Getting there is a much easier drive for you-know-who."

Jana's brows shot up again. "Dylan's going, too?"

Reed shrugged. "Sure. We're a package deal."

Jana came around the desk and braced herself against it.

Thoughtful eyes studied him.

"Reed, why don't I keep Dylan tonight?"

His heart tripped. "Nah, that's not what—"

"You and Kristen need some time to talk, right?"

"I—" His thoughts raced ahead. Could he actually get some time alone with her? Hope pulsed in his chest. "Right. Are you sure?"

"I'm sure." She reached out and touched his sleeve. "You go."

Reed didn't need any further encouragement. Fortunately, he hadn't told Dylan of the plan, so he wouldn't know he'd miss out on seeing Kristen. Launching into action, he retrieved Dylan's bag from the car and told him goodbye, then headed back to the parking lot. But before he got to the car, an idea stopped him cold. He looked at his watch. He'd have to burn rubber. He wanted to do something for Kristen—a peace offering of sorts to make up for his stupidity. Could he pull it off?

****

The crunch of tires on the gravel drive interrupted Kristen's mental designing Friday evening. Maybe Nate noticed the lights on in the farmhouse and stopped for a quick hello. She hoped that was all since she didn't have time for socializing. She needed to get the colors nailed down before Jana arrived tomorrow.

Paint chips in hand, Kristen twisted around and pushed back the curtains from the living room window. Her breath caught in her throat. In the dim light from the porch, she recognized Reed's SUV—pulling a trailer. *What in the world?*

She stepped onto the porch of the farmhouse. Ignoring twenty-some years of upbringing, she let the screen door slam shut behind her. Heart pounding, she watched Reed stride up the walkway to the porch. Still in his business suit. And still making her go mushy inside. She gripped the railing for support. What was he doing here? How had he known…

He hesitated at the bottom step. "Hey."

"Hey." She glanced at the car. "Where's Dylan?"

Slowly, Reed advanced up the stairs. "This is one thing that isn't about Dylan."

Kristen's gaze locked with Reed's. "What one thing?"

Reed took another step forward, wagging his finger between them. "Me and you."

"Two things," Kristen whispered through her dry throat.

A slow smile spread across Reed's face, and he shook his head.

He was inches away from her now. Pressed back against the porch column, she could hardly breathe.

"Us. One thing," he corrected.

Kristen stood still, waiting. What was that supposed to mean? "Us?" she echoed finally.

"Can you forgive me?" He searched her face, and he reached for her hands.

The blood pounded in Kristen's ears. She'd asked herself that question, if they ever got to this point. Could they have a future together? Until this moment, she wasn't sure. Her answer depended on one thing. "Can you trust me?" Regret ravaged his face.

He lifted her hands to his lips. "With my life." He shook his head. "I'm so sorry."

She heard sincerity in his voice. If he didn't mean it, why would he be here?

"I brought you something."

His words were warm and carried a hint of

something she couldn't put her finger on...pride? Appeal? "Yeah? Like what?"

He tugged on her hand. "Come here."

Wrapping her sweater tighter, she followed him down the steps and toward the car. "Why are you pulling—" She broke off when a horse whinnied and poked its nose through an open window of the trailer. *Not just any horse.* "Oh, my gosh!" Kristen squealed. She ran the last few steps to the trailer. "Star, baby. What are you doing here?"

She let the horse nuzzle her a moment before she turned, grinning, to Reed. "What's going on?" For a second, she froze, her smile faltering. *Wait.* He was returning Star? Didn't want her on the ranch anymore? No, that didn't make sense with—

"Thought you might like some company when you're here writing."

Kristen smiled again. She didn't have the farmland anymore, but plenty of open spaces nearby gave her and Star opportunities to ride. Oh, but that would only be once or twice a month. So much time between visits wouldn't be fair to Star. "I would, Reed. That's really nice of you to think of, but...I'm not planning to live here full time, so I couldn't leave Star unattended that long. She'd—"

Reed put a finger to her lips. "I've already talked to Crenshaw. He can have his people feed and exercise her when you're not here. Thinks your neighbor might help out, too. You're keeping the barn, right?"

"Yeah," she said softly, her breath uneven. "I thought people could use it for some private space in nice weather." She looked at Reed again. His face was almost silhouetted in the darkness. "Thank you. I know it took some effort to get her."

"I've missed you," he whispered.

With a tiny step forward, she buried her face in his shoulder. "I've missed you, too." Kristen rocked against him, lost in time. Long moments later, she pulled back and tugged on Reed's arm. "Come inside."

"Let me take care of Star first. I brought hay and oats."

Kristen followed and helped spread the straw, put hay in the bin, and fill buckets with water then guided Star home. When she stepped out of the stall and looked back over her shoulder, laughter welled at the picture in front of her.

Reed twisted, his brows pulled together. "What?"

She swung against the door. "What's a cowboy like yourself doing in a barn wearing a fancy suit? It's probably ruined." She thought of the orange designer tie she'd bought him as a Christmas gift—the one she'd slammed inside a drawer in her bedroom. She planned to return it to the store and get her money back, but... maybe not?

With a lopsided smile, Reed shrugged. "I was in a hurry and didn't want to take the time to change."

His words warmed her again. He'd been in a hurry to get to the farm. *To her*. Not trusting herself to speak, she nodded. A few minutes later, she took his arm and ushered him back to the house. "Brrr, let's get inside." She led him to the kitchen.

"Something smells good in here," he said.

"Baking some enchiladas" A spicy scent filled the kitchen. "I'm sorry there's no furniture. I'm just getting started on re-furnishing the place. Also, I don't have much to drink." She glanced around, aware that she sounded nervous.

"I don't need anything."

With a little distance between them, Kristen took a sip of what was once hot tea and considered broaching the topic of Dylan again. Their relationship was not about Dylan, but he was an important part of their lives. She took a deep breath. "What happened with Dylan the other night? What made him so upset?"

Reed rubbed a hand across his jaw and blew out a heavy breath. "That was my fault. I said something stupid that set him off. Scared him."

Sensing he had more to say, Kristen waited.

"I feel like such a screw-up. I messed up with you and with Dylan. And I don't like it. This isn't how I want to be." He looked past Kristen and cleared his throat. "The thing is, he's—he's my kid now, and I...I want to get this parenting thing right."

Tears welled again, and Kristen pressed her lips to keep from blubbering as a mix of emotions swept through her. Dylan had officially taken hold of his uncle's heart. Reed was ready to be a dad.

He held Kristen's gaze. "That's not all."

She cocked her head. "What do you mean?"

"I hated you being disappointed in me."

The dam broke, and tears streamed down Kristen's cheeks.

"Words with razor-sharp edges from an angel."

Swiping at her eyes, Kristen attempted a smile.

"Scarred me for life, I'm sure," Reed said.

Humor laced his words, and the self-effacing demeanor tugged at her heartstrings.

"But I admit I deserved them." He moved toward her and lifted a strand of hair stuck against her cheek.

"I'm making some changes."

"What kind of changes?" Her voice was barely louder than a whisper.

"I quit my job."

Gasping, Kristen searched his face. "Seriously? Why? I mean, you—"

"The Viking job doesn't work with Dylan. My goal was to advance to the executive level, and I did. That achievement can be enough for now."

"How can you be sure?"

"Because my goals have changed. And I found out I really hate long, boring meetings. I don't like being the last person to pick up my kid at day care. I need to take a step back and start over. Maybe explore other options." He linked his fingers with hers. "And I want to go to Sunnypoint."

She looked from their joined hands to his face. "What?"

"I know it's asking a lot. I don't know if you can forgive me, but I'd like to try again. If there's room for one more, I'd like to tag along on your spring break adventure."

Kristen caught her breath. "Really?" The three of them together…they'd look like a family.

"I've wanted to tell you all of this for a few weeks, but I had to wait until I could get here in person." He gently tipped her chin. "No more misfires and miscommunication."

Nodding, she turned. "Just a minute." She pulled the rough storyboards for *The Awful Waffle* from her leather bag then held them out to Reed.

"What's this?"

"Something I want you to see."

He took the bundle of papers and flipped the pages. Then he read the simple words out loud.

"For Dylan
In loving memory of
Amy, Brian, and Hannah"

Silence settled between them. "I did sell the waffle book," Kristen said. "Not for the figures you saw and not with anything about Dylan—other than that dedication. But you need to know the publishing house has the book on its fast track, and it's set to release this summer."

Reed slowly set the pages on the counter, took a step toward her, and placed his hands on her shoulders.

Blood pounded in Kristen's ears, and her throat went dry as trail dust. Here was the moment of truth. Would he change his mind? Regret coming to see her? Turn and walk back out of her life? She watched emotions flicker across Reed's face and saw his chest rise as he took a deep breath.

"Your books are helping Dylan through a really tough time." He brushed away the tears that spilled under her lashes. "I'm sorry if I gave you the impression that I don't respect your career, angel. I never meant that. You have the coolest career of anyone I know. Hell, without your career, Dylan wouldn't have dragged me to a book signing, and we wouldn't have met."

He pulled her into a quick, tight hug. "I would never ask you to give that up. How could we disappoint the adoring fans waiting for the next Kristen Hanover book?"

At his validation, relief surged through Kristen. She sputtered a laugh, loving his words and loving the sincerity on his face. "Speaking of my adoring fan, where is he?"

"Dylan is with his favorite teacher and your astute friend who thought we might need some time to talk alone."

"Ah. Astute, indeed." She'd have to remember to thank Jana. At least she'd understand why Kristen wasn't ready when she arrived tomorrow. No way would the rest of her to-do list get done tonight.

"She's the one who told me you'd bought this place. But you're not moving back?"

"Not really. I…" She wet her lips and swallowed hard, ready to watch his reaction. "I'll probably move to the Dallas area this summer so I can be closer, though. I want to use the farmhouse for writer's clinics, book club retreats, that sort of thing."

A slow grin spread over his face. "Sounds great. I like the part about moving to Dallas."

"Well, I can think of pros and cons. I like Denver but don't really have the strong ties to—"

He put a finger under her chin. "Where do you want to be? Because you have two people who would very much like it to be Dallas, but who are likely to follow you wherever you go. You know, like stalkers."

Kristen gave a breathless laugh. His presence and his words finally sank in. Like a rosebud in the sunshine, her life was blossoming before her eyes.

He cocked his head. "Did I mention I'm job-hunting? I can go anywhere, but the Dallas area would be nice since I'm likely to be one of the most over-qualified ranch hands in the whole southwest for a while."

"Well, I doubt that'll last long. But," she drawled.

"Did I ever mention how good you look in a saddle?" She hooked a hand around his arm.

Grinning, Reed slowly bent his head, kissing her forehead, then her cheek.

The heat from his lips left a trail of seared skin along her jawline and down her neck.

He slid a hand under her hair and locked his lips onto hers.

Her initial shock gave way, and she melted into the delicious warmth cascading over her. His hands slid across her back, pressing her closer, every movement sending shivers ricocheting through her body.

"So, here's the deal," he said long moments later. "I love you. Unless you kick me out, I'll pick up the young fan in the morning."

His words pooled like lava in Kristen's middle. She let her hands wander across his chest and around his neck, hardly daring to breathe—hardly able to believe he was here.

Standing in his arms felt so right. He'd tracked her down at the farm—found her in her happy place.

Epilogue

The warm, sunny day melted into a cool evening, and Kristen let go of Dylan's hand long enough to slip on her denim jacket in the light breeze. Sunnypoint didn't afford a view of the sunset, but tomorrow, only a short drive down the coast, she hoped for a spectacular scene. Years had passed since her last trip to the beach, and this would be Dylan's first time. She couldn't wait to see the awe in his eyes, to build sandcastles, and to watch him discover the tide pools. She glanced up at Reed and smiled, contentment washing over her.

He squeezed her shoulder and returned the smile.

So far, the trip was perfect. She would enjoy three days with Reed and Dylan before her brother and his family joined them. So far, the biggest surprise was how much she looked forward to introducing her brother to Reed. They'd slipped into such a natural rhythm over the past few weeks Kristen could hardly remember when Reed and Dylan weren't part of her life.

Celia would join them, as well. Kristen couldn't say she had the same level of anticipation to Celia's arrival but gave Reed credit for making the effort to include her, when possible, in Dylan's life.

"Kristen, my feet hurt."

Kristen ran her free hand over Dylan's head. They'd had a ton of fun. She could still see the joy on his face whenever a ride took off or he met a new park mascot. She couldn't wait to look through all the pictures. Dylan was at a great age for a theme park, but dealing with the crowds and lines all over the park made for a long day. He was too young to have a lot of stamina and too big to ride in a wagon or stroller. She took his hand. "Okay, kiddo, let's find a place to sit down. We can chill until the fireworks start."

"We can go back to the hotel. I can see the fireworks next time."

"Nah," Reed chimed in. "They'll start soon, so we might as well wait. Let's find a spot, and I'll get some ice cream or something. How about that?"

She and Dylan settled onto a bench facing the small lagoon, and Kristen let her packages drop to the ground. Her feet were fine, but she felt like a Sherpa.

"What'll you have?" Reed pressed a light kiss to the top of Kristen's hair.

She caught his hand. He'd been such a good sport all day. He pretended he had to be dragged to the park, but she could tell by his good-natured smile and relaxed stance he was enjoying the day. "Popcorn and iced tea if you can find them," she told him.

"Dylan? A frozen lemonade?"

"Yeah."

"Be right back."

As Kristen watched his retreating figure, love warmed her insides. He'd relaxed so much since leaving his executive job. She worried he'd regret the decision, but he seemed to be truly embracing his dad role—and enjoying life so much more without the stress and pressure of that high-profile position.

By the time Reed returned, Dylan's head bobbed

against Kristen's shoulder.

"Sorry. He's worn out, I guess." Kristen reached for the cup in Reed's hand. "Thanks. Do you want to stay or go?" His warm hands landed on her shoulders.

"Let's stay."

Kristen tucked the box of popcorn beside her, then she leaned back and grabbed Reed's hand. Fine with her. She liked fireworks as much as the next kid, after all.

The first shower of light exploded above them twenty minutes later.

Kristen put a hand to her chest. "Oh, my gosh, it's beautiful."

The show was magical, and the crowd erupted in oohs and aahs with each new burst.

When a large white starburst showered sparkles around them, Kristen couldn't help squealing. "These are my favorite."

Reed knelt beside her and leaned in close. "They're pretty spectacular."

"Yeah."

"Big sparks."

Something in his voice made Kristen shift to get a better look at him.

"Remember when we were talking about kindling at the ranch?"

Heat shot through Kristen. The conversation seemed like eons ago, but she remembered well. At one time, she feared their spark had gone out for good. She held his steady gaze in the soft glow of light. "Uh-huh."

Reed reached for her hand, caressing a thumb across the top. "I think I forgot about fireworks. Sometimes a spark fizzles out. But sometimes—on very special, rare occasions—you get fireworks." He held out a small box.

Kristen caught her breath. Sitting straight, she stared at Reed and carefully re-adjusted the sleeping boy beside her. "Reed."

"Open it."

Heart pounding, she lifted the lid and removed a tiny velvet box. With another quick glance at Reed's face, she flipped open the box. Bursts of light from a giant explosion overhead twinkled on the slim, emerald-cut diamond ring nestled there. Kristen gasped. "Oh, Reed. It's beautiful." He pressed closer, his breath warm against her cheek.

"Will you marry me?"

Fireworks reflected in his eyes, illuminating his hopeful, boyish smile. She smoothed a hand over his brow and remembered how tired he looked when they met at the bookstore in Dallas—that day when she felt the first tiny spark. He'd been overworked and overwhelmed. They'd weathered so much since then. Tonight, the stress lines were gone, and he looked happy. Now, he looked relaxed and content and ready to start a new life committed to being a dad and sharing the future with her. Now, she couldn't imagine a life without this man.

Love surged inside her, and Kristen twined her arms around his neck. "Yes," she whispered as fire and light danced around them.

A word about the author...

Darlene Deluca writes contemporary romance and women's fiction, and likes to explore relationships—what brings people together or keeps them apart.

Her intent is to bring to life interesting characters that readers can relate to in real-life situations that combine a little fun, plenty of drama (with perhaps a tear or two), and big helpings of friendship, love, and self-discovery, and will leave you either cheering or sighing with a satisfied smile as you turn the final page.

With a degree in Journalism, she started her career as a newspaper reporter. She writes day or night, whenever the words/mood/deadlines strike, and almost always has a cup of tea and a bit of dark chocolate nearby!

Visit her at:

http://www.darlenedeluca.com

CPSIA information can be obtained
at www.ICGtesting.com
Printed in the USA
LVHW051113300820
664580LV00003B/628

9 781509 232574